Blood and Judgment

Blood and Judgment

JONATHAN HAVARD

2026 042 03
29.7.85

Heinemann: London

William Heinemann Ltd
10 Upper Grosvenor Street, London W1X 9PA
LONDON MELBOURNE TORONTO
JOHANNESBURG AUCKLAND

First published 1985
© J. Havard 1985
SBN 434 31382 3

Photoset in Great Britain by
Rowland Phototypesetting Ltd, Bury St Edmunds, Suffolk
and printed by St Edmundsbury Press
Bury St Edmunds, Suffolk

To Jack, to Tony and to the late, much loved Megan –
with memories of all those Mondays and Wednesdays

Contents

bless'd are those
Whose blood and judgment are so well commingled
That they are not a pipe for Fortune's finger
To sound what stop she please.

Hamlet, III. ii. 73–5

Acknowledgments

It is with gratitude that I acknowledge the expert advice, help and encouragement given me so generously by Professor Lee Sheridan, Professor of Law, University College, Cardiff, and by Professor Bernard Knight, Professor of Forensic Medicine, Welsh National School of Medicine.

PART ONE

Friday, 3 May 1974

1

Reluctantly, Michael Brookes extruded his legs from his half-cold double bed. One hand clutched at his pyjama trousers, drooping beneath perished elastic, as he knocked and opened the door to Jonathan's room. His son nestled in his blankets as in a womb, oblivious to the 'Good morning' wheezed into the expired air of his father's yawn. Turning on the radio and letting in the sunlight by drawing the curtains with their faded, torn linings produced no more than a slight tightening around Jonathan's eyes. Brookes turned and left, closing the door behind him, another tiny fragment of precious intimacy unwittingly squandered from an ever diminishing account.

Living together in a rambling old house, they enjoyed the luxury of separate bathrooms. By the time Jonathan reached the kitchen, Michael had laid the table with the same cereal, same toast, same silence. The kitchen needed decorating and the ceiling over the chip pan was brown and greasy. The plates and mugs were taken from the dozen or so that now, alone, were used. The tea cups and the pretty dinner service with the gold edge were stacked away, high in the upper cupboards, cold beneath a two-year layer of dust. There were no plants to catch the morning light on the kitchen window-sill.

The son sat across the table from the father. Aged sixteen and too tall for his clothes, he had long since passed the age when it was dignified for an Englishman to hug. Any show of emotion, paternal or filial, was taboo. They had not touched since his mother had died. Mutual affection was always transmitted across space.

'What shall I do about lunch today? Can you meet me?' Jonathan's mouth was full when he asked the first time and the only response he got from his father was a grunt. He swallowed and repeated his question.

'Lunch? What about lunch?'

'Dad.' The word was drawn out in exasperation. 'I told you, days ago.

We've got the afternoon off. They need the classroom for something or other. I should be finished by about a quarter to one.'

'I'm sorry, Jonathan. I'd completely forgotten.'

'Can you meet me?'

'I don't really see how I can. I'm afraid I've fixed a whole morning's work. I'm so sorry. I remember you telling me now.' Rosemary would have reminded him, or rather, she would have gone herself. He probably wouldn't have known about it.

'What will you do if I can't make it?'

'No problem, Dad. Don't worry.' Jonathan's eyes didn't leave the toast in his hand, his voice flat with resignation. 'If the worst comes to the worst, I'll stay in school and come home on the school bus. Or, with luck, I can scrounge a lift home with Rob. I'll get something out of the freezer; a pizza or something.'

'Good idea,' Brookes smiled weakly. 'I expect Aunt Lissa will be picking Robert up.'

'Oh, she'll be there.' There was no mistaking his accent on the personal pronoun, distinct if unintentional. He stacked his dirty dishes and thrust long arms into a fraying anorak. With books under one arm, he passed so close that they would have touched if his father had not swung his legs away, just in time.

Brookes' conscience broke the surface, awkwardly. 'I'll see what I can do, Jonathan. I'll do my best. But, if I don't make it, I'm sure Aunt Lissa will give you a lift.'

'That's all right, Dad. See you.' With a friendly, understanding smile, Jonathan backed through the kitchen door and out into the porch. As he did every day, Brookes swivelled round on his stool to look out of the window, though not until the sound of footsteps on the gravel had faded and he knew that Jonathan would not return. For this was the time when he enjoyed to the full the sensation of coveting his neighbour's wife.

The beech trees were not yet in full leaf so that, despite the early morning mist that promised a warm day, he could see the white walls of the Barkers' house a hundred yards away. He rolled the warm curve of the coffee mug between his hands as he tried to picture the scene behind those walls. He saw Alison Barker quite plainly. Tall and erect, she always faced him, smiling invitingly, an expression that did not change when he undressed her in his imagination. At times, Larry Barker flitted across the scene, the feckless bastard. He didn't deserve her.

4

The dripping cold water tap distracted him. It was getting worse. He really must fit a new washer.

He tried to relight the flickering images in his mind but failed to keep them steady enough to enjoy. Now a sense of guilt sent memories of Rosemary pushing their way to the fore.

Brisk, businesslike Rosemary. Generous Rosemary who had given her body unstintingly, taking pleasure in his fulfilment. He could still feel her ribs and her firm breasts, still see her face as they made love, slightly anxious as if she were worrying whether she had enough food in for the weekend. Marital unity between loving friends. Yet all that had stopped as she had become weaker, more disfigured, more reluctant for her husband to see her; when Alison Barker had started to nurse her, be around the place, fill the rooms with warm, perfumed attractiveness.

Brookes stood up, vaguely irritated. That was not how he liked his morning fantasy to end. He poured the dregs of his coffee into the sink, put the empty mug under the dripping tap, and left for the four-mile journey to the hospital.

He had been born and bred in the atmosphere of hospital medicine at a time when doctors were revered as demigods. His father was a full-time physician of a 150-bed hospital in the Wirral; a modest, unambitious man in an age, between the wars, when some of his colleagues strode the profess-ional world like feudal barons. Exploited, spinster ward sisters baby-sat when his parents, resplendent in evening dress, attended BMA functions. They also provided the biscuits and sweets, smiles and winks, in their ward offices, while endless clinical gossip washed around the child Brookes, slowly but surely impregnating a young mind. The winter evening bridge fours were doctors; the coffee drinking wives all ex-nurses. At Hoylake, the golf foursome was occasionally infiltrated by a solicitor or two.

Brookes could never remember any discussion about whether to study medicine or not. Looking back he thought it unlikely that the subject was ever raised. He was told he would go to Liverpool rather than London because of the air raids. A pliant, dutiful son, he allowed himself to drift into a world of tedious fact absorption, exams, sexually frustrating love affairs, exams, cut-rate golf on deserted golf courses, exams, and sudden stark brutality. In his clinical years, he was just in time for the last of the major air raids on Liverpool. As a surgical dresser, he helped stretcher blood-soaked bundles along corridors lined with sobbing relatives. He had dissected cadavers without thinking but he was not prepared for the Nazis' assault on his senses; the sight of pulsating bowel dancing between curtains of torn, filthy, cotton vest, the sound of abject suffering, the smell of a burnt child. Nothing in his gentle upbringing had prepared him for this. Nothing he had learned in the dusty lecture theatres seemed to apply. But Brookes worked painstakingly; his simple procedures being guided by common sense in the absence of any real surgical experience. He drew unsmiling glances and nods of approval from harassed resident surgical officers and snapping, tired theatre sisters.

Technically he was adept and decisive. Here was something he could do and do well. The issues were clear and demanding; he envied the surgeons lounging, blood-stained and exhausted, in their sanctum. He vowed that one day, he, Michael Brookes, would sprawl there, hammered down by that unique combination of mental and physical fatigue. Physically strong, outwardly calm, he felt a restless turmoil that clamoured for the masochistic exhaustion he saw in those men. He looked at them again. Expressionless eyes in flaccid faces. Poor lucky sods. Too tired to talk. Just leaned back. Closed their eyes. It was over. Done their best. To think that most people went through life never feeling like that. He would. One day he would. He made himself a promise.

Qualification was a minor anticlimax on his chosen path. His two years' National Service was spent in Berlin, happily drinking harder than he would ever again, assiduously pursuing the Queen Alexandra's Nursing Service and strangely oblivious to the surrounding devastation and hunger. He returned to Liverpool to begin his climb up the surgical tree. The speed with which he acquired the necessary degrees and publications was clear evidence of the intensity of his ambition. In fact, in the race for consultant status he was considered the local pace-setter, with more than enough ability and a flair for teaching that marked him, except to those who knew better, a certainty for a teaching hospital appointment. But his virtues were offset by an abrasive independence of spirit that had rubbed sparks off those chiefs who had not liked him and dismayed those who had. His more voluble and self-assertive competitors had also welcomed the true amateur's modest indifference to ability that Brookes studiously maintained. Brookes had sufficient insight to realise how his determination to be his own man was prejudicing his prospects, but failed miserably in his attempts to conform. He found it impossible to say 'yes' when he meant 'no', whatever the consequences.

It was when he was Senior Registrar, seemingly dead on course for promotion to the highest ranks, that the new House Surgeon joined the

6

firm. Brookes remembered her as a student, never failing an exam, never excelling; giving answers born of memory rather than understanding. He had been enchanted by her pert, extrovert vitality. Outwardly, at least, they seemed to complement each other; Rosemary determined and pragmatic, Michael easy going and idealistic. She was the only one to see just how hurt Brookes was as plum appointments went to others he felt were no better qualified than he. She was always around to comfort him with her clear-headed sympathy. If Rosemary felt disappointment that the man she had decided to marry was not going to realise his ambition, she never showed it. As the only child of a wealthy builder, she was not concerned that he was now unlikely to make a large amount of money. All she asked was that he should love her and give her the family she longed to cherish. She would provide the rest.

And so Brookes found himself married, with a new car and no mortgage and all financial spurs dulled, and it was with comfortable acceptance that, a year later, he slid into the position of Consultant Surgeon at Dunbridge General Hospital, fifty miles up the coast, an appointment neither he nor his friends would have dreamed of only two years previously.

'It's a dump,' was Rosemary's opinion. They had been driving around Dunbridge, house-hunting. She glanced at her husband nervously, anxious that he might have already formed some sort of loyalty to the place. 'I'm sorry, darling, but I must be honest. It is a dump. Grey, featureless, and heartless. It's not even an honest-to-God industrial town. It's certainly no Cotswold village. It's . . . nothing.'

Brookes laughed. 'Spare a thought for your old man, Mary. I've got to work here for the next twenty or thirty years, you know.'

Rosemary caught her breath as she put her hand gently on Brookes' left sleeve. 'I do tend to put my foot in it now and again, don't I?' The one street of bigger houses differed only in size from the rows of identical semis they were cruising aimlessly along. 'What is the hospital like?'

'Just about the oldest building in the town. It was the workhouse, originally. Parts of it are over two hundred years old. Honestly, it's true. The pathology department is in the cells where they used to doss down the vagrants overnight. They used to have a pile of rock put in the cell with them and they didn't give them their breakfast until they had broken it up into pieces small enough to push through the grilles in the windows. The original grilles are still in the windows. They used to sell the rock for road making.'

'My God, what's the surgical department like?' Not for the first time, guilt flashed through Rosemary's mind. Have I done this to him? When she had been a student, Michael had been pointed out to her as a future staff member, the up-and-coming young man. And now he was going to be a surgeon in a distant, small, provincial hospital, far from the august surgical mainstream. Had that been her fault? Might he have fought on longer in Liverpool if he'd been free? Had her longing for a secure home and a family dragged him into a job that he would come to resent? Would he become bitter as he would stand aside and watch others become successful? Would he hold it against her; feel cheated?

And, if she were to be honest, was Michael the only one who might feel cheated? Had she not thought of Michael at first as certain to become a fashionable surgeon at the centre of a great city's professional society, with herself at his side at elegant dinners and important conferences? There was no chance of that now. Would there be sufficient in Dunbridge to compensate for the loss of that dream? Would she, in turn, hold that against Michael?

'Not to worry, love. The theatres are brand-new. They look like the Hilton stuck down in the middle of Toxteth. New wine in a hell of an old bottle. I wouldn't have taken the job without those theatres. I wasn't that desperate, you know. I did look the place over first.'

'And you'll be happy there?'

'Promise.'

'All right then. Let's go and look for a house somewhere else.'

Rosemary turned her back on Dunbridge. It was as if she refused to accept its existence. She took no part in its society. She avoided all contact with the hospital. Dunbridge was the place her husband went to work each day, no more. Without trying, she gave the impression that Dunbridge was not good enough for her husband, certainly not good enough for her.

Dunbridge was built at the site of the lowest ford over the river Grayling where it widened out into an estuary that curved northwards into the Irish Sea. They drove the six miles to Westmere, a seaside resort to the south-west. Bleached and sterilised by the salt-laden westerlies, it was a high-class geriatric ghetto, financed entirely throughout the long winter months by unearned income. The sandy beaches had attracted a large shanty town of caravans, funfair and garish bingo halls. To Brookes the only attraction was the Royal Westmere, a fine links course, stretching along the dunes to the north. He had played there once with his father.

'And what on earth is that, that dreadful place over there?'

Brookes looked where his wife was pointing, over and beyond the golf course. 'That's Teflo. Some sort of petro-chemical refinery. Something to do with plastics. Impressive, isn't it? Keeps Dunbridge going. I'd hate to think what would happen to Dunbridge if that closed down.'

From where they stood Teflo was partially hidden from their view by the sandhills on the west bank of the Grayling estuary and five to six miles distant. Even so, the effect of this black slough on the coastline was awesome. The multicoloured blanket of smoke, which lay over the works like a pall, was licked by tongues of flame from the tall, narrow towers. As the fumes rose the colours mixed to form a grey slick of smoke that drifted inland, spreading malignantly in the prevailing wind.

Rosemary shivered as they turned away, alarmed by what she saw, and thoroughly disheartened. 'That just leaves Shepworth.'

Shepworth looked perfect. An old market town with its High Street so narrow it had been bypassed in the thirties, its tranquillity was further ensured by the M6, several miles to the east. The shops bustled. The streets were full of children from the local grammar school. The estate agent's Harris tweed and hand-made brogues predicted the houses he had to offer: large, solid and expensive. He was surprised at the price range they quoted and intrigued when all the negotiations were done by the tiny wife, punctuated by phone calls to Daddy.

The Old Mill would suit them admirably, subject to Daddy's survey. Stone-built, and with a vestigial mill wheel, it was surrounded by a paddock. The mill stream ran through a spinney of tall beech trees. Two or three white houses, near but not too near, formed a small cul-de-sac, the Old Mill at its focal point. If Rosemary was not going to live in a large town house at the centre of urban society, this was the best possible alternative.

They drove back to Liverpool, late, tired, each imagining what the next twenty years might bring.

Rosemary thought, 'There will never be a better time.'

'Michael,' she said, shyly. 'I'm pregnant.'

Jonathan was fourteen years old when their fragile happiness crumbled. One Sunday morning, any Sunday morning, Michael lay on in bed, reading the newspapers, blankets strewn with breakfast debris. The beat of a pop record pounded through the walls from the next bedroom. Splashing noises came from the bathroom. There was a pause while their world changed course.

'Michael? Could you come here a moment?'

'Be with you in a second.' Brookes did not lift his eyes from the paper, intent on finishing what he was reading.

'Now, please, Michael.'

Brookes looked up, a tiny niggle of fear growing deep inside him. Rosemary was physically shy, unaffected by eighteen years of marriage. Sex had never thrown off the discretion of sheets and blankets. No full-frontals. No bathroom romps. Certainly no urgent calls to join her in the bath.

A bath towel around her, coyly clutched at her chest, Rosemary stood in the bath. She bent her head backwards and downwards over her left shoulder. She wobbled as she tried to lift her left foot behind her.

'There's something bleeding on my leg. On the back of my left thigh. I just can't see it properly. Will you have a look at it for me, please, darling?'

She turned through ninety degrees to let him see her leg. One glance was enough. He had seen so many over the years. 'How long have you had that, Mary?'

He was fighting for time. Not time to make his mind up. He wished to hell there was some doubt. No; time to learn how to behave when the malignant melanoma you are looking at is not eating away at Mary Jones or Janet Smith – he would know exactly what to say then – but his wife, mother of his son.

'No idea. I just noticed some blood on the towel.'

'Difficult to see in this light, Mary. Jump on the bed and let me have another look.'

Buy time to think. Not easy to examine face down on a soft bed. Don't examine her glands. Will only worry her. He stared at the brown and black mole, its edges fading into the surrounding skin, its surface wet with ulceration and crusted with bloody discharge. A small satellite growth alongside winked its evil message.

'Are there any glands? Do you think you'd better look?'

Already he had let her down. His hesitation indicated how serious it looked. Rosemary turned on her back and Brookes' fingers probed her groin. She did not take her eyes off his face.

'Nothing there, Mary love.'

'Well that's good, isn't it?'

Down to earth, practical Rosemary took charge again. Cursed with her training, already she was one step ahead of her husband. The sadness within slowed him, dumbfounded him. Words of love never reached the surface. She made no demands for a diagnosis. Rosemary had seen just enough to be frightened. Brookes' silence simply confirmed her fears. There was no need to put it into words.

'What happens now?'

'It needs to be removed, darling. Let's hope it's only a haemangioma. I've seen sclerosing haemangiomas look like that,' Brookes lied. At last he was able to help her. He had solid practical ground under his feet. 'Shall I ask George to have a look at it? Or perhaps you would rather see someone in Liverpool?'

'No. George will do me fine.'

George Harrington, Dunbridge's senior surgeon, dear old avuncular George. He could be relied upon to handle the matter with delicacy and compassion, and he would do the operation well, too. Anything more radical or tricky, especially on your wife, well, that might be different.

'Good. I'll give him a ring this morning. I'll see if he can do it for you tomorrow. No point in waiting and worrying, is there?'

'Michael?' Rosemary managed to keep the towel in front of her as she rose to kneel on the bed, facing Brookes. 'I love you.'

The statement included the question. Brookes had to take her in his arms before he could answer, the words being spoken over her shoulder. Why did he always find it so difficult to say? It didn't sound convincing even to himself.

'And you'll stay with me? Promise you'll always be around?'

Later next day, Brookes trudged, cold stone step by cold stone step, up to the histology laboratory. He had hardly given time for the ellipse of skin, fat, fascia and melanoma, removed by Harrington, to be frozen, cut and stained. Stephen Gracie, the Consultant Pathologist, looked up from the microscope, his eyes weary with what he had just seen.

'Hullo, Michael. Come and sit down.'

Brookes did what he could to help Gracie by meeting him half-way.

'I take it it's malignant, Stephen?'

''Fraid so, Michael.'

'And a melanoma?'

'Yes.'

Simple as that. Two professionals who knew exactly what they were talking about. The only unusual feature was that the tiny red and blue sliver still casting its shadow under the microscope was a fragment of one's wife. Clinical honesty over, there was time for trying to blur the stark truth.

'We'll have to wait for the paraffins, Michael. As you know, the cells get a bit distorted in the frozen section. It may not look so bad in the paraffins. Perhaps you would like me to get someone else to have a look at it?'

Smiling gratefully, Brookes shook his head.

'There's no doubt in your mind, is there, Stephen?'

'No,' Gracie conceded reluctantly. 'But they're quite unpredictable. You know that as well as I do. The clinical picture doesn't always fit in with the histology. Some of the worst looking ones go on for years and years, and sometimes get away with it altogether.'

The future was never mentioned. When Rosemary was conscious enough to see that Brookes was struggling to say what she did not want to hear, what his eyes had already told her, she simply put her fingers over his lips.

For five months they tried to recapture the affectionate contentment of the previous fourteen years, the three together, propped up by brittle hope. Her life of providing for husband and son was lived by Rosemary with the intensity of someone who knew time was limited. *Angor animi* gave her a fierce perception.

A lump appeared in her groin and X-rays of her glands confirmed the melanoma's spread. She was torn from her home for Harrington to remove the glands in her groin *en bloc*. Later came the chest X-ray and the cannon ball deposits. A skin deposit in her cheek sloughed to discharge inky, foul-smelling filth. Soon a pair of eyes, searching, yearning from deep in the folds of perfumed silk scarves, was all that Jonathan was allowed to see of his mother.

In the terminal few weeks it was Alison Barker who stayed with Rosemary, supplying the warmth and softness that was absent in an otherwise male household. Rosemary, now hideously disfigured, had been at peace in the presence of this beautiful woman, restless when husband or son was near. Apart from short periods of mute hand-holding, Brookes had seemed incapable of comforting his wife. It had only added to his despair. To the last they had been unable to find that last piece of the jigsaw.

He had woken in the early hours to find Rosemary dead beside him. No goodbyes. Just cold.

2

Laurence Barker raised his head and opened one eye, only for it to be pierced by lancinating pain. The early morning sun, streaming through the bedroom window, stabbed him like a stiletto. He let his head fall back into the pillow with a moaning sigh. Larry Barker drank, heavily.

He heard voices from downstairs. Blindly, he stretched one arm sideways, just managing to bridge the gap between his bed and his wife's, finding the sheets rumpled, warm, but empty. The voices below became more insistent, more demanding.

'Goodbye, Dad.'

No reply.

'Larry. Robert is just off to school.'

'Goodbye, Dad.' Robert tried again.

'Goodbye, Rob. Have a good day. Take care.'

Barker spoke the words to the bedroom ceiling, his eyes still tight shut. He heard his son's footsteps on the gravel drive before nature protected him with a shallow, noisy sleep. He gave a snort as he was woken again by his wife, carrying a breakfast tray.

'Good morning, Larry. How do you feel?'

Alison Barker leant down to balance the tray on his lap as he struggled painfully to the sitting position. She placed the formality of a kiss somewhere above the stubble line. He took some time to answer.

'Awful. Absolutely bloody awful. What's the time, love?'

'About a quarter past eight.'

The answer was thrown over Alison's shoulder as she turned to gaze wistfully out of the window, not the sunlit bay overlooking the close but the small window set in the bedroom's side wall. Soon, those beeches would be in leaf. Then, it would be another six or seven months before she could see the Old Mill again each morning. She heard her husband talking. She crossed to sit on the dressing-table stool from where she could talk to her husband and still keep the window in view. Her mind began to function on two planes simultaneously. Superficially, she heard what her husband was saying, made suitable noises in reply, smiled and nodded in all the right places. More deeply, her heart and mind wandered restlessly.

'What one does for England, home and beauty,' she heard him say.

'Rough night, was it, darling?' Alison said, trying to sound interested.

'You could call it that.' Barker gulped at a glass of orange juice but balked at the toast.

'What happened?' A question that might provoke an answer long enough for her mind to float free again.

'It was all John's fault. You've got to hand it to the old sod. He's got stamina. We played bridge until God knows what time. Helped him make a slam he swore wasn't on. I think he was quite impressed. I'm playing golf with him today; or against him, rather. It seems I've been drawn out of the hat to play with some big shot over from Canada, against Sir John, no less, and the Secretary.' He laughed cynically. 'Funny how Sir John's drawn the Sec for the last three years running.'

'There must be some perks if you're President of Teflo and the Royal.'

'I suppose you're right. I shouldn't really complain. Plenty of young creeps around who'd give their eye teeth to change places with me today. And it'll give me a chance to have a word with John. You know our contract comes up for renewal shortly?'

'Yes. I realised it must be getting close. There won't be much trouble, will there? Not worried about it, are you?'

Alison looked directly at her husband for the first time since entering the room. He found it impossible to look directly back. 'Not really, Lissa, but it is getting harder. We only got through on a majority vote last year. There are two or three firms who would give a lot for our little slice of Teflo.'

'What would happen to Northweir if we lost that contract?'

'We would go under. Simple as that. No doubt about it. Our other work would never keep us going any more. They must renew. They must.'

'Poor Larry. You can't be looking forward to today. Not the best way to enjoy your golf.'

'Not to worry, my darling.' Barker faked confidence. 'The old Barker charm will see us through. Hasn't let us down so far. And how are you going to spend your day?'

'Me? Picking up flowers in town, taking them to the Royal, help arrange them for the dinner tonight, take Joan to Lady A's coffee morning, meet Robert from school at one o'clock and take him out to lunch somewhere.

14

Afternoon free. Then the dutiful wife at your Royal Westmere dinner tonight.'

'That's nice. Sounds fun.'

Fun. The highspot of the Shepworth year. The annual meeting of the Teflo hierarchy with their attendant acolytes, ambitious industrial novices, postulants from other companies and less fashionable courses, all thinly disguised as the local golfing society. The air they would breathe would be polluted by Teflo. The word Teflo would be printed all over the balls they would use. Alison often wondered how she had come to marry a golfing man. She hated golf. She hated her subservience to the sport, her golfing husband, the Royal Westmere, the Society, the President and Teflo, ever Teflo, bloody Teflo. For how many years now had she done it? How did she tolerate it? Could she have stood it if she had not been happy? Perhaps she had been content to submit to this life of sophisticated amentia in return for Robert. Was this the price she had been expected to pay for her son? Would she have pulled herself free from the cloying comfort if Robert had not been born? She knew she had ability; far more than her husband. Why then had she stayed? What held her? Love and loyalty to that man in the bed, inadequate, pathetic, but still Robert's father? Fear of competing in a man's world? Sheer bloody laziness?

'What time are you playing?'

'Ten o'clock.'

'Then I suggest you get a move on, my lad. I've got a hair appointment at nine, so I'm off. What time shall I see you? Six? Half past?'

Barker looked at his wife with admiration he tried to conceal. Tall for a woman, she stood as if proud of it, head held high. He looked at the curves the plain but elegant suit failed to hide; the silk blouse gaping at the neck, sexy but not vulgar. How long was it since he had slid his hand in there? There had been a time when he would not have let her get away with looking like that, hair appointment or no hair appointment. There had been a time when she would not have minded either; positively bloody randy she had been. You would never have thought it to look at her. But now she would wriggle away; find some excuse. Good thing really, he supposed. He would only look a fool again. This bloody impotence. It was the booze, almost certainly the booze. She never made fun of him though, he had to give her that. Strange, but he was not really missing it any more. As long as he had the old Scotch, he could put up with anything. He wondered whether Alison was missing it – she couldn't be having any on the side. In Shepworth? Everyone would know about it. Can't turn over in bed in this place without the neighbours knowing about it. Still they say the husband is always the last to know. Don't be ridiculous. The booze is getting to you, mate. Who would there be around here, anyway? She would be pretty fussy; would have to be her type; fellow would have to have a mind as well as a body. Not many of those to choose from in Shepworth. Who were the possible runners? Someone like Michael Brookes. He could not think of anyone else. Michael Brookes? Steady as a rock, solid old Michael? Now you really are going daft.

'Did you say anything?' asked Alison.

'No. Just thinking.' Barker laughed.

'Well stop thinking and get shaved. Otherwise you are going to be late.'

She bent over him to kiss him goodbye. He smelt her perfume and imagined her breasts hanging inside her blouse.

'Oh, Larry, I nearly forgot,' Alison called from the top of the stairs. 'Bill Rothwell rang several times yesterday. Said it was most urgent. He even rang about eleven last night. Said he'd rung the Royal more than once but they couldn't find you. He wants you to ring him at Teflo first thing this morning, without fail.'

'Blast that man.'

'He sounded very worried, Larry.'

'All right, all right. I'll ring him as soon as I get up.'

''Bye then, Larry. See you this evening.'

Blast the man. Alison must have known all along there had been no high-powered game of bridge with Sir John Anderson. Yet there had been no flicker of reaction to his lies. Snooty bitch. Early in their marriage Barker had flaunted his wife's intelligence to his friends like some prized possession. Now he resented it, resentment that broke silence when he was drunk, with sneering remarks about having married above his intellectual station. That damned legal brain. Probably guessed he'd spent the night in the Harbour Club, that the game had been poker and that, as usual, he'd been too drunk to win.

With a glance at the clock, Barker got out of bed, shuffling to the bathroom to be confronted with his reflection in the mirror over the handbasin. Bloodshot, watery eyes were deep-set in sagging features, the folds of inelastic skin beneath his chin belonging to a man of sixty-one, not forty-one.

'Christ.'

He tried to clean his teeth but the brush in the back of his mouth made him gag. Taking his pyjama jacket off, he shivered as he washed. He began to shave. His shivering condensed to a coarse tremor which made even his electric razor unmanageable. His arm ached and he began to sweat. He switched the razor off and put it down. Placing the bathroom stool in front of the airing cupboard, he climbed unsteadily on to it. He opened the top compartment, unused but for storing spare linen, slid his hand in, thief-like, and withdrew the bottle of whisky. Ten minutes later, more erect, more confident, he finished shaving. The strain of being his father's son was becoming intolerable.

Tom Barker had been a twenty-one-year-old unemployed garage hand in Dunbridge when his wife had presented him with twin sons, Laurence and Adrian. Untrained, and penniless, ambitious and energetic, he had joined the Army as a driver in the Royal Army Service Corps. He had had a 'good' war. At Alamein he had been a Company Sergeant Major in a Royal Electrical and Mechanical Engineers Tank Recovery Unit. Between the North Africa campaign and the Western Offensive he had been commis-sioned and, at Wesel in 1945, he had got his MC just in time, driving a bulldozer under sniper fire to clear road junctions which had been over-bombed.

Demobbed in 1946, he had returned to Dunbridge where his wife handed over the thirteen-year-old twins as she waved him goodbye and crossed the Atlantic to the arms of the American Army sergeant who had been such a comfort to her during Tom's absence. With two army surplus lorries, Tom started a small haulage firm, assisted by Yorkshireman Bill Rothwell, his ex Company Sergeant Major, a man as reliable as he was unimaginative. As the years had passed, Barker's drive and integrity had obtained regular contracts from the local fertiliser firm producing ammo-nium sulphate. The lorries had multiplied; they had acquired a bulldozer; they had rapidly become the recognized experts on the use of mobile cranes. They had gone into plant hire. Northweir Plant had been born and had flourished.

Northweir Plant had come of age when the local fertiliser firm had been taken over by Teflo. Vast constructional work had come their way in preparation of the plant for the production of caprolactam, a basic material in the manufacture of nylon. Tom Barker had worked so well with John Anderson of Teflo that Northweir's new offices were built within the Teflo compound. Tom had been a guest at Sir John's post-investiture party at the Savoy, shortly after the royal opening of Teflo in 1964. It had been boom time.

But such success bore a price, total commitment to the task in hand,

17

leaving little time for anything else, certainly not for his sons who were frequently left to their own devices as they grew up. Adrian had not suffered from this neglect. He seemed barely to have needed his father, easily making his way from school to St John's, Cambridge, with an open scholarship. He came down with a first in law and, at the Inner Temple, a brilliant future was predicted for him, an opinion with which Adrian, supremely confident, cold and utterly ruthless, wholeheartedly concurred, not doubting for a moment that he would take silk or that a lucrative practice within walking distance of the Law Courts was no more than his just deserts. He had viewed Dunbridge as no more than a stumbling block in his path out of the mediocre, only conceding when pressed that his father's sheer energy and the success of Northweir Plant had fortunately provided the funds to prime the pump.

Laurence Barker had never experienced his brother's vaulting ambition, nor his success. A talented athlete and ball player, he had scraped through his accountancy finals after endless examination resits, crammer courses and private tuition but it had been obvious to Tom that his playboy son was quite incapable of making his own way in competitive commerce. The sinecure of Company Secretary was created at Northweir for Larry, to the open disgust of Bill Rothwell. Tom's hopes for his wild son had glowed temporarily when Larry had married a girl Tom had adored. Alison had been swept off her feet by this extrovert, good-looking son of success. Her law degree had also been obtained with first-class honours, albeit red brick, and a sprinkling of distinctions had followed this in her Law Society examinations. Several practices in Dunbridge and Shepworth beckoned. But the career she had planned for herself had been snatched from her. When she finished her articles in 1958, she had found herself married, pregnant and installed in the house next to the Old Mill in Shepworth. Trapped with love and comfort.

In 1968, Tom Barker had gone to see Michael Brookes. Just a bit of indigestion. Lost a bit of weight. Six weeks later, he was dead. The linchpin had fallen out of Northweir and the plant wobbled, sending shudders through many lives. The old man had left forty per cent of Northweir Plant to Larry, forty per cent to Adrian and twenty per cent to Alison. Adrian had appeared for the day of the funeral. Sentiment had not clouded his judgment. They should sell Northweir as a going concern and Larry should start a small accountancy practice or take some full-time managerial post. Alison's loyalty had outweighed her reason and she had supported Larry in his decision to keep Northweir going. Washing his hands of the whole affair, Adrian had made one further comment. As Alison had seen him on to the train at Preston, he had turned to her with the nearest to confusion she had ever seen in her brother-in-law.

'And I think you ought to go out and get a job too,' he had blurted, disappearing into the carriage before Alison could reply.

And so the disintegration of Northweir Plant had started. Plant hire had become a cut-throat business. Indecisions, bad decisions, no decisions, and lack of confidence in the founder's son blighted the company; gold of the Barker Midas touch had turned to lead. There had been a bad winter and a road construction contract with penalty clauses; should he not have been around instead of off skiing for three weeks? Was it true about his drinking? And his gambling debts? Rumours abounded.

As Larry reflected on the growing mantle of problems, he took another gulp of whisky, this time without even the ceremony of pouring it into a glass, before tucking the bottle back under the blankets.

'Aaach! Bugger them all,' he snarled as he dressed, suddenly aggressive, temporarily assertive.

He let himself out through the back door, omitting to lock it behind him. The car's wheel spun, making the gravel fly, as he let the clutch out viciously.

3

Michael Brookes parked his ageing Rover in front of the forbidding grey stone hospital entrance. He did not lock the car, its wings mottled with rust; with luck someone might steal it. He had been due to change his car when Rosemary had been taken ill. Since she had died he simply had not bothered.

He ran up the steps and pushed through the swing door. 'Good morning, Mr Hook.'

'Good morning, sir.'

Dunbridge General Hospital still clung to its Head Porter, ensconced behind his gleaming mahogany desk in the main entrance hall. 'Just a relic of the old voluntary hospitals,' Councillor Rothwell had complained at the first meeting of the new Area Health Authority. 'He's only there to touch his cap to these bloody consultants coming in and out. I propose, Mr Chairman, that he be moved where he can do some real work, not just ponce around for the sake of the doctors.'

Hook had stayed where he was. Fortunately there had been enough old hands on the new committee to understand what Hook represented. To appreciate Hook was to comprehend the ethos of a district general hospital. Dunbridge General was a family. It was housed in substandard buildings, in keeping with so many families in that part of the north-west. The hospital was big enough to be efficient, small enough to give everyone an identity. There were quarrels, love affairs, scandals, marriages, births, deaths. The whole family felt a loss, shared in a happiness or a guilt. There were black sheep, wheeler-dealers, moonlighters, hard-working intro-verts, maiden aunts, father figures. Consultants drove into reserved park-ing spaces in gleaming new cars; cheerfully profane ladies earned a pittance slopping out the distant geriatric blocks. If there was a centre to this sprawling jumble of buildings, it was the entrance hall, the desk within the hall, the man behind the desk. For thousands of anxious patients he was the first impression of a hospital that might mean life or death to them. Hook shepherded, reassured, counselled, communicated. With the telephone switchboard at his back, he was the hospital's most vital link. If the communication system was busier on the day of a big race, who was going to complain?

'Mr Harrington's compliments, sir, and could he have a word with you at your convenience?' An imaginary speck of dust was flicked from a sleeve. 'Had enough papers with him for a court martial. Not been up to anything you shouldn't have, have you, sir?'

'Not that I know of, Mr Hook.' Michael laughed. 'You tell me, you'd probably know first. Nothing much gets past this place. Where did he go?'

'Up to his room, sir.'

'Then I'll see him later in theatre, no doubt.'

The entrance hall had been tarted up with terrazzo floor, veneered chipboard panelling and modern light fittings in a vain attempt to bring it into the twentieth century. The main corridor, though, had defied mod-ernisation. The green-tiled walls were mottled with age; plaques in mem-ory of long-forgotten medical honoraries were ignored by all who passed; boards with long-discontinued lists of charitable donations held the plaster up in places. The dead past looked down on the lively bustle beneath. This

20

corridor was the heart of the hospital, through which circulated red-cloaked nurses, and white-coated doctors, whirled along in a plasma of porters, patients, secretaries, clerks, technicians, radiographers.

Brookes turned into the new theatre corridor, leaving the sturdy protection of Victorian stone masons for the doubtful durability of modern technology. In a few strides he moved from Lister to Barnard, from antisepsis to asepsis, from carbolic to transplants, from chloroform to controlled respiration. It had not been many years since Dunbridge General's theatres had matched the rest of the hospital. That was before the tragedy – a routine clean operation, then tetanus, death, the scandal, the enquiry and condemnation of outside experts who had ignored warnings for years, the magical appearance of money previously denied, the three glistening new theatres. George Harrington's babies. Harrington had fussed over their conception, driving architects and builders to despair, but the theatres had been born as near perfect as Harrington could make them.

In the surgeons' room six battered chairs were arranged haphazardly around the chipped coffee table. Many were the times that Michael had sat there, head back, eyes closed, sweaty, dry mouthed, cold where patches of blood had soaked through trousers he was too tired to change, experiencing the emotions he had glimpsed in those faces so long ago, in another operating theatre, during an air raid. Over the years, there had been the teenager on the go-cart and his ruptured liver, the young butcher's assistant slicing his own femoral artery, the close range shotgun wound of a *crime passionnel*, the attempted suicides, the car crashes. He had felt it all. Exhaustion buoyed with exhilaration when things had gone well. Exhaustion multiplied a thousand times by failure tinged with guilt. Could he have done better? Would someone else have done better?

Like all surgeons, he was addicted to the operating theatre and its atmosphere. He would be drawn back time and time again, like the single-handed sailor to the sea. More at home in theatre or boat than anywhere else, surgeon and sailor respect the menacing calm, are kept alive by eternal watchfulness, are shriven by the exhaustion of sudden catastrophe, wonder why they ever do it. And why? Because they become part of an élite; not above his fellow man, just apart. Someone who has experienced an intensity of feeling not given to everyone. An élite of airline pilots, miners, deep-sea fishermen, soldiers in Belfast, rock climbers. All the same, all different. Yet the surgeon's life is never at risk. Did this not exclude him from this élite? Brookes thought not. There is a fear other than the fear of death. Looking at the soldier dying in a Belfast street with a bullet in his neck, is a comrade who knows it might not have happened if he had not taken cover in a doorway. The miner whose life is being squeezed out by a roof fall is watched by another who put up the props that failed. A rock climber's mistake will cause his best friend to fall to his death. The surgeon might watch the post mortem on the patient he has failed to save – because death was inevitable or, perhaps, because, in his own judgment, negligence, technical ineptitude or cramping fear had taken the upper hand? For the surgeon, the insistent unanswerable self-question would not be a once in a lifetime affair but, as Brookes knew, would be asked repeatedly until the day he retired.

He looked at the typed sheet pinned to the board. His morning's list. A biopsy of breast, perhaps a mastectomy, a gastrectomy for carcinoma, two hernias and a piles. The hernias and the piles he dismissed from his mind. All straightforward. The Registrar, Shah, would do those. The lump in the breast; he remembered her. Terrified as usual. All those blasted women's magazines. He thought it would be benign. He hoped so: she had a couple of kids. The stomach; that was different, and certainly serious. Brookes suddenly realised that he had not seen the report on the barium meal; only heard it second-hand. He must ring Max Verney. He stretched for the phone on the wall, checking the patient's name on the list as he did so. Gregson. James Gregson, aged seventy-two.

On the ward round the day before, Gregson's wife had sat at his bedside, holding his hand. She had looked frightened, quiet, no trouble, so Brookes had not asked her to leave. Gareth Pritchard, Brookes' House Surgeon, had given him Gregson's history.

'Have you any pain, Mr Gregson?'

'None, sir. That's the strange thing. None at all.'

'Just off your food and vomiting a bit?'

'And as weak as a kitten, doctor. Sorry, Mr Brookes.'

'But no pain? None in your back.'

'No, sir.'

Brookes had perched with one buttock on the edge of the bed, clearing a gap between pyjama jacket and trousers. He had felt gently below the ribs. No lump. No liver. He had turned his head over his shoulder towards Pritchard.

'Barium meal?'

'Neoplasm pyloric antrum, sir.'

There had been a pause as patient and surgeon smiled at each other, one searching for hope, the other endeavouring to give it. A picture of

22

Gregson's stomach had flashed through Brookes' mind with textbook diagrams of all the possible surgical procedures. Should he tell Gregson he had cancer if Gregson didn't ask? Brookes still didn't know the answer to that one. Should he explain to Gregson all the possible operations, their pros and cons? No. He was sure of that one. He'd made that mistake before. That was his job. Any doubt about what should be done, should anything be done at all, was for him, not Gregson. For Gregson there must be nothing but reassuring certainty, even if its provision involved Brookes lying his soul into perdition. He must not sell Gregson short.

'Well, what are you going to do with me, Mr Brookes?'

Brookes had seen the hands squeeze tighter.

'You've got an ulcer, Mr Gregson.'

'An ulcer, is it?'

'Yes. An ulcer in your stomach. And it's beginning to block the outlet. That's why you're vomiting.'

'It's a bad one then?'

'Yes, but nothing we can't put right for you.'

No hesitation. No flicker of doubt in voice, eyes, lips.

'What does that mean exactly?'

'It means an operation.'

'When?'

'Tomorrow.'

Gregson had turned to his wife. 'An operation tomorrow, love.'

'Will he be all right, doctor?'

'Mister, love. Mr Brookes is a surgeon.'

'Yes, of course, Mrs Gregson.' Brookes had smiled as he had looked her straight in the eyes, thinking: 'How the hell can you say that when you know damn well it's probably inoperable?' But his confidence trick had worked; after all, he was an expert.

'Then you'd better carry on, Mr Brookes. I know I'll be in good hands.'

'I'm sure it's the right thing to do, Mr Gregson. Your vomiting is only going to get worse if you don't have something done.' There had been enough truth in what he had said to make it acceptable to him, enough bullshit to make him wonder. Before passing on to the next patient, Brookes had patted Gregson's foot through the blankets, a deal struck between friends.

That had been yesterday. Today he must see just how far he could keep his word. He dialled a number on the internal telephone.

'X-ray. Can I help you?'

'Mr Brookes here. Can I speak to Dr Verney for a moment, please?'

'He's only just started screening, Mr Brookes. Is it urgent?'

Smiling at her apprehension, Michael reassured her: 'Don't worry. I'll take the blame. Tell him it's about a patient I'm operating on this morning.'

'All right, sir. Wish me luck. I'll see what I can do.'

Brookes imagined Verney's language and heard his rapid footsteps.

'Yes, Michael?' Friendship encased in irritation.

'Sorry, Max. I should have had a word with you yesterday. Patient called Gregson. Nice old man about seventy. You did a barium meal on him last week.'

'I remember. What's the problem?'

'I'm operating on him this morning. What did you think?'

'What I wrote in the report.' Not one of Verney's good days. 'He's got a carcinoma.'

'No doubt? He looks very fit and there's no pain at all.'

'No doubt. Bloody big ulcer. Mostly posterior wall. No peristalsis in a wide area around. Through to the pancreas too. You'll be bloody lucky to get that out.'

'Thanks, Max. That's all I wanted to know.' A grunt and the line went dead.

With a grin, Michael passed through into the surgeons' changing-room to find David John Williams standing in his shirt tails, hairy legs disappearing into bright red socks. A few years older than Brookes, Dai Jack's war service had probably robbed him of a Welsh cap at scrum-half. Now the stocky strength of youth was giving way to fat. Out of theatre he was fiery and unpredictable; curse you one minute, buy you a drink the next. In theatre his anaesthesia was based on artistry rather than science. Patient and doctor became as one. He handled newborn babies and crumbling geriatrics like Dresden. During the worst cases, Brookes never gave him a thought, the highest compliment he could pay.

'Good morning, David.'

'Morning, Michael.'

The words stimulated a fit of coughing. Williams' face became congested as he coughed up the previous night's nicotine.

'I see you have kept the pick of the litter for me, as usual. The breast has got asthma, one of the hernias is a diabetic and the piles had a coronary last year.'

'Take it as a compliment to your skill,' Brookes laughed.

24

'Balls. The poor old bastard with the carcinoma is about the fittest of the lot. What do you intend doing to him?'

'A gastrectomy if I can. If not, some sort of bypass. Must stop him vomiting to death if we can. Hell of a nice old boy.'

As Brookes followed Williams out into the corridor between changing-room and operating theatre, he passed Henry Orme, head down, pushing a respirator festooned with cables, plastic tubing and corrugated hose.

His rank of Consultant Anaesthetist was equal to that of Brookes and Williams, Harrington and the rest, but intellectually he existed on a different plane. He was the hospital medical odd bod and rarely gave an anaesthetic. Dunbridge General was sufficiently well blessed with anaes-thetists that cover could be given for colleagues on leave without having to bother Orme, for which Brookes was not the only surgeon to give thanks. For Orme was not an attractive man and, denied the comforting anodyne of stupidity, he had become embittered by the constant small withdrawals, both mental and physical, of those he worked with. His was an active, analytical mind trapped in a repulsive body and he cursed the Creator who had made such a mismatch. He felt sure that, somewhere, a village idiot was walking round in the body of an Adonis he did not deserve.

Orme had been the professor's nightmare, the research assistant who was far cleverer than he but whom no one would take off his hands. It had taken many sleepless nights to come up with the solution of the super-numerary consultant post with a generous research grant, and Dunbridge General had, at the time, felt honoured to be chosen for the purpose. The professor had been happy to shunt Orme and his beloved respira-tors into an obscure siding and, as time had passed, so had Dunbridge General.

'Strange beggar,' Brookes thought, the only thought he gave Orme as he pushed his way through the spring-hinged door into the scrub-up room. Scrubbed and gowned, he walked into the operating theatre to give his last 'good morning' to Sister Kay, standing stiff and erect, hands resting on the instrument trolley. Normally, by now, the patient would have been somewhere between anaesthetic-room and theatre and Brookes raised an eyebrow and nodded enquiringly towards the anaesthetic-room.

'Bit of spasm, I believe, sir. Poor woman is terrified.'

As she spoke the doors were opened and Williams appeared, syringe in hand, with orderlies pushing the patient, temporarily disconnected from any machine. Quickly, wordlessly, she was connected to the machine in the theatre, the orderlies expert from constant repetition.

'Sorry, Michael, but she's got a bloody awful chest. I hope you don't have to do a mastectomy.'

Within minutes the terrorising piece of flesh was removed, bisected, inspected, remarked upon, dropped into a plastic bag and despatched for frozen sectioning. Brookes, confident that it was benign, closed the wound. He perched on the edge of a stool to wait for the report that would prove him right or wrong. The patient lay with the blissful inattention of the anaesthetised. Williams hovered with his finger over the receive button of the intercom and Pritchard leant against the patient, mentally undressing the swab nurse. Sister Kay stood erect.

'How is Jonathan, sir?'

'Very well, thank you, Sister.'

'I haven't seen him since last Christmas but he was growing so tall; good gracious me.'

She lifted both hands from her instrument tray as she ground out the guttural sound that belied her otherwise immaculate accent. Michael looked at her and smiled affectionately. An amazing woman, he thought. She had been a theatre sister when he had been appointed and he knew no more about her now than when they first met. All he knew was that she was the best theatre sister he had ever worked with. But outside the hospital she vanished. In all the years she had been there no one had got close enough to get a glimpse of her private life.

The intercom buzzer had only sounded once when Williams pressed the button. He grinned as he inclined his head towards the wall.

'About time, young Gracie. Bit early for coffee, isn't it?'

Gracie's voice sounded as if it came from lunar orbit.

'Morning, Dai Jack. Any chance there's a proper doctor down there who can take a message?'

The banter confirmed that the lump had been benign and it was with a 'humph' of pleasure that Sister Kay scooped up her instruments between her hands. Middle-aged nursing sisters ask not for whom that particular bell tolls.

After handing his patient into the care of the recovery-room staff, Williams went back to the anaesthetic-room. Gregson lay there, smiling as he chatted quietly to the escort nurse, his quiet bravery typical of a man who thinks he's of little importance. The ward check-list was handed to Williams, consent, temperature, blood pressure, number, identity disc, time of premedication, drugs given, passed urine, false teeth, rings, contact lenses, wigs; the list seemed endless. A forthright character, Williams had

Gregson laughing gently as pentothal flowed through the cannula in his vein, carrying him down to a few moments of deep sleep into which nearly two hours of real time would be telescoped. Williams paralysed Gregson, passed an endotracheal tube, pushed him into the theatre and connected him to the machine which was waiting with its gases flowing. Shah had now joined Brookes at the table.

Michael opened the abdomen automatically, his mind no more than a jumble of thoughts, not all related to the patient. He turned to wash away the blood and dusting powder caked on his gloves. He then eased his right hand into the abdomen, intent now only on gathering evidence, applying knowledge born of experience, making a decision. He leaned forward, his right hand buried to the wrist, his eyes focused on the middle distance over Shah's right shoulder. Pritchard, Sister Kay, Shah, Williams all looked at his face.

'Carcinoma. Big one. Seems pretty mobile though.' His forearm changed its attitude slightly. 'Liver's clear. Let's see if there's anything in the pelvis.' Changing hands, Brookes' left arm disappeared up to midforearm as his finger swept the pelvic cavity. 'Clear. No peritoneal deposits that I can feel. Now it all depends on whether it's fixed to the pancreas. Let me open the lesser sac and see. A self-retaining retractor, please, Sister.' Four clamps, a few snips of the scissors, four catgut ligatures tied with conjuror-like dexterity, and he probed behind the stomach with two fingers. Delight was obvious in his voice. Delight for the patient or because he had been proved right and Verney wrong? Both.

'The pancreas is free. No reason why we shouldn't do a gastrectomy if you're happy, David.'

'No problem my end. Depends a bit on what you intend doing exactly. What are you going to do, a total?'

'No, a Polya subtotal. I reckon that's all he needs.'

And so, two decisions were made, one easy, one difficult. Like all such decisions there was a time limit. No going away and thinking about it; can't go and read the books again. Decisions made under a merciless light before half a dozen critical witnesses. No one really to discuss it with. The Registrar, perhaps, but he'd be biased. Always anxious to see radical surgery done, the youngsters. And Brookes must appear decisive whatever went on behind the poker face. The great leader must not be seen to dither; bad for morale and a good theatre is based on good morale.

The first decision was the easy one. A cancer with no secondary spread, technically capable of being removed, with the alternative being death by continuous vomiting. Easy.

The second decision was much more difficult, more complex, more personal, more worrying. Option one: to remove the growth locally, stop the vomiting, with low risk to the patient but increased chance of recurrence. Option two: remove the stomach totally together with the spleen, omentum, lymph glands and a bit of pancreas, a radical excision carrying a high risk to the patient with, it was believed, less chance of recurrence. Does the surgeon buy extra years for the few with the lives of others? He can't ask the patients. He alone must decide. He will not be short of advice from those who do not have to make the ultimate decision. Inevitably the surgeon's personality becomes a factor. Throughout their careers some, by their very nature, are radical operators, certain in their belief, while others are more conservative, open to doubt. Most, wherever along the scale they begin, tend to become more conservative with age and experience. It is rare indeed for a conservative surgeon to become more radical.

Instinctively, Michael was a conservative man, sensitive enough to have cracked under the mortality rate some other surgical disciplines would demand. He did not find it easy to live with. Was he truly conservative from conviction or just frightened of the big stuff? He did not think it was the latter. In his younger days he had performed extensive ablations at times just to show he could do them. To show whom? Himself? His Registrar? The GP? The patient? Whom was he trying to impress? There was no doubt that it was the radical surgeons that got the limelight, the reputations. Was he jealous? Who cared at the end of the day, anyway? Brookes looked around him. The patient would not know the difference. David Williams, he knew, felt the same way as he. Pritchard was only doing six months' surgery as required by law. Sister Kay was blindly devoted to him, and the swab nurse did not know what the hell was going on. That left Shah. Brookes could feel the waves of disapproval coming over the table. But was that good enough reason for doing an operation you thought ill-advised? Hell, no. Do what you think is right; always providing, of course, you are sure it is right.

'A Polya gastrectomy then, Sister.'

The atmosphere relaxed. This was an operation Brookes liked and, therefore, did well. It was an operation with predictable stages which pleased Sister Kay. There were no special problems for Williams as he sat on his stool, doodling in Biro on white trousers, stretched across broad thighs. Shah wondered whether the old man would give him the anastomosis to do, compensation perhaps for not seeing a total gastrectomy performed. The only difficulty Pritchard was experiencing was deciding whether the swab nurse was wearing a bra.

Brookes freed the greater curvature of the stomach, tied the right gastric artery, clamped and divided the duodenal stump. Crisply relaxed, no problems.

'That's the duodenum closed, Sister.' Time for a short pause in concentration before the next stage. 'Now, young Pritchard, what artery is that?'

'Artery, sir?' Pritchard was startled out of his reverie. His arm ached from holding a retractor for the last twenty minutes.

'That one there.'

Pritchard looked along the forceps pointing at the pulsating tube.

'No idea, sir,' he replied, not unduly ashamed of his ignorance.

'Gastroduodenal, Pritchard. Gastroduodenal. The one that bleeds like hell in duodenal ulcer sometimes. I seem to remember your father was not much of an anatomist either.'

Pritchard's father, now cloistered in a country practice, had been a student contemporary of Brookes.

'No, sir.'

'How is your father? Is he fit?'

'Yes, thank you, sir. He reckons he has got the secret at last. Does his practice with his spinal cord and uses his cortex only to catch the salmon.'

While Williams and Brookes laughed, Sister Kay frowned over her mask at the brash young man who could be so familiar with his chief. Brookes looked paternally at his young assistant. A nice lad that, he thought. A chip off the old block. A bit of a ram, if all he heard was correct, but good luck to him as long as he kept it out of the hospital. Good houseman. Often the way with these rather wild young bucks. Plenty of guts too. Enjoyed watching him play rugby last winter.

Michael turned his attention to his Registrar. 'Now then, Shah. The next thing is to ligate the left gastric vessels. What do you think is the better way of getting at them, from the front or the back?'

Critically viewing the stomach as it was held out of the wound, Shah decided, 'From the back, sir.'

'I quite agree. A Moynihan please, Sister.' Brookes held his hand out without raising his eyes from the plexus of artery and veins he was about to tie off. 'Still the best instrument for doing this, I think.' He waved the instrument briefly in front of Shah before pushing its point through the tissues behind the artery.

29

'Bloody hell!'

Relaxation became tension. Everyone hunched forward a little as their eyes tried to peer into the wound. Brookes rarely swore. There must be some good cause.

The cause was a sudden gush of blood from the region where he had been inserting the points of the forceps. The tip of the instrument disappeared rapidly into a dark pool, the level rising at an alarming rate in the confined space in which he was working. The site of the bleeding was already out of view, hidden beneath the glinting surface. Again Brookes experienced that sharp, chest-constricting moment of complete loneliness. It was as if a ground-glass cylindrical screen had descended, isolating him with this warm, pulsating, rapidly deteriorating problem. Beyond the screen he was aware of vague faces, voices, shapes, all anxious to help, but unable themselves to do what he alone could do. God, how he wished he were somewhere else; anywhere else. Meeting his son from school; seeing Alison. Come on now. So the buck stops here. Get on with it. You have been in worse spots before. A few minutes and all will be peace again. Now. Slowly. Gently. No panic.

It was a moment when mistakes could be made by mentally freezing and doing nothing, or by flying into furious hyperactivity. The happy mean was only reached after coping with many such incidents over the years. The momentary panic did not last as long now, but Brookes knew it would never be overcome completely.

Brookes withdrew the forceps and laid them down rapidly but deliberately; no place these days for forceps flying all over the theatre. Inserting his left hand into the abdomen and squeezing the region of the bleeding point with his index finger and thumb, he turned to Williams at the head of the table.

'Bit of a problem, I'm afraid, David.'

All he got was all he wanted at that stage: a friendly nod and an encouraging smile. Williams walked round his machine to peer unobtrusively over Brookes' shoulder. That is a fair bleed, he thought. Looks venous and awkward to get at. Still he seems to have got it under control at least for the moment. He looked at Brookes' profile, as much as was not hidden under cap and mask. He looked calm enough. He wondered what went on inside. He was sure that Brookes was not as unruffled as that underneath. Why did not Brookes curse and swear a bit when things went wrong, like he did? Much better for you. Why did some people have to keep up the façade? He must get another couple of units of blood cross-matched.

'Would you get the sucker going, sister, please, and give it to Mr Shah. Thank you. Suck around now, Shah, until we have got a dry field again.' His voice calm and polite, Brookes spoke appreciably more slowly. 'May I have another Moynihan's, please, Sister?'

Sufficient control from the surgeon to say 'please', and it was 'please', 'please', 'please', all down the line. Panic spread twice as fast.

The problem was now temporarily stabilised. With the Moynihan artery forceps poised in his right hand and the bleeding controlled by his left hand, Brookes paused to compose himself both mentally and physically, like an athlete balancing himself in mind and body before a high jump. Why the hell had he done a thing like that? How many times had he been round those vessels before without any trouble? Hundreds of times. Still, no doubt better surgeons than he had made the same mistake. Now take it slowly. He must go and meet Jonathan from school today. He would have plenty of time whatever happened here. Now, come on, get that forceps round the back of that vein. Alison would be there, meeting Robert. What would happen if he put the forceps through the vein even higher up? Well, he would have to cope with that too, wouldn't he. He wanted another man's wife. Oh God, please don't let me tear the vein higher up. He really must spend more time with his son. Christ, there must be easier ways to make a living. Perhaps they could have a weekend in Liverpool together, just the two of them; perhaps go to the theatre. Why not a weekend in London? Easy now. He could feel the forceps' points almost safely through the resistant flesh. This was the crucial moment; that thin layer between his finger and the cold metal might be nothing more than the vein again. Got it. It's through. Thank God for that. Nothing to go really wrong from here on. He's bound to lose some more blood when I take my fingers away, especially from back bleeding, but it should come right now. Now where the hell is that aneurysm needle?

'An aneurysm needle with thread, please, Sister.' Brookes' voice was still matter of fact. Nothing was rushed. Nothing got dropped at the crucial moment.

'That is fine thread, Mr Brookes,' said Sister Kay, handing him the loaded aneurysm needle.

'Will do well, thank you, Sister,' replied Brookes, passing the instrument around the vessels through the hole he had just made with the Moynihans.

'Would you please tie that for me, Shah, while I keep my hand in place.'

Brookes watched critically as Shah tied the ligature. Shah had a good pair of hands but Brookes would put another ligature around himself later.

31

Another ligature on the other side of the torn vessels and Brookes was able to divide them. There was more bleeding on the stomach side as small veins slipped out of the mass ligature but it was easily managed.

'Well done everyone, panic over. That can be quite nasty.' Brookes looked across at his Registrar. 'Never, never dive for one of those with a forceps. Bound to make it worse. Always try to get some sort of control first. It's one of those times when he who hesitates is saved. Now that's something you've learned this morning. Much better than watching a total radical gastrectomy being done.'

He must keep up the old pretence, making them think that the episode had taken nothing out of him. He breathed not a word about the hundred gut-aching episodes as a junior that had given him the competence to deal with such crises. He looked at the nurse opposite: she probably hadn't taken her mind off her boyfriend the whole time. It was at times like these that he wondered why he never shouted a bit, demanding that someone should share the load. Yet reason always regained the upper hand. Michael knew it was the way he had wanted it, and there was always the fact of the difference in pay cheques to be borne in mind. He looked across the table and smiled. 'I think I deserve a cup of coffee after that, Sister. In any case, I know Shah won't talk to me for a week if I don't let him do the anastomosis.'

He backed away, pulling off his gloves. A nod from Sister Kay brought the swab nurse to Brookes' back. She fumbled at the tapes nervously under Sister Kay's scrutiny.

'Thank you, Sister Kay.'

'My pleasure, Mr Brookes.'

The nod as she spoke was no more than a tribute from one hardened professional to another, but there was a fleeting softening in her features, not amounting to a smile, which said, 'I know. I know.'

4

By the time Larry Barker drove into the crowded car park of the Royal Westmere, he was late. He had begun to shake again and the sight of

Anderson's shining red Mercedes in its reserved space, attended by Sir John's uniformed chauffeur and patiently waiting caddie, did nothing to raise his spirits. It took some time for him to find space for his ageing T-type Bentley. Larry remembered his father taking Robert to London to collect the car; they had made a weekend of it. Then the car had been immaculate, worthy to park alongside any in the Royal. Now it was dented and scratched, the exhaust blowing through cheap repairs. Barker could not maintain it, had no hope of replacing it, yet hung on to it in the same way he hung on to Northweir Plant, refusing to acknowledge his inability to cope.

At the door to the clubhouse Barker met Alex Finlayson, the club Secretary and, together, they went in to find Sir John Anderson who was standing there, empty coffee cup in hand.

'You are late, young man.' There was a smile on Anderson's face but a cold edge to his voice.

'I'm sorry, Sir John, but I had my Plant Foreman on the phone early this morning and there was something at the works that I had to fix before I came. It took a bit longer than I thought.' Traces of the earlier liquid confidence still lingered as he added, 'Not all of us can manage to take two whole days off, you know.'

'Fair enough, Larry,' Anderson laughed. 'Now let me introduce you to your partner, Pierre Beaupré. Pierre is Chairman of one of our rival concerns in Toronto. We're hoping to make a partner out of a competitor, so be nice to him, d'you hear? Pierre, this is young Barker who looks after most of our mobile plant up at Teflo.'

'Pleased to meet you, Larry.' An enormous man uncoiled himself to take one of Barker's hands in both of his and pump it heartily. 'I'm so pleased you're to be my partner today. I need a strong young fella to steady me up. I tend to be a bit wild, I'm afraid.'

Everything about Pierre Beaupré was larger than life. A huge hairy frame, covered in a check shirt of bold colours, was surmounted by a shaggy head split by a massive, friendly grin. Barker felt crushed just to look at him.

'Seems I've been lucky enough to draw the Sec again this year.' Anderson smiled. 'I can't imagine how that happens.'

Barker began to be conscious of that pain over his eyes again. No one could remember when the Secretary had last lost a match. An extremely fit fifty-five-year-old redundant civil servant, Alex Finlayson ran the club with quiet competence, playing golf almost daily, always with the same dour efficiency. Barker was suddenly desperate for a drink but a 'Get changed then, young man' from Anderson made that impossible. By the time Barker reached the first tee, Anderson and Beaupré were fidgeting like men who had been kept waiting. Two caddies hovered disapprovingly behind them. The first green was empty. They were the last off. Anderson's voice, sharpened by a thousand board meetings, cut the soft morning air.

'Right, Larry, what's your handicap?'

'Twelve, Sir John.'

'Pierre here is a Canadian fourteen which makes you twenty-six. Alex is ten and I'm eighteen, which makes a difference of two. Three-eighths of two is six-eighths; that gives us one stroke.'

Brave the man who would argue with the President's maths. Similarly, there was no argument about the pairings.

'Pierre will drive the odds with Alex. We'll have our own little duel on the evens, Larry. Your honour, Alex. Off you go.'

The Secretary, his simple compact style drilling the centre of the first fairway, drove 180 yards into the breeze that always blew at Westmere from one direction or the other. Beaupré took two or three scything practice swings, holding his club like an ice-hockey stick with no over-lapping of his hands. He despatched his ball thirty yards beyond the Secretary's, in spite of lifting a sizeable divot.

'Sorry about that, Larry. Didn't quite catch it properly.'

Anderson, playing from where the Secretary had left him, pulled his shot into a bunker short of the green. Barker, now left with a seven-iron shot to the green, addressed the ball. He was quite unable to concentrate. He made a conscious effort to prevent his tremor starting again. He felt the presence of these hard, successful men. For all their *bonhomie*, they frightened him. He felt threatened by them. They would crush him; take away all he had. His arms felt like rubber. His topped shot scuttled along the fairway to end in the middle of the green.

Two putts saw them down in four to Anderson's and the Secretary's five.

'Well played, partner,' boomed Beaupré as Barker and Anderson walked to the next tee. Anderson said nothing.

With the combination of Barker's nervous jerky stabs and Beaupré's inaccurate, booming flyers, they were lucky to get to the ninth tee only two down. Beaupré and Finlayson had a long walk to the next tee, the Canadian's giant strides contrasting with the shambling trot of his aged caddie, bent so low by the bulging golf bag that his long shabby mackintosh brushed the grass. They were held up further by a slow foursome in front. Anderson's caddie knew almost to the yard where the Secretary's ball was going to land. He handed Anderson the iron club he had decided he should use, sat on a tuft of coarse grass, lit a cigarette and gazed out to sea. Anderson swung the club gently, to and fro, to and fro, deep in thought. He was irritated when Barker interrupted his thoughts but managed to smile. After all, this was not the office; he was meant to be enjoying himself.

'It's a gorgeous day, Sir John.'

'Yes, it is,' replied Anderson, looking around as if he had just noticed it.

There was another strained pause. Desperate to put in a word about the Northweir contract, Barker searched for an opening but failed to find one. They had so little in common that they had nothing to talk about to pave the way. Anderson knew what Barker wanted, but hoped he would not get around to it. He was not going to help him. It was very unlikely Barker would be part of Teflo next year: nervous, apologetic, getting to look scruffy, not eccentric scruffy, dirty scruffy. To think he is Tom Barker's son and married to that beautiful girl.

'How is Lady Anderson?'

'Very well, thank you, Larry.'

Out of the corner of his eye, Barker could see Finlayson preparing to drive. Panicking inwardly, he tried to make his tone light-hearted, like a man simply confirming a foregone conclusion. He stumbled over the words which tumbled out one moment, dried up the next.

'Northweir's contract, Sir John. No problem I imagine this year? We are in good shape, you know.' Should he have said that unless there was some doubt about it? 'Can't imagine not working at Teflo after all these years.' Should he have admitted the possibility? 'I've got quite a few plans for improvements and expansion next year; should improve our service to you a great deal.' That's better. 'I hope you're going to give us the chance to put them into effect.' He laughed. 'I think poor old Dad would turn in his grave if we ever lost our contract with you.'

There, he had said it. He had got it out; for better, for worse. Within seconds he knew which; for the worse. The club in Anderson's hands came to rest. There was no smile on his face as he looked at Barker. He wanted nothing from Barker that several others were not queuing up to do better. But he was not going to tell Barker just yet; the contract still had some time to run.

'Look, Larry. Over there is a man I want a favour from.' Anderson pointed his club in the direction of Beaupré, just moving off the tee. 'Even when you get to be President of somewhere as big as Teflo, you still want things from people. Beaupré can mean a whole lot of money to Teflo, money lost or made. I know it. He knows it. That is why he is in this country. However, at the moment, all I am anxious about is that he has a good round of golf, that he enjoys himself. I don't know yet whether he has any other sporting interests but, if need be, we'll slip a blonde in his bed tonight as well. But I would be crazy to go and start talking mergers in the middle of a round of golf if he didn't feel like it. If he started the conversation, that would be different. Do you get the difference, Larry?'

'Yes, I understand,' Barker replied, head down like an admonished schoolboy.

'The only thing that worries me,' Anderson went on, 'is that Beaupré is not going to win this match. You know our Sec; too bloody mean to lose a match and too straight for me to ask him to throw it. So I'm rather depending on you to win it for me, Larry.' Anderson managed a smile. 'I'll do my best not to stand in your way.' Anderson had relaxed a little as they walked to where their partners had driven. 'We all loved your father, Larry. We would all hate to see what he built up go down. On a personal basis, obviously I would like to help as much as I can, but I have a Board of Directors, you know. Some of them are new. Not all of them remember your father now. And you must have learned by now that business is never run on sentiment. Are you in trouble?'

The question was blunt, direct, but did not specify any particular kind of trouble.

'No, of course not, Sir John.'

'Tell you what, Larry. Come down and see me in Liverpool sometime soon. Ring up and make an appointment. Let's have a chat about things.'

'That would suit me fine, Sir John.'

'Good. Let's leave it at that then.'

Could he do nothing right? Larry felt that fine tremor that went with the void in his belly. No breakfast and at least another hour away from his next drink. The last ten holes back to the clubhouse and the bar stretched away interminably. Anderson had told him, Beaupré must win. Anderson would make sure he would not play as well as Beaupré. All Barker had to do was to play better than Finlayson and they were already two holes down and the stroke hole to come. His head ached and the palms of his hands sweated as they tried to grip the club. They went another hole down.

It was the tenth hole that finally destroyed Barker, almost literally so, had anyone bothered to trace back the sequence of events fate held in store for him. The stroke hole, it was imperative that they made a good show of it if there was to be any hope at three down.

Anderson drove first, the ball flying away sliced but curling back viciously to land in the middle of the fairway 150 yards on. The obsequious 'Good shot' this badly struck ball extracted from all those watching was accepted as homage due to the club President. Barker took his stance in front of the widest fairway on the course, mentally locked in the certainty that his drive would never lie on it. A desperate, rubber-legged, eyes-closed slash, saw his ball hook agonisingly out of bounds into some bracken. In complete silence, Beaupré walked back the hundred yards or so from where he had been waiting for Barker's drive, teed up and put his drive fifty yards beyond Anderson's. Barker walked up the fairway as if through a long cavern of black despair to stand and watch while Finlayson played their second shot. Without hesitation, Finlayson took a five iron, lazily putting the ball within a few yards of the cross bunkers 150 yards on – there for one, stroke gone.

The flag on the tenth green, another hundred yards beyond the cross bunkers, mocked and beckoned in the wind. In a wild swing of mood, Barker's despair was replaced by blind, furious arrogance. He'd show them. He could be as forceful and as dynamic as anyone there. With his brassie clamped in the vice-like grip of desperation, he took a quick back swing, despatching the ball at tremendous speed. Never rising more than three feet above the fairway, it embedded itself in the far wall of the cross bunker.

'Shit.' All polite conventions down, the raw obscenity, snarled in a thick Canadian accent, revealed the ruthless competitor that was the true Beaupré. A savage hack with a sand iron only buried the ball further in the sand and, with a bitter 'conceded', Beaupré picked up without a word to his partner.

By the time the game was lost, six and five, and they had played the bye, Barker and Finlayson for another ball, Anderson and Beaupré double or quits for the original twenty-five pounds, all seemed amiable enough. As they entered the clubhouse, Finlayson went directly to his office, Anderson and Beaupré went to change their shoes and put on the ties that even the club President was required to wear in the dining-room, while Barker homed in on the bar. By the time Anderson and Beaupré joined him, he had already knocked back two large whiskies.

'A bit early for that, isn't it?' Anderson asked, nodding at the large whisky Barker took as he bought pints of lager for Anderson and Beaupré.

'Just trying to blot out the memory of the tenth. I shouldn't think that Pierre here will ever forgive me.'

'Nonsense, Larry. Just wasn't your day.' Beaupré was back to the bluff, affable guest again. 'No doubt we'll get our revenge this afternoon.'

He was interrupted by the steward pushing the telephone across the bar towards Barker.

'Sorry to butt in, gentlemen. It's for you, Mr Barker. A Mr Rothwell. He's getting a bit steamed up. Says he's been trying to get you since last night. He rang earlier but I didn't think you would want to be brought off the course.'

Sensing Anderson's eyes on his back, Barker said, as lightly as he could, 'Thanks, steward. I'll take it in the hall. Don't want to bring business into the bar, do we?' He turned to Anderson and Beaupré. 'If you'll excuse me a moment.'

'Same trouble you were dealing with this morning, d'you think?' asked Anderson, his skin wrinkling around half-closed eyes. Beaupré watched, interested.

'Possibly, Sir John. My foreman is normally a very steady reliable chap. Not like him to be confused. I'd better have a word with him.'

That was the second time that bastard Rothwell had dropped him in it. It was almost as if he was trying to do it. When Barker re-entered the room he smiled, loose-lipped.

'I'm afraid I'm going to have to leave you two gentlemen to lunch alone.' Barker hoped he was giving the picture of the over-worked executive. 'There's another small problem at the plant that it seems can't be fixed without me. I'm sorry. I was really looking forward to another round this afternoon. However, duty first, as they say.'

Barker extended his hand to Beaupré to have it grasped perfunctorily without being shaken.

'I'm so pleased to have met you, Mr Beaupré. Goodbye, Sir John. I'll be in touch as you suggested.'

From Beaupré he got courteous insincerity.

'It's been a pleasure, Larry, and thanks for the game.'

From Anderson, he got no more than a nod.

Barker had never realised how far it was to walk from the bar to the door, imagining, quite wrongly, that Beaupré and Anderson were watching him leave. Long before he had reached the door, the two men were surrounded by those hoping, determined to buy them a drink.

Conditions in the Royal Westmere's common-room and bar were atypical in that they had been temporarily infiltrated by outsiders, in the form of a large golfing society, an event the hard core of members did their utmost to avoid. Even so, anyone with an analytical mind could still define at least three sub-groups amongst the members that lunch-time.

There was the relatively small group which drank, gossiped, played cards and never put a foot on the first tee. Small, quiet men, their eyes wet with the tear that never drops, they were rarely seen standing, the glass in their hand a small one, never full, never quite empty. Many had joined this group through age or illness. Most were happily bound to its nucleus by the natural laws of mutual affinity.

Another group were the keen golfers, clear-eyed, early to bed, low-handicap men. Immaculate in their matching trousers and jumpers, the lunch-time maximum was a pint of shandy because of that important afternoon foursome. At tea-time they were first in, showered and changed, to settle to their poached eggs and pot of tea. Inability to remember in detail every stroke of the day's two rounds led to immediate disqualification from this group.

Finally came those who, unless exhausted by a disastrous round of golf, did their drinking standing up. Mostly big, noisy, successful men, favouring tweed sports coats or blazers and club ties, they formed the smoke-screened barrier other groups had to penetrate to get to the bar. They tended to start with beer, always pints, but rapidly progressed to spirits. Buying a round in that company was no mean undertaking. All played their full rounds of golf, tending to go out late after lunch, their faces aglow. Many newcomers with the temerity to play with them in the afternoon, looking for easy pickings, had played the eighteenth hole regretfully, wiser and much poorer men. They had found to their cost that this band of sportsmen included many a good golfer with a competitive nature matched only by his ability to metabolise alcohol rapidly.

Excited by the presence of Anderson and Beaupré at its focal point, the group at the bar was dense and agitated. Shoulders jostled to get closer to the great men, to buy them a drink, get an introduction, register a name, a face. Anderson and Beaupré glowed with geniality, shook hands, roared with laughter. Behind each façade, however, stood another man, flint-hard and ruthless. That man whose drink they have just accepted, next week they might crush him into bankruptcy or swallow him in a merger, spitting out him and his golden handshake without noticing it.

Teflo, large as it was, was only a part of a large conglomerate of chemical industries, mainly in the field of plastics. Nitromid International, of which Anderson was Chairman, had their headquarters at Liverpool but their interests were spreading worldwide, particularly in Australia and Canada. It was in Canada that their development had slowed almost to a stop. In Beaupré they were up against a man they could not hope to beat. Competitive, strike-free, he was considered the man most likely to survive the recession everyone said was coming. Perhaps more worrying, Beaupré was showing signs of competing nearer home. He was pushing his UK markets hard and there were rumours that he was looking for a suitable site; he had been spotted in South Wales surrounded by Welsh Office under-secretaries, all eager to please. Anderson had cracked first. Unused to the role of supplicant, he had arranged for Beaupré to come to Liverpool; the golf was convenient window-dressing. The two men, sizing each other up, stood amongst the crowd at the bar like two heavyweights before a fight. Soon they would be alone in the ring, stripped of all the ballyhoo.

On instructions from Anderson, Finlayson had reserved a table for two for lunch; opportunity for an opening round if Beaupré so wished. They had only just sat down when Finlayson came across to whisper in Anderson's ear.

'First class, Alex,' Anderson said. 'Well done.' He turned to Beaupré 'Alex has fixed a new partner for you this afternoon, Pierre. The assistant professional will go round with you. Give you a chance to get your money back.'

Good humour restored, lunch went well. Anderson was careful not to drink too much, stayed on his guard. Beaupré seemed unaffected by the drinks that had progressed from beer, via spirits and wine, to a glass of kümmel. Oblivious to the fact that no one else in the dining-room was smoking, Beaupré produced a cigar which had been rolling loose in his inside pocket. He lit it and smiled at Anderson.

'All right if we leave business until Monday, John?' He turned sideways so that he could stretch his legs. 'I'm just beginning to enjoy myself.'

'Not at all, Pierre. I shall be in Liverpool all day. You pick a time.'

'Nine a.m. do you?'

'Look forward to it, Pierre.'

'Just one thing, John. That fella Barker. How big a wheel is he at Teflo?'

'Not very big, Pierre. He's not that important.'

'What did you say he did?'

'He has the plant hire firm that looks after all our mobile work.'

'And that's not important? Do you mean to say that you don't have your own plant?'

Anderson squirmed. Beaupré was talking to him like a man who held all the cards.

'No, but it's a thing we are looking into. It came about in rather a peculiar way. Barker's father was a great chap, built the firm up from nothing after the war. He got the contract when Teflo was being built and just stayed on. If he had lived, I have no doubt he would have been on the Board of Teflo by now.'

'How long a contract has this guy Barker got?'

'It used to be a five-year contract when his father was alive. Now it's renewed annually.'

'Why the change?'

'Just being cautious. New hand at the helm and all that.'

'The truth is you don't trust him.'

Anderson was not used to having words put in his mouth. 'I must admit he's not the man his father was.'

'How much more of his present contract to run?'

'Not long. It's on the agenda for the next full Board meeting.'

'He wouldn't work in any organisation of mine,' Beaupré said, forcefully. 'No backbone. Christ, did you see him shaking? Any chance he's on the sauce?'

'Not that I know of. The Royal Westmere isn't exactly the local headquarters of the Temperance Society but I don't know that Barker drinks much more than the rest of us.'

Beaupré looked around at the early afternoon faces at the other tables. 'That doesn't say much,' he growled. 'I can only repeat, I could never have a man like Barker working for me in any position of responsibility.'

To Anderson, Barker suddenly became disposable, a sacrificial lamb. Perhaps it wouldn't be a bad tactical move to give Beaupré the first round. The first round didn't matter. It was the last round on Monday that he must win.

'Perhaps I shouldn't say it, Pierre – obviously it's a matter for the Board to decide – but I think you can take it that the Barker contract won't be renewed. I know of at least two other firms that are only waiting to take on the work.'

And so, the first casualty fell, after no more than a few ranging shots from the big guns.

5

It was warm enough for Alison Barker to wind down her window as she sat waiting in the school car park. She was early. She opened a paperback on her lap and tried to read. Half a paragraph and she had given up, restlessly throwing the book over her shoulder on to the back seat of the Mini. She had just tiptoed through the minefield of a Lady Anderson coffee morning. She would have preferred a morning in the company of the KGB rather than be grilled by that red-taloned, nosey old bitch. That wasn't fair. Alison liked her; brassy, vulgarly rich but basically kind. If only she did not wear those pink, tight-fitting, trouser suits. Perhaps that was what turned Sir John on. How old was he? Sixty-five? Looked about fifty-five. Fit, active chap. A thruster if ever there was one. Alison tried to imagine Sir John and Lady Margaret in bed. She laughed quietly to herself and shook her head. She wondered what Sir John's secretary looked like.

Alison looked up sharply as another car nosed its way tentatively into the car park. She smiled as three attempts were made to reverse a car into a space large enough for a juggernaut. Another mother with the job of fetching son or daughter from school. Where was father? Playing golf too? Alison looked at her watch once again. Another twenty minutes. She beat a gentle tattoo on the steering-wheel. Would he come to fetch Jonathan? Something told her, today he would. If not, she couldn't let Jonathan go home to that empty house, and would take him out to lunch with them. He was so much his father's son, and would never ask for anything. How had they managed these last two years, she wondered. Just that Mrs Fairclough coming in for a few hours a day, cooking the odd meal. That great big house.

Two years and more. Alison remembered the guilt; she still felt it. Side by side, looking down at Rosemary dying. Side by side, feeling the warmth, enjoying it, thrilling to it, courting it. So close, Rosemary's eyes looking from one to the other. Never touching but attracting, body, voice, eyes, perfume, movement, closeness, wanting. Leaving Rosemary for the coffee

42

downstairs; murmured conversation, intimacy under a fragile veneer of good taste that she knew she could have shattered with the crook of a finger. She had only needed to put her body against his.

So why not? Sense of decency? Maybe. She hoped so. Fear of rebuff perhaps or of losing him afterwards from feelings of remorse, recrimination? Alison again felt the guilt. She remembered sitting there, listening to Rosemary. What had she said? Poor Michael; how he was so helpless; how would he manage; how lonely he was. Not would be; was. Not Jonathan; Michael. And finally, she was gone. The funeral, the mourning, the decent interval. And then, slam. Down had come the shutters, opaque with politeness and good manners. Behind the screen, father and son, indivisible.

With small fretful movements, Alison shifted her cramped position. She looked towards the school entrance gates once more. So stupid. Like a lovesick teenager. She ached and wriggled in her seat.

It was only a question of time. That screen would shatter. She knew it. Jonathan was two years older now, and he would understand, perhaps. She sensed Michael's despair. She ached to hold him, help him. There had been no rumours of dirty weekends even though he worked amongst women all day. And she remembered that night when Larry had been drunk – was there a night when he wasn't drunk? – when Larry had told Michael about his impotence, made a great joke about it, saying she would have to avail herself of Michael's services soon, goading him, enjoying it. She remembered Brookes' face: a mask. So, there they were. He, a pillar of local society, and his dead wife; she and her sexually crippled husband, their marriage as good as dead; two vulnerable boys; all under the dissecting microscope of local gossip. But she wanted mystery, tenderness. She knew it was there.

Larry's love-making had always been of a sporting nature: orthodox, enthusiastic, no frills. He had used her body like an exercise machine, gratefully accepting physical relief; he had needed her like he needed a good game of squash. He had expected as much reaction, participation, from Alison as from a bicycle or squash court. As a result, his impotence had come as a relief; thank God, no more acts of sham affection, as someone she no longer liked grunted to his solitary satisfaction. But it was bloody nonsense to say that you don't miss what you have never had. Alison knew what she had never had and there was little doubt she was missing it.

The familiar car bonnet swung through the car park entrance. Moving slowly, Brookes seemed to be having difficulty deciding exactly where to park though there was space either side of Alison's Mini. The car cruised past, with a small smile only from Michael. Friends laugh and wave; lovers steal glances. He parked and walked towards the Mini. He had to bend low to look in through the small car's window, only to see Alison's back as she leant across to open the passenger's door. Both tall, they had trouble swivelling around to face each other, their knees meeting above the gear-lever.

'Hullo, Michael.'

'Hullo, Lissa. You look beautiful.'

They smiled at each other, open smiles, knowing smiles. The beginning. At last.

'You've come to fetch Robert.'

'And you've come to fetch Jonathan.'

And they laughed as if that was the funniest thing they had heard in ages.

'I didn't think you would come.' Alison blushed. 'What I mean is, don't you operate on a Friday morning?'

'I do and I have. Dr Kildare Brookes has been saving lives like the devil all morning. Well, part of the morning.'

'Why the sudden change of heart then?'

'A sudden urge,' Brookes said, with more emphasis than the words seemed to warrant. 'Something happened in theatre today; the sort of thing that makes you see more clearly for a while. It wears off though. Doesn't always help to see things too clearly, does it?'

'What happened exactly?'

'Oh nothing. Nothing that should bother you on such a beautiful day. Tell me what you've been doing this morning.'

Gone again, infuriating man; back behind that screen like a ship appearing, disappearing in a fog bank. 'Me? I've had a wildly exciting morning. Lady A's coffee morning.'

'Of course. It's the Teflo golf meeting today. I'd forgotten.'

'Right. Fortunately I managed to get away before the sherry. Said I had to pick up Robert from school.'

'And Larry? Is he playing? He usually does, if I remember correctly.'

'Yes. He's coping with the other half of the terrible duo, poor devil. He's playing with Sir John.' Not 'poor lamb' or 'poor dear' or 'poor man', but 'poor devil'. 'You're lucky in the medical world. You don't have any of this nauseating back scratching.'

'Don't you believe it,' laughed Brookes.

'Do you? I always envied Rosemary. She never had to do any of this

44

business entertaining. No dinner parties for jumped up entrepreneurs, all velvet jackets and purple ties; just people you liked. And you don't have Larry's business lunches to cope with.'

Brookes laughed again. 'Oh, yes we do. Except we're the entrepreneurs. I've had the odd wild night out in Liverpool; ten-minute film about a new antibiotic, sometimes they even forget to show that, and then wine, women and song. I use the word women figuratively, of course.'

'Of course, sir.' Alison frowned in mock disapproval.

'Think of the temptation if you're a consultant radiologist or cardiologist when they're building a new teaching hospital, or even a new district general for that matter. You may have the final say in the choice of equipment costing hundreds of thousands of pounds, maybe millions these days, for all I know. Just imagine the high-class reps chasing those fellas around. I bet there've been a few velvet-jacketed medicos in the fleshpots of Rotterdam or Hamburg over the last twenty years.'

'Yes, but pretty rare, aren't they?'

'Maybe, but you take your average GP. He could probably have lunch out three days a week with some drug firm if he chose to.'

'Yes, but he's not obliged to. In big business, if you want to survive, you have no choice but to join the merry-go-round. You've got to suck up to the likes of Sir John Anderson. The power they wield is frightening. You surgeons are not the only ones with the power of life and death, you know.'

'No, but there's big business in medicine too.' She was so beautiful, so close in the tiny car. What the hell were they doing, talking about money and medicine? 'If you want to make the real money in medicine, you've got to start way back as a junior. Yes, sir, no, sir, three bags full, sir. I don't say you don't need ability too; most of the people at the top these days are pretty able. But, from the beginning, you've got to stand up at meetings, keep talking, get your face known, keep on the right side of the Sir John Andersons of our business. Then, if you go into private practice, you've got to cultivate that. However good you are, it's hopeless just sitting in your rooms expecting the patients to start rolling in. You've got to go out and make yourself available. And, of course, if you choose to go into medical politics, God help you.'

'But you don't have to do it just to survive,' she insisted.

'No,' conceded Brookes, laughing. Looking the way she did he'd concede anything. 'No, you can do what I did, take a job in the periphery, opt out of private practice, just do your job and go home.'

'And are you glad you did?'

No one had ever asked him that question and expected an answer. He had asked it of himself a hundred times. He knew that Rosemary had been too afraid of the answer to ask the question. And Alison knew she had asked too soon. There would be a time for confidences like that.

'Well, I'm glad you did.'

Her hand was half-way to touching him when there was a bang on the roof of the car.

'Hi, Mum. Hullo, Michael.'

'Uncle Michael to you, young man,' Alison said severely to the grinning face that peered at them through the window. She withdrew her hand as unobtrusively as she could. 'Don't be so familiar.'

'Not at all. I like it. Makes me feel young.'

'Morning, Jonathan.' Alison had to bend her head low to see the quiet form behind her son.

'Morning, Aunt Lissa.'

'Are you coming to have lunch with us?' Robert squatted on his haunches to talk to Michael in front of his mother. 'Mum's promised to take me to the Harvester's.' A nervous tic pulled at his grin. 'Smashing steak and chips.'

'Robert.' The severity now was patently bogus. 'Jonathan and his father probably have their own plans.'

She tried to look flustered but only succeeded in looking appealing.

'What do you say, Michael?'

'Thought you'd never ask, Robert.'

'Smashing. Mum you take Jonathan and I'll go with Michael. We'll race you.'

The powerful V8 followed, purring sedately, as the Mini picked its way through the lanes. The Harvester's was a forbidding, stone-built pub. Its only saving grace, its antiquity, had been taken away by the addition of a plastic-roofed extension, one window as brown as a nicotine-stained fingernail around a thundering ventilator fan. Everything with chips. The only others in the bar were two travel-worn reps, comparing order books. George Shearing and Nat King Cole crackled through a nicotine-stained amplifier. Michael reached for his wallet.

'We lost the race so I suppose I had better buy the drinks. Alison?'

'Gin and tonic, please, Michael.'

'Jonathan, a Coke?'

'Please, Dad.'

'Robert?'

46

'Lager and lime. Pint, please, Michael.'

'No.' This time, true severity rang through Alison's voice. Brookes looked at her, one eyebrow raised enquiringly.

'No, Michael. He's too young, apart from the fact he's under age. He is too young to be drinking beer. He should have a Coke, like Jonathan.'

'But Mum, when I'm with Dad . . .'

Alison cut him short.

'You're too young to be drinking beer,' she repeated. 'You have a Coke.'

Michael looked at Robert with a smile and shrugged his shoulders. 'Better do as your mum says, old son.'

The young lad accepted the Coke with bad grace but his ebullient good nature returned with the sight of the food. The sirloin steak, with the consistency of rump and the price of fillet, was garnished with youthful chatter. Alison watched Brookes' enjoyment as Jonathan joined Robert in the verbal assassination of some wretched schoolmaster's character. Brookes winked at Robert as he poured him a glass of wine without asking Alison. Contentedly full of wine, beer and companionship, Brookes paid the bill and walked to where the three waited near the parked cars, the boys drooling over a new Jensen Interceptor, probably a defaulter from the Royal Westmere.

'Thank you, Michael, that was lovely.' Alison paused, uncertain what to say. 'What do you do now? D'you have to go back to hospital? It's such a beautiful day. It seems a shame to be indoors. I thought I might take Robert along the beach for a walk.'

'May we join you?' Michael felt a surging ache in his belly, a quickening. 'My contract says Friday afternoon is for administration and travelling time. In other words, my afternoon off.'

The four piled into the Rover for the drive of a mile or so to the beach at Westmere. A family heading for the seaside. Without comment from Alison, Brookes paid to enter the public car park, though the Royal's was no more than two hundred yards away. They made their way down to the beach along the public footpath, for all the world like some family up from Preston for the afternoon. They turned north along the beach, parallel with the golf course.

'See you at the wreck,' shouted Robert, as he and Jonathan disappeared into the dunes, leaving Alison and Brookes alone to walk the mile and a half to the reef where the blackened remains of a coaster were visible above the low spring tide.

'They get on so well, those two. I hope they'll always be friends. And yet they are so different,' Alison said. She put her hand in his, interlocking their fingers. 'Jonathan adores you, you know.'

And so, it began. The ground was even; they did not have to look where they were going. The day was just warm enough to raise a vibrant sheen above the distant beach. There was a lazy buzz; the hiss of the receding tide, to and fro, to and fro, as if the sea was breathing, in and out, in and out; the gentle murmur of banal conversation about sons and schools and examinations, but spoken in lovers' tones. There were distant voices, young and boyish from the dunes, old and angry from the Royal's fairways. For a moment Brookes felt himself once again in that cataleptic state, so seductive that morning when faced with a man bleeding to death, with the hypnotic sibilance of the anaesthetic gases in their tidal flow in and out, in and out, with distant voices, vague peripheral shapes, out of focus, dream-like, bereft of substance.

Alison half turned towards Brookes to look at his face. What was he thinking, this timidly brave man, whose grip was beginning to hurt. Brookes felt the pressure of her breast on his arm. He thrust his free hand into his trouser pocket towards the bulge in his crotch, trying to hide the erection he hoped she had seen. It had started. It would never be the same again. What would happen to them now? And Jonathan? They bent their entwined arms at the elbow, allowing their thighs to brush rhythmically. What more could she do to help him, help herself? She longed for his hand on her breast, to hold him, comfort him. She bent her head towards him.

They sprang apart, disturbed by two teenagers running at their backs. Robert was sure the tide was low enough for them to reach the wreck. He asked Jonathan's opinion but Jonathan was looking at his father, puzzled uncertainty on his face. Brookes looked longingly at his son, appealing. Please understand. Don't go away.

They heard Alison complaining, laughing.

'But I'm dressed for coffee mornings not for clambering over rocks.'

'You'll be all right, Mum. We'll help you,' Robert shouted as he dashed away ahead.

Jonathan stayed behind but stood apart as Brookes helped Alison as she slithered over the rocks in her flimsy shoes. On the return up the beach, that hint of jealousy evaporated in the heat of races and games invented in fertile young minds, and all four collapsed into the car, hot, flushed and sweaty. Alison pulled down the sun visor and looked in the mirror.

Brookes watched as she tried to push into place thick, heavy tresses, the colour of beaten copper.

'My God! Look at my hair. All that money wasted this morning. I'm going to look a mess at the dinner tonight.'

She was still drawing a comb through her hair, at times swinging her hair like a burnished cloak around her shoulders, when they reached the Harvester's car park and the Mini. Robert was first out but Jonathan stayed, watching, allowing Alison and Brookes only a few urgent, stolen words as they walked between cars.

'Michael. Come and see me soon. Make it soon.'

'I will.'

6

There was only one thought in Larry Barker's mind as he escaped from Anderson and Beaupré: a drink. The nearest pub was the Harvester's. A drink and maybe even something to eat, but first a drink, perchance with some soulmate ready to listen to his troubles for the price of a beer. At the Harvester's he recognised the two cars, parked side by side, so close. He cursed and drove on. What the hell; there were other pubs.

Some time later, there was breezy confidence in his wave to the guard at Teflo's main entrance as he swept through the security gate. Everyone knew Larry Barker and his Bentley. His self-assurance crumbled as he stepped out in front of Northweir's office block. Behind the stubby red-brick building reared flame stacks, reactors, cooling towers, rising out of a complex of hissing pipes, whirring ventilator fans and high-tension cables. The air was thick with sweet smelling pollution. Tom Barker had helped build it all, and stood enthralled, marvelling, feeling the vibrant energy all around, seeing nothing but challenging opportunity. In Larry it only instilled fear, a feeling of claustrophobic panic. He wanted to run. Fear born of ignorance. He did not understand the simplest detail of the processes that throbbed around him. All he felt was terror of the giant standing over him, hot, pulsating, evil. He lacked the intelligence to learn, to understand; the basic steps to conquering his terror. To him, fear was not a spur but a crushing burden.

Two prefab huts and a caravan had stood on that site when Tom Barker had moved in. Now his son looked up at his office window on the first floor. He imagined the pile of paper work. He turned and started to walk towards the wharf. It was a quarter of a mile away but he did not take the car; put the problem off that little longer. As he turned the corner to follow the estuary towards the wharf, he saw a group of men standing around a mobile crane.

A coaster moored alongside, with its hatches open, listed a few degrees as it took the muddy bottom in the spring ebb tide. It looked deserted. A row of railway trucks, half of them empty, stood the other side of the crane. One of the group of men detached himself and walked to meet Barker. Barker had little difficulty in recognising the clean, ill-fitting, double-breasted suit, the shining, heavy shoes. Once a warrant officer, always a warrant officer. No smile moved the deeply etched naso-labial folds that bracketed the thick moustache that covered Rothwell's upper lip.

'Thank God, you've come at last, Barker. Where the hell have you been? I've been looking all over. I had a right job getting through to you at that snooty bloody golf club, I'll tell thee. Didn't Mrs Barker tell you I'd rung?'

Larry knew to his shame that no other foreman spoke to his boss like that. Rothwell had been privileged in his father's day; after all they had been under fire together when there had been no such thing as Northweir Plant, no such persons as boss and foreman. For years Tom had not known what to call him, but both had known who was master, who was man. And that was how Rothwell had liked it; firm orders carried out to the letter, grumbling, criticising constantly the while. Without detailed instructions, he became confused, aggressive. His devotion to Northweir as it sank slowly towards bankruptcy was accepted as loyalty. His wife and children knew better. The loyalty was not refusal to leave the sinking ship but fear of the solo swim to another. To add to Barker's troubles, Rothwell was now TGWU plant convenor for the whole of Teflo. There was enough union trouble at Teflo as it was, without sacking the plant convenor and having Sir John Anderson breathing down his neck.

Rothwell turned and walked, in step, alongside Barker.

'Tha can't afford to play golf while things like this are happening, y'know. Nero fiddling while Rome burns, that's what I call it. Don't you know what's going on?'

'All right, Bill. Take it easy. It's not as easy as it sounds. It may have looked like playing golf but what I was really doing was trying to make sure our contract gets renewed. You try a day with Sir John and his cronies some time.'

'That's as may be, Barker. But there's damn all use in getting contract renewed if we don't have plant to work with. We couldn't find you yesterday or last night. Mrs Barker didn't seem to know where you were, neither. Time's money, y'know.'

'I'm sorry, Bill. I was busy.'

'Busy. Try telling that to coaster's skipper over yon. He has missed a couple of tides already. That's brass to him. And there's another anchored down river, waiting. If we had plant, we could off load both the same time. Time was when we could cope with three ships at same time.'

Time was. In the old days. Before your father died. When your father was alive. As Mr Tom used to say.

Barker groaned inwardly. They moved over to the crane. The small knot of men parted, heads down, hands deep in pockets, to let them through. One or two nodded or smiled; no one spoke.

'There you are. You don't have to be an engineer to see what's wrong. Reckon even an accountant can see that.'

There was a snigger from behind Barker's back. Barker looked at the crane's caterpillar track while the men looked at him. One of the tracks had broken, one end draped over the driving wheel, the other trailing flat along the concrete.

Though Tom Barker had favoured the Jones KL 77 and KL 44 mobile cranes on tyred wheels for the smaller tasks, and later the Priestman Bison 11 with its broad-tracked base for the heavier loads, the NCK Rapiers had been his favourites. Capable of being fitted with tracks, or even lorry loaded, their versatility suited the extremely varied tasks demanded of them at Teflo. The crane they were ruefully surveying was an ageing tracked Rapier. Much of the raw material at Teflo was delivered by rail and road but most of the pyrites and sulphates were delivered by coasters negotiating the estuary only at high water. The mobile cranes were equipped with luffing jibs and a grab, moving along the wharf on their tracks as the coasters emptied.

'That track went about midday yesterday. I rang Grimthorpe's straight-away and they said they had a spare in stock. Trouble was, they wouldn't send track over without word from you. Seems our credit is not too good at present.'

Rothwell looked accusingly at Barker. His remarks were all made within earshot of the men. Feet shuffled uneasily.

'That's crazy, Bill. I don't know what's got into Grimthorpe's these days. They were always happy enough to have our business in the past. Is there any chance of repairing this on site? What do you think, Albert?'

The question was directed at a huge, fat man dressed in overalls, whose straining buttons gaped from hairy chest to sagging crotch. His head was topped by a thick, knitted woollen disc, like some oily religious skull cap. It had never been known to leave his head, indoors or out, fine weather or foul. Albert Crampton was the oldest crane driver at Teflo. Many times, young Mr Larry, the boss's son, had sat on Albert's wide acreage of lap, had driven cranes under the tuition of those podgy, capable hands.

'Nay, lad. Won't do. Happen it's been repaired once already. Tha's only throwing good brass after bad. T'would only last a few days. Nowt you can do about it. Best get a new one, lad.' Crampton's hard-headed, North Country common sense was not really needed. It was already obvious to Barker that there was no other valid option.

'There would have been none of this trouble if you'd done what I suggested years ago. Put these cranes on rails along the wharf, I said. It's the only answer.' Rothwell's voice was beginning to saw away at Barker's frayed nerves. One or two in the group grinned sheepishly and winks were exchanged. Hell of a boy, Bill Rothwell. Did you hear him talking to the guvnor?

'I know, Bill. But that makes them fixtures here and they wouldn't be available for any work anywhere else in the plant.'

'When was this crane away from wharf last? Not for last twelve months, I'll be bound. Tha's plenty of work here for it. Fact is, work load's going up. Teflo's expanding and we're not keeping up. And that's the truth of it.'

'Maybe you're right, Bill. Anyway, I'll go and get a new track for you. If I can get Grimthorpe's to deliver it first thing in the morning, when could you get things moving again?'

'Mid-afternoon, I reckon. If you could get Grimthorpe's to deliver tonight, we could get an early start. Just means paying some driver a bit of overtime.'

They all gazed dolefully at the immobile crane, one of them moodily kicking at the broken track. The group parted as Barker moved to leave.

'All right, lads. You'll have the track tomorrow. Can't have you standing round all day or Albert here will get fat.'

Barker tugged at Crampton's straining buttons and got a grudging laugh all round. Rothwell shook his head as Larry walked away, hands deep in pockets, chin on chest. Barker had hardly entered his office overlooking the main gate, when he was followed in by Mrs Hillard. Competent and experienced, she had mothered Tom Barker, forever urging him not to work so hard. Her task with his son was somewhat different.

'I'm so glad you've called in, Mr Barker. I'm afraid there's a mountain of work piling up for you. Some of it is rather urgent, if you wouldn't mind, Mr Barker. It can't really be left much longer. The most urgent seems to be some trouble with a crane down on the wharf.'

'Now don't you start, Mrs H.' Larry smiled affectionately. 'I've already sorted that little problem out.'

'D'you mean you've seen Bill?'

'Yes, Mrs Hillard.'

'Down at the wharf?'

'Yes, Mrs Hillard.'

'And you've been able to fix it?'

'Yes, Mrs Hillard.'

'And there's no need for me to worry about that again?'

'No, ma'am.'

The mock humility of someone completely in control of the situation failed to impress. Mrs Hillard knew Tom's son too well.

'It's just that Bill has filled in this requisition for a new track, but said not to send it until you'd seen it and signed it. I rang up and priced a new track. You'll find the figure down at the bottom.'

Mrs Hillard selected a sheet from the sheaf in her hand.

'That's all right, Mrs H. I'm going to ring Grimthorpe's now. Let me see the requisition for a moment.'

As she handed him the sheet, Barker looked at the figure at the bottom of the right-hand column. He closed his eyes and whistled softly.

'As to these other letters,' Mrs Hillard began.

'Later, Mrs Hillard,' Barker broke in.

'They really are rather urgent.'

'Later, I said,' snapped Barker. 'Please?'

With a sniff, his secretary turned and stalked out of the room. Barker rose from his chair, closed the door behind her and moved over to the window. For several minutes he stared down blindly at the bustle ebbing and flowing through the factory entrance. Finally, with a sigh, he lifted the receiver and asked the operator to connect him with Grimthorpe's. Twenty minutes of discussion with a hard-nosed sales manager ensued, Barker effusively confident, the sales manager unconvinced. When Barker replaced the receiver, its handle wet with sweat, the arrangements had been made for delivery of the track the following morning, but it would not be off-loaded until the driver had been handed his personal cheque. Barker signed a cheque, drawn on his own account, gazing at it for a moment before sealing it in an envelope, together with the requisition. He must ring his bank manager first thing in the morning.

There went any hope of a summer holiday, or next winter for that matter. He would have to explain to Alison and Robert. He supposed Alison would start her bloody nonsense about going out and getting a job again. She had dropped enough hints recently. No doubt she could earn more than he was getting out of this bloody shambles at the moment. And, if Northweir went through altogether, what then? Where was he going to get another job? Failed accountant. Over forty. Unable to keep a thriving business going. He could hear the interviews.

On a wave of self-pity, Barker threw the pile of correspondence on the floor, slammed past an open-mouthed, protesting Mrs Hillard and out to his car.

The security guard saluted respectfully as Barker drove out.

'And fuck you too,' roared Barker above the squeal of tyres as he accelerated viciously towards Dunbridge.

7

'Poor bastards.'

There was genuine compassion in Rothwell's voice as he leaned across to lower the car's nearside window for a better view. He had come to a halt half-way along the only link between Dunbridge and Teflo, the road and rail embankment that ran like a curved spine with the Grayling estuary on one side and low, reedy wasteland on the other. Northweir Plant had helped build the road and railway, levelling the mass of hard core that had been sunk into the marshy ground. Heavy lorries, bound for Teflo, pounded the road, day and night. Rothwell was held up at one of the temporary traffic lights permanently to be found bracketing road repairs at one point or another. His two-year-old Granada shone like his shoes and his conscience. He had done his best; it wasn't his fault those houses had not been demolished.

Through the open window Rothwell gazed at Monkey Island, a council housing estate surrounded on three sides by the dank marshland and extending to within two hundred yards of Teflo's boundary fence. Just below sea level at high-water springs, Monkey Island flooded repeatedly in winter. In Teflo's lee, the prevailing westerlies polluted the lungs, stained the grey roughcast and bleached the couch grass, seared the skin. It was a scene of peeling paint, vandalised phone boxes and skulking mongrels.

'Poor bastards,' he repeated, moving on as the lights turned to green. A staunch Labour member of Dunbridge Borough Council, Councillor Rothwell saw the inhabitants of Monkey Island as the poverty-trapped stratum, crushed thin by the toffee-nosed gentry of Shepworth and the Royal Westmere. Short on oratory and with a limited vocabulary, this thick-skinned, well-meaning man had wagged his politically motivated finger at his fellow Councillors on innumerable occasions, all to no avail. They all agreed with him that houses should not, would not, be built so close to somewhere like Teflo again, but that Teflo had been built near the houses, not vice versa.

What Rothwell failed to appreciate was that he was up against the vested interests of the Housing Department and the local police. Monkey Island served its function as a repository for all the rent dodgers and vandals while the police looked on Monkey Island as an animal pound where they could corral the majority of the local villains, drunks and wife-beaters. But what Rothwell lacked in intelligence he made up for with brass-necked persistence; they hadn't heard the last of him yet.

At the landward end of the embankment he turned left and, passing some derelict shops whose boarded-up windows pronounced that Preston North End Rules, OK, left again. With the car crawling in low gear, Rothwell drove along Piggott Street, Monkey Island's one sizeable street pointing directly back towards Teflo. Its pot-holed dead-end fell away into the two hundred yards of salt marsh between it and Teflo. Fed by innumerable subterranean streams, constantly changing course, the marsh was dank and wet.

Rothwell pulled up outside number 62 but did not get out immediately, taking in the view as if replenishing the feelings of social injustice which this invariably inflamed. To the right, the houses were interrupted by the old brick primary school, vandalised out of all practical use. To his left the terraced houses stretched unbroken, though some, roofless and hollow, looked like decaying teeth, their windows filled with corrugated-iron sheeting like shoddy amalgam fillings. Amongst the rubble glinted broken glass. From where he sat, the marshland was below the line of sight, giving the impression that anyone venturing beyond the street's end would be swallowed up in the great works' vibrant maw. Cars littered the street, mostly propped on bricks, one or more wheels missing. About ten doors down, one of the cars, in better repair, was being washed in dirty water from a yellow plastic bucket by a woman in tight, ill-fitting, pink trousers. Above the waist she wore a bra only, though a flimsy yellow headscarf did its best to conceal the multicoloured rollers in her hair.

With a sigh Rothwell got out, knocked at number 62, pushed the door open and walked in. A woman leaning in the next doorway watched him, idly swinging a slippered foot at a dog cocking its leg at her doorpost.

Within ten minutes, Rothwell was on his way home again, shaking his head in wonder at the mess some men made of their lives. Liam Murphy, the man he had been to see, had been one of his union members at Teflo until he had been crushed between a stone wall and a reversing truck, leaving him paraplegic. He had always had a way with him, had Murphy, must have been a good-looking fellow when he was young. But what Rothwell couldn't understand was what the hell he had done with the fifteen thousand pounds compensation the union had fought hard to get for him. Surely even an embittered man like Murphy could hardly drink his way through that amount? Still, Rothwell supposed, all you need is a television, a phone by the bed and a bookie's account. Murphy had always been a compulsive gambler. It was amazing how his wife stayed with him. She was a fine looking woman, with more than a touch of class. One glance and it was obvious she did not belong in Piggott Street. Murphy must have dragged her down with him. Rothwell had been relieved that she was not in when he called; he always tried to arrange it that way. There were not many women who frightened Bill Rothwell but this one did. Always kept Murphy so spotless. Must have been a nurse at some time or other, the way she refused any help. Rothwell had often thought to find out more about her but there was something about her, that look of hers, that somehow forbad him. She even made the packet of fags he slipped Murphy look like charity.

Rothwell lived in a cedar-porched, green-tiled bungalow on a private estate in that part of Dunbridge that was spreading inexorably along the Shepworth Road.

'I'm home, mother,' he shouted from the hall.

As Ivy Rothwell came out of the kitchen, her cheek was already turning for the kiss.

'Hullo, dear. You all right? You look tired. Come on in. Your tea is on the table.'

Tea was a beef casserole with potatoes, peas and dumplings. A large egg custard waited on the sideboard and a thick brown teapot nudged a hissing kettle. Thick slices of bread, already buttered, lay on a plate in the centre of the table. Rothwell hung his jacket behind the door. He smiled at the food and at his wife.

'That looks grand. Always said I married best cook in ATS.'

His wife did not smile back; she said 'Yes, dear' in that abstracted tone that suggested she might have heard that phrase before.

'Busy today, dear?'

Ivy sat facing her husband, eating nothing. Thin and patient, she watched him fill his mouth with so much steak, dumpling and bread, that he found it impossible to swallow without the lubricating effect of a mouthful of tea.

'I've spent most of the morning chasing after young Barker. And where was he? Playing golf with Anderson when he should have been at Teflo. We weren't able to unload coaster because of breakdown and Grimthorpe's don't give us anything on tick any more.'

'Surely you've more than one crane, haven't you?'

'Not one that's serviceable, Ivy, not a suitable one; not one with a grab, you'll understand. We've taken bits off others just to keep this one going. The only decent crane we've got left is that old Rapier of Albert's. I tell you, Ivy, I don't see the end of it, and that's a fact. Told him so, in front of lads. Those cranes just aren't up to it any more, I said. Teflo's expanding, I said, and we're standing still.'

Rothwell dipped his gravy-stained knife into the butter dish to augment the layer already spread on the slice of bread balanced on the palm of his left hand. Ivy looked at the gravy smeared over the butter dish, her face a mask. Rothwell gave a loud belch as Ivy filled his cup once more. He tapped his chest, knife in hand, and winced.

'Pain again, Bill? You shouldn't eat so fast. I keep telling you.'

Rothwell ignored her. 'Should have made Barker an engineer. I told his father that, but no, it had to be an accountant. Engineer wasn't posh

57

enough. Should have made him work with his hands, learn business from the bottom. Anybody can see he hasn't the brains to go with accent. And that brother of his.' Rothwell waved a meat-laden fork in the direction of his wife. 'He's no better and all. Owns nearly half Northweir and never comes near the place. He hasn't put foot in Dunbridge since the day we buried his father.' He suddenly clutched at his belly and his face contorted as a spasm of pain peaked and fell away again. 'Happen he's going to cost me my job and no mistake.' Rothwell had to speak louder as his wife moved to the kitchen. She returned to place his bottle of antacid on the table. When his pain had subsided, Rothwell reached for the egg custard. 'I can see crunch coming when our contract runs out. I reckon Teflo will kick us out then, you wait and see.'

'Don't worry, love. We'll manage. After all, you are sixty-three. Lots of people are retired much younger than that. It's not as if you've been extravagant. We can live quite comfortably. And you've got the Council.'

Ivy rose as the telephone rang. She called to Rothwell from the hall. 'It's for you, dear. Someone from the fire service.'

She held the receiver until he took it from her. He placed his hand over it while he struggled to control a spasm of explosive belching.

'Rothwell here.' He listened intently without interrupting. 'That's fine, John. I'll leave at once. Should be there in ten minutes. And John? Thank you for letting me know.'

He hurried into the bedroom and began to change. Ivy stood at the bedroom door.

'What's happening, Bill? Are you going out?'

'Yes, love. That was the fire service. Major Accident Alert. I must get along at once. John didn't know what it was about but they might need me.'

'D'you think you ought to go out like that, straight after your tea? I can see you're in pain. Shouldn't you let your tea go down first?'

'You fuss too much, woman.'

'Well you know what Dr Sturdy said.'

'Bloody doctors. What do they know? Stomach like an ox.'

Rothwell made his point by striking his belly with his fist.

'You've got a waterproof of some kind, dear?'

'You should know by now, Ivy, I keep everything for an emergency in the boot. Now stop fussing. And don't wait up for me; I may be late.'

'Very well, Bill. Take care.'

In its early days, Northweir had helped the local fire service with lifting gear and Rothwell, for a while, had become a part-time fireman. Now the

58

plant had nothing to offer, leaving Rothwell useless in any local catastrophe, but always conspicuous in his yellow hat and oilskins, amongst the reporters and voyeurs at the fringe of the drama.

Ivy Rothwell cleared away the dishes, washed and wiped them, put them away. She wiped the stainless-steel sink unit until not a molecule of water remained. She looked round the silent, shining kitchen, sighing when she could find nothing more to clean or tidy. She turned off the light, walked to the living-room, switched on the television, to sit erect, oblivious of the programme. She wondered if one of the children might ring. It would be nice to hear their voices again.

8

The stillness pervading the Old Mill was in harmony with the tranquillity of a beautiful May evening. It was broken only by the gentle sounds of the *Blue Peter* programme. To two shy people living together, the television was a boon, filling in large gaps where, otherwise, conversation would be a painful necessity. Of the thirteen rooms in the rambling house, seven were kept in a state of suspended animation, dusted and polished from time to time but never tidied, never disarranged. Brookes and his son had a bedroom and bathroom each and they ate in the kitchen. There was a small study where Brookes voluntarily immured himself at times, but, in the main, Michael and Jonathan Brookes lived out their peaceful coexistence in one living-room. Rosemary had always resented Mrs Fairclough calling the room 'the snug' – it sounded like a pub – but the name had stuck. Three armchairs, deep and worn, were the only furniture of substance in the room, two facing the television, the other now pushed into a far corner, watching from the shadows. A small oak gate-legged table stood against the wall, spreading its legs only for weekend lunches.

A gas fire was set in the wall. Pretty, coloured tea and coffee sets smiled down hopefully, hopelessly, from glass-fronted shelves above a chest of drawers, difficult to open, impossible to close, so full of Scrabble boards, tattered Monopoly sets, Leggo boxes, loving Christmas mornings of yesteryear. A sturdy nest of oak tables supported a cut-glass vase, its facets dull with disuse, and an empty fruit bowl. The carpet was stained alongside the arms of the chairs, a testimony to hands groping for coffee mugs with eyes glued to a flickering screen. Uniformly distributed was the litter of bachelor existence: socks, slippers, month-old *Radio Times*, T-shirts, junior squash rackets, paperbacks.

Everyone had been quite sure that Brookes would marry again. Give him a year; you'll see. Not natural, well set-up man, good-looking. That big house and just one son. There had been winks and nods at Medical Benevolent Fund coffee mornings and at weekly Sisters' meetings. 'I bet that she wouldn't mind parking her boots under his bed anytime.' In particular there had been speculation about Sister Kay.

But slowly, sensitively, Brookes and his son had survived. There had been nothing insincere about Brookes' distress at Rosemary's death but the pain had not lasted. He had not loved Rosemary deeply enough to sustain intense grief. Now she was dead, he could say it. He had cherished and cared for Rosemary; he had certainly been faithful to her, even happy to be organised by her. But love? Can you love, be dreamily romantic with, the captain of the women's hockey team? He supposed not all captains of women's hockey teams remained unloved. Who might love them? Captains of men's hockey teams? Could be. But not he. Someone would need to be more yielding, less strident. He accepted that the mind would still be female, hard, realistic, but it would be embodied in softness of heart and voice, with rounded limbs and gentle hands. Someone like . . .

But that was another story. His fantasies about Alison had started long before Rosemary had died. The closeness of Alison as she had nursed Rosemary had simply added substance to them. But when Rosemary had died, her bed cold, the relatives gone, the parson and the solicitor paid, Jonathan had remained. The adored son with his mother's face. To have lost him also would have been beyond endurance. And so Brookes had watched over his son as he would over some vulnerable, wobbling, spindle-legged foal. He had held his arms out to his son not to restrain but to protect, not to smother but to ensure freedom, not to direct but to guide, unable to hold tight for fear of damaging this fragile immaturity. Ready to give the help that was never asked for, subjugating all his own needs, he had watched as Jonathan had slowly found his own feet, stood tall. There would be time enough for Brookes to think about himself.

As the months had gone by, they had become inseparable though apart.

They had come to live in parallel, never distant, never touching, their lives never really crossing. They had taken a boat on the Broads, just the two; a sure test of friendship and they had both enjoyed every peaceful moment. Brookes had invited sons of colleagues for the weekend; disaster. There had been that French boy from Lyons, who stayed a week on an exchange arranged by the school; prolonged disaster. Robert Barker had provided the only close friendship Jonathan seemed to need. Jonathan had been studious, polite, never bored, never withdrawn. But he had never chattered, confided, touched. Their life had become one of companionable solitude, the solitude being mutual as much as individual. A kind of contentment had settled over them that had done nothing to dull Brookes' needs, desires; merely made them endurable. To have done anything about his personal loneliness would have extracted a price he had not been prepared to pay. Nothing, no one, would harm his son.

But that had been two years ago. Jonathan was now two years older. In two months he would be seventeen, with the serious maturity of someone years older. Solid as a rock now. Wasn't he? He would understand now. Wouldn't he? Understand what? His father making love to a woman, to a married woman, to Alison, to his mother's friend, Robert's mother? And would he understand the possible aftermath; gossip, scandal, admissions, divorce, talk of moving from Shepworth, losing his only friend, peace and security split end to end? Happiness bought with misery; Michael's happiness, Jonathan's misery.

Not that Jonathan would show his misery. Michael knew his son as well as he knew himself. The son, like father, would never show how he felt, as if it were a matter of pride not to do so. He remembered how differently Jonathan and Robert had reacted to childhood injuries. Robert had thrown things, bawled his head off and run for solace; Jonathan had stood back, eyes closed, fists clenched and lips pursed, fighting back the tears and any offers of comfort. And wasn't this how Michael had reacted to disappointments in his professional life, to Rosemary's death, to his loneliness? A Brookes never complains. But he doesn't tell anyone he loves them, either. Not even his son.

Jonathan interrupted his thoughts. 'I'll turn it off if you like, Dad.'

'What?' Brookes looked up, startled. It surprised him to hear the voice he had just been listening to in his imagination. 'I'm sorry, Jonathan. What did you say? I must have been dreaming.'

'Shall I turn it off? You were looking pretty bored and I can't say I'm all that interested.'

'Perhaps we have both grown out of *Blue Peter* at last,' Brookes said, smiling.

Jonathan got up, switched the television off, but did not sit down again. Too polite simply to walk out of the room, too diffident to say anything, he stood, grey school trousers shining at the knees, an open-neck grey shirt under a crested navy pullover. Traces of Westmere sand clung to his shoes.

'Enjoy this afternoon?'

'Very much, Dad. It was magic.'

'Did you enjoy the meal? I thought the steak was quite good for one of those places. I noticed that Robert had about half of yours.' Jonathan laughed. 'Do you want some supper now?'

'A bit soon yet, Dad, after that lunch. Can I make myself a sandwich later on? I've got some work I must do by tomorrow.'

'Yes, of course. Your mock As. How are they going?'

'Well enough, I think. I'm not worried, anyway.' Simple statement of fact.

'I must say, it's a great comfort to have a genius for a son. Cuts out a lot of the worrying.'

'I'm no genius.' Jonathan laughed. 'I just work hard. I enjoy it. Anyway, what else is there to do around here?'

'I know,' Brookes murmured, understanding. 'I was only joking. The fact is that I'd be more worried if you were a genius. The one or two so-called geniuses I had to compete with in school haven't come to much in the end. Give me a hard worker anytime. Still going to do medicine?'

'Yes, I think so.'

'When will you have to decide?'

'I'll have to apply in the autumn. I should be having interviews about this time next year.'

'Never thought of doing anything else? You don't have to do medicine, you know. Just because your Mum and Dad . . .'

'I know.'

'I mean, judging by your O-levels, you could have done anything. At one time I thought we might have a lawyer in the family, just for a change. Someone like Robert's uncle. I'm told he's very successful. Be a judge some day. Sir Adrian Barker. How would you like to be a successful London barrister?'

'I don't know. I've never met one. Have you met Rob's uncle?'

'No, never. I'm told he's making a pile of money.'

'That's not everything, is it ?' Youthful intensity of feeling snapped the words out like a reprimand.

'I suppose not, Jonathan, though it is quite a useful commodity at times.' Brookes grinned at his son. 'What about Oxbridge? Are you going to try?'

'They've asked me to.' Jonathan shifted his weight guiltily from one leg to the other and stood, silently embarrassed. 'I don't want to do it though. Do you mind?'

Brookes felt inept in the presence of a youngster who had made all the decisions without help from him. 'Mind? Of course not. All I want is for you to be happy. It's just that I would have given my eye teeth for the chance.' The moment had produced a fragile bubble of intimacy that Brookes strove not to burst. 'Wherever you go, this place is going to be very quiet without you. I'll miss you.'

'I know, Dad.' Jonathan's voice was resonant with adult understanding but he seemed to be struggling to find the right words. His attention was still focused somewhere in the garden. 'Do you ever get lonely?'

'I miss your mother very much, if that's what you mean.'

'Not exactly, no. Do you ever get, well you know, lonely? What I mean is, if you ever wanted anyone to stay,' his words became jerky, higher pitched, 'I mean some of your doctor friends.' He turned his head to look at his father, his face flushed but his eyes level and true. 'I wouldn't mind if it was a lady, Dad. I think I understand about these things.'

Brookes almost wept. His eyes filled and he could force no word past the tight constriction in his throat. Inwardly, the tears flowed; tears of pure paternal love, tears of guilt for Rosemary, tears of frustration for an overpowering longing he could do nothing about, tears of self-pity previously kept at bay.

The telephone had rung several times before it registered in either's mind. Unable to speak, Brookes sat, incapable, while Jonathan walked over to stop the clamorous intrusion.

'Yes?'

Silence.

'Hullo, Dick. I'm very well, thank you. D'you want Dad?' Jonathan did not wait for an answer. 'It's for you, Dad. It's the hospital.'

He handed the phone to his father and walked out of the room. Brookes watched him go, almost gagging with emotion. He held the receiver against his chest as he struggled for self-control. The operator's calls were becoming more frequent, less patient. Brookes tried to speak, failed, cleared his throat and tried again.

'Brookes here.'

'Good evening, Mr Brookes, sir. I'm afraid you'll have to put the gin and tonic down. We've got some work for you.'

Robert Turpin, known hospitalwide as Dick, was as irrepressible, as courteously irreverent as ever. A long-distance lorry driver admitted to the hospital over fifteen years before with fulminating ulcerative colitis, the young, new surgeon, Michael Brookes, had removed his colon. Sporting his ileostomy bag, Turpin had become the hospital's best-known telephone operator, secretary of the local Ileostomy Association and noted raconteur.

'Hullo, Dick. What do you want?'

'Something tells me I've rung at the wrong time. Sorry, Mr Brookes, if I've interrupted anything. Shall I ring back?'

'No, no. Carry on.'

'Something a bit unusual for you, sir.'

'You mean the Major Accident Alert? Is that what you've rung about?'

'Mr Brookes sir. My moment of drama for the day and you have to go and ruin it. And I suppose you know it's only an exercise and you needn't come in?'

'Yes, Dick. Mr Harrington told me this morning.'

'Now isn't that typical of the ruling classes. Now, we of the proletariat, nobody tells us anything. You wait. Come the revolution.' He paused. 'Anyway, I'm going. Take care, sir.'

A click and silence. Brookes replaced the receiver and stood still, as if any movement might impair his recollection of his son's last remarks. What would he have replied if the telephone had not rung, snapping the first fragile tendril of manhood Jonathan had extended towards him? What had prompted it? Had Alison and he been so obvious on the beach? What had Jonathan meant by 'lady'? Alison? Any woman? Any woman but Alison? What had he pictured in his mind? A succession of local friendly ladies? Or just one lady, Alison, in his mother's bed, the smallest sounds audible through the door between them? God help them both. What an impossible situation.

He snatched up the folder containing Harrington's Major Accident Procedure from the table where he had thrown it earlier. He supposed he would have to read it sometime. Brookes took it into the study, sat in a high-backed, winged chair and reluctantly took out the thick wad of foolscap paper, neatly arranged in multicoloured layers. He wasn't going to go through all that word for word. He had virtually no interest in it.

George Harrington would have spent hours on it; Brookes was not going to improve on that. He would treat it in the same way that he read any surgical literature in which he had little interest; skim over it with a quick but lazy mind and extract enough salient points to impress the likes of Harrington, but no more.

He looked down the index; Hospital Services – pink section. He isolated the pink coloured sheets and groaned as he flicked them over this thumb. He read the headings, discarding anything he thought would not apply to him. His son's face blotted out the description of a designated hospital as compared with a support hospital. A trance-like fantasy of making love to Alison blurred the details of Dunbridge General's expected capacity in the event of an emergency: ten serious patients and twenty-five minor cases in the first hour.

With a conscious effort, Brookes cleared his mind enough to register that the Site Medical Officer would be the Consultant Radiologist. He smiled at the thought of Max Verney clambering over twisted railway carriages in a yellow tin hat. He would dictate priority to the rescue services and ambulances. In hospital, one of the orthopaedic surgeons would act as Assessment Officer, sending the critical cases to theatre, serious injuries to casualty and minor cases to the outpatient department. Orthopaedic surgeon be damned. Fat chance of that. That would be George; tailor-made for him. No orthopaedic surgeon was going to get a look in there. Surgical triage would appeal to George's orderly mind, demonstrate his ability to make decisions, delegate to others a great deal of the operating responsibility. Brookes' duties seemed simple enough; they must be, they only took three lines to define as compared with two foolscap sheets of instructions for the Head Porter. He would proceed to the theatre and operate on those abdominal and thoracic cases that Harrington would direct. Nothing to it. Piece of cake.

So, there it was. Brookes threw the folder on the floor, stretched his legs and yawned. While everyone was dashing here and there, all he would have to do was to walk into theatre, scrub and wait. Nothing there to worry about. He turned his head to marvel at the twilight amongst the trees, watched it succumb to darkness. He was still outstretched and pensive when he heard Jonathan in the kitchen. A short while later the door opened.

'There's a sandwich on the kitchen table for you, Dad. I've still got some reading to do and I thought I would do it in bed. Are you all right?'

Brookes could see his son peering around the darkened room.

'Yes, of course. I'm just sitting here thinking. Goodnight, Jonathan. Sleep well.'

9

It was impossible to tell the exact moment when the turbulent phantasmo-goria that barred the way to sleep merged with the black and white silent bedlam of Brookes' chaotic dream-world. The car he was driving was slowly, inexorably gathering speed over the greasy surface of a gentle slope. His foot searched unavailingly for a brake pedal. He spun the steering-wheel with no effect. Jonathan sat in the passenger's seat, scream-ing soundlessly at him to stop it, pleading that he would be a good boy if only Dad would stop the car. Someone ethereal, faceless, calm, sat in the back seat. Suddenly, blocking the road ahead, was a milling crowd, seemingly unaware of the onrushing car; Sister Kay, Harrington, Dai Jack, Larry Barker. Brookes furiously pressed the horn; blah-blah, blah-blah, blah-blah.

Blah-blah, blah-blah. Brookes, sweaty and heavy-eyed, found the bedside telephone and rolled on his back. He fought his way up to a level of consciousness capable of a degree of reasoning. It was the tele-phone, cradled in folds of his blanket, that was insistently calling his name.

'Michael. Hullo, Michael, are you there? Hullo, Michael. Oh, dear.' There was despair, exasperation, in Alison Barker's voice. She wondered whether the line had gone dead.

'Michael. Hullo, Michael. Hullo.'

What female from the hospital would be shouting 'Michael' at him at this time of the night; at any time of day? 'Hullo. Brookes here.'

'Michael. Thank God for that.'

'Alison? Is that you?'

'Michael. I am so sorry to ring you this late but I didn't know what else to do. Michael, I've got trouble.'

66

There was a pause as Brookes wriggled upright, almost fully awake. He screwed his eyes shut as he switched on the bedside light.

'What sort of trouble, Lissa?'

'It's Larry. I don't quite know what to do.' There was a tearful tremor in her voice.

'Do you want me to come over?'

'Please, Michael, if you would. As soon as you can.'

The telephone clicked dead, leaving Brookes gaping stupidly at the receiver. Slowly, he replaced the receiver, pulled back the bedclothes and drew trousers and polo-necked sweater over his pyjamas, his movements accelerating as reason returned with reality. He puffed and blew as he bent to tie his shoes, tucking the bottoms of his pyjama trousers into his socks. He was sufficiently vain to glance at his reflection in the dressing-table mirror, running his fingers through wiry hair and feeling the rasp of the stubble on his chin. He pushed Jonathan's door ajar to see his son sleeping deeply, under the blankets.

He was awakened fully by the clear air on the short walk between the houses. He looked at the stars, shivered and ran the last few yards. Alison was at the window as he ran up the drive but met him at the open front door. Without a word, she put her arms under Brookes', pressing her body to his. Both tall, her head, turned sideways, was cushioned against the side of Brookes' neck by thick soft hair. Eyes closed, she clung and squeezed. She was wearing a long velour housecoat over her lace night-dress and to Michael, she seemed irresistible. Through his thin jumper and pyjama jacket, he thrilled to the soft mobility of her breasts. Alison felt his arousal and gently broke away.

She took his hand and led him into the house. With all the ground floor lights burning Brookes instinctively turned left towards the lounge but pressure on his arm diverted him to the right, through the living-room door.

'He's in here,' was all Alison said, as she guided Brookes through the living-room to the kitchen.

The kitchen strip light shone into every corner with cold, clinical brilliance. Larry was lying on the floor in the angle between two kitchen units, his head propped up by a cushion. He appeared to be unconscious, the right-hand corner of his mouth flapping in a frothy slobber with each breath, stains of vomit drying on his lapels and shirt. The whole room reeked: of alcohol, vomit, and that other odour Brookes had smelt a thousand times on a hospital ward. He looked at Barker's crotch to see it soaked with urine. The stench of whisky came from the sodden pocket of his dark blue, pin-striped, Chester Barrie jacket. Pieces of glass from a broken half-bottle lay on the draining board where Alison had placed them. Larry's eyes were half-open, the lower lids hanging lifelessly. Brookes raised the upper lids to look at the pupils without inducing any reflex blinking, then pressed hard with his thumb over the supraorbital nerve. There was no response to the pain.

Taking the pillow away, Michael made Larry lie flat by pulling on his ankles. With all the grunts and strains of humping human dead weight, he managed to turn him on to his right side, and replaced the cushion under his head. It had been a miracle that Barker had not drowned in his own vomit. The floor around was wet but clean and Brookes looked at Alison's housecoat to see stains, not only of vomit, but blood. He felt the tacky warmth of blood on his own hands that had come from a scalp wound on the back of Barker's head.

Brookes straightened up from his crouching position to sit on a pinewood kitchen stool. He leaned forwards, elbows on knees, sticky hands extended. As Alison stood alongside him, they gazed silently down at the bundle of human wreckage. Without a flicker of movement other than his breathing, Barker passed a long-drawn-out bubbling fart.

Embarrassed, Alison left, saying she would get a blanket. While she was out of the room Brookes looked round at the spotless elegance and back to Barker at his feet. A Skid Row derelict in a glossy page of *Homes and Gardens*. What he saw and what he smelt took him back to those casualty departments on Saturday nights when, even as an idealistic youngster, he had found it difficult to keep his patience with the fighting drunk he was trying to sew up; the sterile trolley sent flying, the drunken lechery as blood-stained hands mauled the young nurse trying to restrain him. He tried but could find no pity for another of their kind who now lay mute at his feet, demanding his help. Alison returned with a blanket and, as she tucked it around her husband, Michael studied her face, seeing none of the revulsion he felt and showed. She looked at Brookes nervously.

'What now, Michael?'

'Depends rather on what's wrong with him.'

Alison inclined her head, showing her surprise. 'But surely, he's, well, just drunk, isn't he? I mean there's not much doubt about that, is there?'

'I'm sure you're right. Everything points that way. But this is the Casualty Officer's nightmare. Is he drunk or has he got a head injury? It happened to a great friend of mine, years ago when we were housemen.

68

Drunk brought in by the police. Has he got a head injury? No. Is he just drunk? Yes. Found dead in the cells the next morning from brain haemorrhage. You can imagine the inquest. It really is very difficult to tell at times, and he's got that scalp wound on the back of his head. How did he get home?'

'I don't really know. We should have gone to the dinner at the Royal but Larry didn't appear. So I rang up and made an excuse. I stayed up till gone midnight but I must have been asleep when he came in. I imagine he must have had a taxi.'

'I noticed his car wasn't outside when I came in. What's the time now?'

Alison glanced at a china-plate kitchen clock hanging on the wall. 'About three thirty.'

She came to sit beside Brookes, their backs to the kitchen table, Barker still slobbering stertorously at their feet.

'Look at his hands and knees.' She pointed at gravel abrasions on his palms and dusty tears in his trousers. 'He must have crawled up the drive.'

Her voice quivered and she leaned towards Brookes. Awkwardly, he put his right arm around her shoulders, reluctant to touch her with his filthy hands.

'Oh, Michael. I don't want Robert to see his father like this.'

She was about to break into tears when Barker's head jerked momentarily as he gave a snort. His left arm moved as if to brush something from his face but it fell away as he lapsed back into coma. Brookes disengaged his arm, leaned down to Barker and pressed hard against his boney orbit once more. Again, no response.

'Head injury or no head injury, I think he's just dead drunk.' There was vicious delight in the pressure as his thumb bored in again. 'Come on, you bastard. Wake up.'

It was as if Barker heard him. Perhaps it was the sort of language most likely to penetrate to whatever sodden layer of consciousness remained to him. His hand moved once more to sweep something from his face. His eyelids opened to bare glazed eyes, staring fish-like a few inches above the floor tiles. Painfully, he rolled on his back, striking his head against a cupboard door, his lower jaw falling, dragging his mouth open. His parched tongue rolled, looked for saliva that was not there. He made two or three abortive attempts to raise his head.

'Wake up, Larry. Come on, wake up.'

Alison sponged her husband's head and face then stood by Brookes, watching as Larry struggled up to a sitting position.

'Christ. Where the hell am I?' His speech was thick and dry.

'You're at home, Larry. You're quite safe.' Alison bent forwards at the hips, hands on the thighs, as if talking to a small child. 'What on earth happened to you?'

'God knows.' Barker looked at the floor around him and down at his clothes. 'Must have been quite a party.'

He sniggered oafishly. His focus moved laboriously from Alison to Brookes. There was a spark of recognition.

'Michael, you old bastard. What the hell are you doing here?' His eyes wavered uncertainly between Brookes and his wife. He sniggered again. 'Or perhaps I shouldn't ask.'

'I called Michael because I didn't know what else to do. I woke up because there was the most terrible bang. You must have fallen. I found you lying there and just couldn't wake you up. So I'm afraid I panicked a bit and rang Michael.'

'And up rode gallant Sir Michael on his white charger. Good old Michael. Steady old Michael.'

Barker had woken up still fighting drunk. Alison, despairing and apologetic, put her hand on Michael's arm. Brookes shook his head to show he understood.

'Had us both worried for a moment, Larry. You've got quite a bang on the back of your head, probably been a bit concussed. The sooner we get you to bed the better.'

Larry managed to rub the back of his head. He looked at the blood disinterestedly. 'God, I'm dry. Give me a drink, love.' The glass of water Alison handed him slopped over. 'Help me,' he demanded, querulously.

Alison held the glass to his lips as he sluiced the water around his mouth. The first mouthful squirted to the floor, narrowly missing Alison. Between swallowing the rest, he watched Brookes wash blood and vomit from his hands.

'Makes himself quite at home, doesn't he,' Barker scowled. In an instant the scowl was transformed to a smile. 'Sorry to spoil your beauty sleep, Michael. Need your sleep in your job, don't you, all this life and death stuff.'

'It has its moments,' Brookes said, trying to smile. 'What about bed for you? D'you feel up to managing the stairs?'

'Tension. That's it, pressure. You guys think you're the only buggers to feel it. Life in their hands and all that balls. You should try it in industry, mate; a real man's world. Then you'd know what real tension was. How long does yours last? Few minutes every now and then? You try having business troubles, day in, day out. You people sit there on a nice fat salary, comes in regular as clockwork. How many surgeons d'you hear of being made redundant at fifty, with a couple of kids to bring up? How many surgeons get the boot in the course of the year? How many d'you have to bump off before you get the push, eh?'

Larry drifted off into maudlin ramblings. With her hands over her ears, Alison looked pleadingly at Brookes.

'I want a drink. I want a drink. I want a drink.' As he repeated the words, so Larry grasped a cupboard door, using it to beat time. He changed tempo and rhythm as he varied his slurred chanting to 'Why are we waiting?'

'Larry, darling, please. You'll wake Robert in a moment. Please stop.' Alison knelt beside him. 'Please, Larry, come to bed.'

'I tell you what.' Barker became decisive. 'Leave me here with a drink and you two go to bed. All be happy then. Haven't been much use to her lately, you know, Michael.' He winked. 'You'd be doing both of us a favour.'

Alison shrank back as Michael, with one stride, bent down, caught Larry by the lapels and hauled him, limp and unresisting, into the sitting position. Swaying, Larry winked again at his wife.

'Strong, isn't he? Often the way with these silent types. Must be a tiger in bed.'

Michael tried shaking Larry into some sort of reason, then propped him up against the cupboards once more. He turned to Alison, now weeping softly. 'Where do you keep your drink?'

'Living-room. Welsh dresser.'

Brookes fetched a whisky bottle and poured half a tumbler. He placed it on the kitchen table, in full view of Barker but out of his reach.

'You get that when you are in bed and not before. So the sooner you help me get you upstairs, the sooner you get your booze. Right?'

Gone now was any vestige of professional attitude towards Larry, the patient. This was now Michael Brookes and Larry Barker, the stinking shambles of a man he was trying to get upstairs and put in her bed. Thou shalt not covet thy neighbour's wife. Did that apply when your neighbour was that miserable soak who was alternately grinning and scowling at him as he tried unavailingly to reach for that glass of whisky? Did he really have to worry about Larry? Did Larry really stand between him and Alison?

Miraculously, Barker tottered to his feet.

'Masterful types, these surgeons, darling,' Barker said, as he put one arm round his wife's shoulders, the other around Brookes. When they finally reached the bedroom Brookes stripped every vestige of clothing off Barker, dumping the foul smelling heap in the bath. He watched as Barker swallowed the neat whisky, like some mother making sure her child took his medicine. Without a word, Barker turned on his side, drew his knees up and, within minutes, was snoring loudly.

In a vain effort to rid himself of the smell, Brookes washed his face and hands in the bathroom. The stench, he knew, would stay up his nose and in his sinuses for days. As he dried himself, he surveyed the pink, yellow, blue bottles, jars, sprays; sweet-smelling femininity, missing from his bathroom for so long. He smiled at the red lace briefs hanging from the tap in the shower. Downstairs, he found Alison sitting in the living-room before the empty, cold fireplace, a steaming cup in her hand. She pointed to a similar cup, balanced on the arm of the chair alongside.

'I've made you a hot chocolate. I hope you like it.'

'Anything so long as it isn't whisky.' Brookes pulled his lower lip down in distaste. 'I don't think I'll ever touch the stuff again.' He gave a deep sigh as he lowered himself carefully into the chair, protecting the cup as he did so.

'I'm sorry you had to see us like this, Michael. I didn't want to involve you but I just was at my wit's end. Forgive me?'

'Don't be ridiculous. How long has it been going on, Lissa?'

'Difficult to say. A long, long time. It all happens so gradually, you can't really say when it starts. I think that Larry was drinking very hard for some considerable time before even I realised. It's amazing how devious they can be, you know.'

Already she was talking of Larry as 'one of them', someone apart. It was the first crack in her loyalty that Michael had sensed, and he knew in his heart that he was going to take full advantage of it. Any feeling of guilt that he may have had for lusting after another man's wife had been dispelled by the disgust he had felt over the last hour. Sipping at his drink, looking at Alison over the rim, Brookes said nothing.

'It builds up so gradually. Poor man. Trying to live up to his father and his brother. Trying to keep the plant going when, frankly, Michael, I don't think he is up to it. His worries at Teflo make him drink and then he goes to work looking like death. He goes to some meetings in Liverpool, at Nitromid, I think, for a day or so every month. Lately he's had to have a day in bed after coming back from those. And now he's very concerned that Teflo is not going to renew our contract. And if they don't . . .'

72

As her voice trailed away in despair, Brookes put his cup down, stretched and took her hand. Keep your mouth shut and let her tell it all.

'Why didn't you tell me? I had no idea. I was only just over there, you know.' Brookes nodded his head in the direction of the Old Mill. 'You only had to call.'

'I know.'

'Then why didn't you?' Michael accentuated the words by beating their clasped hands gently on her knee. Their heads were now close. 'Why didn't you?'

'I was afraid,' Alison replied, hesitantly.

'Afraid?'

'Yes.'

'Of what?'

'Oh, you and your son.' There was a hint of bitterness in Alison's voice. 'For that matter, why haven't you come to see me? Don't you ever need help?'

'I was afraid too.'

'You afraid? Of what?'

'That –' Brookes hesitated over the word, 'man upstairs.'

They both laughed.

'Michael, we mustn't laugh. He wasn't always like that, you know. It's a disease, isn't it? He can't help it. It's that thought that has kept me going these last six months. He is going to drink himself to death. He is dying of a disease as surely as Rosemary was. The only difference is that this takes longer, with less dignity.'

Brookes raised his eyebrows as if prepared to challenge that. What could have been more degrading than the disease that had destroyed Rosemary?

'Oh, yes, Michael. Rosemary was able to keep her personal dignity to the end whatever her disease did to her and she made sure her degradation spread to no one else.' Alison paused as if hesitating to go on. 'We haven't always had single beds, you know. They are fairly recent. And do you know why? Because I couldn't stand it any longer; waking up to find myself soaking in his urine. Sometimes too drunk to realise he was peeing all up the stairs as he made his way to my bed.'

Defences down, the heartbreak tumbled out.

'But these are just the outward,' she struggled for the word, 'manifestations, I suppose you'd call them, of the disease. It's what it's doing to Larry himself that upsets me most. It's much more personal, internal if you like, the way he's destroying himself. Do you remember how he used to be?

He was a fine-looking man, you know, Michael, when we got married. And just look at him on that kitchen floor tonight. He used to be such a big strong man. He was Robert's idol. It's broken my heart to see Robert pretending the man he sees falling upstairs or retching his heart up in the bathroom in the morning, is still the same man who taught him to ski and used to go swimming with him.'

'It's only going to get worse, Lissa. He's an alcoholic, you know. It's not only the patient who has got to be convinced of that. You've got to accept it too if he's to have any chance of fighting it; not curing it, fighting it. Please let me help.'

Alison's face wore the impenetrable mask of someone totally reluctant to accept what they know is true.

'Look. Let me arrange for someone to see him, get him some treatment. A psychiatrist. There's one of the saner ones, nice chap, does a clinic once a week at Dunbridge. Let me fix for Larry to see him. What d'you say?'

Alison showed no enthusiasm.

'I've already suggested it to him. I doubt whether you'd succeed. And, at the moment, I must admit I can see his point. Northweir's on the brink of collapse, desperate to have its contract renewed. Without it we're finished. The news that Larry was seeing a psychiatrist for alcoholism would be the final straw.'

Brookes opened his mouth to speak but Alison cut in. 'Oh, come on. You know everyone in Dunbridge would be talking about it in a week.'

'Let me see what I can fix for him in Preston or Liverpool, then. I'm sure we could keep it quiet. Let's face it, Lissa, he needs treatment. He needs to be dried out.'

'And that would mean staying in Preston or Liverpool for a while?'
Brookes nodded.

Alison shook her head. 'I just don't see it. Larry would never agree.' She paused. 'Let's leave it until this wretched contract is renewed. Once that's over, I'll do my best to make him go for treatment.'

'Promise?'

'Promise.'

There was a pause, a moment for relaxation, as though having done their best for others, they could now, perhaps, have a little time for themselves.

'And what about you, Lissa?'

'What about me?'

Brookes clumsily reached for her hand and tried to sit on the arm of her chair. Alison gave a little laugh at his shy awkwardness, stood up also and led him over to an old leather chesterfield. As they crossed over, Brookes glanced out of the window.

'My God. Is that the dawn?'

Alison did not answer but drew him down to sit alongside her.

'It's not fair, is it?' Alison said.

'What?'

'Us. It's just not fair.'

'What do you mean, us?'

'Oh, stop being obtuse, Michael. You know perfectly well what I mean.'

She took his hands firmly and shook them, in exasperation, in encouragement. The poor man. He wanted her so much you could feel it. Yet he was tongue-tied. What was he afraid of? Her? Afraid of committing himself? Afraid of his own drive? Afraid to start something he couldn't stop? She smiled. She would have to do the talking, at least at first. Lead him along as if cajoling someone edging nervously across a very narrow bridge.

Face to face, they leaned their heads against the back of the chesterfield, their shoulders sinking into the welcoming comfort. For a while, their eyes met and held, level, unwavering, undemanding, giving, not dominating, as they wordlessly declared their love, one for the other. Brookes seemed content to stay like that indefinitely and it was Alison who finally broke away. Lifting her head, she looked down at Brookes.

'My God! Just look at us.'

Brookes lifted his head and looked from himself to Alison. They both laughed. Alison saw a man, tired, prickly chinned, physical want struggling with shyness. She put her hand to his face, ran her fingertips over the stubble, felt his small laugh of apology. Brookes could see nothing but beauty in the dishevelled hair, the stained curves of the housecoat. He saw her eyes close, felt her cheek press against his palm as his fingers explored her neck, deep in the coppery warmth of her hair. With lips just open, they kissed like sipping a fine wine. They knew there would never be another kiss like this one, the first one. They drew it out, lingered over it, as long as they could, supporting their heads against the cushion, their cheeks held in the clean, dry caress of the supple leather.

No sooner had it ended than Brookes asked breathlessly, lovingly, 'Can I have another one, please?'

'You know what happened to Oliver Twist?'

'I'll risk it.'

Their pillow talk murmured on for an hour and more, their entire world encompassed by no more than a pair of arms. Daylight turned the lamplight yellow. Now he knew what it was to feel her hair brush his face, her mouth searching, her voice caressing. For a while she had felt secure, encapsulated in the tenderness that this gentlest of men had wrapped round her. Both felt taut with aching excitement but were too sensitive to let it dominate and destroy. Both took pleasure in its control. They knew that one plunging grope would instantly dispel the enchantment, the innocence. Passion was something to contemplate pleasurably for another time they both knew would certainly come. Nothing now could prevent it; Shepworth, husband, Rosemary, gossip, Jonathan. Jonathan? Brookes raised his head to look through the window.

'Lissa, darling, I must go. It's broad daylight.'

'What time is it?' asked a voice muffled by the folds of a sweater.

'I don't know, but the boys will be awake soon. You don't want Robert to come down and find us like this, do you?'

'Don't care,' said the voice.

'Now come on,' Brookes said, laughing as he struggled to his feet, Alison still hanging around his neck. 'Break it up, Mrs Barker. I've got to go home.'

Alison stood back a pace, her eyes dancing.

'Can I come with you?' Teasing, Alison put her hands behind her neck. Lifting her hair behind her, she braced her elbows backwards, showing sensual delight as Brookes lowered his gaze. With the torpor of a sleep-walker, he stretched out his hands to cup, to mould her breasts. She watched, exultant for a moment, then pushed herself between his arms, thrusting her body against his.

'That wasn't fair either, darling. But there will be a time soon. I promise you.'

Brookes, dry mouthed, could say nothing, only allow himself to be led gently to the hall. Before opening the door they held each other once more. Alison felt Brookes shake his head over her shoulder. Pushing him away just far enough to see his face, she asked, 'What's the matter? What was that for?'

'Nothing really.' Brookes laughed. 'I was just thinking it's been quite a day one way and another.'

'What d'you mean?'

'Well, you could hardly call it a typical day in the life of a provincial general surgeon, now could you?'

'I wouldn't know. I don't know what you surgeons get up to in a typical day.' Alison paused. 'But I'm dying to find out. I can't wait to find out what goes on in there,' she softly patted his chest with the flat of her hand and, with a sudden change of mood, kissing him, full of mischief, 'amongst other places.'

'Lissa!'

Unrepentant, Alison said, 'Michael, I haven't felt like this for years. I'm not sure I've ever felt like this before. I didn't think it could happen any more. I want you. I want to make love to you. My only problem is going to be hiding it from the general public.'

'So you wouldn't say it's been a typical day in the life of a Shepworth housewife either, then?'

'No, but I don't imagine I'm unique either. There must be hundreds of Shepworths up and down the country. Odds on there's some other housewife somewhere, in Torquay, or Aberdeen, who's got an alcoholic for a husband and a sixteen-year-old boy as a rival.'

Brookes stood back, startled.

'What d'you mean,' he asked, sharply, on the defensive.

'You know exactly what I mean.' Alison took hold of his hands, pleading. 'Don't be afraid, Michael. We'll be lovers but I won't do anything that will hurt Jonathan.'

She looked lovingly at Brookes.

'Michael, I'm no fool. I know what a local scandal would do to you and to Jonathan. You'd hate it and then you'd hate me.'

Alison put her fingers on Brookes' mouth as he tried to protest.

'I know how you feel about Jonathan. You can't expect me not to be a bit jealous. I know how close you are, how you love him. Don't imagine I haven't known what's gone on these last two years. You chose him before me then and you'd do it again. I love you, Michael, but you needn't worry. I'll be discreet. I'll never do anything to harm Jonathan. I wouldn't want to anyway, but I have a much more selfish reason. If I hurt him, I lose you.'

PART TWO

Operation

10

'Good morning, Mr Beaupré.' The receptionist's smile was as bright, professional and artificial as the décor. 'Would you come this way, sir? Sir John is expecting you.'

Teflo (UK) Ltd occupied the top two floors of Nitromid International's office block in Liverpool. Beaupré had just penetrated the outer bulwarks of this industrial fortress and was being escorted into the last line of defence, Anderson's personal secretary's office. The girl knocked on the door and opened it, standing so that Beaupré was obliged to pass through the maximum flux of her body's magnetic field. Signal received and understood. No need for him to be lonely while in Liverpool.

'Mr Beaupré,' the girl announced, lingering long enough to confirm any impression she may have given earlier.

Anderson's secretary's words of welcome were addressed to the back of Beaupré's head. He turned rapidly, apologetically, as the welcome was repeated.

'Good morning, Mr Beaupré. My name is Mary Jamieson. I'm Sir John's secretary.' She had been amused at the sexual semaphore between Beaupré and the receptionist and her smile showed it. She walked around her desk, taking the initiative, to shake Beaupré's hand. 'I won't ask you to sit down; Sir John has asked me to let him know the moment you arrive.'

She returned to her desk and pressed a button, leaving Beaupré standing, silently appreciative. He saw a woman of near forty, sexy in a lofty, you'll-have-to-work-hard-to-get-me, kind of a way. He looked at the large desk, piled high, but neatly so, with files; a separate table with a typewriter for the confidential stuff. She wore a wedding ring but she must be widowed, divorced or separated to keep that job down, Beaupré thought. The whole office reflected competence.

For a moment, there was no reply to her call and she smiled apologetically. She felt her advantage slipping away to the man standing there, massively silent. His very presence was dominating. Quite relaxed, he none the less oozed power, without the slightest hint of nervousness or shyness in his spade-like hands or craggy features. She was accustomed to Savile Row greys and blues in her office and Beaupré's well-cut check made him look even larger. Gentle giant, maybe, but someone well able to settle an argument with his fists if all else failed, if the shape of his nose was anything to go by.

'Yes, Mary?'

'Mr Beaupré is here, Sir John.'

'Thank you, Mary. I'll be right out.'

Beaupré clearly felt there was no need to fill the short period of silence that followed with any polite chit-chat. In the few moments before Anderson opened his door, Mary Jamieson changed her mind. This was no gentle giant but a hard man to whom any woman was someone to be taken or left, either option being exercised without emotion. She was relieved to hear Anderson's voice.

'Pierre. Nice to see you again. Come in. I'm sorry if I've kept you waiting.'

'Not a bit, John. Good morning.'

Beaupré gave Mary Jamieson a curt nod as he headed for Anderson's office. The large room was divided into two by a wrought-iron screen of the most delicate filigree design and two curved, thickly carpeted steps. The screen divided the hard sell from the soft; the black leather and stainless steel contrasted with the inlaid Regency sofa table, the steel grey carpet with the enormous Persian rug; the vast window and its view of Liverpool's dockland with a smaller window, softened by curtains of thick brocade; the cold efficiency of the space capsule with the faded gentility of the London club. On one side, a silver-framed picture of Anderson shaking hands with royalty at Teflo's opening; on the other, a Lowry original and a vibrant charcoal-and-wash drawing of miners' heads. Hard seats, designed for the discomfiture of supplicants, desperate to please, were divided from body-enveloping comfort for the seduction of bankers and politicians. The two halves were unified only in cupidity.

Too short to reach around such massive shoulders, Anderson took Beaupré's elbow in his hand and led him to one of the deep leather chairs. Both sat to face each other.

'Sorry to arrange this for the lunch-hour, Pierre. I know how early you North Americans like to start work but I thought you might like to meet the directors.'

82

Beaupré gave a non-committal grunt. He noticed that Mrs Jamieson had followed them into the room.

'What can we get you to drink, Pierre?'

'A pink gin, if that is possible?'

'Yes, of course,' Mrs Jamieson said in answer to a questioning glance from Anderson.

She crossed to the Sheraton sideboard with its flower arrangement partly concealing the cluster of decanters. From the cupboard she deftly, unhurriedly, produced some bottles.

Beaupré watched, amused, as Mrs Jamieson, poised and chic, skilfully twirled the glass, wetting it with the bitters, before throwing the excess away. Slowly, she added the gin until stopped by a sign from Beaupré. Without asking, she poured Anderson a whisky. Beaupré followed her hand, saw the soft ruff of silk around her wrist. She made the simple act of dropping an ice cube into Anderson's glass look sensual. And there was the giveaway; that hand on Anderson's shoulder, so softly, as she leaned over to give him his drink. The lucky old devil. The door shut behind her, leaving them alone.

'Don't your directors start work before lunch-time, John?'

'Of course they do, Pierre.' Anderson laughed as he made the ice in his glass tinkle. 'It's just that some of them have had to come from some distance.'

'Oh?'

'Yes. We make it more or less a condition of employment that the Managing Director lives locally, or at least reasonably close, but we are not too concerned about the others. Three have come up from town this morning, the other two from the Midlands.'

'Part-timers, you mean.' There was an overtone of contempt in Beaupré's voice as he went on. 'Let me guess. At least one titled gent, preferably a peer, maybe even a hereditary one if he's on Nitromid's Board as well; at least one distinguished soldier with a string of gongs; at least one hyphen, preferably joining two foreign-sounding names, French rather than German; and fill up with old Harrovians with contacts in the City. All looks good on the company's letterhead. Who is your Managing Director?'

There was sufficient truth in Beaupré's resumé to force Anderson to laugh.

'I am; at least, I'm acting Managing Director. We appointed Jeremy Whitlam recently but he won't be starting here for a while, probably a few months. He is Managing Director of our plant in Victoria and doesn't want to leave until he has seen some scheme of his down there working. Good man. You'll like him. A very able chap. Qualified as a chemical engineer before he became an accountant. Knows the business backwards.'

'But, in the meanwhile, you are virtually running Teflo, John?'

'Well, with the Board, of course.'

'Bullshit. How often do you see these directors of yours? How often do you have a Board meeting?' As Anderson started to object, Beaupré drove home his point. 'Tell me, John, honestly; if you have a day-to-day problem at Teflo, who do you get in touch with?'

'Man called Fred Richmond.'

'Who is?'

'The General Works Manager.'

'In fact, you are, at the moment, the next man up from the Works Manager. To all intents and purposes, you run Teflo.' Not a question now but a statement and Anderson's conceit allowed him to concede the point with little more than a nod. 'But I still have to meet these Boardroom puppets of yours. When do I get to having a look at Teflo? That's really what I'm here for.'

'I must say, Pierre, you are two different men in a boardroom and a golf club. I say that with every respect, of course,' Anderson added hastily.

'Well,' drawled Beaupré. 'Perhaps I can borrow a phrase from our great southern neighbours; this is an entirely different ball game.'

'There is one man I would like you meet before you go up to Teflo; Fred Richmond, the General Works Manager I mentioned earlier. I've asked him to explain the process at Teflo to you so that you will have a better idea of what is going on when you look around the plant this afternoon. They should all be in the dining-room by now.' Anderson hauled himself out of the deep recesses of the armchair. 'Come and meet them.'

He'd met them all before. All over the world. The cars outside might vary, Cadillac, Mercedes, Ferrari, Citroen, Jaguar; basic English might be butchered by different accents from a Southern drawl to a Royal Mid-Surrey; the hats might vary from ten-gallon Texans to well-brushed bowlers; but the men would be the same, interchangeable, disposable. However, one man stood apart like a curate at a conclave of bishops, a glass, brimming with sweet sherry, held in front of him with two hands like a chalice at Holy Communion. The ritual preprandial banalities did nothing to improve Beaupré's mood and he was almost relieved to find the frightened little man sitting next to him at lunch.

84

'Frederick Richmond, isn't it? I have got the name right, haven't I?'

'Quite correct, sir.'

'May I call you Fred?'

Richmond blushed. 'Of course, sir.' He did not raise his eyes from the soup spoon half-way to his mouth. His left hand was tightly wedged between his knees as if he was afraid of what it might do if set free.

'How long have you been at Teflo, Fred?'

'Just over five years, thank you, sir.'

Full stop. Beaupré tried again. 'Where were you before you came to Teflo?'

'I was a Plant Manager with Courtaulds in South Wales and had a research post in a polytechnic before that.' There was further silence as he continued drinking his soup.

'Sir John speaks very highly of you. Still, I don't suppose you get to be General Works Manager of a place like Teflo without knowing a thing or two.'

'You'd be surprised,' replied Richmond, cryptically.

'Really?' asked Beaupré, beginning to sense hidden depths in the man.

'Yes, really. I reckon there are some plants where the Works Manager knows as much about the process as, as, as . . .' he looked around the table, hesitating, plucking up courage, 'as one of the directors.'

Beaupré's surprised roar of laughter turned several heads. When the surrounding conversation picked up again, Beaupré turned to Richmond once more.

'Any ambitions of joining the Board yourself, Fred?'

With astonishment, Richmond replied, 'What? Join this lot? No thank you. You just leave me in my lab where I'm happy. You can keep the gin and tonic. I'd rather tea out of a beaker any time.'

And so, later, it was with a new respect that Beaupré looked at Richmond, standing in front of a blackboard rigged at one end of the dining-room. The waitresses had cleared the table of the dirtier dishes only, before being hastily shepherded through one door by the Catering Manager; Anderson had swept the directors through another.

Anderson settled Beaupré in a chair facing the blackboard, a goblet in his hand, a bottle of Remy Martin at his elbow.

'I'm leaving you in Fred's capable hands, Pierre, and the best of luck to you. Prepare to be blinded by science. I must admit that he leaves me behind after about two sentences. I'm going up to Teflo now and Fred will bring you up later. Duncan Rae, our Works Engineer, will show you whatever you want to see, warts and all, and then, perhaps, we could have a talk.'

The door closed behind Anderson and Richmond waited for Beaupré to settle. With legs extended, ankles crossed, brandy warming at navel level, Beaupré nodded.

'Right, Fred. Shoot.'

'Well, Mr Beaupré. I am going to assume that you know virtually nothing about the manufacture of nylon. I am going to start from first principles. Now, I give you fair warning; I can bore you to the back teeth on the subject. I'm no good at the social small-talk but, on my own subject, I can talk all night. When you have had enough, please say so.'

Richmond turned to face the blackboard, paused to marshal his thoughts, and drew rapidly with coloured chalks to produce a simple flow chart. With an intensity that surprised Beaupré, he explained the basic process at Teflo, the production of caprolactam for the manufacture of nylon elsewhere. Beaupré was well into his third brandy before Richmond slowed sufficiently for him to ask a question.

'You mention optimum temperature and pressure, Fred. What sort of temperature and pressure are we talking about?'

'Unfortunately quite high, Mr Beaupré. 155° centigrade and 8.8 kilograms per square centimetre, to be exact.'

'And this oxidised cyclohexane, is it inflammable?'

'Yes.'

'Very?'

'Under the right conditions, explosive.'

'And how critical are the conditions in those reactors? Or anywhere else in the system for that matter? How much of a margin of safety have you got?'

'Well, temperature and pressure are interrelated and have to be nicely balanced, but it's by no means a razor's edge.'

'But if things get out of hand, and don't tell me they don't, how do you stop the whole bloody issue going up in smoke?'

Richmond, as relaxed and in control as he had been tense and at a loss in the lunch, smiled as he replied.

'All catered for, Mr Beaupré, chemically and mechanically. The pressure valves you must talk over with Duncan Rae this afternoon but, chemically speaking, you simply turn the heat off and blow inert nitrogen through the reactors, a so-called nitrogen purge.' With a few more squares and arrows, he added the nitrogen circulation to the flow chart.

Beaupré put his brandy aside, leaned forwards, elbows on knees and his hands together like a child praying. His eyes screwed up as he asked, softly, 'Is it safe? Honest opinion now, Fred. Is it safe?'

Richmond considered for a moment. He replied, slowly at first, then more rapidly as his opinion crystallised.

'No process at high temperature and pressure can ever be guaranteed totally safe. However, I think there are sufficient safety measures built into this process to make it an acceptable risk.'

'Right then.' Beaupré stood up abruptly. 'Let's go and have a look at the place.'

When Richmond saw Beaupré walk towards the Aston Martin DBS, he had a premonition that he was not going to enjoy the drive north. Beaupré drove with a furious intensity, taking advantage of the slightest timid concession from another driver. Richmond spent the first quarter of an hour anxiously recalling the number of brandies he had seen his driver put away. By the time they reached Dunbridge, he was smirking at the lesser mortals, such as himself, left standing at traffic lights in their family saloons. It was almost with a swagger that he got out and introduced Duncan Rae to Beaupré in Teflo's directors' car park.

'Mr Beaupré, may I introduce Duncan Rae. He's our Works Engineer here. Duncan, this is Mr Beaupré.'

'Good afternoon, Mr Beaupré. Welcome to Teflo.' Rae held out his hand.

'Hullo, Duncan. I'm pleased to meet you.'

Richmond, although senior to Rae, once more became the odd man out. It is doubtful if either Beaupré or Rae heard Richmond say that he would see them both later in the Boardroom; they were too preoccupied sizing each other up. They might have been father and son.

Aged thirty-five, Rae was tall with a mass of red hair protruding untidily from under his yellow protective helmet. A thick tartan shirt, open at the neck, revealed a deep chest covered in a mat of hair. From a square, weather-beaten face, blue eyes danced with the lively arrogance of some-one physically hard and fit. Beaupré looked, and saw himself twenty years before. Too big a man to be jealous, Beaupré took to him at once.

Handing Beaupré a helmet, Rae asked, 'Where would you like to start, sir?'

'I'm in your hands, Duncan, but Fred started his talk at the reactors so, perhaps, we could start there too?'

With a farewell nod to Richmond, Beaupré and Rae began the two hundred yards' walk to the reactors, directly behind the car park and office block. As they walked, conversation came easily.

'Well now, Duncan. Tell me about your part in all this. What exactly do you do?'

'Where do I come in the pecking order, do you mean?' laughed Rae. 'Fred Richmond is my boss and is responsible directly to the Managing Director. I am the Works Engineer and, with six other executives, I am responsible to Fred.'

'Bit young for Works Engineer, aren't you?' Beaupré said, but did not wait for an answer. 'Who or what are the six executives?'

'Three Plant Managers, a Technical Manager, the Chief Chemist and the Instrument Engineer.'

'What are you trained as, Duncan?'

'I am a chartered mechanical engineer, Mr Beaupré.'

'And the Plant Managers?'

'Chartered chemical engineers.'

'Does that mean you are the only mechanical engineer at this level?' Beaupré asked, with some surprise.

'That's right, sir. And I shan't be here much longer.'

'Oh?' Beaupré showed surprise. 'You're leaving?'

'Yes,' Rae replied.

'Why?'

'Oh, I don't know. Generally fed up. Fed up with management that won't move with the times, fed up with bloody minded unions.'

'But it'll be the same wherever you go.'

'Oh, I'm getting out. I have a motto: if you can't beat them, leave them. I'm off to your country. I've got a two-year research fellowship in Toronto, studying ergonomics.'

They had reached the reactors and were joined by an overworked, strained-looking Mark Dixon, Area Engineer for that part of the plant. With their voices raised against the hum and hiss, with arms sweeping and necks craning, Rae and Dixon explained the mechanics of the valves that controlled the heat exchanger, the safety valves on the off-gas line, the mechanism of the nitrogen purge.

'And is there a fail-safe on the heating?' Beaupré asked.

'Yes,' Rae replied. 'Fail-safe position is closed.'

'And the safety valves, once more?'

'Vent at 11 kilograms per square centimetre and the nitrogen purge is at 12 kilograms.'

'All blowing out to the waste-gas line?'

'That's right, sir, and ultimately, to the flare stack.'

The three men walked through the plant, stopping at times for Rae to point to something of interest, Dixon standing a respectful pace away. They emerged the other side to follow the off-gas line which ran parallel to the roadway as far as the base of the flare stack. Beaupré raised one eyebrow at Rae. There didn't appear to be much more to see.

'Just one more thing, Mr Beaupré. Just come and look at what I mean.'

He guided Beaupré to a group of absorber towers, the final processing plant before the flare stack, a group of cigar-shaped towers clustered together with only the narrow roadway separating them from the gantry that carried the off-gas line.

'D'you see what I mean, sir.'

Beaupré stood back amused as Rae ranted at the morons who could have a sixty-acre site and still end up with such a cramped lay-out, while Dixon explained to Beaupré the difficulties of the site; that, in places, rock gave way to marshland and they couldn't always pick and choose where to put the plant.

'All right, you two, stop arguing,' Beaupré broke in. 'I take both your points but forget that for a moment and let me see if I've got things right. The waste gases, the off-gas if it's ever blown off through the safety valves and the nitrogen after a nitrogen purge, they all come down that pipe there' – he pointed to the long gantry and then swung his hand in the direction of the flare stack – 'and blow off to the atmosphere there.'

Rae and Dixon nodded simultaneously.

'Right then.' Beaupré started walking back. 'I'd just like to see the control-room before I finish.'

In the control-room on the first floor of a red-brick building at the heart of the complex, Rae introduced Beaupré to the Shift Superintendent, Jack Summerbee, and the young Process Control Technician, Philip Dodd. Summerbee, upright and immaculate, looked in danger of snapping to attention and saluting Beaupré, while Dodd, seated at a control panel, stared Beaupré down with an assurance that verged on insolence. Beaupré marked him down as a man to watch. Beaupré was led dutifully around, his hands behind his back, his interest seemingly as intelligent as the local mayor's on open day. When he had gone full circle, however, he turned to Rae.

'Why are your nitrogen tanks only sixty per cent full?'

Taken aback, Rae did not answer while Dodd sniggered.

'If nitrogen is your main safety measure, why keep the stock so low?'

'Best ask the bloody unions about that,' Rae replied.

'What d'you mean?'

'Well, we've got a leak that's a bit of a problem. It's not much but we can't even find if it's leaking into or out of the system. But the main trouble is the supply. The unions are limiting the supply.'

'Why?'

'Best ask Sir John that one, Mr Beaupré.'

'But what happens if your level drops any further? Aren't you worried?'

'Not really, sir. Not in safety terms. There is a sensor which automatically closes down the whole process with a nitrogen purge if the level in the tanks falls below a certain point.'

'But the unions could close this place down any time they wanted, without the management being able to do a thing about it?'

'That's right, sir.'

There was another snigger from the control panel. Dodd thought about showing Beaupré those other controls on the back of the main panel, out of sight, out of mind, that enabled him to override that automatic nitrogen purge. What the hell; no skin off his nose.

Before leaving the control-room, Beaupré paused to look out of the window, Summerbee standing quietly at his elbow. Beaupré pointed to the reactors and heat exchanger, seemingly no more than a stone's throw away.

'They've built this place a bit close to those reactors, haven't they, Mr Summerbee?'

'They have indeed, sir.'

'Any reason for that?'

'None that I can think of, sir, no.'

Beaupré glanced around the room behind him.

'D'you have any sort of shelter you could run to in an emergency?'

'None, sir.'

'Not much chance for the lads in here if that lot went up, then.' Beaupré jabbed his thumb in the direction of the reactors.

'Not much, sir, no.'

'Humph.' Beaupré paused. 'Tell me, Mr Summerbee. If there was some sort of major accident at Teflo, if this control-room was destroyed, do you have anything resembling an aircraft's black box to give some clue afterwards as to what went wrong?'

'No, sir.'

'Interesting. Thank you, Mr Summerbee.'

'Thank you, sir.'

Anderson and Richmond stood up as Beaupré came in. They must have had little common ground for conversation and both looked relieved. Their tubular-framed chairs scraped the floor.

'There you are, Pierre. I hope Rae has been looking after you. Have you seen all you want to see?'

'I think so, John; yes.'

At a nod from Anderson, Richmond and Rae left the room like seconds leaving the ring.

'I'm sorry to meet you in a place like this,' Anderson waved around at the small, no-frills dining-room within earshot of the clattering canteen kitchen, 'but I thought the fewer people who know you're here the better.'

'Suits me fine,' said Beaupré, lowering his bulk on to one of the chairs while Anderson stood in front of him.

'Well, Pierre, what do you think of Teflo?'

'Impressed, John. That's a whole lot of engineering you've got out there. Yes, sir.' Anderson's smile of self-satisfaction faded as Beaupré continued. 'But you've got snags, John. All right, I know it's not possible to have a perfect set-up, especially one as big as Teflo, but you've got problems, potentially dangerous problems. No two ways about it, John, I wouldn't accept them in any plant of mine.'

Anderson looked hard at his opponent. He began to walk restlessly around the tables. Like a terrier with a bull, Anderson circled looking for an opening but Beaupré gave him no chance.

'Why are you letting Rae go?'

'What do you mean?'

'Exactly what I say. You're losing a first-class man and you seem to be doing nothing to prevent it.'

'He's a mixed blessing, Pierre. First-class man, agreed, but like a red rag to a bull where the unions are concerned.'

'Have you got a replacement for him?'

'Not yet. The Services Engineer is going to fill in temporarily for him.'

'Filling in temporarily.' Beaupré repeated Anderson's words. 'Why not give him the job?'

'Because we must advertise the job first.'

'And, if this Services Engineer applies, will he get it?' Beaupré insisted.
'No.'
'Why not?'
'He's not a sufficiently qualified engineer,' admitted Anderson.
'So, for a while, he will be doing a job for which he is not qualified?'
Anderson did not answer as Beaupré pressed home his advantage. 'You already have Dixon, an unqualified engineer, doing two men's jobs.'

Once he had his man cornered, Beaupré was not likely to let Anderson slip. The best he could hope for was to ride the punches until Beaupré chose to change his line of attack. Systematically he drove home all Teflo's weak points; the senior management, top heavy with accountants and chemists; the nitrogen leak and the low reserves; the union troubles. Anderson felt crushed by the man's grasp of the working problems in a plant he had only seen for the first time that day. Northweir Plant was only mentioned briefly, with a few scathing words that were virtually its epitaph. By the time Beaupré had finished, he had depicted 'that complicated pressure cooker out there' as a lethal machine being tended by a strike-prone labour force with a depleted, poorly qualified management team.

As Beaupré's relentless goading continued, Anderson's face became suffused with suppressed irritation. Suddenly his eyes closed and his face wrinkled in pain. With the knuckle of his right index finger, he bored into his right temple as if trying to trepan his skull and evacuate some agonising tumour. Beaupré half rose from his chair in concern.

'John. Are you all right?'

Anderson's irritation broke the surface.

'Yes, of course I am,' he snapped, turning his back on Beaupré as if to hide any sign of weakness. But the pain persisted and he was forced to sit for a while, his back still to Beaupré.

Beaupré felt that he had made most of the points he wanted to and, in any case, he would have found it difficult talking to Anderson's hunched shoulders. He walked deliberately to a window and gazed at the plant. Below him, a tanker driver leaned from his cabin window to gossip with a mate standing alongside. Opposite, and at a comparable level, two men erecting scaffolding around a distillation tower shouted at each other, their voices lost to Beaupré in the overall din of the plant. Throughout the engineering jungle spread out before him, human animals walked, climbed, communicated, made diminutive by the machines they had created. If Beaupré noticed them at all, he would have seen them as no more than moving parts in an industrial complex he was determined to control. He would not have seen breadwinners, gamblers, loving husbands, wife-beaters, lay preachers, alcoholics, the daughter in university, the spina bifida in the parlour. He would have been quick to spot the fatigue of the man promoted beyond his ability, the financial worries of the compulsive gambler, the shakiness of the alcoholic, only in that they represented signs of stress in the plant rather than in the man. He saw a man as a part of the plant as liable to a stress fracture as a pipe weakened by zinc embrittlement. To Beaupré, redundancy was the removal of a part of the plant that was surplus to requirement, employment of extra manpower as a necessary part of plant expansion. Neither would cause him emotion.

Beaupré returned to the table, towering over Anderson for a moment before he sat down. No doubt now who was the stronger man, with Anderson looking haggard and tormented.

'Right, John. No bullshit. Time's come to wrap this one up.' Beaupré made no allowance for Anderson's appearance. 'We don't have to spell it out, do we? The problem is that we are both too strong to break, too big to take over. I can see the sense in not knocking financial lumps out of each other competing for world markets, if we can come to some arrangement, merger, call it what you will. But let's get one thing straight; you want me more than I want you. If you want a fight, we are more than ready. It would cost us both, John, cost us a lot. But, after what I've seen today, I've no doubt who'd go to the wall and it wouldn't be us. So you're asking, I'm telling. Agreed? And this is what I'm telling you.'

Anderson fought to concentrate on Beaupré's face as Beaupré laid down his conditions in a quiet, precise voice. No table thumping.

'I'm not having anything to do with your company until some serious flaws are ironed out, and so, here are my conditions. I agree that our bankers should meet in three months' time if, during that period . . .' Beaupré began to count off the points on his fingers. 'One: there has been a minimum of eighteen thousand tons of caprolactam produced. Two: no stoppages in the process other than due to acts of God.' Anderson pulled a face but did not interrupt. 'Three: an overall reorganisation has taken place to strengthen the mechanical engineering management. And four: the decision to shut down oxidation is taken no lower than General Works Manager.'

Anderson stared into Beaupré's face as if waiting for further conditions but Beaupré had finished. Once again, Anderson rose to pace nervously up and down, up and down. He produced a bunch of keys from his trouser pocket and began to throw them, hard, from hand to hand.

'Production and stoppages go hand in hand, Pierre. If we meet the production figures easily, would you forgo the condition about the stoppages?'

'No chance. Rather the other way around. I wouldn't mind if you just missed the target if I knew there had been continuous production.'

Anderson had not expected it to be easy. It was no worse than he had hoped for and he delayed his reply only to hide his readiness to agree.

'All right. It's a deal, Pierre. I think you've been a bit tough about the stoppages but we'll have to see what we can do. We'll meet again in three months' time.'

'Look forward to it, John. Do you want anything in writing?'

Anderson thought for a moment.

'I think not, Pierre. If the unions get to hear that we've got a deadline to meet, they might take advantage of that; might hold us to ransom. I think the fewer people who know about it the better.'

They stretched across the table to shake hands.

'Now, what about a drink?' Anderson said, selecting a key from the bunch in his hand. 'Do me a favour and call those two in, Pierre. I think they deserve one too.'

When Richmond and Rae entered, Anderson was already behind the small bar in the corner of the room, rolling up the grille with a clatter. Though now exuding professional *bonhomie*, he held his head and neck quite still as he bent to reach for bottles on the lower shelves, his carotid arteries banging out their painful warnings on the base of his skull. He talked Richmond into the second sherry of the day and listened as Beaupré talked to Rae.

'I give you six months, Duncan. You don't look the university type to me. Just promise me one thing.'

'What's that, Mr Beaupré?'

'When you get fed up, as I am sure you will, don't take another job until you've had a word with me?'

'You have my word on that, Mr Beaupré.' Rae raised his glass. 'Your good health, sir.'

Anderson and Richmond murmured assent as they put their glasses to their lips. Beaupré acknowledged the toast, raising his glass also.

'Here's to profit.' He smiled.

11

Whilst Anderson and Beaupré were discussing the future of Teflo, another meeting was being held in another Boardroom not six miles away.

'Bloody monumental waste of time,' was Dai Jack's opinion.

Several other members of the Dunbridge General Hospital Medical Staff Advisory Committee would have agreed.

In one Boardroom, two ruthless professionals, in half an hour of uncompromising dialogue, had made decisions that would affect the lives of hundreds of people for whom they felt little concern. In the other, a motley group, for the most part reluctant, amateur administrators, their main vocation being the well-being of their fellow men, would, in a welter of words, come to few decisions of any consequence. Gone was the efficient, all-powerful triumvirate of Medical Superintendent, Matron and Hospital Secretary. Gone also the Boardroom of the days of the voluntary hospital, the medical sanctum sanctorum with its solid mahogany table, panelled walls, hat stand for the bowlers, leather-bound visitors' book for the visiting honoraries' signatures. Now the NHS table-top was warped and stained, the dry, unloved panelling split, the hat stand gone, the lectern for the visitors' book demoted to supporting cold tea cups, tea-soaked fag ends in their saucers, relics of the afternoon's meeting of the Catering Committee.

George Harrington and David Williams, Chairman and Secretary respectively, sat at the end of the room farthest from the door, watching the members drift in singly and in groups. The evening was fine and warm, the agenda long and chill, all portents of a low attendance. The tendency was for the seats nearest the door to be occupied first, facilitating early defections and thus leaving gaps on either side of Harrington and Williams. In contrast, the sturdy figure of William Rothwell thrust through the gentle gossip near the door, to stride across the room and take the seat next to Harrington.

His 'Evening, Harrington, Williams' was received by Harrington's polite smile and Williams' scowl. Harrington looked at his watch, coughed and tapped ineffectually on the table with his pen. The early formalities of a committee meeting were lost in the chatter of the late arrivals. Last to arrive, Michael Brookes found that the nearest vacant chair was that next to Rothwell. Deliberately, Brookes lifted the chair, carried it to the back of the room and sat down behind those already at the table. Rothwell flushed, Harrington frowned his disapproval and Williams grinned openly.

Brookes found one other isolated from the rest at the back of the room: Henry Orme. Instinctively, Brookes shifted his chair a few inches. Orme saw the movement and smiled his knowing, flaccid smile. There was little love lost between the two of them. Orme's reputation throughout the hospital for silently touching any part of a female form that came within range of those pale hands, failed to cement a trusting relationship. His single package holidays to Majorca or Tenerife were always booked with fantasies of the raving nymphomaniac he was to meet in airport bar or hotel lounge, fantasies never translated into fact. Michael remembered the occasion when a widowed staff nurse who had gone on a walking holiday in North Wales with Orme returned early to her silent flat, determined she was not that desperate yet. And, more importantly, the one time he had made it all the way he had been discovered, grunting sweatily with the Night Sister in the Duty Anaesthetist's bed. She had been sacked and he had suffered the ignominy of chastisement by Dunbridge General's 'three wise men', one of whom happened to be Brookes. Michael and Orme now sat close to each other, the space between them as vibrant as between the like poles of two bar magnets.

A month earlier had seen the first meeting of the Advisory Committee under the local government reorganisation. By invitation, the Chairman of the new Community Health Council, a kindly, apologetic, retired head-master, had attended with his deputy, William Rothwell. Diffidently, the Chairman had told of complaints about the accommodation for parents in the paediatric ward and had accepted gracefully an invitation to be shown around the ward. All consistent with the watchful courtesies of strange bedfellows. All too polite for Rothwell, determined to make his mark. His uninvited diatribe on appalling waiting lists which he attributed to ob-vious bad management and inefficiency, led to a head-on clash with Brookes, who had been in the hospital service for thirty years and was not going to let any jumped-up teachers and plumbers tell him how to run his unit.

Rothwell and Brookes had met before, long before Rothwell's election to the Community Health Council. Their very first meeting had been bitter and recriminatory. Rothwell's daughter, Sheila, three months' pregnant, had been admitted with abdominal pain and Brookes' Registrar had removed a doubtfully inflamed appendix. There had been some doubt about some symptoms of urinary infection the next day but no doubt at all about the miscarriage of what would have been Rothwell's first grandson. The Registrar had not called Brookes, but Rothwell had always held Brookes responsible. He should have come in, Rothwell had complained. If Sheila had been one of Brookes' snooty friends' daughter, not just a working-class lass, then he'd have come in all right. Perhaps if he had done the operation, not one of these foreigners, perhaps she wouldn't have lost the baby. Perhaps he wouldn't have operated at all. He had no right to get away with it.

Now Harrington tried to instil a little discipline into the crew of free-thinkers that faced him. Long war service in destroyers had earned him a DSC in Atlantic convoys but his navy, double-breasted suit, white shirt and dark blue silk tie was the nearest to a uniform he could now wear. Bluff and formal, he sat erect, enjoying the father figure image he took pains to keep in sharp focus.

'Well, gentlemen. Perhaps we can get on. As you can see, we have a long agenda to get through.' He turned his head towards Rothwell beside him. 'Perhaps we could start by welcoming once more our friend from the Community Health Council. I know he is a very busy man so I intend to deal with item three first; the matter of the accommodation in the paediatric ward we discussed last time. Mr Rothwell, would you like to say what developments there have been since the last meeting?'

'Yes, thank you, Mr Chairman. I would like to come in here.' Rothwell spoke with the measured rhythm of the well-rehearsed speech. 'As you know, we were in receipt of certain complaints at the Council, due to certain representations made by some parents. Naturally we were only too glad to carry out an in-depth investigation of the situation as it existed at that point in time.'

David Williams sat back and seemed to become totally engrossed in something he could see on the ceiling.

'I suggested to my Chairman that he should arrange for us to visit ward in question, as this was obviously an on-going problem situation, and he agreed.' Rothwell, with a friendly gesture, smiled at one of the younger consultants opposite him. 'Dr Meyrick was kind enough to accompany us around the ward with Sister.'

Rothwell turned and spoke directly to Harrington as if to emphasise the effect.

'Both I and my Chairman agreed that, with the difficult situation you face in that old building, you are doing all you can under the circumstances. We have been in communication with the parties who made those representations and have informed them of our findings and I hope they won't bother you again.'

David Williams' gaze swept along the line of his colleagues' faces, all registering surprise at Rothwell's conciliatory tone. Harrington's mouth gaped slightly in astonishment until he regained his composure.

'Well, I'm sure we are all grateful to you, Mr Rothwell, for that report; and to your Chairman also, of course. It will be very encouraging to Dr Meyrick and his team. I am sure we are all grateful to you for coming this evening.'

Harrington's tone was obviously valedictory but Rothwell made no sign of taking the hint.

'It has been a pleasure, Dr Harrington. As we have always said, the aim of Health Council is to help.'

As he spoke, Rothwell's gaze rested squarely on Brookes. Harrington left an embarrassingly long pause for Rothwell to retire but Rothwell sat back, well pleased, his skin thick enough to resist any pressure Harrington was likely to apply. Too much of a gentleman to ask him to leave, Harrington finally went on to the next item.

'So, gentlemen, if we can now go back to item one, which is a proposal put forward for your consideration by Mr Lithgow. This is something of a hardy annual that tends to rouse emotions, but I would be grateful if you would all allow Mr Lithgow to put his case. Mark?'

All eyes turned on Mark Lithgow, tall, thin, elegant to the point of foppery. Face flushed, long fingers nervously playing with a solid gold pen, he began to put his case.

'Thank you, Mr Chairman. As everyone knows, we are legally entitled to two private beds in this hospital and that there are no other private facilities in Dunbridge. As things stand at present, a private patient is put in whatever bed is available at the time. As a result, I think the service we give the private patient for the amount the hospital charges him is disgraceful.'

Several heads nodded in agreement.

'I feel that the least they should expect to get is a single room and privacy; that is what most people pay for. Now I know that it has been proposed before that two single rooms be allocated for private patients and that there have been objections to this, but what I want to suggest is this. I feel this committee should approach local industry for money to upgrade two single rooms in the hospital with possibly the addition of a bathroom and toilet. After all, industry is the main source of private work around here and it has been done elsewhere. Private wings have been built by local industry and I . . .'

'By local industry, happen you mean Teflo?' barked Rothwell.

'Principally, yes,' admitted Lithgow, glancing at Harrington for support.

'Then I can tell you now, you're wasting your time.'

Harrington held his hand out, palm down, in front of his neighbour. 'Please, Mr Rothwell. I must ask you to allow Mr Lithgow to have his say.'

'I don't think I have anything to add, Mr Chairman,' Lithgow said feebly. 'I just thought it was an idea the committee might find worth discussing.'

Rothwell, the experienced, semi-professional committeeman, gave the others no chance.

'Through you, of course, Mr Chairman,' he said, with exaggerated politeness, cold eyes above a fixed, disingenuous smile, never wavering from Lithgow's direction, 'I can save committee a lot of wasted effort. If you think workforce at Teflo are going to stand by and watch profits they create go to provide private facilities here, and line consultants' pockets, tha's got to be crazy. What you consultants must also realise is that we have a number of our union members here in hospital, some in key posts, and . . .'

Harrington managed to stem the flow.

'Mr Rothwell.' Harrington used his quarterdeck voice. 'Even if you were a member of this committee and not here simply by invitation, I have no intention of allowing this committee to become a forum for union negotiations and threats. Mr Lithgow is perfectly within his rights to put forward his proposal and it is now open to the members for discussion.'

No one spoke. Many were full-timers, not involved in private practice. Most were apathetic, all certain that Lithgow's plan stood no chance of success. It was pointless to raise the blood pressure over a cause already lost. The silence dragged on long enough for Harrington to find it impossible to prevent Rothwell from speaking again.

'I would only like to repeat, Mr Chairman. While I respect what you said about this committee, I'd not have you labouring under any illusions. Any action along these lines and I'd not stand idly by. Let's be quite clear about this, one word from me to Executive Committee and we could close Teflo tomorrow.'

A pause, filled with hostile silence, was cut by words from the far end of the room, sharp in their cynicism. Brookes had taken no part in the proceedings. Hunched behind the row of his colleagues, with no table to lean on, he sat, elbows on knees, glowering at the floor.

'I must agree with Councillor Rothwell on this one, Mr Chairman,' Brookes said, without raising his head. 'We can't possibly lose those two single rooms. After all, where would we put the doctors' wives, County Councillors and union officials when they come in for their operations?'

The sniggering laughter around the table was the background for glances at Rothwell. If they were hoping for any over-reaction, they were disappointed. The fixed smile never wavered, if anything becoming more set in a subtle hardening of Rothwell's features. Harrington, torn between pleasure at Rothwell's discomfiture and irritation at Brookes' discourtesy, strove to stabilise the meeting again. He was grateful for Stephen Gracie's suggestion that everyone should be given the time to consider Lithgow's proposal and that it should be discussed again at the next meeting.

Another hour of grinding monotony brought them to the last item, the Major Accident Procedure. Hospital tea, Marie biscuits and the stuffy atmosphere had dried mouths and distended dyspeptic stomachs. A sufficient number had drifted away already to leave embarrassingly large gaps around the table; the remainder would have to see the meeting through. Harrington, uniquely upright in his chair, held up his multicoloured sheaf of foolscap.

'Last item, gentlemen. You will all have had a copy of the procedure by now and, hopefully, one or two of you might even have read it. You will be pleased to hear that I have no intention of going through it paragraph by paragraph this evening but our new lords and masters at Area seem to be in a hurry to have it. So, if anyone has any queries perhaps they would raise them now. I know that some of the orthopods want some amendments to the lists of equipment and they have promised to let me have these soon. Otherwise, any problems? Yes, Dr Gracie?'

'Mr Chairman, on behalf of everyone, I think I should congratulate you on your drafting of the procedure.' He waited for the murmur of assent to die away, while Harrington's smile of gratification threatened to lift his glasses off the bridge of his nose. 'It obviously represents a great deal of work on your part. However, several people have mentioned to me that they do not think the Consultant Radiologist the most suitable choice for

Site Officer. I feel, we feel, that someone with surgical skills and who is not needed at the hospital, would be more appropriate; in other words, the Consultant Gynaecologist. May I propose that amendment, Mr Chairman?'

'Second that.' Curt words from Brookes at the other end of the room.

Harrington registered the nods of bored approval from colleagues, anxious to be away, before looking at Lithgow's vacated chair.

'Mark is not here to defend himself, so I think we can take it that Dr Gracie's amendment is carried unanimously; that will teach him to leave early.' He paused. 'Well, gentlemen, if there is no other business . . . ? Yes, Mr Rothwell?'

Rothwell, gently insistent, began to speak, his tone subdued and suppliant, impossible to deny. Harrington held his papers vertically in front of him, signalling the end of the meeting, but Rothwell paid no heed.

'If I might come in here, Mr Chairman, on one small point. I know how busy you gentlemen are, but, if I may?'

He raised his eyebrows towards Harrington who, wearily, put his papers flat again.

'Thank you, Mr Chairman. Naturally, I have not had the opportunity to read your plans for a Major Accident but I'm interested, not only as a member of the CHC, but also as a member of the rescue services.' He leaned back in his chair, opened his jacket and stuck his thumbs in the armholes of his waistcoat. 'We would be reassured to know that services in hospital are as efficient as outside. For instance, was there any problem in contacting senior staff in recent exercise?'

'None that I know of,' replied Harrington.

'Might that be because you did not enquire, Dr Harrington? We all know the junior doctors will be around; it's ridiculous the hours you people expect those youngsters to work. But it seems to me that consultants can't always be depended on to be available.'

'Mr Rothwell, when you have had more experience of the Health Ser –'

Harrington's attempt to resume command of the situation was interrupted by a voice from the far end of the room.

'It seems to me that Councillor Rothwell is determined on a witch hunt against the wicked consultants, Mr Chairman, and, with respect, I don't think anything you say is likely to have any effect. Discussion is impossible with anyone as prejudiced as this and I think we all ought to go home.'

'Running away, Brookes? Got summat to hide, have you?' Rothwell sneered, yet still managed to smile.

In an attempt to smooth matters over, Gracie spoke directly to Rothwell.

'There is, as I am sure you know, an on-call system for the senior staff which has always worked very well in the past.'

Harrington also tried to help.

'The other evening was, after all, only an exercise. It is difficult to simulate the real thing in hospital without causing the in-patients undue distress and discomfort.'

'That is not the point, Mr Chairman. What if the other evening had been real thing? Where, for instance, was the Site Officer at the time?'

Harrington and Brookes exchanged embarrassed glances. Was it by chance or design that Rothwell had picked out Lithgow? They knew that Lithgow, at the time of the exercise, had been in the middle of a lengthy operation on a private patient in a Preston nursing home, fifteen miles away. Gracie, ignorant of the fact, came to their rescue.

'It is impossible, even when you are on call, to be eternally on the end of a phone. If there is any difficulty, a colleague can always be relied on to cover temporarily.'

Rothwell shifted his sights. It was as if the preamble had been no more than an opening barrage, a smoke screen, to cover his main attack.

'No doubt you would be one of the stars of show, Brookes. No doubt you were called. Were you happy with what you found when you came in?'

'I didn't come in,' snapped Brookes.

'What did you say?' asked Rothwell, having heard every word. He sprang for this unexpected gap in Brookes' defences, while feet scraped the floor in embarrassment around the room. 'Didn't come in, did you say? Just like you did once before?'

Rothwell's position alongside Harrington gave false authority to his words. Brookes, exposed at the far end of the room, felt like some admonished schoolboy.

'No.'

'Why not, pray?'

'Because I knew it was only an exercise and that it would only be a waste of time. I know what I have to do in the real thing.'

Harrington tried to intervene but it was like trying to separate two spitting cats.

'And, of course, your time is more valuable than anyone else's. We can go, missing our suppers, just to attend an exercise, but you? No, you're too important. Hell of an exercise it would have been if we'd all behaved like that.'

Brookes was seething with fury, and no opposition for Rothwell in such a slanging match. The best he could manage was a muttered 'Damned if I know why you bothered', which Rothwell, now grinning triumphantly, heard.

'Vocation, Brookes, vocation. Remember word? The thing only you doctors were meant to have. Tha couldn't believe that someone in a nine to five job could have it, could you? Well, they can. And I'll tell you this to think on. If you want privileges of a profession, you've got to earn them with responsibilities. And that's where vocation comes in, Brookes. Fail to deliver with the vocation, I tell thee, and you'll find your fancy privileges gone, and all; unions will see to that.'

Rothwell looked round to see nothing but stony faces and he laughed outright.

'Reckon I'll see you buggers clocking on shift system yet, and that's a fact.'

12

The ageing car took the full brunt of Brookes' ill-humour. Normally a meticulous driver, he thrashed through the gears, pushing the rev counter through arcs it had not swept for years. Through the windscreen he saw nothing but Rothwell's face, grinning, triumphant. What fuelled Brookes' wrath was the thin vein of truth that had run through all that Rothwell had said, and the distance between Dunbridge and Shepworth, covered at a furious pace, was not long enough to damp down the fire that burned in his chest and throat. With tyres squealing, he pulled viciously into Old Mill Close. As he passed the Barkers' house, he saw the Bentley parked in the drive. On impulse, he braked savagely, reversed, got out and slammed the car door shut.

A prolonged ringing of the door bell brought Alison Barker to the door, surprise, fear, excitement, all competing for expression in her face when she saw Brookes standing in the doorway.

Laurence Barker lounged, feet up, on the chesterfield, his back propped against one of the arms. A glass in one hand, the other hung vertically, just above floor level, smoke from the cigarette it held weaving its way upwards through the brown stained fingers. An ashtray, heavily laden, rested on the carpet within easy reach. He had heard Alison's surprise as she had opened the front door. The door closed. Barker's head inclined as he listened intently. He heard the momentary whispering, smiled as Alison called out, too loudly, 'It's Michael, Larry.' A warning to Larry that Michael had arrived, or a warning to Michael that Larry was in the living-room? He made no effort to rise as Brookes followed Alison into the room but waved him to a chair facing him.

'Michael, old son. Nice to see you. Alison, get the man a drink. He looks as if he needs one.'

Brookes smiled and nodded to Alison.

'Please. Whisky and water; about fifty-fifty.' He turned his smile to Barker. 'I was on the way home when I thought I should pay a follow up visit to my patient of last Friday.'

'Did you now? That was very thoughtful of you, I'm sure.' Barker paused as he inhaled deeply from the butt end of his cigarette. He leaned over to stub it out in the ashtray, holding his breath as if to extract the full effect of the drug from his smoke-filled lungs. As he spoke again, his words were carried on blue hazed air. 'All I know is that it must have been quite a party. The pity is that I can't remember a thing about it.'

'How do you feel?' asked Brookes, taking his drink from Alison.

'Great,' replied Barker. 'Back to work tomorrow. Couldn't quite make it today. Bit of a headache.'

'How is that bump on the back of your head?'

Barker searched the area with his free hand, wincing when he found the wound.

'That seems to be better too, but I wouldn't like to wear a halo just for a while.' He laughed.

'I see you have got your car back. What happened to that?'

Alison answered. 'The manager of the Harvester's turned up with it on Saturday morning. Apparently he took Larry's car keys off him on Friday night and stuck him in a taxi. I ran him back on Saturday and paid him for the taxi.' She turned accusingly towards her husband. 'Not many managers would do that for you, Larry, and I doubt whether he'd do it a second time.'

'Why not?' sneered Barker. 'I must be about his best customer. Which reminds me; get me another drink, love.'

He held his empty glass towards Alison who looked appealingly at Michael, hesitating before taking the glass.

'Brave little woman is trying to ration me now. Man's not master in his own house any more.'

'It's not that, Larry, but,' Alison turned towards Michael, 'he has been drinking pretty steadily all weekend. And I just cannot get him to eat anything. He's hardly touched a thing for days.'

'Stop blathering, woman, and get me another drink.'

Michael watched Larry as he lit another cigarette. He saw the creased trousers, the waistband pushed down, cutting into him below his belly, so swollen as to show bare skin between straining shirt buttons. Must be his liver. Should have put his hand on his belly when he had the chance last Friday night. Might even be ascites by the look of it. Christ, what a mess he looked. It was there on that sofa that they had sat last Friday night; where he had made love to that man's wife. Perhaps he hadn't been 'inside' her, perhaps 'intimacy' had not taken place, as they say, but he had been inside her mind, and she in his. He could still feel her breasts through that housecoat. And that pickled, nicotine-stained apology for a man was now lying there, on their first love bed.

'You haven't come to lecture me, have you?' Larry's jaw stuck out truculently. 'I've had enough of that from her in the last couple of days. Even talking about psychiatrists. Come to that, you don't look too bloody hot yourself. What's the matter with you?'

'Oh, nothing.' Brookes gave a short laugh. 'It's just been one of those days.'

'I must say, it's not often we see the Brookes' feathers ruffled. Something finally got under your skin?'

There was no ring of friendliness in Barker's question. He did not take his eyes off Brookes as Alison handed him his drink, his peripheral visual fields sensing the movement rather than seeing his wife return behind Brookes. He changed his focus, seeing her hovering around Brookes' chair, too restless to sit. Lucky bastards; they both looked so fit. He used to look like that once. Could play tennis all day; or squash. Used to get so randy; still did; just couldn't do anything about it now. God, if they only knew how he felt – to know you couldn't keep your wife. Not money, though that was bad enough. No; love, sex. So empty; might as well be dead. And there they were; look at them. Made a handsome pair. He'd keep her happy all right. Come to visit his patient, his arse. That man there wanted his wife and he was the stumbling block. Better off dead, out of their way. Wouldn't mind really. Wonder if he has had her already. Wonder where. Oh, God!

'As a matter of fact, it was that bloody foreman of yours; that man Rothwell. He is on the new Community Health Council. I ran head on into him in a Medical Staff Committee meeting this evening and came off second best; the supercilious bastard.' He looked apologetically at Alison. 'Forgive the language, Lissa, but he really got me on the raw. These professional committeemen, they sit there, big smiles on their faces; never lose their tempers. I just get furious and tongue-tied and always think of what I should have said half an hour later. I should have learned by now to keep my mouth shut but I just can't resist arguing with the devils.'

Brookes began to laugh, feeling himself relax.

'He's not a bad chap at heart,' Barker said, 'but spare a thought for me. I have had to work with him every day for the past six years.' He raised his glass before gulping down another mouthful. 'Enough to make anyone get drunk now and again. No, to be fair, Bill Rothwell is as solid as a rock but, unfortunately, just about as imaginative. Give him a dull, repetitive job and he is totally reliable, completely honest. But give him problems involving decisions, especially quick decisions, and then he starts to dodge and weave.'

'But he can look after things when you are away, such as today?'

'Oh, yes. Whole blurry place is so run down now, compared with what it used to be, that a high-grade ape could run it.' Barker's speech began to slur and his gestures became more expansive. 'We have had to lay off so many that we only do a few routine jobs now. Anything special and they have already started to bring in outside firms. Mrs Hillard looks after the pay as well as everything else. That's why I have got to go to Liverpool tomorrow; to try and save our contract for what little is left. And where will our Bill Rothwell be then, when I am crawling on my belly to that bastard, Anderson?'

His face made vicious by self-pity, Larry drank the remnants of his whisky. Without tasting it, he threw the fluid into the back of his throat where it disappeared with scant evidence of swallowing. He stood up, steadied himself, and set off in the direction of the bottles, determined not to risk refusal by asking for another drink.

'Did you say you were going to Liverpool tomorrow? Are you fit enough?' asked Brookes.

106

Alison answered for her husband.

'Michael, I have tried to stop him but he says the appointment is already made. Apparently he has got other meetings at Nitromid as well, so he says he'll stay the night at his club as usual. He won't let me drive him down but at least he has agreed to let me drive him as far as Preston and catch a train from there. But I don't think he is fit to go and I wish you'd tell him so too.'

Larry did not give him the chance. Sympathy and concern only increased his self-pity. Without looking to see the level in his glass, he stopped pouring from the bottle which he grasped high around the neck. He used the bottle to point at Brookes, oblivious to the whisky he spilt over trousers and shoes in so doing.

'What the hell does he know about it?'

He moved to stand with his back to the fireplace, swaying, one arm bent to support his glass, the other hanging vertically, heavy with the weight of the bottle he still held by the neck. His eyes glazed, his voice became maudlin.

'I wasn't cut out for this sort of thing. Fancy having to crawl to a bastard like Anderson for favours.' Alison and Michael watched, silently fascinated, as he rambled on. 'Struts round the place like a little dictator. Talk about Hitler. And there is no way you can fight him. What can you do? If only there was something physical I could do about it, I'd do it tomorrow. I'm just no good at this clever, dirty fighting. They fought cleaner in a war. I would have been better off in a war. I've seen pictures of me, leaning against my aircraft, leather flying helmet, silk square around the neck, top button undone. Trouble with me is that I was born a generation too late. God,' he called, his jaw clenched, looking upwards momentarily, 'you and your atom bombs did me out of a war. Why couldn't I have gone out; nice and clean. End up just a faded black and white smile on some ageing parent's mantelpiece. They shall not grow old and all that. Much better for everyone except I haven't any ageing parents either; unless, of course, I still have an errant mother around somewhere. Only a son who can't look at me any more. Just think of the son I would have been in the great Tom Barker's imagination if I'd been killed in a war. I would have played rugby for England, been head of an industrial empire, probably knighted. And look what reality brought him.'

'Darling, you do say the most foolish things at times.'

Alison's voice was full of compassion and understanding as she moved towards her husband, only to be fended off by the arm holding the bottle.

Ignoring her, Larry focused his attention on Michael. Self-pity gone, his face haggard from prolonged self-torture, he pleaded for help, not to his wife but to another man. The fact that the man was probably his wife's lover was suddenly irrelevant. Only a man would understand what he was trying to say. He wanted comradeship, not sentiment; understanding, not forgiveness. He wanted Brookes to get drunk with him, stand shoulder to shoulder with him in a bar-room punch-up; not Alison making soothing noises, forgiving him for not being everything she had hoped for. In that fight, he would not want to hurt so much as be hurt, would probably buy his antagonist a drink afterwards. He would welcome the pain of physical injury as a form of spiritual catharsis, purging him of his fear of inadequacy, of intellectual impotence. He longed for the comforting banter of friends and enemies who had been just as frightened, just as cowardly, that day; not the one-way grille of the confessional, draining away dwindling self-respect.

'I have inside me, Michael,' – the liquor he held slopped around as he clawed for expression – 'a – a – a – a monstrous sadness trying to get out. And it is tearing me apart. It goes everywhere with me, looking for peace. I can knock it on the head with this stuff for a time,' he waved the bottle, 'but it keeps coming back. Or is it restlessness? No. Why don't we admit it, it's fear. We are all frightened.' He swept the bottle through a wide arc, overbalancing for a moment as he did so. 'But some are more frightened than others. That's the truth of it; fear. We used to have a gardener, delightful old boy, dead now. Used to come up from Shepworth. I say, Michael, I am sorry. You haven't got a drink.'

He thrust the bottle in Alison's direction.

'Give the man a drink, Lissa. Poor bugger can't sit there listening to my rantings without a drink. Give him a drink.'

Brookes began to refuse, saying he must go home soon but handed his glass to Alison when Barker became agitated.

'Have a drink, you prissy bastard. I hate drinking alone, specially when I'm baring my soul. Now where was I? As I was saying, we had this old gardener, over eighty when he died. Now there was a man at peace. And do you know what? That man went through four years of war from 1914 to 1918, Ypres, the Somme, Passchendaele, the lot. A lot of those old sweats looked like that. Known such terror that it leaves them in peace. Do you know what I mean?'

The two men looked at each other and, in a moment of clarity between them, smiled. Alison, standing alongside, for that moment, need not have existed. The bond snapped as her husband plunged back into his drunken oratory.

'I've got a theory. I don't think a man is ever free from fear until he has experienced total terror. Don't know about women; never did. But men; yes. Why do you think they go climbing rock faces and killing themselves with hang-gliders if they are not looking for terror? I tell you, there have been many times when I would have settled happily for a Passchendaele if I had known that I would have come out of it either dead or at peace with myself. I suppose people still have their own personal Passchendaeles.'

His voice trailed away to an unintelligible mutter as he stared out of the window. Michael, seeing an opportunity to break away, made a show of tossing back the last few drops from an already empty glass. Suddenly, feeling exhausted and hungry, he longed for the loving calm of his son's company. He got as far as putting his hands on the arms of his chair.

'Oh, don't go, Michael. Stay a little longer.'

No polite insincerity, born of good manners, but a genuine plea, a cry for help from Alison.

'I'm so sorry, Michael. You must be starving. Can I make you a sandwich?'

Michael had to abandon all hope of immediate escape from the highly charged atmosphere, but he did not want to commit himself to a longer stay than was absolutely necessary. He felt confused, wanted time to think. The man he had learned to despise, almost wished dead, had shown him a completely new mien, one he understood, respected. Dammit, they had something in common. He might even get to like him. But, for now, he had had enough. He wanted to get away.

'No, thank you, Lissa. I must get home shortly and make sure Jonathan has something to eat.'

'Are you sure? I'm sorry you let yourself in for this; as if you haven't got enough troubles of your own. He's not like this very often.' She spoke of her husband impersonally, as if he were not in the room.

They watched Larry in silence before he interrupted their thoughts. 'Never met my brother, have you?'

'No,' he answered.

'Not when he came to Dad's funeral? Why didn't you come to Dad's funeral?'

'I don't know. I think it was due to the fact that I had operated on him. I don't like going to patients' funerals. Stupid, I know.'

'We are identical twins, you know.'

'So I believe.'

'Yes. The only way you can tell us apart is that I am the one that's drunk.' Barker laughed, adding bitterly, 'Of course, he was born first.'

Alison and Michael looked at each other, wondering what was coming next. They watched his features take on a cunning, inquisitive aspect as he fought to keep Brookes in focus.

'You're a doctor. Is it true – I'm sure I read it somewhere – that we are all a mixture of the sexes; that a man has a bit of female in him and vice versa?'

'Yes. I suppose you can say that,' laughed Brookes, looking puzzled. 'At a very early stage of development it's almost impossible to tell whether you are going to turn out male or female.'

'So the sex chara, charact,' He gave up struggling with the word. 'So your sex is in the balance in everyone?'

'Yes.'

'Too much male in the female and you're butch, too much female in a man and you're a poofter?'

'Yes.' Brookes was both amused and intrigued.

'Yes,' repeated Barker, as he took a few moments to contemplate ponderously before speaking again with the forceful deliberation of the lounge bar philosopher. 'And do you think that could apply to chara, charact, things other than sex? What about other things being in balance? Love and hate; fear and, and, and confidence; sadness 'n joy? Can't think of any others. Do you think we are all a balance of those things too? What d'you say? You're meant to be a bloody genius.'

'You could well be right, Larry. I've never thought of it in that way.'

'Ah. So you see. There's more to Larry Barker than meets the eye.' He winked one eye and put his forefinger alongside his nose. He nodded with alcoholic sagacity. 'Didn't think I thought thoughts like that, did you? Think I thought thoughts; that doesn't sound right.' Barker shook his head from side to side. 'That sod of a brother of mine, born first, took my birthright with him.'

'What on earth do you mean, Larry?' Alison asked. She sat on the arm of Brookes' chair, searching for his hand as, frightened of what she would hear next, she stared at her husband.

'Identical twins come from the same egg, don't they?'

Brookes nodded.

'Well. Why are we so different? Tell me that.'

'I don't know that I can, Larry. I'm no expert in genetics but I know you must have been born alike. At least there are some things which must have been identical, like blood groups and eye colour. On the other hand . . .' Brookes hesitated as a thought struck him. 'Perhaps I am wrong when I said you must have been born identical.'

'Ah,' said Barker.

'Yes,' Brookes went on. 'I still say that you must have been identical at the stage when you split off from each other; when you were no bigger than a few cells. But that doesn't mean, of course, that you have to be absolutely identical when you are born. After all, things can change in the uterus. Sometimes one twin can grow at the expense of the other, one of them being no more than a disorganised mass of tissue, a monster, attached to the other twin. It's called a teratoma.'

'Well, I reckon I'm Adrian's monster,' Barker snarled.

'Larry, don't be so stupid.' Fear, compassion, irritation, all modulated Alison's voice. 'You are talking rubbish; just being melodramatic.'

'Am I? I don't mean physically. I could always thrash Adrian. I mean mentally. I reckon Adrian took more than his fair share before we split. Not just brains. Took my confidence and my joy; not that he has made much use of that, the miserable bastard. Hate too. He could always hate more than I could. All I wanted to do, ever, was to . . .'

As Barker's voice faded away, Michael thought he might cry. His face a tragic mask, Barker let his face fall sideways, to rest against the back of the chesterfield, rather as Brookes had done some days earlier. Brookes made his apologies once more and started to leave. Larry watched as Lissa took him to the door, and began his accusations the minute she returned.

'Seen our local Christian Barnard safely off the premises, have we? Took you long enough. Kissed him goodnight, I hope? Must be hospitable. What he came for, after all. Mustn't let him go home without what he came for.'

'Larry, you really have talked some nonsense tonight.' Alison felt herself blushing as she turned her back to her husband to pick up the empty glasses. 'I don't know what's come over you. Michael has been a very good friend to you, especially last Friday.'

'Of course. That's it. Why didn't I see it before? It was out of friendship for me that he called tonight.' He peered into his empty glass, balancing his need for another drink against the physical effort of struggling to his feet to get it. For the moment, he decided to endure the former. 'And there I was, thinking all the time that he was in love with you. Silly me.'

'Larry, I'm tired and I'm going to bed.'

'Friendship, be damned.' Barker spoke to his empty glass, then looked unsteadily at his wife. 'The man's in love with you, as if you didn't know.

Follows you round the room with his eyes like a dog on heat. Had a hell of a job to keep his tongue from hanging out. Could almost hear him panting.'

'I'm going to bed and I suggest you do the same, Larry. You've got to be up early tomorrow and it's going to be a long day.' Alison headed for the safety of the kitchen. 'Can I get you a sandwich or a milky drink? You have had virtually nothing all day.'

As she passed where Barker was lying, he put his arm out to stop her. His hand and forearm came to rest against her upper thighs and he felt the warm lure of her body. His mood swung in an instant as his wife backed away, out of contact, to look down at him, coldly.

'I'm sorry, love. I don't really mean it. I'm so miserable.'

Alison's guilt gave way to compassion. She saw once more someone ill and vulnerable. Emptying her hands on to a table, she knelt besides her husband, taking his hand in hers. With a small cry from somewhere deep within his chest, he leaned his head on her shoulder. Unable to support his weight, Alison slumped awkwardly against the sofa.

'I'm sorry, Lissa. I'm a failure. You married a loser. I'm losing my job, my son, and I'm frightened, Lissa. I'm frightened I'm losing my senses. And I know I'm losing you. I don't know why you haven't left me. Wouldn't blame you if you did. You and Robert would be better off without me. Much better if I died out of your way. I certainly would die if you left me. Don't leave me, Lissa.'

Within minutes, like a child, he was asleep. He did not waken as she managed to shed the weight of his head from her saliva-wet shoulder or as she tucked a rug around his legs. She left the glasses unwashed, undressed and got into bed to stare, dry eyed, at the ceiling, a sense of hopelessness banishing all hope of escape into sleep.

13

Larry Barker's *via dolorosa* started from that most unlikely spot, the approach to Preston's railway station. Through tear-filled eyes, Alison watched him, shoulders now typically hunched under the weight of his own particular cross, as he walked down the slope to disappear into the station without even glancing back. He looked crushed, defeated. It was more than ten minutes after the 9.15 a.m. to Liverpool had left when Alison drove away, tears of shame now mixing with those of pity. Could she not even trust him to catch a train?

He had sat, knees together, staring straight ahead, with a lightweight plastic raincoat over his arm, while Alison had driven, chattering intensely about matters of little consequence, like a mother taking a child to a new school. His tongue dry and feeling twice the normal size, Barker had said nothing except 'Goodbye, Lissa. I love you.' He had looked longingly at Alison for a moment but had made no attempt to kiss her before hauling himself out of the car, leaving Alison to lean across and close the door behind him.

In Liverpool the Nitromid Building towered above him, impersonal, uncompromisingly efficient. The revolving door sucked him in like a piece of fluff into a vacuum cleaner. He was whisked up to Anderson's floor in a lift full of brisk, ambitious men and women. The receptionist did not smile when Barker apologised for being ten minutes early.

'Take a seat, please, Mr Barker.'

The girl became engrossed in a card index as three typists behind her typed and gossiped, gossiped and typed, oblivious of the man seated in the corner. Ten minutes later, Barker looked at his watch for the third time, caught the girl's attention and smiled. However, it was not until he stood up and walked to her desk that she picked up the internal phone.

'Mr Barker is here, Mrs Jamieson.'

She had replaced the receiver and was concentrating on her index cards again as, with thinly veiled insolence, she pointed vaguely to her right.

'Through there, Mr Barker.'

She ignored Barker as he searched for somewhere to leave his raincoat. Mary Jamieson's smile was genuine enough but she did not get up from her chair.

'Go straight in, Mr Barker.'

He tapped on Sir John Anderson's door and entered.

Anderson had three methods of welcoming visitors. The Beauprés of this world he greeted in Mrs Jamieson's office, to usher them personally to the comfort of an armchair. Other industrialists, respected for their success, however attained, asking for favours that might be turned to Teflo's advantage, were shown in by Mrs Jamieson, Anderson timing expertly his walk across the room to meet them, hand outstretched. The likes of Barker opened the door themselves to cross the long room and climb the steps to the cold ruthlessness that awaited them at the far end.

'Well, Larry. It's good to see you again. How are you?'

'I'm very well, thank you, Sir John.'

Barker screwed his eyes into wrinkled slits against the glare from the window that framed Anderson's head. As he looked up at the man from his low, uncomfortable chair, Barker could not see Anderson's features clearly. His eyeballs began to ache.

'And Alison? We missed her at the dinner. How is she?' Missed her, not you.

'Very well indeed.'

'Ah, good. And your boy; Robert isn't it? How is he doing?'

'He's fine. Working hard for his O-levels this year.'

'Good. Now, what can I do for you, Larry?'

Forty love down in the first game, on what should have been his service. He could not remember how many children Anderson had, let alone their names. He struggled to ask after Anderson's wife but, dithering as to what to call her, found her Christian name blotted out in a panic-stricken mental blackout.

'What's the problem?'

'No problem, I trust, Sir John. I felt it was time I came to see you, out of courtesy, to confirm the renewal of our contract. I didn't want you to think that we were taking you for granted. I do apologise for bringing the matter up on the golf course the other day. I realise now that it was quite the wrong place to do it. And so, here I am, as you suggested.'

It was impossible to read any reaction in the shaded mask that stared impassively at him, giving him no help, waiting. Sink or swim, Anderson was not going to throw any life-lines.

'The answer is no, Larry.'

'What do you mean, no, Sir John?'

'Just what I say, Larry. Your contract is not to be renewed. As simple as that. No need to beat about the bush.'

Barker's jaw dropped. The decision was no more than he had expected but the little man's brutality made him wince. He put his elbows on his knees, his head in his hands, as beads of cold sweat began to show at his temples. He looked like a defeated boxer, driven into a corner, his guard permanently up around his head in expectation of further blows to come. Anderson stood off as long as he could, hoping Barker would either throw in the towel or come out fighting. Anderson had not expected Barker to put

114

up much of a fight but he was surprised how quickly Barker had sought the refuge of a submissive fugue.

'If you were sitting here, Larry, would you renew the contract?' Once again he waited hopefully for some form of reaction. 'Give me one good reason why we should.'

The prolonged silence would have been embarrassing if it had not been between one too dominant, the other too bankrupt of morale to notice it. Barker finally forced sound between leaden lips.

'We've served you well for many years,' Barker monotoned, his words directed downwards at the carpet.

'Not strictly true. I walk around Teflo now and again. I don't always sit behind this desk. Your plant is becoming a bit of a joke. Personally, I think it has got beyond a joke. You are now a liability. We nearly had to close down the other day because of some difficulty in offloading at the wharf.'

'That's been fixed,' snapped Barker.

Anderson relaxed, relieved to find some reaction in Barker. Even Anderson derived little enjoyment from hitting a defenceless human punchbag indefinitely.

'I am determined that there shall be no more shutting down at Teflo for reasons that we can control. And you are suspect. If I thought that Northweir had the ability and drive to get back to where it was, I would consider taking the chance, but it hasn't.'

'When you say Northweir you mean me, of course.'

Anderson did not answer for a moment.

'Larry, you're not your father's son. Why don't you face the fact? There is no disgrace in it. You should have sold up when he died and gone off and done your own thing, whatever that may be. You haven't really run Northweir ever. Tom Barker got the contract renewed after he died; on his good name. You might say that he has kept Northweir going from beyond the grave. Then someone like Beaupré comes along, someone who never knew your father, and he sees Northweir for what it is, not what it used to be. I'm afraid you didn't make too good an impression on Beaupré.'

'And is that so important? Who is running Teflo, you or Beaupré?'

Anderson smiled at the brief spark of resistance. The *coup de grâce* delivered, he allowed his manner to soften imperceptibly.

'I'll tell you what I'll do, Larry. When does your contract end?'

'On 31 July.'

'About two and a half months?'

'Yes.'

'By that date, we intend to have our own mobile machinery. Beaupré was surprised that we bothered with an outside contractor.' The only movement Barker could see in Anderson's shaded face was from his mouth. For a moment, he had a vision of a ventriloquist's dummy manipulated by a third presence that filled the room, compelling, prevailing. 'He felt we should have our own maintenance and repair shops. We will take your drivers on if they want to; with the exception of that fellow Rothwell, of course. And there would be a job for you, Larry. We would want someone to look after the books for us, someone who knew the business. What would you say to that?'

'Salaried, nine to five job?'

'Yes. Out of the rat race. No more worries.'

'And would I be in charge?'

'No, Larry. I'm putting an engineer in charge. We are short of mechanical engineers throughout Teflo and I think it is a job for an engineer like your father. What do you say?'

'A nine to five office boy.'

'Hardly that, Larry.'

'Can you see me going home, telling my wife and son that I've got the job of wages clerk in my own firm?'

Anderson looked at his watch and stood up, the thrusting tycoon once again. The interview was over. He pressed a button on his desk as Barker rose slowly. They walked towards the door.

'Think it over, Larry. If I haven't heard from you in a week I'll take it you're not interested. It's the best I can do for you. Goodbye. Remember me to Alison.'

It was over. He was escaping. Soon he would be alone to find the blessed oblivion of anonymity.

But Larry still had a part to play. Anderson used him to set the scene for his interview with his next client, now within earshot.

'It's the best I can offer, Barker. Take it or leave it. I don't want to see Northweir go; no one does. Too many memories. But Teflo must be protected. There's too much at stake to allow for any sentiment. We'll honour our contract until 31 July, of course, but, after that, Northweir is finished.'

Barker had vague sensations only of Mrs Jamieson passing him with another shadowy figure, but it was with biting clarity he saw his creased plastic raincoat held at arm's length between the receptionist's right finger and thumb, as she studiously examined a split nail on her other hand.

116

14

The following day dawned fresh and misty. The cloudless sky merged into the lush green of early May through a haze that foretold another warm day. Michael had been awake since first light. He had washed, shaved, dressed and breakfasted by seven thirty. He had seen Jonathan off to the school bus, and now sat on the low stone wall, nursing a cold coffee cup. He threw the dregs on the lawn, watching the line of drops arc away to lose their identity in the wet grass.

The crunch of footsteps in the gravel courtyard behind him made him turn to see Alison walking towards the house, head down, deep in thought, her hands dragging down the pockets of a loose-fitting cashmere cardigan. She gave a start as he stood up.

'Good morning, Lissa.'

'Hullo, Michael. I didn't see you sitting there.'

She tried to smile but did not succeed completely in wiping away her look of concern.

'I've just seen Jonathan off and it was too warm to go in again. Spare a thought for me in theatre on a day like this.'

'What time do you have to go?'

Brookes looked at his watch before replying.

'I should leave in about fifteen minutes but it wouldn't matter if I were a few minutes late for once.'

'Do you have time for another coffee?'

'Yes, of course.'

He put his arm around her shoulders as they walked into the house, felt her softness, felt himself stir. Behind closed doors the urgency of his kiss met reservations, tension. Alison sat while Brookes boiled the kettle and made the coffee. He removed Jonathan's cereal dish from the tiny kitchen table to make room for her cup before sitting opposite her. He tried again.

'Do you always look so gorgeous this early in the morning?'

Alison smiled. 'I'm sorry, Michael, but I'm so worried.'

He reached for her hands. 'I love you, Lissa.' He paused for a moment. 'And do you love me?'

'Yes, I do.'

'Then what in hell are you worrying about?'

'It's Larry again. Michael, he's missing.'

'Good.' He laughed jokingly, to be answered by the briefest of polite smiles.

'I'm serious, Michael. I suppose it's a bit melodramatic to say he is missing but I don't know where he is; I can't find him.'

Blast the man. Even *in absentia* he managed to keep them apart. A beautiful morning; never been alone with her before; they wanted each other; painfully obvious; he could get Shah to do the list; Jonathan and Robert in school; a bed upstairs.

'What's the silly bastard up to now?'

'He's ill, Michael.'

'I know that. But why doesn't he go and do something about it instead of making a bloody nuisance of himself?' He reacted to the frown of disapproval on her face. 'How do you expect me to feel about him? You couldn't expect me to shed many tears if he decided to push off altogether, now could you? How long has he been gone? It can't be very long. He was at home the night before last, as we both know to our cost.'

'I drove him to Preston yesterday morning to catch the Liverpool train and I haven't heard from him since.'

'But you said that he was going to stay the night.'

'Yes, I know. I'm probably being a complete fool but something tells me that something's wrong. He always rings me early in the evening when he's away. Last night he didn't. I rang his club this morning, just before I came over, and they haven't seen him since lunch-time yesterday. He didn't sleep there last night.' In an unconscious attempt to hold on to comforting normality, she started to pile dirty dishes on the kitchen sink. 'Michael, I'm frightened.'

'And you want me to find him?'

'Could you?'

'You want me to go out and find the one man I wish would disappear from the face of the earth?'

'Michael, I'm sorry. But I have no one else I can turn to.' Her lips became hard to prevent them trembling as her eyes filled with tears. 'I'm so frightened of what may have happened to him.'

Brookes sat looking at her for a moment. Saying nothing, he got up from

118

the table and went into the hall. Alison heard him pick up the phone, dial a number and start talking. By the time he had returned, she had washed and stacked the dirty breakfast dishes.

'Right, that's fixed. Dai Jack will arrange for Shah to do my list this morning.'

'God, I'm being an awful nuisance. Can you take a day off just like that?'

'Fortunately there is nothing major on the list this morning and it's about time I had a day off, anyway.'

'And what will you say if Larry turns up while you are on your way to look for him?'

'I'll think of something. You'll be required to pay a forfeit of some kind.' Brookes grinned. 'Perhaps I could cancel another Wednesday list when we know exactly where he is.'

'I could hardly refuse under the circumstances, could I,' Alison replied, smiling fleetingly. 'Michael, you don't think he has done anything silly, do you?'

'You mean committed suicide?'

'Yes, I suppose I do.'

That inner voice said 'No such luck', but Brookes made no outward remark as they walked towards the door, his arm around her shoulders.

'Now don't worry. I'll find him. He probably got caught up in some party last night and I'll get hell from him for turning up.' He hesitated. 'No chance, I suppose, that he has got a girlfriend in Liverpool? I mean these regular overnight trips. I know he always rings you but do you ever ring him?'

'Do you mean does he ring early in the evening so as to leave the rest of the evening free?'

Brookes nodded.

'Don't imagine I'm so naïve that I haven't thought of that but I really don't think it very likely.'

'Why not?'

'Now you are being naïve. Let's just say that she must have been a very understanding girlfriend over the last few years.'

She blushed as she pressed her face into his shoulder and felt Brookes laugh.

'Sorry, Lissa. I didn't realise it was like that.'

'Where will you look for him?'

'I don't really know. I imagine I start at his club and play it by ear from there.'

119

'All I ask is that you don't go to Teflo if you can possibly avoid it. Things are so bad that one word of this to John Anderson and Larry would be finished.' She stretched to kiss him, murmured 'I'm sorry', and was gone.

There was little urgency about Brookes' driving. Heavy lorries thundered past him as he day-dreamed his way down the inner lane. His confidence sank, the further he was drawn into the dusty heart of the city. Gratefully he abandoned his car to the hollow security of a multi-storey car park, nodded to the attendant whose complexion blended into the surrounding dusty concrete, and found his way to the Mersey and County. He looked at his watch. It was past midday.

Built in 1880, the Mersey and County Club had been formed by those who had made their money so quickly that they had not been stamped with the hallmark of one of the better public schools as demanded by the Athenaeum. Red-brick and solidly flamboyant, it was a mass of bay windows, balconies and porches.

He ran up a few steps, pushed through swinging glass doors with gleaming brass fittings, to find himself in a large hall, being frowned on, smiled or scowled at, by several heavily framed portraits around the walls. Through one door could be heard subdued voices and tinkling glasses. Through another door he saw two elderly waitresses patiently leaning against an enormous mahogany sideboard, fresh linen napkins draped over thick-skinned forearms. The hall porter, in smart navy uniform and guardsman-like boots, emerged from behind the glass screen.

'Can I help you, sir?' Sydney Ransome's voice was deferential, his manner protective.

'Good afternoon. I'm looking for Mr Laurence Barker.'

'I'm afraid he's not here at the moment, sir. Did you arrange to meet him?' Ransome enquired.

'No, I didn't. I happened to know he was in town and I was rather looking for a free lunch. Did he stay with you last night?'

'No, sir. Mr Barker has not stayed with us for quite some time. Must be a year or more.' He scratched his chin and laughed. 'Rather looks as if you will have to buy your own lunch, doesn't it, sir.'

'Yes.' Brookes smiled. 'But I am anxious to see him. Did he call yesterday at all?'

'He did, sir. In fact I believe there was someone making enquiries about him earlier this morning.' Ransome's voice, though still respectful, rose a semitone as he scented a story. 'No trouble for Mr Barker, I hope?'

'Not at all,' Brookes said hurriedly. 'I believe he had lunch here yesterday?'

'That's right sir, or rather he had some calories, mostly liquid, if you know what I mean.' Ransome made an oscillatory movement with curved thumb and forefinger. 'I remember because I had to get a taxi for him when he left at about three o'clock.'

'Perhaps you would know where he went in the taxi?' Brookes asked hopefully.

'I'm sorry, sir, I don't, but,' said Ransome, encouraged by the sight of Brookes reaching for his wallet, 'perhaps we can find out. We always use the same taxi firm around the corner from here. I'll give them a ring and see if they can help. Thank you, sir.'

The note Brookes gave him disappeared into his breast pocket as he returned to his small office to pick up a telephone and plug it into the club's switchboard. As Brookes, now feeling hungry, paced the hall, two members thrust through the swing doors, nodding to him as they passed. The waitresses moved expectantly but resumed their long-suffering vigil as the two men disappeared into the bar.

'The driver who picked up Mr Barker is not on duty until two o'clock, I'm afraid, sir.' Ransome put his head around his office door, still grasping the receiver in his hand. 'What would you like me to do?'

'Please ask him to come around and pick me up as soon as he comes on duty.'

Ransome's head disappeared once more to emerge once more, smiling broadly.

'All fixed, sir.'

Brookes spent the lunch-hour in the stark sleaziness of a city pub, eating a lunch any ploughman would have thrown in the hedge and watching paunchy young reps playing darts. As he approached the Mersey and County again, he saw a taxi parked outside. Inside the hall stood a young man in a dirty sweat-shirt, his tangled hair merging with an unkempt beard.

'Are you the driver who picked Mr Barker up from here yesterday?'

'I certainly picked someone up here and I'm told that he was a Mr Barker though, of course, we were never formally introduced. In what way can I be of assistance, sir?'

His unexpectedly cultured voice was modulated by mockery born of class-consciousness.

'I'll tell you when we are in your taxi. Are you free to take me somewhere?'

'Sir, your word is my command.'

In the taxi, out of earshot of the hovering hall porter, Brookes leant forwards to speak to the driver.

'Can you remember where you took my friend from the County Club yesterday?'

'Yes.'

'Can you take me there?'

'Yes.' The driver made no attempt to start the car.

'Well?' enquired Brookes.

The young man turned and looked coolly at Brookes. Reassured by the lack of any affected condescension in Brookes' voice, the youngster's defensive mockery had vanished.

'You a copper?' Again he surveyed Brookes. 'No. Professional. Certainly not business; not like those berks in that County Club. Not a solicitor; wrong suit. Not the Church.' He made up his mind. 'You have got to be medical. Are you a doctor?'

Brookes grinned, warming to the puckish character.

'All right, so I'm impressed. Now will you get on with it and help me find my friend? Where did you take him?'

'The Bexham Hotel,' the driver answered, starting the engine, engaging first gear, releasing the handbrake and moving the indicator control, seemingly all in one movement. 'It's about a mile away.'

'The Bexham Hotel,' repeated Brookes, as if talking to himself. 'Now why the hell would he have gone there?'

'Well, doctor,' said the young philosopher at the wheel, 'I drive this taxi part-time for my uncle to top up my grant but I reckon I have learned more sitting behind this wheel than I ever do sitting at a desk. Do you really want to know the reason he wanted a dump like the Bexham?'

Brookes nodded.

'Because he wanted to bend one on in a place he was not likely to be recognised, cheap so that he would have more money for booze perhaps, though it's strange how these guys go for such places even when they have plenty of cash; almost as if they enjoy dragging themselves down in some peculiar way. I've seen them all now. With some it's any hotel with any woman, if he can wait to get to the hotel, that is. Felt like putting a flashing red light on the roof sometimes. Now and again it's two consenting males looking for a bit of privacy. Well, what the hell. Takes all types. With your friend it was any room with a bottle. He was half-stoned when he came out of the County Club; it was like being down wind of a brewery. We had to stop at an off-licence on the way and the plastic bag wasn't loaded down with crisps. So you see, any genius could have worked it out.'

Brookes slid back into the rear seat, slightly resentful that the young man had painted the picture he had persistently refused to contemplate. The taxi squeaked to a halt, Brookes got out and thanked the driver as he pocketed his money without looking at it.

'Pleasure, sir. I hope you find your friend. The best of luck; I think you are going to need it.'

The houses in the long, wide crescent where Brookes now stood were huge, solid, three storey and a garret, stone-built status symbols of the professional class when servants were cheap and plentiful. Some, Brookes noted, were still privately owned, probably flats, he thought. Others had solicitors' or dentists' plates half-hidden by straggling, diesel-dewed privet. The Bexham Hotel had been formed from the amalgamation of two such houses. The tiny front garden had been levelled and concreted. A standard glass and aluminium front door and porch led Brookes into the hall. There were men still drinking at the extensive lounge bar to the left. To the right was a dining-room with a peg board outside announcing that a well-known drug firm was entertaining their local representative to lunch. The thick maroon wall-to-wall carpet extended up the stairs which faced the front door.

Brookes approached the small office to one side of the stairs.

'Yes, sir?'

The man behind the counter did not look up from writing in a ledger as he spoke. Brookes waited until he did so before replying. They glowered at each other in instant mutual antipathy.

'Good afternoon. I'm looking for a friend of mine who, I believe, booked in here yesterday.'

'Name?'

'Barker. Laurence Barker.'

'No one of that name staying here at the moment, sir. Sorry I can't help you.'

The man returned to his writing as Brookes consciously strove to control his rising blood pressure. Michael kept his voice soft and deliberate but could not control entirely the tremor of inward anger. 'May I have a look at your register?'

'Sorry, sir. I'm afraid we don't show that to any stranger walking in.'

'In that case, would you rather show it to the police?' When he looked into the eyes that now were peering at him, he knew that he had won.

'No need to take that attitude, sir. Only trying to protect the privacy of our clients, you know.'

'May I see the register, please,' Brookes repeated.

A book was produced from under the counter and pushed across to Brookes. He turned it round, opened it and found the page. Amongst the four who had registered the day before was the name Tom Shepworth, London. With a flash of pity for the anguished mind that must have thought that name up, Brookes said, 'I believe that may be the man I am looking for.'

The manager spun the book back and looked at the name Brookes indicated. He began to show concern.

'He checked in about tea-time yesterday, went upstairs and we have not seen him since. He rang down for a bottle of brandy about ten o'clock.' He paused to respond to the expression on Brookes' face. 'We don't mind sending up the odd bottle as long as they pay bar prices. It's usually for a party. But I don't like these loners. They usually go in for women but, of course, I don't allow any of that here.'

'Is there any chance he may have left without you knowing?' asked Brookes.

'No chance. The maid tried to take his breakfast in this morning and failed. I went up but all I could hear was loud snoring.'

'I think you had better take me up.' Brookes backed towards the stairs but the manager hesitated to follow him. Brookes emphasised, 'if I have got the wrong man, I will apologise to him. If I am right, you have a man staying here under a false name and who is very sick indeed. Now are you going to show me up?'

The manager took the pass key from the rack behind him and led Brookes up the stairs. The thick fitted carpet gave way to thin at the point where it was no longer visible from the hall. On the second floor, there was only a threadbare runner in the corridor, and the stairs to the rooms in the roof creaked as they climbed. Conscious of Brookes' attitude of increasing distaste the manager shrugged his shoulders.

'I'm afraid it is what he asks for. It's either he can't afford anything better or he just wants to get as far away from people as he can.'

'You mean he has been here before.'

'Hell, yes. So he wants to have a drink now and again. We can't pick and choose in this business. There are another six hotels like this in this road alone. We can't afford to be choosey.' The manager stepped over the breakfast tray on the floor and turned the lock with the pass key. The door gave only an inch or so. Putting his considerable power behind the door, there was a clatter as a chair, propped against the inside, fell over. Both men's faces wrinkled at the stench that greeted them. The curtains over the tiny window were closed and the manager crossed the room to draw them back and open the window rather than turn on the light. His foot caught in some bedding on the floor and he cursed. The sunshine flooded the room imprinting an indelible picture in Brookes' sensitive memory.

'Jesus Christ!' The awed whisper came from the manager, just behind and to one side of Brookes.

Barker was lying on a low divan bed in the corner, most of the bedclothes strewn on the floor around. He lay on his back, rolling eyes wide open. He was silently mouthing unintelligible words to himself while appearing to to pluck some invisible objects out of the air in front of him. At times his face was contorted with some inner terror and he would feebly roll his shoulders on the bed as if trying to get away from some danger. His tie was loose and he still wore his jacket, but he had tried unavailingly to remove his trousers. The one leg he had managed to free had been the instinctive action to avoid soiling with the faeces that fouled the bedding.

Michael crossed to the bed and tried to turn Larry on his side. For the second time in less than a week, he had avoided drowning in his own vomit by some miracle. Barker started when first touched and resisted any attempt to be turned. Michael said nothing, the sightless eyes telling him it would be useless, and raised one of Barker's eyelids. There was an obvious tinge of jaundice and one hand slipped briefly under the wet shirt confirmed the large liver he had suspected.

The manager had been picking up bottles, glasses and bedclothes and overturned chairs. He was the first to speak.

'We must get a doctor. We must get him to hospital. The poor bugger's got DTs. We always use Murphy from up the road. I'll give him a ring.'

'I am a doctor.' The manager opened his mouth to say something when Brookes added, 'For God's sake, shut up and let me think. Leave me that blanket and take the rest of that mess away. I'll let you know what we are going to do as soon as I know myself. I'll see you downstairs.'

Obviously relieved, the manager left. Michael covered Larry with the blanket and sat on the end of the bed, gazing at the tremulous, terrified man. If Barker had been Joe Bloggs, then the manager would have called Murphy and the end result would have been the alcoholics' wing of the local mental hospital. Brookes could see it all. Just imagine taking Alison to see him in a place like that. There had to be another way. He could not

125

get Barker back to Dunbridge, that was certain. So he must be looked after here in Liverpool. But by whom? Alex Tibbs. It would have to be Alex. He must ring Alex.

Alex Tibbs and Brookes had been contemporaries at Liverpool Royal Infirmary at senior registrar level. Tibbs, tall, aquiline and abrupt, had gone on to consultant rank in the teaching hospital. His large private practice was ample evidence of his great ability, because with no stretch of the imagination could it have been due to his notoriously crusty bedside manner.

The manager took Brookes into a tiny inner office, pointed to the telephone and went back to his desk.

'Liverpool Royal.' The brisk voice, uttering the two well-remembered words, was like the first touch of solid ground to the struggling swimmer. 'Dr Tibbs? Just a moment, sir.' There was a pause. 'You are through to Out Patients, sir.'

'Dr Tibbs' outpatients. Can I help you?'

Another pause and Tibbs' unmistakable voice.

'Hullo, Michael. Long time no see. How are you? What the hell do you want?'

'A favour, Alex. I'm in a spot and I'm looking for help.'

There was no more than a non-committal grunt from the other end of the phone.

'A friend of mine has been taken ill in a hotel here in Liverpool. I am here with him now.'

'Which hotel?'

'The Bexham.'

'Never heard of it. Go on.'

Brookes took a deep breath.

'He is my next-door neighbour back in Shepworth and he and his wife were extremely kind to me when Rosemary died.'

'What's the matter with him?'

'He's got liver failure, Alex. He is semi comatose, jaundiced, flap and big liver; the lot.'

'Is he a boozer?'

'Yes, Alex, he is. The last thing I would want to do is to con you. He's got DTs as well, though he isn't violent. Can you help?'

'He had better come into one of my beds here, hadn't he,' Tibbs said, gruff but kindly.

'Thank you, Alex. I'm most grateful but I am going to ask an even bigger

126

favour.' Brookes crossed the fingers of his free hand and closed his eyes. 'Would you take him into St Saviour's?' St Saviour's was the Roman Catholic nursing home where Brookes knew Tibbs treated his private patients. Brookes sensed rather than heard the indrawn breath at the other end. 'Believe me, Alex, I know exactly what I am asking. This is the last sort of case you would want to look after there, I know. But I am anxious to keep this as quiet as possible as his business is almost on the rocks, and one word of this to his lords and masters and he is out on the street. And I owe him, Alex. I owe him.'

Reluctance on Tibbs' part produced a long pause. 'Oh, all right, you bastard. I'll get my own back on you one day. I can't promise you that they will take him but I will ring you back. You are sure he's not violent?'

'Quite sure, and I promise you that as soon as he is out of his coma I will get him up to some place in London to dry out. The farther away the better. I promise.'

Brookes whistled quietly as he replaced the receiver. The door opened and the manager put a tray of tea and sandwiches in front of Brookes.

'Any luck, sir?'

'I think so. Someone is going to ring me back and let me know where to take him.'

'In that case I will just go up and keep an eye on him.'

Brookes watched the manager's broad back recede. Half an hour ago and he would happily have stamped on Brookes' face. Now, he felt the glow of his protective bulk. It was well past four when Tibbs rang again.

The ambulance men did not need the manager's offer of help to carry Barker's emaciated frame, and he was soon lying within the whispering compassion of the Sisters of St Saviour's. Tibbs had examined the wasted, pot bellied, unresponsive body as it lay, washed and talcum powdered, within the white, shroud-like theatre gown. He had also set up an infusion into Barker's fragile, collapsed veins before he sat wearily in the silent day-room with Brookes. In the quietness, Brookes smiled at the thin, rose-patterned cups, the hand-knitted cosy over the teapot, the thin sliced, crustless bread and the pot of strawberry jam. He thought of the thick mugs of hospital coffee in the clatter and bustle of his own ward back at Dunbridge.

'I'm afraid your friend is a very sick man, Michael. Even a surgeon couldn't miss those physical signs.'

'Sorry to give you a liver problem, Alex. Bit out of your line if I remember correctly. Can you remember what to do? Perhaps a second opinion?'

'Cheeky bastard.'

Michael grinned, their banter engendered by mutual professional respect.

'I'm partly to blame; letting things get this bad. I always knew he was a fair performer but I had no idea he was this bad until just a few days ago. I should have guessed.'

'You can't blame yourself, Michael. It happened with one of our colleagues only recently. Working with him every day. No one had any idea. His ward sister found him blind drunk in his office. Called me. You know the rest. Three wise men; suspension on full pay; off to take the cure. Back at work now with everyone watching him like a hawk. Very unpleasant.'

'Good of you to say so, Alex, but I still feel guilty. He was so kind to Rosemary when she was ill. I'm grateful to you for what you have done. Now, you just tell me when he is fit to travel and I will get him up to London; he has a big shot barrister for a brother up there and I'll get him involved that end.'

'Fine,' said Tibbs, rising, his cup still half-full. 'It's amazing the power of recovery the liver has. Get him over this and, if he stays dry, who knows? He could outlive us both.' He changed the subject, dismissing Barker, to him no more than a clinical problem. 'You must be hungry. Come and have supper with us. Mary would love to see you again.'

'That is kind of you, Alex, but I must get back. There is another wife up north who is waiting anxiously to hear what's happening.'

'Give her a ring.'   ·

'I'd rather not, Alex. I must get back. Give my love to Mary, won't you.'

'Yes.' The word was drawn out as Tibbs looked hard at Brookes. Did Brookes come looking for all his patients when they disappeared in Liverpool? Did he always rush back to tell their wives personally? Well, they were neighbours. But the fellow could not look him straight in the eye. Well, well.

A boorish grunt, a wave of the hand and Tibbs was gone.

The phone hardly had time to ring before Michael heard Alison's voice, husky with anxiety.

'Yes?'

'I've found him.'

'Thank God for that.' Brookes could hear her struggle to control her tears. 'Where is he? Is he all right?'

'He's quite safe, Lissa. But he is very sick. You must be prepared for a shock when you see him. He is in hospital, being looked after by an old friend of mine from the LRI. But, as I said, the important thing is that he is safe.'

'Thank God,' Alison repeated. 'Where is he?'

'In St Saviour's.'

'And what is the matter with him, Michael?'

'He has damn near drunk himself to death.' A jealous pleasure in denigrating Barker in Alison's mind broke the surface. 'He's got DTs and his liver is affected. He's a sick man and likely to be one for some time. These famous meetings of his in Liverpool, they have all been drinking bouts. He has never stayed in his club. That is why he always rang you.'

'Where did you find him?' Alison almost whispered.

'In the attic of a third-class hotel.'

'I'll come down, Michael.' The words came out flatly as a matter of form, lacking any semblance of conviction. 'I have already sent Robert to stay the night with Jonathan.'

'There's no point, Lissa. Larry's unconscious, in a coma. He won't even know you are here.'

His inner voice almost screamed at him. 'Stay there. That drunken sod is not going to stop me going to bed with you tonight; this is one chance I am going to take. Doctors, patients, ethics, wives, sons, neighbours, scandal; I couldn't care less. I want you. I won't let you come down just to hold that drunken bastard's hand. He's not worth it.'

'Leave it until tomorrow. Wait until he is conscious. He's in good hands.'

'What happens then, Michael?'

'We will have to get him dried out. Somewhere in London, I thought.'

Both felt spent, exhausted for the sake of another, impatient to be done with him.

'Michael, you must be tired.'

'Relieved more than tired. I had no idea what I was going to do if I could not find him.'

'Come back, Michael. And come here to me. Please don't go home. I want you. It's awful, I know, but now that I know he's safe I don't care about Larry. I'll worry about him tomorrow. I want you to stay with me tonight.'

15

Although it was well past nine o'clock when Michael pulled up in the Barkers' drive, Alison had been standing at the window for more than an hour. The living-room table had been laid for two as carefully as her plans for the night that lay before her. She had known exactly what was going to happen when she had sent Robert to sleep the night with Jonathan. No one, sons or sick husbands, nothing was going to prevent her savouring every moment. Please God, just don't let them ring up to say Larry's dead and spoil it all. Guilty feelings of complicity had bounced off a conscience rendered impervious by a longing, a lust, that demanded gratification. She stood, erect and relaxed, her mind cleared by the honesty of her attitude. She had tried to picture herself as the loving wife, hastening to her sick husband's bedside, her face distorted with concern, mopping his brow. But now she simply felt that Larry owed her. For years she had given and now she was going to take.

She watched Michael as he levered himself stiffly out of his car, throwing his jacket over his arm. She saw the creased, sweat-stained shirt sticking to his back as he walked wearily to the door. He looked exhausted. The stench of human degradation pervaded his nostrils, submerging a great deal of what was to happen that evening beneath the surface of his already blurred awareness, and the warmth, food and alcohol Lissa offered him were to combine to drag him even further into a dream-world. Thankfully, snatches of thoughts and sensations would rear above the fog to lodge in his memory: the embrace, the sensual kiss, broken off by him with Alison's tongue still flicking. That first sip of whisky as his head fell back against the chair. The aura of femininity in the bathroom. His instinctively modest clutch for a towel as an arm demurely passed a clean shirt round the door. Putting on a man's shirt to steal his wife. A bottle of claret, fumbling fingers and a broken cork. A discussion of Larry's illness in the emotionless tones of a surgeon telling his wife of an interesting case he had seen that day, a mere libation to the God of Decency, no more. The glass of brandy. And

130

then the warm blur of the bedroom, with Alison standing silent, smiling, arms hanging invitingly to her sides. The tingle in his hand as he caressed breast and buttock. Alison stepping back, her nightdress hissing silkenly as it curved over her head, and the toss of her hair as she stood there, absorbing his parched stare. Guilt momentarily shaping the fog around him into a boy's face, earnest and enquiring, wiped away in an instant as Alison came forward, rubbing her flesh against his, to and fro, to and fro. Then panic: nothing there, and a sense of failure. The blind agony of frustration as he shrank further at the touch of those cool hands. Their frenetic despair as they fell on each other with hands and mouths to fight for his arousal.

Brookes' premature ejaculation left them both sticky-handed, gasping, wide eyed, haunted. A short silence smothered cries of defeat as they clung to each other in tense shame and humiliation. Brookes screwed up his eyes as if to shut out all sight of his failure.

'Lissa, I'm so sorry.'

'Don't be silly. What for? What for? There's nothing to be sorry for.'

She wrapped herself around him, vainly trying to impart some strength and self-respect back into his cringing frame.

'But I'm so ashamed, Lissa. What a bloody pathetic display. I usually manage a bit better than that.'

'I'm sure you do, darling,' Alison said, standing close to him, beginning to feel her nakedness. 'Just out of practice, that's all. At least, I hope you are?'

''Fraid so.' Brookes managed a smile. 'I wanted it to be so good.' He saw Alison raise as eyebrow. 'For both of us. Both of us. It's been such a long time. I do want you. You must believe that. Perhaps I want you too much. But I love you too. It isn't that I don't love you.' A note of panic crept into his voice. 'That wasn't the reason why . . .'

He tailed off as Alison looked into his face, as if sifting evidence, making a decision. 'I know,' she said, slowly. 'You do love me. I'm sure of that.'

With pressure against his arm, Alison led him towards the bed, his gait shuffling from tiredness and the shackling of his ankle by the crumpled trousers.

'You look worn out, darling. You've had a rough day. Don't worry. Get some sleep.'

When she returned from the bathroom, Michael was already deeply asleep, lying on his side, one hand under the pillow, his knees drawn up. She smiled at the pile of creased trousers, underpants, socks and shoes beside the bed. The collar of Larry's shirt smirked at her from above the

131

sheets. She reached for her nightdress from the foot of the bed. After a moment's thoughtful hesitation, she threw the flimsy garment back and crossed the room to scrutinise unhurriedly what she saw in the dressing-table's mirror. Standing back far enough to see herself from head to thigh, she was not deceived by the flattery of the distance and softness of the light. Even so, she drew satisfaction from what she saw. She was beautiful, not pretty but beautiful; she had been told that often enough for her to believe it. Her hair was that of a young woman. Her breasts sagged a little but from fullness, not from atrophy, and she pinched her nipples into prominence as if to emphasise their thrust. Her hand felt the flatness of her belly, though she held her breath as she did so, enjoying the suppleness of skin spared the disfigurement of stretch marks. Her thighs were long, lean and athletic, the skin over the inner surfaces still taut and in seductive apposition.

'Then why?'

The words were whispered through a confusion of self-satisfaction and reproach. Then reason stirred her intelligence: what had she expected? Had it not been as much her fault? Had she not helped to bring about his failure? The man had been nearly out on his feet when he had arrived. Had she not taken what he had done that day as being no more than you would expect from any emotionless, detached surgeon to do on any old working day? And then she had filled him with food and drink, plied him with alcohol. Slowly she began to realise her part in the fiasco, began to share his feeling of failure. She had gone at him like some cold-fingered virgin teenager in the back of a parked car. But how was she to learn? The only love-making she had known was that with Larry who had always orchestrated the event, set the pace, discouraged reaction, disapproved of any sign that she might share his pleasure if allowed to, assiduously maintaining physical dominance, fearfully scorning anything that might lead to a meeting of minds where he knew he would be no match.

How could she have made the mistake of expecting Brookes to react the way her husband used to, years ago? Had she expected Brookes to take her with about as much feeling as an errant husband on a rugby club tour? Had she not failed this gentle, almost timid man the first time his sex drive had been released after two weary years of self-imposed celibate fatherhood? Had she done anything to help him blot out those constantly whirling emotions that had finally inhibited him? Images of his son, no more than a few hundred yards away; recently engrained pictures of Larry, a defence-less friend and patient who would need to be talked to and smiled at tomorrow; the realisation that he was trampling all over another man's

132

home, eating his food, drinking his wine; the guilt that would not be denied, that he had come as a thief in the night to steal another man's wife? And she had even given him that bloody shirt to wear.

'You really didn't do very well, did you, madam?' she asked of the image in the mirror, and watched a smile of quiet resolve spread over its face.

Stealthily, she slid between the sheets in front of Brookes and, with back, buttock and thigh, began cautiously to uncoil the foetal curve of the body behind her. Twice she stopped to hold her breath as Brookes stirred in his sleep. Ultimately she felt her aim achieved as he nuzzled forwards. When his erection came it was sudden, the only warning Alison had being an urgent quickening in his breathing. With the deft precision of a preplanned movement, she gently drew back the bedclothes, allowing her to bend her trunk forward, raise her thigh and lovingly lead him into her. Brookes was already thrusting savagely though still half-asleep and Alison waited until she was sure he was sufficiently awake. As his hands gripped viciously at her loins, she tore herself free, turned Brookes, unresisting, on his back to straddle him, leaning forwards to sway her breasts within reach of his outstretched hands. Although Brookes' perception, like his inhibitions, was dulled by sleep, his ferocity frightened him until he realised that it was being matched in everything except physical power. This beautiful woman, whose *soigné* tranquillity he had adored for years, was astride him, meeting him appetite for appetite, thrust for thrust until they jerked and grunted wordlessly to a mutual noisy climax.

Too fearful to speak, too frightened to look for the reaction in the other's face, both awed by the power of a sexual drive which they had never experienced before, both wondering whether to be ashamed, they collapsed into the pillows, both now longing for time-lapsing sleep. It came but not before Alison had felt Brookes' tears on her shoulder, heard his first wet-eyed crying since childhood, wondered at the storm that was blowing itself out within him.

Brookes woke first. Daylight diffused through and around the curtains. He lay for a moment surveying the unfamiliar surroundings, savouring the ambient smells and sounds peculiar to any house. With distaste he saw the shirt he wore, tore it off and hurled it from him. He turned his gaze on Alison where she slept, facing him, one breast pressed against the other by the weight of her arm. With his finger he traced the curves and slowly wooed her awake. She wriggled, smiled without opening her eyes and whispered 'Good morning'. Sleepily, she teased out of him caresses, murmurs, protestations, until she could stand it no more and opened herself to him, felt his penis nudging, confirmed it with caressing hands.

'My God, what's this? Three times in one night?'

'Well, two and a half,' laughed Brookes.

'Fancy yourself all of a sudden, don't you?'

'You can always say no.'

And so, with gentleness, in an act of giving, they made love. Michael took Alison to the moans of frenzied distraction, always holding back his own climax that he knew would end it all. In time the pursuit of his own orgasm became beyond his power and they both collapsed into laughing, loving helplessness.

'Stay there, superman. I'll get you some coffee.'

When she returned, dressed in her housecoat, Brookes was sitting up in bed. She sat on the edge and noticed his frown. 'What's the matter?'

'I just wondered what happens if Robert suddenly walks in. What the hell do we say?'

'You weren't worrying too much about that half an hour ago, were you?

'True,' admitted Brookes.

'Well, you can stop worrying. The school bus went some time ago.'

'Is it that late?'

'It is.'

And the outside world came flooding in.

'They'll know all about this, of course,' said Michael.

'They?'

'Robert and Jonathan.'

'Yes, they will.' Alison looked at him closely. 'Does it bother you?'

'Yes, it does.'

'Why? Are you ashamed?'

'No.' Brookes hurriedly stretched out his hand to lay it, palm down, on her thigh. 'Not after this morning. That really was something, wasn't it?'

Alison nodded.

'There had to be more to that than sex, surely?' he asked. 'That had to be love, didn't it?'

Alison nodded again, smiling at his earnestness as she answered. 'As you say, that was something. Have you ever felt like that before?'

'Never.'

'Neither have I. To think that some women go right through life, probably happily married, and never feel like that. The way I feel at the moment I couldn't care less what happens.' She saw concern spread over

134

his face. 'Don't worry. I shan't do anything stupid. Tomorrow, no doubt, I'll see reason again. I too have a son, you know. I need his love. You're not the only one. I only hope he is old enough to understand.'

'So, where do we go from here?'

Alison laughed at his glum face, that of a small boy whose new toy has been snatched away from him.

'You go to work. I go to London to look after this husband of mine. We both ultimately will have to face our sons. After that,' she shrugged her shoulders, 'who knows?'

'Tell them in St Saviour's that I'll be down sometime this afternoon. I've promised Alex Tibbs that I'll get him moved as soon as he's fit to travel.'

'You did say to London?'

'Yes. The further away from the north-west the better, I thought.'

'Where exactly in London, Michael?'

'Good question. That's where I rather hoped you could help. I wouldn't know where to look around here let alone in London. D'you think Larry's brother would know of anywhere? Find somewhere to look after him? His own doctor up there would probably be able to help. After all, where do big-time lawyers with a drink problem go in London?'

'You'd like me to ring Adrian, see if he can make arrangements that end?'

'Would you?'

Alison nodded. 'Of course. And what about Robert? He ought to know about his father. I should have told him last night. I shouldn't have let him go to school this morning without knowing.'

'You leave Robert to me,' Brookes said, a little uncertainly. 'Jonathan and I will look after him. He can stay with us. Give him a ring tonight from Liverpool. I will have had a word with him by then.'

A shiver of guilt ran through Alison as she walked over to the window.

'All looks different in the daylight, doesn't it? Doesn't feel right any more. All of a sudden I see little joy in this for us, Michael.'

16

Duncan Rae groaned as the phone continued its clamour. Who the hell would want him on a Friday night? He had made a formidable investment in the lissom young lady, sitting on the rug at his feet, in the form of an excellent meal at the Dunbridge Country Club, followed by expensive brandy, and there was ample evidence already that his speculative venture was going to mature. By way of a bonus, she was intelligent, as might be expected in a research chemist at Teflo, and showed no interest in any matrimonial merger. It made a change from some of the buxom blockheads whose mind-blowing stupidity Teflo's most eligible bachelor had to plough through to get at their bodies. Rae had just decided to make his takeover bid when his whole strategy had been shattered by the telephone. Finally capitulating, he made a wry face at the girl, turned the record player down and lifted the receiver.

'Rae.'

The brusque monosyllable was meant as a warning to any junior engineer at Teflo that he had better have a good reason for ringing him.

'Good God! Good evening, sir.' The respectful cadence made the girl look up in interest, mischief in her eyes. Further conversation became impossible as a highly trained, experienced, research chemist carried out an uncontrolled experiment on the effect of female incisors on the ears of male engineer, while her hand searched for evidence of response. Rae finally broke down.

'Excuse me a moment, Mr Beaupré, while I explain to this sex-starved moron that you're a big industrial tycoon and that I may be looking for a job in Canada one day.'

Beaupré chuckled as he heard Rae tell someone to sit down and behave herself.

'Right, sir. Sorry about that. By the look of her I've got about five minutes at the most. What can I do for you?'

'I'm sorry, Duncan. What time is it over there?'

'Just about midnight, sir.'

'Hell. I didn't realise. Perhaps I came back to Canada a bit too soon; perhaps your friend has got an older sister.' They laughed and, within moments, were talking as if women did not exist. 'Duncan, something's bugging me. Ever since you showed me round Teflo.'

'Oh?' Rae said. 'What's that?'

'That's just it, I don't know.'

'Bit difficult to help you then, isn't it, sir.' Rae laughed.

'Quite.' The line went quiet long enough for the girl to stick her tongue out at Rae who shrugged his shoulders in reply. 'It's got to be something to do with safety.'

Rae said nothing.

'It can't be anything to do with the chemistry. Fred seemed happy enough and I don't know enough about the subject to get worried about that. No, it's got to be safety. Take me through those safety valves again, Duncan.'

With ill-concealed sounds of irritation which Beaupré chose not to hear, Rae sank resignedly into an adjacent chair. He struggled to visualise the valve system at Teflo as one of the plant's most attractive employees threw off her shoes and swayed seductively into the bedroom, holding a brandy glass like a lamp. In strangled tones he once more explained how the valves on the heat exchanger failed-safe closed, and how the other safety valves had dual controls, either from the control-room or manually on site. His fraying temper became audible as he finished.

'And, overall, we have a set of valves, preset, never altered, that blow off if the pressure anywhere in the system rises above 11 kilograms. I don't know what the hell you're worrying about, Mr Beaupré.'

'And where do they vent to?' persisted Beaupré.

'Through a pipe that runs alongside the off-gas line on the gantry. You know the one, sir. Where we were arguing about the plant being so close together, Dixon and me.'

'And that goes to the flare stack too?'

'And that goes to the flare stack too.'

'I'm sorry, Duncan,' Beaupré laughed, 'and my apologies to the lady. I realise what I'm probably doing to both of you but one last thing, this nitrogen leak.'

'Bloody hell.'

Beaupré took the curse as directed at him. He was not to see the naked figure leaning against Rae's bedroom doorpost, the tip of her tongue languidly tracing the rim of an empty brandy glass.

'Duncan, it's important.'

'Mr Beaupré, sir, with the greatest respect, sir, bugger your nitrogen leak. Good night.'

As over three thousand miles of cable went dead, Rae thought, 'Well, there goes any future I may have had in Canada. She'd better be worth it.'

17

Monday morning, 8 July, found Sir John Anderson ploughing through the weekend mail. The heat wave showed no sign of abating and already, at nine thirty, he was in his shirt sleeves, Mary Jamieson hovering at his shoulder, cool in a button-fronted shirt dress, just open enough for Anderson to be conscious of the fact. The telephone rang loudly.

'What the hell, Mary. Didn't you tell them we weren't to be disturbed?'

'Yes, John, I did,' she answered quietly, as if soothing an unruly child.

She put the phone to her left ear, deftly sliding off a troublesome earring as she did so.

'Sir John Anderson's office.' A pause. 'Just a moment, Mr Whitlam, I'll see.'

Mary Jamieson, discreet and unfailingly polite, still managed somehow never to call anyone 'sir'. She placed her hand, the earring dangling from her index finger, over the mouthpiece.

'It's Jeremy Whitlam. Must see you this morning, without fail. Says it's urgent.'

'Blast the man. What does he want? For God's sake get rid of him. I'm too busy.'

'He sounds worried, John. I think you'd better see him.'

'God, but you're a bloody slave driver,' he laughed wearily. 'What's fixed for today?'

'Our plane leaves Manchester at three, and don't you dare cancel that. You know how I love Amsterdam. Before that you are having lunch with the new Chairman of Cumbrian Airways. Otherwise there is only our friend Rothwell to see at eleven. So, what shall I say?'

'The bastard has only been here two minutes and he's after my job already. You realise that, don't you?'

'When?' she pleaded.

'Oh, whenever he likes. As long as he's out before Rothwell gets here.'

When, later, she showed Whitlam in, Anderson was surprised to see Fred Richmond, stooped and anxious, glide in behind him.

Whitlam, short, forty and beginning to show the physical defects of affluence, was a thruster. He had always had that fat and hungry look. As a young man he had been flabby and neurotic, a hypochondriac who bore with fortitude diseases he did not suffer from. When he failed to get the first in chemical engineering he had promised himself, he had turned to the study of converting money into power. At this he had excelled. His neuroses were cast out by driving ambition as his unsuspected flair first for making, and then breeding, money had swept him through his training as an accountant. Proud of a mirthless sense of humour, totally devoid of charm, he had pushed his ever-expanding chest up through the crowded ranks of junior management, pinching the secretaries' bums, unclipping their bras, while still demanding their respect as due to someone above their class, someone with more money.

He leered at Mary Jamieson as she left the room. She felt his eyes on her back, making her flesh creep, making her feel as if she were walking out in her bra and pants.

Anderson welcomed them with minimal warmth. 'Morning, Jeremy.' He nodded in Richmond's direction. 'Fred.'

Richmond perched himself on the nearest available chair but Whitlam, brash and confident, walked past Anderson to look out of the window.

'Good morning, John.'

Large as it was, with its view over the docks towards the Liver Building, Nitromid's headquarters was itself dominated by the mass of the Anglican cathedral; God's and Mammon's cathedrals both towering over the inhabitants of Toxteth. As he looked out from this armoured-glass pulpit, Whitlam felt again the thrill he had known as a lay preacher in his pimply, black-shoed youth. But he turned his back on the scene, knowing that, one day, he would be high priest of Teflo, draped in the vestment of knighthood.

'I'm sorry to bother you with this one, John. Under normal circumstances, you understand, I would deal with it myself.' He kept his back to

139

the light, irritating Anderson to see him so much at his ease, like some predator certain of his kill. 'But as it was you who made this agreement with Beaupré, I thought you had better make the decision about shutting down.'

'Shut down? What d'you mean, shut down?' Anderson almost shouted.

Whitlam's smile broadened into a grin. Excitable little bastard, wasn't he? It was going to be a pushover. Only a question of time.

Anderson turned to Richmond. 'What does he mean, Fred? What's this about a shut-down?'

Richmond wriggled to the edge of his seat, a puppet in the hands of two manipulators, one amused, seeing nothing but advantage in it for him, the other intent with sudden alarm.

'It's a question of one of the absorption towers, sir.'

'Absorption towers?'

'Yes, Sir John. I'm sure you remember. They are the very tall columns on the off-gas line very close to the flare stack. One of them has got to be replaced. They have a normal useful lifespan and they need to be replaced from time to time.'

'Do you have a reserve or spare or whatever you call it?' Anderson began to get irritated as he began to feel technically out of his depth. His knowledge of the process was minimal while that bastard, Whitlam, of course, had a degree in that sort of thing.

'Yes, sir. Like all the absorption towers, it is duplicated to allow for breakdowns and maintenance. Unfortunately the stand-by column has also developed a fault and has become most unreliable.'

'How unreliable?' asked Anderson. 'How long do you think we could keep it going? Could we make another six weeks, say?'

'I'm no engineer, Sir John. I can only give you Mark Dixon, the Area Engineer's opinion and he reckons it could fail any day. As far as I can see, it's only due to almost day and night minor repairs on his part that the thing has been kept going at all. He looks an extremely tired man to me.'

There was a lull in the conversation as Anderson digested what he had heard so far. Abruptly, he started again. 'You still haven't told me why you have to close the whole process down just to replace one tower. If there's another tower working at the moment, where's the problem? Are you having difficulty getting a new tower?'

'No, sir. There's a new tower out there on the perimeter, ready to be installed. The problem is the site.' As he came to the crux of the problem, Richmond, dry-washing his hands nervously, edged sideways until only one buttock supported his weight. 'It's so restricted. There has been so

140

much development in that region recently that the towers have become almost completely surrounded. Duncan Rae warned us about it. The outcrop of rock suitable for building these towers on is very limited just there, with marshy land all round. In Dixon's opinion, the waste off-gas line would have to be dismantled just short of the flare stack to allow access.'

'That's Dixon's opinion. What does the Works Engineer think about it?'

'We haven't got one. If you remember, Duncan went to Canada last month.'

'Blast. Of course.' Anderson turned to Whitlam. 'Haven't you replaced him yet, Jeremy?'

'Already appointed,' Whitlam replied, unruffled, 'but can't start for another week or so.'

'I see.'

Whitlam and Richmond watched Anderson press his fingertips together and close his eyes. What they were not to know was that he was trying to dispel an aura that there was another man in the room, watching, waiting, dominating.

'If you had to turn the process off, Fred, could you call that an act of God?'

'No, sir, not really. It's a straightforward result of poor forward planning by the engineering side in that area. Simple as that.'

'And d'you think Beaupré would know about that?'

'I'm sure he would. In fact I think I can remember Duncan complaining about it when he showed Mr Beaupré round.'

'Bugger it.' There was silence. 'Is there nothing we can do?' Anderson's despairing question was not directed at either of the two men specifically but it brought a twitch of reaction from Richmond.

'Yes, Fred? Any ideas?'

'I wouldn't call it more than a faint glimmer of hope, sir. It's pretty common knowledge at Teflo that we're on some sort of three-month trial period.' Anderson raised his eyebrows. 'Well,' said Richmond, 'one would have to be deaf, dumb and blind not to see the reaction from on high at the very mention of a shut-down these last few weeks. So I made a few enquiries of my own on the engineering side. I went to see the managers of two of the local plant-hire firms.'

'And you've found someone who can do it?' Anderson broke in.

'No, sir, I didn't.'

As if to gain assurance from his moment of importance, Richmond got up to stand beside Whitlam at the window. Anderson peered at them, the glare making his head ache again.

'But I did find out one thing. As I was following a man out from one of the firms, he turned and started talking. Seems he used to work for Northweir before they started laying people off. He seemed to know why I'd been there and he reckoned he knew a way round it.'

'Well?' Anderson said.

'Well, I'm not at all sure it would be altogether acceptable to you, Sir John.'

'What do you mean?'

'It would involve using Northweir Plant to do it. This driver reckoned they had a crane at Northweir when he worked for them that was specifically designed for working in confined spaces. He seemed to think it was still on site though it may not have been used for some considerable time.'

'Have you looked into it?' Anderson became purposeful again, leaning forward. 'What have you done about it?'

'Nothing, Sir John. It's also common knowledge around Teflo that Northweir is almost finished and that they had great difficulty in paying their men last month. Add to that Larry Barker's recent illness and I didn't want to entrust such an important undertaking without Mr Whitlam's consent. Frankly, Sir John, it's not my job. It's the Works Engineer who should be here with this problem, not me.'

The spark of rebellion brought an apology from Anderson. 'I'm sorry, Fred. You're quite right. I'm grateful to you.' He turned towards Whitlam. 'Well, Jeremy, what d'you think?'

'I don't see we have much alternative. It looks as if this chap Barker is our only hope.'

'I'm afraid I have to agree with you,' Anderson replied, grimly, curving his mouth downwards to show his reluctance. 'There doesn't seem to be any way round it, does there? Right,' he said, a decision made. 'I'll see to Barker myself. Only fair under the circumstances.'

'One further suggestion, if I may, Sir John?'

'Yes, Fred?'

'Could you possibly leave your meeting with Mr Barker until tomorrow? That would give me time to get his driver to see the problem first. He could tell you "yes" or "no" then, when you see him.'

'All right, Fred. But you just put the technical problem to him, nothing more, d'you hear? Leave the rest to me.'

142

From being Anderson's saviour, Richmond returned to the role of employee and it was with obvious irritation that Anderson saw that Richmond was not finished yet.

'Yes, Richmond. What now?'

'I really don't want to add to your troubles, Sir John, but I think you ought to know that nitrogen is leaking again. It seemed to have cured itself for a while but I was told yesterday that it was back as bad as ever if not worse.'

'Are you working on it?' asked Anderson.

'It's an engineering problem, Sir John. I can't help. It was difficult enough coping with it when Duncan Rae was here. If you must let people of the calibre of Duncan go, you mustn't blame the rest. They're doing their best. It's not our fault we're dangerously short of top-class engineers at Teflo.'

'Yes, all right, Fred. Point taken,' Anderson replied, testily. 'Something we need to put right as soon as we can, Jeremy.'

'Absolutely. I'll get on to it right away.'

As Whitlam and Richmond left the room, Anderson pressed the intercom button.

'Yes, Sir John?'

'Mary, I would like to see Laurence Barker here again tomorrow.'

'You can't.'

'Why not?'

'Because we won't be back from Amsterdam.'

'When do we get back?'

'Not until late tomorrow night.'

'Wednesday morning, then.'

'What time?'

'Any time to suit him. And, Mary . . .'

'Yes?'

'Be nice to him. Pass it down the line, would you?'

'Yes, Sir John. And your next appointment, Mr Rothwell, is here.'

'Send him in.'

'Mr Rothwell, Sir John,' Mrs Jamieson announced from just inside the door, as Rothwell strode past her. Being kept waiting in the outer office had done nothing for his blood pressure. He shook hands with Anderson.

'Good morning, Sir John.'

'Good morning, Mr Rothwell. I'm sorry you've been kept waiting. Won't you sit down.'

143

Rothwell ignored the hand directing him towards the chair in front of the desk and, like Whitlam before him, walked past Anderson to look out of the window.

Though Liverpool still simmered in the sultry heat, away to the north the horizon was leaden, shimmering with distant, silent lightning.

'Quite a view, Sir John.' Rothwell threw the remark over his shoulder, without so much as a glance at Anderson. With a chuckle, he added, 'On a clear day, happen you could see Monkey Island.'

'Monkey Island?' asked Anderson, blankly.

'Never heard of place, I suppose.' Rothwell crossed to the chair, sank into it and calmly crossed one leg over the other. 'All you can see when you come to our part of world is Teflo, spelt profit. I don't expect you give a thought for poor sods living in that estate near Teflo. Still, I don't suppose for a moment that's why I'm here today. What can I do for you, Sir John?'

'Nothing specific, Mr Rothwell. I just felt we ought to meet now and again, in your capacity of convenor at Teflo, of course.'

'Well, I guessed that.'

'Bit unusual, I know, but, as convenor at Teflo, you're the most influential man union-wise and I thought it could only do good for industrial relations at the plant if we were to get together now and again. Talk over any problems, you know. Utmost confidence, of course.'

His tone had the desired effect.

'I think it would be reasonable to say t'lads would do more or less what I told them and I'm sure they wouldn't object to top levels of unions and management getting together like this. Happen you've got a particular problem in mind?'

'Not really, Mr Rothwell. I think that, overall, Teflo has a pretty good record, due mainly to your good offices.'

'True,' Rothwell conceded.

'But, in a plant the size of Teflo, there are always some difficulties, aren't there? Some things best sorted out between the two of us.'

'What sort of thing did you have in mind, Sir John?'

'Well, for instance, this business of the nitrogen supply.'

'Ah, so that's it. That one beginning to pinch, i'n't it?'

'It's of no great consequence to us at the moment, of course,' Anderson replied smoothly, 'but we are particularly interested that nothing should rock the boat at Teflo over the next few weeks. I don't mind telling you that developments are going on at the moment that could mean great things for the future of Teflo, if they come to fruition.'

'Fruition? You say fruition? And where will fruit go? To shareholders, I'll wager, not to poor buggers who grow it.'

'You know as well as I do,' Anderson retorted in crescendo, 'that Teflo depends on making a profit and that Dunbridge depends on Teflo for its prosperity as much as any shareholder. You cut off the nitrogen supply and you put thousands of livelihoods at risk, directly or indirectly.'

'Tha don't frighten me, Sir John.' Rothwell still looked in command of himself though his colour was high and the veins in his neck congested. 'Tha knows what action is all about. We want closed shop at Teflo and we won't rest until we have one. We'll never stop supplies altogether, we're not that daft, but we know all about this Beaupré fellow. We know what's going on.' Rothwell's finger began to wag rhythmically in Anderson's direction. 'We know you've got a production target. And we know we can get you to close down any time we want by letting tank levels fall. And it's no good putting in extra tanks, we won't fill them.'

'You're playing with fire, Rothwell.'

'No we're not. You've got remedy. Ball's in your court. You let us bring in closed shop and you can have all nitrogen you want.'

'I don't want you to be under any illusions just how close you are sailing to the wind, Rothwell. There is a leak. The plant is losing nitrogen and they can't find out where.'

'Your problem, Anderson, not mine.'

'If there is an accident as a result of your cutting off the nitrogen supply,' – Anderson stood up to thump his desk top – 'I will hold you personally responsible.'

'The remedy is in your hands, like I said. Close down, Anderson. That's my advice if you're worried about accidents. Close down. I don't see how you can have an accident in a plant that's closed down.'

Anderson's face was as pale with impotent rage as Rothwell's was red with the flush of hatred.

'So long as I'm Chairman of Teflo, there'll be no closed shop. There seems to be little to be gained by prolonging this interview. We'll just have to hope you come to your senses and realise that profits mean jobs. Remember, Rothwell; no nitrogen, no profits, no jobs, including yours.'

Rothwell rose, insolently turning his back on Anderson once more to look out of the window. He watched, far below, two coloured youths kicking an empty can in a cratered road between two derelict buildings.

'Happen anyone would tend to think he was God, looking down at people from this height, day after day. No reason, I suppose, why you should be any exception.'

18

Larry Barker had made a remarkable recovery.

At St Saviour's he had gradually emerged from his coma over two or three days, and his jaundice had faded. As the level of his consciousness had improved so had he become increasingly violent and his transfer to a private clinic, arranged by his brother Adrian, had involved Alison and a nurse from St Saviour's in a harrowing journey to London by road. There Larry had dried out, cold turkey. Whatever sewers of his own particular hell he had been swept along, whatever torments he had suffered on the way, lucid moments, short at first, had become more frequent. Each time he had surfaced, Alison had unfailingly been present to comfort him, help him keep his sanity through the next spasm of racking horror.

After a week, Larry had fallen into the sleep of an innocent; dark, tranquil and dreamless. As if shriven by the scouring convulsions, he had woken gently, as helpless as a child. Alison had slept at Adrian's flat and many times he had taken her place at the bedside. The *rapprochement* between the twins had touched her deeply. There had come the day, three weeks after Larry had been found in Liverpool, when Adrian had driven both home to Shepworth.

In those three weeks, Brookes had suffered his own withdrawal symptoms. With a perfunctory 'Thank you for having me', Robert had left to go home, leaving the house to Brookes and a polite, remote son. He had waited, aching, passive, but the two households had remained discrete. Only when he had been sure that Adrian had left, Brookes had walked that short distance and knocked on the door. Within moments he had sensed the old barriers of conformity and loyalty. For six weeks he had been obliged to watch Barker regain his strength, mental and physical. The Mini and the Bentley had gone, replaced more realistically by the Cortina. He had watched Alison drive her husband to Teflo, going earlier and returning later each day. He had seen Barker begin driving again, carefully, purposefully, Alison always beside him. Gone were the braggardly histrionics.

At Teflo, Mrs Hillard had worked and watched with the awe of someone witnessing a miracle, but fearing that it has come too late. She looked perplexed as she knocked and entered Barker's office. 'Sir John Anderson's secretary on the line, Mr Barker. He would like you to go and see him in Liverpool on Wednesday. It seems he won't be coming up for a few days and he wondered if you would mind going to see him.'

'Good God! Are you sure you have got that right? Would I mind going to see him?'

'That's what he said.'

'Well, I'm damned. Yes, of course I'll go. Ask him what time?'

She returned a few minutes later. 'Curiouser and curiouser. He is having a working lunch in his office and would you care to join him. Twelve thirty. Also she said that Fred Richmond wanted to see you. Could he see you as soon after three o'clock this afternoon as he could make it? She said it was some technical problem and that he wanted your best crane driver to be present if possible. I imagine you will want Albert for that.'

'Something's up. I wonder what he could possibly want me for? Tell her I will be delighted.'

'I already have.' Mrs Hillard smiled and nodded at the window against which drummed slanting rain, sudden and torrential.

'The weather has broken at last. It's been too hot too long. Perhaps your luck is going to change with it. I'll go and make sure I know where to find Albert this afternoon.'

Two days later, Alison peered anxiously through the Cortina's windows, obscured by the driving rain, as she gingerly manoeuvred the car into the slow lane of the M6. It had been raining continuously for two days and clouds of spray from thundering lorries combined with gusty crosswinds to make driving difficult. Concentrating on her driving, she found conversation difficult.

'How do you feel?' she asked.

'I feel great, thanks.' Larry Barker stretched his legs, rested his head back to stare at the car's roof, relaxed in the middle of the motorway's hissing frenetic tension.

'Sure?' Alison risked a momentary glance in his direction.

'Of course I'm sure. I haven't felt better for years. To tell you the truth, I have never felt better. Still feel a bit weak, but I expect that. But it's different. I can't explain. I feel . . .'

He tried to imply with his hands what he could not put into words, clenching both fists in front of him, brandishing them as if shaking someone by the shoulders, his jaw tightly clenched.

'Are you nervous?'

'Not a bit.' He chuckled as he gazed through the arc of the windscreen wiper, his eyes unfocused. 'I reckon it's Anderson who is nervous this time. Or ought to be. Richmond showed us the problem on Monday and I talked it over with Bill and Albert Crampton yesterday. I reckon we've got him by the short and curlies.'

'But why the Chairman, Larry? How is he involved in this? Surely it's a purely technical problem?'

'Agreed. There has got to be more to it. But do you know, now that Duncan has gone, there is no one on the plant at the moment above the level of Area Engineer? On the engineering side that is. It's virtually straight from him to the Chairman at the moment. The Managing Director is new to the job and another chemist, according to Fred.'

'What is the problem exactly?'

'Changing an absorption tower. The problem is that the plant there is so congested that everyone else says it can't be done without closing the process down.'

'And can you?'

'Albert reckons we can. He says it will be a tight fit but he seems sure he can do it and I would back his word against anyone's.'

'What about Bill Rothwell?'

Barker laughed. 'Poor Bill. He wouldn't be sorry to see the process shut down. Everyone knows that Anderson is trying to impress this Canadian fellow Beaupré, and Bill is terrified of Teflo being absorbed into something even bigger, more difficult to fight. At the same time, he doesn't want to do anything to prevent Northweir getting back on its feet, what with the jobs involved, including his own. So he has done what he always does; sat on the fence. He thinks we shouldn't do it, that it's too risky and says that he won't take any responsibility if anything goes wrong. But, at the same time, he won't stand in the way of Albert if he is prepared to take the chance.'

'And what did Albert say to that?'

'Unrepeatable.'

'But why Northweir all of a sudden?'

'Fred Richmond admitted that no one else around would touch it. They

148

all reckon Albert to be the best driver in the county and his beloved old Sprawler the best, possibly the only crane for the job.'

Alison waited until she emerged from the blinding spray of another lorry.

'Well, well. It's a funny old world.'

'As you say, my love, it's a funny old world.'

They fell quiet amid the motorway's noise. Some miles south of Preston, Alison became conscious of her husband's stare. She glanced at him, saw that he had turned sideways to look at her.

'All right?' He said nothing. 'Do you want me to stop at the service station for a rest?'

He ignored the question. 'You are beautiful,' he said.

Flustered, Alison instinctively put her hand to her hair. 'What am I supposed to say to that?'

'Nothing. I was stating a fact, not asking a question.' Another silence. 'Correction. You are very beautiful.'

'Larry Barker. For goodness sake, shut up.'

The next pause was short; too short.

'Are you going to leave me?'

Her grip on the wheel tightened. Fettered at feet, hands and head, she felt as if she were lashed to some inquisitional chair, with nowhere to run, hide, turn.

'What a stupid thing to say, Larry. I don't know what you are talking about.'

'You don't?'

'No.'

'Then you are not as bright as you are beautiful; and I always thought you were.'

He laughed at her confusion as she stared ahead, biting her lower lip, her driving reduced to keeping the car straight between two painted lines.

'I'm not cross. Looking back, I wouldn't have blamed you if you had walked out months ago. All I know is that I would not have survived that last piss-up of mine if you had not been around. Wouldn't have wanted to. I must have given you hell. And Robert. It must have been difficult enough for you without having friend Michael pawing the ground outside.'

'Larry, you are talking rubbish.'

'Am I? I may have been drunk most of the last two years but I wasn't always blind drunk.'

The car's speed fell away as guilt undermined her concentration. She cut

149

back into the slow lane too close to a towering juggernaut, its headlights flashing its displeasure.

'For God's sake, don't get us killed. Nothing is worth that. Don't worry about it. I'm not going to challenge Michael to a duel or anything like that. When you come close to death and you survive it, you find you don't make moral judgments any more. You just thank God you're alive. No doubt, once the novelty of living has worn off, I will start getting just as priggish as everyone else again. But poor old Michael. Have you seen the poor sod's face these last few weeks?'

'Please, Larry, don't,' Alison almost sobbed.

'I'm sorry, Lissa. I've been something of a bloody nuisance, haven't I? Not any more. I have this feeling that things are swinging my way at last. I think I may snatch Northweir back from the proverbial jaws today. I'd love to make it a going concern again. Perhaps then sell up, get out; pastures new; start up again somewhere else; find a bit of dignity and self-respect again. Perhaps that sounds a bit dramatic.' He looked at her, embarrassed. 'I'd quite understand if you decided not to come with me. I'd hate it but I wouldn't make it difficult for you.'

If a feeling of guilt had produced the flush on her face, anger now sustained it. Anger and resentment; surprising her with their intensity. Savagely, she pressed her right foot down and the car surged forward. Boxed in, she had to brake sharply to avoid ramming the van in front. Bloody men. What did they think she was? Some prize for the best contender? It was obvious that Larry could only imagine her leaving him if it were to live with Michael. Both of them saw her only in terms of their own existence. Someone incapable of independent existence. And they were being such good chaps about it; damned sporting of them. Bloody men. She savoured the thought of being free of both. Just she and Robert. Free to love anyone. Free not to love anyone. Get a job. As the man said, 'pastures new . . . find a bit of self-respect again'.

Barker laughed. 'Christ. I sounded like a page out of *Woman's Own*, didn't I? But I meant it, Lissa, every word.' He sat up abruptly. 'Now, get a move on or we are going to be late. And when I am in with Anderson, try and think of somewhere expensive to eat on the way back. We haven't been out to dinner together for years.'

At Nitromid, he was met by a very kindly Mary Jamieson, who delivered him into the outstretched arms of Anderson. Sir John shook his hand vigorously and they walked together across the room, Larry to a chair near the table covered with smoked salmon and sandwiches, and Anderson to

150

the sideboard. Larry still looked ill, thin and fragile, but there was quiet dignity too. His emaciated frame was erect, his stride slow and deliberate, his gaze level and unwavering. He looked composed as he sat, dwarfed by the huge chair. He looked unlikely to apologise for anything.

Mrs Jamieson closed the door on them both as Anderson reached the sideboard.

'What would you like to drink, Larry?'

'Nothing, thank you, Sir John. I am an alcoholic.' A simple remark, unaffected by any overtone of guilt or pride. It left Anderson nonplussed and Barker took advantage. 'Don't worry,' he smiled, 'it's not infectious. I can see a bottle of bitter lemon there; do you think I could have that? And, please, don't let me stop you having anything.'

Anderson handed him the glass of opalescent fluid and poured himself a gin and tonic. He sat opposite Barker.

'How are you feeling now, my boy? Are you better?'

'Very much so, Sir John. I'm feeling great. I may not look it but I feel better than I have for years. I'm still physically pretty weak, but I am getting stronger every day. But mentally, I feel great. I find now that decisions don't frighten me any more and I don't give a damn about anyone.'

He spoke with enough emphasis to make Anderson uncomfortable. He edged forwards in his chair to offer Barker some food.

'I'm glad to hear it, Larry. Do you know, you are getting to sound just like your father.'

'No, I'm not; I just sound like me. Tom Barker is dead and the days of the son trying to be the father are over. You are dealing with Larry Barker now, not Tom, and, if you don't like it, Sir John, you can bloody well lump it.'

For a moment, Anderson stared across at him, a sandwich halted half-way to an open mouth. Dropping the sandwich back on the plate, he put his head back and gave a shout that startled Mary Jamieson in the next room. He rose and paced the room once, emitting loud noises of laughter, of astonishment, of delight. He came back to a chair besides Barker and they both turned sideways to face each other. 'That's more like it, Larry.' Anderson reached for his sandwich again and began to eat enthusiastically. 'Now I don't mind admitting that we need your help. Has Richmond been to see you?'

'Yes, he called after Mrs Jamieson rang on Monday. We have been over the problem.'

'Can you do it?'

'Do what exactly, Sir John?'

'Put that absorber tower up?'

It was a moment before Barker answered.

'Why Northweir, all of a sudden? The last time I was in this office, you just didn't want to know. And now we seem to be all-important. What about these other local plant-hire firms you were going on about? Can't they help you?'

'Fair comment, Larry, and I'll admit that we have approached them and they can't help.'

'But I know for a fact that they have plant capable of lifting that tower, so why bother with Northweir who, according to you, are just about finished at Teflo anyway?'

'They all say that it is impossible with what access is available. They all claim that it can only be done by dismantling the off-gas line, or whatever they call it, at the base of the flare stack,' Anderson admitted reluctantly.

'And that means closing the process down for at least a day, possibly two?'

'That's correct, Larry.'

'And Teflo cannot afford to do that just at the moment?'

'No.'

'Amazing how fortunes change, isn't it? Six weeks ago, I sat in that chair asking for help,' – he waved his hand vaguely over his shoulder in the direction of the far end of the room – 'and all I got was a bum's rush. Now it seems that I am about the only one that can help you. You are going to have to make it worth my while.'

'If you can do this for me, Larry, I will renew your contract. I knew that would be the price before you came. But I thought that I would be dealing with the Larry Barker of old and, frankly, it would not have meant much. I would have still gone ahead with my original plans. Now? I'm not so sure. I'm impressed. Perhaps you can make a go of it. You've changed.' He looked as if he meant it. 'The main thing is, can you do it?'

'Yes, we can do it.' Barker's reply was quietly confident. 'After Richmond left on Monday, I went out on site with Rothwell and my best driver. We met again yesterday and decided it was possible. Tricky but possible. As you might have expected, Rothwell has washed his hands of the whole affair; he thinks the whole thing too risky and is going to cover himself by putting it in writing. But the driver has been with us since Dad's day, he is sure he can do it and I would back his judgment against

Rothwell's any time. The only worry he has at the moment is the weather. He says he will have to wait for the wind to drop. He's not too worried about the rain. So you can stop worrying about your tower; we will put it up tomorrow, weather permitting, but only on the understanding that our contract is extended for another year.'

'Good. That's settled then,' sighed Anderson.

'It's going to mean using a crane that has been lying idle for months. It's old and does not have a current inspecting engineer's certificate. The maintenance register is not up to date because there has been no official maintenance on it for at least six months, but it is Albert's pride and joy; he swears by it and he's sure it can do the job.'

'Well, there is no need for me to know anything about that, is there?' Anderson added quickly. 'You just get that tower up and, in a month or so, Teflo will really begin to take off. Perhaps Northweir too, eh? No reason why not, you know.'

Barker looked at Anderson as if seeing him for the first time.

'Strange how things work out, Sir John. I used to be absolutely terrified of you; God knows why. And now, and I say this in all humility, I feel sorry for you. You are cock of the roost, top of a pile of ambitious bastards, and now it's your turn to be frightened. You know perfectly well, make a hash of this merger, or whatever it is that's going on, and they will have you by the balls. And here am I; just about at the bottom. Believe me, where I went six weeks ago, there is nowhere lower. But at least I am not scared any more. As the Americans would put it, I'm fresh out of terror; sort of immune.' He turned to Anderson with a smile. 'Perhaps you should try it, Sir John.'

'No thanks, lad, but I can't tell you how glad I am to see you looking so well again. We must meet again soon; work out some plans for Northweir.'

With a fatherly arm around Barker's shoulders, Anderson, asking after Alison and Robert, steered him through Mrs Jamieson's room into the outer office. The sight of Anderson startled the receptionist. She hurried to open the outer door, hobbling as she lost a shoe en route. Barker took his time as he bent to retrieve the shoe and hand it, at full arm's length, back to the girl as she stood holding the door, a forgiving twinkle in his eye.

Life was sweet.

19

Robert was still in bed when his father slammed the car door shut. The noise stirred him in his sleep but he did not wake. Alison stood at the door, fully dressed, anxiously watching her husband who, for the first time, had insisted on driving alone. The garden was sodden from the days of rain, the shrubs still dripping from the last of the squalls. But the wind had died away, the early morning sun was warm and the steaming road was already dry in patches.

'Good morning, Mr Barker. A better morning,' the Teflo gate attendant smiled.

Barker parked his car, deciding not to drive round the perimeter. He stretched for his yellow protective helmet on the back seat and started the long walk through the centre of the works, warming to the friendly nods from other yellow-helmeted heads, taking pride in belonging, cursing the wasted years. A surge of excitement left him rubber legged and sweaty. He walked between the plant rearing up on each side of him, inspiring in him more awe than any cold, towering Gothic lancets. He felt the warmth of the vibrant chemical life within the hissing monsters, heard clanking noises of metal striking metal, of piping reacting to the forces of heat expansion, as if those monsters were straining to be free from their chains. He remembered how he had walked that way two days earlier with Albert Crampton; how he had sprinkled his words with profanities to show his common touch with the labouring classes. With sudden shame he had realised that Albert never, or rarely, swore, had felt humble in the presence of this gentle man. He had a lot to learn. He was desperate to do so. He had wasted so many chances.

He walked on, dodging around pools of oil-slicked rainwater. One large tower, still under construction, was festooned with scaffolding, men working at different levels, looking like astronauts at work on a missile. Through the main part of the plant and out beyond, he saw the spherical tanks, propped up on spindly, inadequate-looking legs, that Crampton had told him were full of naphtha, benzene, even gasoline. 'Heaven help us if that lot ever go up.' And now the tarmac of the main plant complex gave way to the concrete roadway. He could see the crane with the delicate-looking lattice of its boom high above one of the towers, packed tightly in a group of six on a concrete pad to the left of the roadway. To the right, the gantry with its pipes arrowed away to the flare stack, separated from the road by a few feet of grass thrown up in irregular tussocks. All this against the background of yellow dunes and slate-coloured sea.

As he approached, one of the group standing near the foot of the tower came to meet him. Barker recognised Mark Dixon, a clipboard under his arm.

'Good morning, Mr Barker. You've timed it well.'

'I was hoping not to miss any of the excitement. How are things going?'

'So far, so good. We had a good early start. I'm beginning to believe what I've heard about this driver of yours. He really is quite fantastic. He is all hitched up, ready to take the strain as soon as my fitters get the last couple of bolts undone. We disconnected the piping from the off-gas line yesterday.'

Barker shaded his eyes as he looked up at the tower. White fluffy clouds made it seem as if the tower was falling towards him. With the nausea of vertigo, he looked away hurriedly. Two steel ropes, hanging from the crane's hook and held apart by a steel spreader, were shackled to a collar one-third the way down the tower's length. The ropes were slack, the hook oscillating gently. He could see Crampton waiting patiently in his cab, catching his eye, brandishing an encouraging thumbs-up sign.

The Sprawler stood on the road some way beyond the tower. Developed from the American Koehring machines used by the armed forces, the length of the boom looked hopelessly out of proportion with the rest until one saw the large A-frame high above the cabin, holding the jib with thick steel suspension ropes, the whole balanced by the enormous counter-weights which curved round the back of the cab like some giant skier's waist-belt. Tom Barker had always bought the best, and this crane was powered by a Rolls-Royce C4S unit. The first impression one had was of rust and peeling paint. The NCK Rapier 545 sign was barely visible on the cabin's scratched and dented side. The crawler shoes were red with rust, the cabin windows broken. But all the gearing that was visible, the bearings, cogwheels, linkages, driving chains, all were clean and covered in fresh grease. The cabin controls were immaculate and the panels, giving safe weight–angle ratios, intact and readable.

The tower was 90 feet long, and so the Sprawler had its longest boom in use, 120 feet. The roadway was about 18 feet across, the crane 12 feet wide, so Crampton could not use the outriggers. At 11 tons, he knew the tower was well within the safe lifting capacity of the crane, but the lack of outriggers cut the safe weight by a third, 35 tons to 24 over a 12-foot radius with a shorter boom. Any pendular movement from a 120-foot boom would soon take it over that radius, and he knew that he would have to work at a considerably greater radius than that. The tower was well off the roadway and he knew that he would be working at the very margin of safety. But he felt that, if he could keep the radius to within 20 to 25 feet, he would be all right. Like many drivers, he did not mind turning a deaf ear to warning bells so long as it 'felt right'. He knew that all safety standards always left a margin for error. Just how far he would stray into that no man's land between safety and catastrophe would be governed by experience, by hearsay. 'Pal of mine worked up north some years ago; County Durham; building a jetty. He was using a Sprawler. Reckoned he was lifting 7 tons at 30 feet and more, admittedly with only 80-foot boom. Reckoned it was the only crane that could have done it at the time. No; my main worry i'n't at site, it's at bend in road. That's where I think main danger is; slewing round to take that corner without hitting gantry or stay ropes.' Beyond the towers and before joining the perimeter road where the new tower lay, the roadway was forced away at an angle by the pyramid of steel guy-ropes that supported the slender flare stack.

Dixon suddenly hurried back to the base of the tower as the crane's engine roared and the cables snapped taut. The wheel at the end of the jib turned slowly and the hook was hoisted upwards, the tower coming out of the recess in the base like an old tooth. The boom was directly over the front of one of the crawler's tracks, the point of maximum stability, but Crampton now slewed the jib through forty-five degrees to reach the midline, at the same time derricking in to reduce the radius as much as possible. The slewing motion was started and completed slowly to avoid any unnecessary pendular movement and the slewing brake applied. Slowly, painfully, he now edged nearly 50 tons of crane and tower along the road, the crawler shoes, applying a load of well over 7 pounds per square inch, scouring and fragmenting the concrete as they went.

Dixon and the fitters followed behind as if in some funeral slow march, their eyes raised anxiously to heaven, the hook like some leading star, diverting their attention from what was going on under their feet. Where the crane had been standing, mainly on the side of the road nearest the gantry, cracks had appeared in the concrete.

Crampton negotiated the forty-five degree turn. Reversing all the way, he hung out of the cab door to guide himself. At the corner, with one track stopped, he turned, careful to avoid the tower swinging laterally as a result. The tower cleared the gantry comfortably so that he had no need to add a slewing motion to get round. Once out on the perimeter, he stopped and called Dixon to the cab. A few shouted words, a pointing of arms, and Dixon stepped back to watch him lay the tower down. The skill with which Crampton carried out the complicated manoeuvre was not lost on Dixon. The crane's engine died and Crampton heaved himself out of the cab, an old army side-pack over his shoulder. He saw Barker and Dixon walking towards him. He sat on the crane's track and opened his pack, taking out a huge thermos flask. He smiled and nodded at the two men.

'Half-time; one nil to us,' he grinned. He offered a greasy plastic mug full of indeterminate brown fluid in their direction but they both shook their heads. He drank loudly, belched and grinned again.

'Nowt to it. Now all we have got to do is exact opposite and you can ring your friend Anderson and say whatever you gentlemen say to t'other on such occasions.'

Barker could say nothing. He felt so ineffectual alongside this mountain of a man and his machine. He envied the man his strength, his simplicity. Not for him the power-driven, drug-sustained posing of boardroom or golf club. Just a job requiring strength, skill and courage at which he knew he was the best around. No one to fear unless it was an Anderson or a Barker or a Rothwell, who might take his crane away from him, put him on a street corner.

'Where's Bill this morning?'

'It seems he has an important union meeting in Dunbridge.'

'Best place for him, an' all.'

They grinned at each other, knowingly. With a quickening of spirit, Barker realised that, a few months ago, he also would have found some important meeting to go to, somewhere with a bar. Crampton swilled the dregs around the bottom of the mug, swallowed them and refilled the mug from the seemingly bottomless thermos.

'He's not all bad, is our Bill. His heart's in right place. There's nowt wrong with fighting for lads. It's just that these union fellas get like bosses; get to enjoy power too much. I'll tell thee, t'lads are not too happy about this nitrogen nonsense. Reckon it's getting too personal 'tween him and Anderson.'

He stared straight at Barker. 'You never bring your lad to Teflo, Mr Barker. Why not?'

It sounded more like an accusation than a question. Crampton sat totally at ease while Barker, reluctant to sit and get his suit dirty, stood in front of him, shifting awkwardly from foot to foot like some nervous candidate for a job he did not feel up to.

'What is he going to be? An engineer like his grandfather?'

'I don't know, Albert.'

'It would be nice, working for third generation of Barkers. Happen I'll be on scrap heap by then, though. Too old. But it would be nice. Bring him down, Mr Barker. Let me show him around; meet t'lads. They're not a bad lot when you get to know them, you know, Mr Barker. Bit rough here and there. But Teflo is grand place to work, you know, when you get to know it.'

'I will certainly do that, Albert.' They smiled. 'And thank you.'

Mark Dixon broke the duologue.

'All set then, Albert? They've shifted the cables. They've shackled on the new tower.' He looked at his watch. 'Nine thirty. We've done well. I didn't think we'd be as quick as this. Whenever you're ready, Albert.'

He walked away.

Crampton replaced the thermos in his pack, threw the pack into the cab and climbed in after it. Affection clutched at Barker's throat as Albert instinctively adjusted his oily cap, gave a broad grin and, once more, a massive thumbs-up sign. The hoist ropes were lying loose on the ground near the old tower. He lifted the wires until they were hanging free before derricking in as far as possible and then hoisting the gear to near the maximum. He slewed the jib through 180 degrees and trundled quite rapidly to where the new tower lay. Dixon and the fitters already stood near the attachment collar, two-thirds the way along it. He slowed to within a yard of the tower's foot, lowered the jib until the hook hung vertically above the fitters and dropped the hoisting gear until there was just enough slack in it for them to hook on.

Crampton left the cab for a moment to stand beside Barker, checking that the fitters were hooking on correctly. Neither spoke. Crampton stayed longer than was really necessary and Barker wondered. Was this man afraid also? Was he as much a sham as everyone else? Was he looking for reassurance? From Larry Barker? Someone looking for strength from Larry Barker?

Dixon waved to indicate that they were finished. Without a word, Crampton walked back to his cab. For years it had been his habit to look briefly at wind and weather before starting, but this time his gaze seemed to take in the whole scene around. He wiped sweat from his palms with a cloth, before grasping the control levers. By a skilful combination of luffing and hoisting, he kept the hook so nearly vertical over the centre of gravity of the tower that there was no more than a few inches of pendular movement as the foot finally cleared the floor. Five more minutes and the whole complex was stable enough to trundle off the perimeter towards the narrow-angled bend near the gantry.

As Barker followed behind, the Sprawler crawled nearer to the corner. Dixon and his fitters walked backwards ahead of the crane, signalling directions to Crampton. As there had been room to turn the old tower without moving the jib, Crampton proposed to do the same going back. At the corner, however, Dixon became agitated and stopped the crane. He climbed into the cab to explain that large pieces of concrete had broken away at the corner. Crampton slewed the jib around as far as he could to the right. Gingerly, he crawled around the corner, reducing the slewing angle as he went.

Dixon sighed with relief and, with waves of encouragement, he walked on to the base where the new tower would stand. The fitters stood round the recess, ready to direct Crampton to within an inch of where the tower's flange must engage. Two plant operators, opening the block valves nearby, became interested spectators.

Crampton began the delicate process of lowering a ninety-foot long, complicated tube weighing eleven tons, into a recess with less than one-eighth of an inch tolerance, rotated so that holes drilled in its flange would fit over bolts embedded in the base. He started the manoeuvre by slewing round so that the tower hung vertically over the base, lined up by eye in two planes, by himself in the cab and by Dixon standing to one side. The two fitters waited, eager to feed the tower's foot into the recess and then the bolts into the flange.

From where he stood behind the crane, Barker moved to get a better view. He squeezed passed the narrow gap between the crane and the edge of the roadway. As he rounded the counterweight he gasped, though the significance of what he saw did not register immediately. Two or three feet of concrete between the crane and the grass verge crumbled away as he watched. Out of sight of the others, the noise was lost to them in the roar of the engine. The jagged margins of the concrete were now back to the edge of the crawler shoe, in some places disappearing beneath it. Creaking, grinding, splitting noises were increasing as he listened, the sound of running water now coming distinctly from a muddy torrent which dived under the roadway at that point.

Barker froze with fear. A loud crack and a shock wave he felt through the soles of his feet finally convulsed him into action. He must go back round the other side and warn them. With thin legs trembling, his progress was nightmarishly slow before reaching the cab. Painfully he climbed up to the door. Albert Crampton had just succeeded, at the first attempt, in lowering the tower into the first few inches of the recess in the base. The crane still held its full weight at the limit of its safe radius while the fitters sweated to rotate it so that the holes in the flange would fit over the bolts. Crampton's concentration was intense. Seeing Barker through the cabin window, he swore, 'Bugger off, Mr Barker. Not now, sir.' He turned his eyes to the jib head once more. When the cab door opened and Barker put his shoulders in, Crampton exploded. 'For Christ's sake, can't you see . . .'

His voice trailed away as he saw the terror on Larry's face.

'It's crumbling, Albert; all crumbling away. There's a flood down there.'

'What do you mean?' There was urgency in Crampton's grip as he took Barker by the lapels. 'Where?'

'Down there.'

He nearly fell from the crane as Crampton brushed him aside. He jumped to the ground to join Crampton who was looking under the crane. They could see little. As Crampton walked round the back of the crane, the ground gave a convulsive shudder and the roadway extending some ten feet towards the centre gave way. Two triangular flaps opened like trap doors and the left-hand crawler shoe sank into it with a rattle of straining suspension ropes and groans of bolts and bearings under extreme and abnormal stresses. Water rushed in to fill the defect in the road, splashing half-way up the crawler shoe. The jib head and hook were pulled sideways, dragging the tower with it, wedging it obliquely in its recess. Crumbling, cracking, plopping noises echoed around; the process was not at an end.

'Christ, she's going,' Crampton whispered, appalled. His first reaction was to run; let the whole thing go. So what? Nothing to blame himself for. But what about the fitters? He had better get them out from there. But could he save the crane? All he need do was get the hook above the centre of gravity, just straighten it a few degrees and it might drop in place. Pay

160

out all the cable then and at least only the crane would go; it might not bring the tower down. He wondered if he could. As he ran back towards the cab he collided with Barker.

'Get out, sir. Run as hard as you can. There's no way you can help. Go on; run.'

He hesitated only long enough to see Barker hurrying in the direction of the perimeter. Climbing into the cab was more difficult due to the angle at which the crane now lay. He tended to slide off the sloping seat and he had to take more pressure on one leg. He felt the crane tilt a few more degrees as he looked up to assess the problem.

The tower was pulled over at a very slight angle, unable to tilt further with its lower end just engaged in its recess. The boom, distorted by the strain, had tilted away from the tower. The suspensory ropes and winding gear were ramrod taut. If only he could drop the tower the full distance. To do this he must get the hook above the recess again and this meant slewing. He released the slewing brake to find the crane tilting even more to the left, putting even greater strain on the hoisting gear and boom. The tower was already holding the crane up. Any more subsidence must bring both crane and tower down. There was nothing more he could do with the crane except sacrifice it by winding out more cable, hoping at least to save the tower.

The crane tilted further so that he could no longer stay in his seat. Standing to reach the controls, he cautiously payed out the hoisting rope. The loosened hoisting wire allowed the crane to tilt further, the slack in the wire being taken up rapidly as the distance between tower and jib head increased. The more the crane tilted, the more weight was shifted to the left-hand side of the roadway and larger pieces of concrete fissured and fell away into the underground stream that now poured through the tunnel. Finally, the crane tilted so far as to apply intolerable leverage at the foot of the tower. With a petrifying, wrenching snap, the buckled foot became disengaged from the disintegrating edge of the recess.

It was obvious to Crampton now that everything was beyond the point of no return. He could see that the tower would now swing across like a giant pendulum to take the centre of gravity beyond the base of the crane and bring the crane down. Shouting something unintelligible, he tried to get out of the cab. The floor was rapidly approaching the vertical; he was a very big man and the door had jammed half-open. He had a vague picture of men scattering from the area of the tower's base as one of the beams of the A-frame snapped, and drove its way through the cabin roof. The jagged

161

end caught in Crampton's loose dungaree jacket and forced him forwards and downwards to the floor. It drove on inexorably, sliding between his shoulder blade and chest wall, crushing and lacerating the blood and nerve supply to his right arm before smashing his clavicle and emerging again near the root of his neck. It finally came to rest in the oil-soaked floor boards, pinning him to the wood like a rare lepidopterist's specimen. After a brief, macabre struggle, Crampton lapsed into the blissful unconsciousness of neurogenic shock.

It was from the turn in the roadway that Barker first looked back. He was just in time to see the frantic efforts to release the tower and to watch it break loose from its base. He saw its pendular movement start, slowly at first but rapidly gaining pace, a slight hesitation at half-way as if it had dragged across the road. The weight of the tower and boom, now well outside the base of the crane, destroyed what little stability was left.

One hundred and twenty feet of twisted boom, with the tower attached, fell across the off-gas line and its supporting gantry. The gantry for more than thirty yards on each side was brought down and the guy-ropes of the flare stack a hundred yards away shivered in the shock wave.

On the far side of the road, Dixon had started to run the moment he saw the crane tilt and Crampton hurriedly climb back in. He turned and watched the whole thing in horror, frozen into inactivity. The two fitters had remained at the foot of the tower, unaware of the danger they were in. When the tower tilted slightly to jam in the recess, they expected no more than that Crampton would withdraw it and try again. It was only with the sudden lurch of the crane and the buckling of the tower that they were struck by terror. One, frozen with fear, incapable of making any decision, stayed where he was. The tower passed within inches of where he stood and he walked away unscathed. The other stood on the opposite side, hemmed in by another tower, the block valves behind and the crane alongside. He began to run for safety under the boom. Out of the corner of his eye he saw the tower break free and swing towards him. He threw himself flat, hands on his neck, judging that the tower would pass over him. The boom on the tilting crane had, however, brought the centre of the arc lower, and the tower hit the road a foot short of the fitter. It pushed him along as he frantically rolled to avoid it. Inevitably, the cutting edge of the steel tube caught in his clothing, held him captive while the eleven-ton tube transected him without a noticeable judder as it passed. The two halves of his torso were linked only by fragments of his clothing which had survived the

162

tower's scything action. Small and large bowel were visible in the blood-soaked rents in the clothing, one kidney glistening in the dust three feet away, a ragged length of ureter still attached.

A silence fell over the whole scene. The final creaking of straining metal, adjusting to the new stresses and strains, made the silence more intense. With neck bent forwards inquisitively, his eyes wide open, the dead fitter seemed to survey the scene with interest.

As Dixon walked back towards the shambles, he could hear the surviving fitter vomiting painfully. He tried not to look at the blood-soaked bundles on the road and had almost picked his way passed when he turned to put his jacket over the staring eyes. He shivered as he got nearer the overturned crane.

'Crampton,' he shouted, his voice tremulous and broken. 'Albert, are you all right?'

'Is that you, Mark?' The voice from the other side of the crane was Barker's. 'What has happened your side?'

'There is one fitter dead here and I can't get any answer from Crampton. What shall we do?'

'Go and get help. You will be quicker than I will. I'll try to climb up and see what has happened to Albert. Hurry, for God's sake.'

When the works ambulance arrived, its bell strident above the sounds of running feet and shouted commands, they found Barker in the crane's cab. Pale, but calm and completely self-composed, he sat, cradling Crampton's head in his lap.

20

As usual, Summerbee was two minutes early and Dodd ten minutes late. The fact that they were both to die that day was no reason for any sudden change in their personal behaviour. The shift was from 7.00 a.m. to 3.00 p.m. Jack Summerbee, spotlessly erect from his highly polished shoes to his neatly trimmed military moustache, thrived on regulations and punctuality. Phil Dodd, a lusty and wide-ranging bachelor, while finding no difficulty in playing his part in the 3.00 p.m. *valete*, often experienced trouble meeting the 7.00 a.m. deadline.

It had been a long, worrying and frustrating night and Mathew Sharples, the outgoing Shift Superintendent, watched Summerbee's incoming ritual with something less than amusement. He sighed resignedly as he mentally predicted the stages. Through the door, pause, look at watch, remove hat, wipe immaculate shoes on non-existent doormat, open locker, don white coat, fasten all buttons, secure locker with key chained to belt, turn and acknowledge colleague's presence, stretch out right hand to receive clipboard, say 'Right'. He wondered if Summerbee made love to numbers.

'Good morning, Jack. Can't say I'm sorry to hand this lot over to you this morning.'

Summerbee took a quick glance at the last readings on the chart and whistled.

'Only 3 kilograms per square centimetre and 110° centigrade? What's been the trouble, Mat?'

'We've not been able to keep the plant stable for more than an hour at a time. I'm sure the nitrogen we are losing is leaking into the system somewhere and is giving us these unstable pressures. We just can't get the temperature up without the pressure rising too high.'

'I see you've had to vent quite a few times in the night,' observed Summerbee. 'What about the nitrogen purge control?'

'Set at zero, Jack. I just couldn't abide the damn thing purging automatically as well.' He expected disapproval and Summerbee did not let him down. 'I know. I know. It's not strictly according to the book but you just wait and see how unstable the thing is at the moment. If you ask me, they ought to close down and find the leak or let us have unlimited supply of nitrogen.'

'You may well be right, Mat.'

There was just enough condescension in Summerbee's voice to make Sharples, heading for the door, turn with a flicker of weary defiance.

'I'll bet you a fiver you don't start oxidation this shift, Jack.'

His challenge fell on deaf ears, as Summerbee, who had never laid a bet in his life, was already poring over his control panel. He had every confidence that strict adherence to the manual would stabilise the whole situation. First he must reset the automatic purge control. He passed behind the control panel, moved the control and returned to his dials. He was relieved to see no evidence of a purge; at least the levels were not that low. He made a note of the time. His frown was intensified as a breathless,

164

untidy Dodd burst through the door. Without raising his eyebrows, Summerbee growled.

'In a constantly changing world, it's a comfort to know we can rely on something, young man, if it's only your unreliability.'

Summerbee's mock severity was matched by Dodd's penitence.

'Yes, Mr Summerbee. Sorry, Mr Summerbee. The fact is I'm finding it more and more difficult to get out of bed these mornings, even my own.'

Jack Summerbee laughed softly. He had enough insight to realise that he was at the ceiling of his ability, obtaining and keeping his job only by the rigid application of rules and regulations laid down by brains greater than his own. He had never had an original thought in his life and he knew it. For this reason he enjoyed the company of his junior, with no bitterness in his envy of Dodd's ability. Dodd, a quick and intuitive intelligence, was prepared to challenge the most accepted of theories. In return, he derived comfort and reassurance from Summerbee's solid dependability.

'Take a look at that, lad, and tell me what you think of it.'

Summerbee thrust the clipboard at Dodd as his young colleague was still struggling into his white coat. Dodd placed the board on the desk, leaning forward to read it as he tied a shoe-lace.

'Always said that shift were an impotent lot of bastards.'

'What do you mean?' asked Summerbee.

'Well, they've obviously spent a very restless night without producing any satisfactory result.'

'Come on now, Phil. Be serious for a moment. Lift your thoughts above the navel for a moment and tell me what we're going to do.'

'What I would do or what we are going to do?'

'What we are going to do.'

Both men were now at the control panel, Dodd seated and Summerbee standing at his shoulder.

'In that case, we're going to warm up as per regulations laid down,' smiled Dodd. 'I imagine the purge control is on automatic?'

'Of course.'

'But what if it purges, Jack?'

'That's their problem, not mine. Now get on with it.'

And so they began, first by building up the pressure with nitrogen before circulating the cyclohexane, and then opening the steam valves to the heat exchanger. By 8.30 a.m. the pressure had built up to 8 kilograms but the temperature was only 105° centigrade. Perhaps Mat had been right. Perhaps the nitrogen was leaking in.

165

'You're going to have to vent if it goes on like this, Jack.' Dodd's voice had a goading edge to it, mocking him, prodding at his rule-book mind. 'Don't forget what it says in the regs.'

He laughed openly as Summerbee struggled with himself to break the rules, just once, and failed.

'Vent, dammit; vent,' he snapped.

By 9.45 a.m. they were justifiably pleased with the approach of optimal operating conditions. The pressure was 9.2 kilograms per square centimetre, a little high but not dangerously so. The temperature was 152° centigrade in No. 1 reactor, diminishing in the remaining five. For years Summerbee had never allowed the pressure to rise above the optimum of 8.8 kilograms per square centimetre but Dodd had shown him how the warming up process could be speeded up by letting the pressure rise to anything up to 9.5 kilograms per square centimetre without ill effect.

'That's fine, Phil. I think we can go over to automatic now with full circulation. I'm going out on site to see if I can find Mr Richmond and get permission to start oxidation.'

As Summerbee left the building, Dodd shut the valve on the steam bypass and set the steam supply to automatic. For the first time that morning, he could relax. He stood at the window, paper coffee cup in hand, looking out at the plant. The six reactors were in full view, No. 1 being no more than a hundred yards away. 'My God,' he thought, 'talk about "seated one day at the organ".' It made his spine shiver to think of the fearful power within those black satanic creations, as he sat at the instrument console. He had a mental picture of the superheated fluid kept from boiling by the high pressure of the gases, both kept from exploding only by the strength of the reactor. He was joined at the window by another young Process Control Technician and five minutes of gentle banter and gossip ensued.

As he returned to his control panel, his instinctive first glance at the readings from No. 1 reactor produced an immediate ache deep in his chest and a dryness in his mouth no coffee could remove. The pressure dial that Dodd now gazed at anxiously had a simple linear scale marked on it. The needle now rested just within the danger zone, the red colour beaming its warning on either side of the needle. Dodd, with mounting anxiety, checked all the readings against the last recorded figures on his clipboard. The nitrogen level had fallen sharply.

'Christ. What do I do now?' Dodd's mind began to race. 'More to the point, what would old Jack do? Where the hell is he?'

166

The dials, switches and trace recorders danced before his eyes, incapable of being assessed by a volatile mind, panicking and irrational. Slowly Dodd's intelligence and ability took command again.

'For God's sake, take a grip, you stupid bastard,' Dodd muttered to himself. 'What have you got? You have got a pressure just in the red in one reactor but the temperature is still all right. The nitrogen level is falling, so probably the cause of the rise in the pressure is due to the leak. Now the last thing we want is for an automatic purge to push the pressure up even more, so to hell with Jack and his precious regulations, that lever is going down.'

Relieved to have made a decision and to be able to do something active, Dodd went to the back of the panel and set the purge lever at zero. When he returned, the readings seemed to have stabilised, though the pressure was still high. The time was 10.15 a.m. as he recorded the readings.

'Right,' Dodd thought out loud, 'the block valves are open to the flare stack. The whole system is safety-valved to the flare stack at 11 kilograms per square centimetre so I can't come to any harm. I'll turn the steam supply down a little but I'm not going to turn it off unless the pressure goes any higher.'

Unconsciously, he wiped sweating palms on his white coat and wished Summerbee would come so that he could go to the toilet. The clamour of an ambulance's bell racing past the control block was of no significance to him, totally preoccupied as he was with the needle on No. 2 reactor's dial that was also beginning to creep towards the red arc. He was stretching for the steam supply control when the door burst open and a breathless, plethoric Summerbee entered.

'Nasty accident near the flare stack. Thought I'd better get back,' Summerbee gasped, as he crossed the floor towards his console. 'Those stairs, not so young as I . . . Jesus Christ, what's that?'

His jaw sagged and his suffused face became blotchy with pallid areas as adrenalin, pumped out at his first sight of the pressure gauges, took its effect. For several seconds he could not speak, holding his breath as a wave of turbulent palpitations swept through his chest. Visibly controlling himself, he still shouted as he spoke again, attracting the attention of other staff.

'What the hell has been going on while I was out?'

'Now don't panic, Jack. Everything is under control.'

Dodd's voice lacked conviction. As he spoke, both men could see the needle in No. 2 dial reach the red and No. 1 began to climb again.

'For God's sake, turn the heat off.' Summerbee couldn't hide his fear.

'I was just going to,' Dodd snapped back, 'when you came through the door.'

Another five minutes and it was plain that turning the steam off had produced no effect. The pressure in all reactors was now over 10 kilograms per square centimetre.

Summerbee's voice sounded as if he were reading from a manual as, querulously, he tried to regain control. 'The block valves are open?'

'Been open since 9.45.'

Dodd checked with his record. 'Steam supply shut off?'

'Off,' confirmed Dodd.

'Oxidation off?'

'Never been turned on.'

For the first time, Summerbee noticed the nitrogen level.

'Why hasn't it purged?' asked Summerbee, petulantly like a child with a toy that won't work.

'I put the control on zero,' admitted Dodd.

The words 'Bloody young fool' were flung at him as Summerbee leapt to the back of the console and slammed the lever over. This seemed only to accelerate the rate at which all the needles were climbing. A fatalistic calm now settled over Summerbee. According to the book, he had done everything possible. There was nothing else laid down to cope with this sort of crisis.

'All I can say is "Thank God for safety valves."'

His words were now being listened to by most of the control-room staff who were standing in an arc around Dodd, Summerbee, and their rows of cold, emotionless instruments.

'They must blow off any second now. We will know when the pressures fall. It's never happened before as far as I know. I wonder what Mr Richmond will say.'

He straightened as if about to receive bravely the verdict of some distant court martial. If he heard Dodd's next words, they made no obvious impact.

'Pressure in No. 1 is already well over 12, Jack, and still climbing. The safety valves are set at 11 kilo; they should have blown by now.'

'In that case, Phil, you'd better get on the phone, find Mr Richmond and tell him the position. I don't have the authority to evacuate the plant. For Christ's sake find him and get him up here at the double.'

Several of the older men amongst the onlookers hurried to their panels,

168

turned a few switches and ran for the door. Two fell as they fought to get through the narrow exit. Summerbee walked to the window, a trance-like stare on his face. Dodd, aware of the futility of trying to find Richmond in time, stayed at the console, impotently flicking switches and moving levers in a search for a last-minute miracle, finally hammering the panel with uncontrolled frustration.

Summerbee gazed out of the window, peering from side to side as if to find some clue as to what was amiss. He saw some of the control-room staff, white coat tails fluttering as they ran, urging others, mainly site operators, to run with them. One stopped a tanker driver, begging for a lift. But his eyes were attracted back to No. 1 reactor. Was it his imagination or was the reactor moving? Surely a thing that size couldn't vibrate. The hum and hiss they emitted under pressure, was that louder than usual?

Any doubts he may have had about what he could see or hear were suddenly dispelled. With a central roar surrounded by the ringing sound of metal fracturing, pieces of gantry and scaffolding flew into the air. No. 1 reactor tilted a few degrees. One piece of gantry, weighing several tons, fell obliquely across the cabin of the tanker. A white-coated man leapt from the wreckage and ran, head and shoulders bent; the driver did not emerge. Summerbee watched with horror.

What Summerbee could not see was the block near the flare stack; the pile of twisted crane, absorption tower, gantry scaffolding and pipework at the centre of which lay vulgar, undignified death and tortured human misery. The crash had closed the off-gas line as effectively as any block valve. Also twisted and bent beyond all hope of function was the piping between the safety valves and the flare stack. The valves had operated at 11 kilograms per square centimetre but only into pipes that were themselves blocked. The nitrogen line, at 12 kilograms per square centimetre had only added to the build up of pressure and Summerbee was never to have the satisfaction of knowing that there was nothing in the book to prevent it.

There was another bang, less violent than the first. The reactor shook and a cloud of grey-white vapour appeared between Nos. 1 and 2. As the reactor had tilted, a stainless-steel tube had disintegrated, belching out cyclohexane. The tube, at high temperature and pressure, had been brought into contact with a minute piece of zinc in a badly welded gantry joint. Metal failure due to zinc embrittlement had been instantaneous. Distinct from the ever-increasing hiss, Summerbee could now hear frantic bubbling noises as the superheated cyclohexane fluid, now released to

169

atmospheric pressure, became gaseous. He called to his young colleague who was still reluctant to leave the control panel.

'Leave it, Phil. There's no more we can do now.'

The two friends watched for a few minutes as the cloud increased in size, drifting away from them. There was no sign of it slowing down, the gas still belching from the split reactor in thick, unfolding billows. The leading edge of the cloud was already over Monkey Island, turning Piggott Street into a murky twilight.

'Time for you to go, lad,' Summerbee said, softly. 'There is nothing more you can do. Get out while you can.'

'And you, Jack?'

'I'll stay just a little longer; just in case I'm needed.'

As Summerbee replied, there was another muffled explosion and the cloud seemed to change course. The reactors suddenly disappeared from view as the vapour came their way. With no more than a glance at each other, they began to hurry for the door. They never heard the explosion, having already been reduced to jagged, blackened masses of charred bone and bubbling fat by the fireball that preceded it. So different in life, in death they were differentiated ultimately only by their dental cavities. Their corpses, roasted in milliseconds, were buried under debris as the control-room disintegrated around them. Wrecked panels fell across them, the dials, so vital to them only minutes before, mocking them in death.

Nothing survived beneath the ignited vapour cloud. As the cloud had drifted back towards the plant, it had ignited, the epicentre of the explosion probably being the hydrogen-producing complex. The heat of the ignition sterilised the ground beneath of all animal life, human or otherwise. In Piggott Street, no man, woman or child, no rat, sparrow or cockroach survived. The devastation that followed was covered in the thick, black, oily film of cyclohexane combustion products. Nothing moved in this black chemical desert.

Beyond the area of ignition extended the destruction caused by the explosion equivalent to some sixty tons of TNT. Rows of houses in Monkey Island were razed to the ground. Water mains spouted and crackling high-tension cables straddled splintered beams protruding from piles of masonry. The cries of children were answered only by moans or high shrieks of hysterical terror.

In the fringe zone between the incinerated and the destroyed were those unfortunates who survived the blast but were severely burned. The smell of

Circle 33

CIRCLE 33

Date... 18th NOV '15... 2015

...MARTIN... from Savills called today on behalf of Circle 33 to undertake a survey of your home.

Please call **MARTIN SHIELS** on the number below to arrange a convenient appointment. If we are unable to survey your property, we will not be able to identify what works are required to your home.

07534 854286

Thank you in anticipation.

burned human flesh was soon to pervade the whole area, to rise even above the acrid stench of chemical catastrophe.

For several minutes after the main explosion, smaller secondary explosions occurred as tanks full of naphtha, toluene and benzene went up in sheets of flame. A vertical flame, three hundred feet high, roared heavenwards like some triumphal funeral pyre as the remaining cyclohexane discharged under pressure from the shattered reactors.

Teflo as a functioning unit was wiped out. Its destruction was complete. Few of the tall chemical towers remained erect. One of the absorption towers had toppled to lean precariously against the crawler track of Albert Crampton's crane. One of the ambulance crew nearby, unscathed, lay in the filth, prostrate, racked with convulsive vomiting. His colleague, caught as he clambered over the crane to reach Crampton, was crushed, one eyeball resting sightlessly on his cheek.

There were remarkable escapes. The research laboratories, only two hundred yards from the control-room, were just beyond the vapour cloud. Sheltered by towering surrounding plant, the staff had no warning of the escape of gas and were working normally when they were hit by the explosion. In some freak way protected by the surrounding plant, some got away with no more than minor injuries. Sue Maguire, research chemist and erstwhile bedfellow of Duncan Rae, was the first to stumble from the wreckage of the laboratory. The roadway outside was only just recognisable under the wreckage of pipes, gantries and shattered buildings. Amongst the maze of tangled pipes, darted small tongues of flame. Steam hissed from leaking joints. A tanker lorry lay on its side, opalescent fluid flowing from its split tank. Sue gave a hysterical giggle. They would have to be careful; that might be inflammable. She thought she heard the distant wail of a police car.

She was joined by another dazed, unharmed chemist and, with no thought for those still in the shambles that had been the laboratory, and with no word to each other, they began to pick their way through the wreckage and around the mutilated human remains. Sue Maguire's first emotional response was at the sight of a man who stumbled into view beyond wreckage that made it impossible for them to reach him. Naked except for vestiges of shoes, his body black between raw red areas from whose edges hung tassels of shrivelled dead skin, he stumbled blindly, his eyes opaque. Sue's screams of warning turned to sobs of horror as the man slipped and fell in the pool of fluid from the tanker. The grey smoke of the corrosive action of concentrated sulphuric acid on human flesh rose from the now motionless form.

Ten minutes later, Sue was still racked with gibbering sobs as she walked into the arms of a grey-faced policeman, his car incongruously white in the distance.

21

'What the bloody hell is going on?'

Brookes snarled as a cloud of dust, together with some larger pieces of plaster, fell all over him. Instinctively, he threw his forearms over the open wound on which he was working, but too late to prevent gross contamination of the red raw tissues. With eyes narrowed to protective slits, he looked up to see a jagged, deep crack traverse the whole width of the operating theatre ceiling. As he watched, the two halves of the ceiling moved on each other with a grinding, tearing crunch, sending down further showers of debris. This sound was immediately drowned by an awesome, booming explosion which left them all shaken and silent. The silence was broken first by the soft whimpering of the young swab nurse, cut off at a glance from Sister Kay.

'What the hell do you think that was, David?' Brookes spoke quietly, as if in a holy place. 'Do you think that was an earthquake?'

'I wouldn't have thought an earthquake would make a noise like that. Sounded more like a bomb to me. What shall we do with the rest of the list, cancel it?'

Brookes nodded. As Dai Jack left the theatre to reach the phone, Brookes turned his attention back to the problem under his hands. Fortunately, he had already closed the peritoneum but the wound was full of grey dust and larger pieces of plaster that he began to remove with dissecting forceps. The particles became so small that he could no longer pick them up.

'Give me something to irrigate with, please, Sister. After that I will want to leave some antibiotic in the wound.'

The muscle layers he sutured with interrupted stitches, leaving wide gaps

172

for the discharge he knew would be inevitable in a few days' time. The skin he left wide open, to be closed days later with the stitches he had inserted in the edges but left untied.

Brookes was peeling off his dusty, blood-stained gloves when David Williams returned through the anaesthetic-room door. Williams' Registrar was already disconnecting the patient's endotracheal tube and Sister Kay was clearing away the dust-laden drapes, her nose wrinkled in distaste. Across the activity, Williams called to Brookes.

'I've cancelled the rest of the list; told Sister to use her discretion about sending patients home if she thought they were fit to go. I haven't told them to come back next week; I don't think we will be operating in here for a while.'

Brookes turned his head to look where the anaesthetist was pointing. A large piece of concrete ceiling lay wedged at a precarious angle.

'What is going on outside, David?'

'Mostly rumour so far. Most people seem to think there has been an explosion at Teflo.'

The two consultants watched as the patient was lifted from the table and wheeled to the recovery-room. They passed through the theatre door into the corridor to see groups of housemen, nurses and orderlies whispering together in excited gossip. They were joined by Andrew Stafford-Wills, the senior orthopaedic surgeon who had been working in 'B' theatre, to become a slightly more select but equally ignorant group. Sister Kay put her head around the door, barked a command and several nurses and orderlies scurried back into 'A' theatre. Williams grinned at Brookes and returned to lounging against the corridor wall. He straightened and turned as George Harrington strode through the door at the far end.

Alison Barker's back felt as if it was breaking. She straightened painfully and looked around with some despair. They had a large garden, looked after in previous years by a gardener, sacrificed, like so many luxuries, on the altar of Larry's drinking. Her mood brightened at the sight of Robert and Jonathan Brookes, their O-levels behind them, animatedly discussing a technical problem in an old go-cart they had bought between them. Jonathan, tall, slim, clean and full of quiet serious logic, stood over a supine, oil-streaked Robert, blood trickling from knuckles injured in a furious attack on a particularly stubborn nut and bolt.

With a sigh, Alison bent her back once more. The tangle of bindweed, the target of her outstretched hand, survived as she was struck immobile by the noise of the explosion. She stared quizzically at the soil beneath her as waves of thunderous noise surged over her, eddying and swirling around her as they rebounded from the hills to the east. Smaller explosions seemed desperate to keep the cacophony alive but finally peace descended again.

Stunned by the suddenness of the noise, Alison looked to the sky, instinctively looking for thunder clouds. All she saw was a column of smoke just coming into view above the beech trees to the north-west. With increasing urgency, she walked, then ran, down the drive to the centre of the Close. There, plain to see, was a mushroom of smoke, the top only just beginning to be frayed by the wind, the base flickering and changing with a central incandescence.

She left Robert and Jonathan, gaping in silence, and ran back into the house to grasp at the phone. She did not get as far as to dial the number of Larry's office, the sinister high pitched whine emitted by the receiver only adding to her increasing sense of terror.

Slowly, she rejoined the two boys. They were arguing where the fire was exactly. Could they go and watch? A glance at her face quietened them and Robert was surprised by the force with which she pressed his dirty oily body to hers. With her other arm, Alison reached for Jonathan but he, with an embarrassed smile, stayed just out of range. They watched the cloud grow.

The button glowed instantly at the touch of Rothwell's finger. No need for the effort of actually pushing the device in this, the only modern block of offices Dunbridge possessed. As he waited for one of the two lifts, he looked at the plush entrance hall with smug self-satisfaction. When Heritage House had been built three years before, the TGWU had rented rooms on the third floor and it added to Rothwell's egotism to spend as much of his time as possible in their hushed, thick-piled modernity. Today he was calling to ask for a meeting of shop stewards at Teflo and those involved in the transport services. This nitrogen supply caper, he felt, was getting a bit hairy, like, and perhaps he could get the lads to change tactics, perhaps block supply of pyrites at the wharf.

Totally preoccupied, he entered the lift, pressed the plastic square for the third floor, and sensed the doors glide shut. After rising a few inches only, the lift stopped with a jerk and the lights went out. The void that Rothwell felt suspended in, shook and rattled as the shudder ran through the whole building. Calmly, he searched for and found the row of rectangular plastic buttons, systematically pressing each one in turn. If one was an alarm button, it did not appear to be working either. There was now the sound of hurrying feet and shouting in the hallway. High in the building, he heard someone screaming. Somewhere above the lift cage, he could hear the crackle of short circuiting electricity, sniffed its acrid smell. He started to beat on the door, to shout for help. It was several minutes before he got any response. Someone stopped long enough to say he would get help but did not return. The sweat of vocal and physical exertion in a closed humid box was now mixed with the cold sweat of fear. He removed his jacket and tie, breaking fingernails, a comb and two pens in quite illogical attempts to prise open the doors. After a period of sullen resentful silence, crouched in a corner, he attacked the door again with his fists.

He screwed his eyes up as the shaft of light split the blackness. A crowbar, wielded by a young man in dungarees, grated and scraped at the paintwork. With a loud snap, the doors broke free and Rothwell, pushing one door aside, jumped down to the hall floor. Without waiting for thanks, the man ran up the stairs, looking for the other lift. With eyes still aching from the sunlight, Rothwell stumbled into the street. Everyone seemed to be moving at twice the normal speed. He tried to stop someone to ask what had happened and someone finally flung the words over his shoulder.

'Explosion. Teflo.'

He listened uncomprehendingly to the wailing of police cars and ambulances, a puzzled look on his face as he was almost run down by a swerving taxi, a girl propped up in the back seat, blood pouring profusely from her neck.

With a sudden sense of purpose, he headed for the Fire Service Control Centre. He saw the bays all empty, the glass in the open doors shattered. It was a harassed controller that saw Rothwell rush in. He had never liked the bastard and he knew that, with Teflo wiped out, what little use Northweir Plant had been to them over the last few years, had gone also. He had little to lose.

'Sorry I couldn't get here sooner,' Rothwell said, breathlessly. 'Is there anything I can do to help?'

'Yes.' The controller faced him squarely. 'You can bugger off.'

Mary Jamieson leaned forwards between the two men to pour their coffee.

Beaupré's visit had been totally unexpected. There was still a month to run of the trial period set by Beaupré, and here he was, wanting to go back to Teflo, to be shown round again.

'What's the matter, Pierre? Don't you trust us?' asked Anderson.

'It's not that, John. I was over here on some other business, had a couple of days to spare. I've asked my top engineer to come over too; should be arriving tomorrow. I'm sure your boys up at Teflo won't mind; probably teach him a thing or two, I wouldn't wonder. Yes, sir. I thought I'd take in another round of golf while he's looking around. Why not come up with me, John? Do you good.'

'I second that,' Mary Jamieson said, from the other side of the room. 'I've been trying to make him take a break for some time. He's working himself to death.'

Anderson bestowed on her a half-vicious frown only to evoke a pouting smile in return. Beaupré felt that, had he not been there, she would have put out a pink, moist tongue at him also. He wondered, amused, whether Lady Anderson knew. Both men beamed as they watched her cross to answer the phone. Two men, at the peak of their power, secure in their wealth and position, shortly to bring about a merger that would raise eyebrows in Stock Exchanges around the world. Two signatures and a handshake, moulding thousands of lives, involving millions of pounds, would give them the orgasmic thrill felt by the compulsive gambler risking all on the spin of a wheel.

'Oh, my God! No!'

Beaupré and Anderson looked across the room to where Mary Jamieson stood at Anderson's desk. Startled, they fell silent until she spoke again.

'Oh, my God,' she repeated. 'Has anyone been killed?'

After a few seconds as someone replied, Mary Jamieson dropped the receiver on the desk, and slumped into Anderson's chair. Anderson was the first across the room.

'Mary, what has happened?'

The only reply he got was a gesture of the hand towards the telephone. Anderson picked it up.

'Anderson here.'

He spoke with the self-assured authority of a man at the head of an international business empire. As he listened, mute, Beaupré watched him shrink in stature. From erect, brisk, thrusting tycoon the metamorphosis to shrivelled, stooped, defeated old man was rapid and complete. He had already replaced the receiver, cutting off the metallic voice it was emitting, when he whispered 'Thank you.' As if walking in a trance, he moved to the window, his eyes trying to focus on the horizon to the north. Beaupré was at his side, trying gently to turn Anderson towards him.

'John. What has happened?' Beaupré asked.

'Gone,' was all Anderson could say.

'What's gone?'

'Wiped out. Teflo. Completely wiped out by an explosion. They think there will be very few survivors.'

Beaupré took the news with the genuine shock and sorrow that is felt at the news of a death in someone else's family.

'Jesus Christ, John. What went wrong?'

'No one seems to know. Just one big bang. The whole area is devastated.' With an effort, Anderson tried to pull himself out of the pool of trance-like inertia into which he had fallen. 'I must get up there. I must get a car. I must ring . . .'

His voice became choked as his face took on a look of surprise, of bewilderment. He pressed the pulps of his fingers against his right temple. With the smile of fear, he stretched his left hand towards Mary Jamieson but it refused to leave his side. He stumbled to his left for Beaupré to catch him and lift him, like a child, into his black, high-backed chair that Mary Jamieson hurriedly vacated. Within seconds he was unconscious, his chin on his chest, his tongue slobbering from the drooping corner of his mouth.

'Stay with him, Mary. I'll get a doctor and an ambulance.'

Beaupré strode to her office rather than use the phone on Anderson's desk. She heard him rap out orders to the operator at the switchboard. Then the door between the two offices closed softly and when Beaupré whispered the Toronto number, the operator had to ask him to repeat it.

22

The National Health Service frequently acknowledges its debt to the Victorians who built their workhouses so well. Dunbridge General Hospital was one of many which had stood the test of time, but the two-feet thick, solid stone walls of the outpatient department shook to their foundations as the shock wave reached them.

George Harrington's right index finger, suitably gloved, was searching the confines of a patient's rectum when the window alongside him shattered, showering him and his patient with fragments. Completely nonplussed, Harrington removed his finger with as much clinical decorum as he could muster under the circumstances. Gingerly, with his left hand, he removed several jagged glass slivers from the couch so that the patient could turn on his back once more. The whole ludicrous situation was retrieved by the patient's North Country humour.

'I trust that doesn't happen every time you examine somebody's back passage, doctor.'

Ignoring the sounds of confusion outside, Harrington washed, explained to the patient his proposed treatment for his piles, wrote a few notes and filled in a waiting-list card. Only then did he open the door leading to the waiting-hall. It was the first public sign of Harrington's steadiness that was to underpin the behaviour of the entire hospital staff during the hell of the next twenty-four hours.

The waiting-hall was large and graceless. Narrow, ugly columns supported the high ceiling with its chipped and dusty coving. Rows of tubular-framed chairs faced one end where, from wall to wall, ran the appointments desk and records office. A WVS canteen at the other end struggled bravely to bring some cheer to the drab surroundings. Large wooden double doors in one wall opened directly on to the street.

Harrington stepped out into an atmosphere of stunned fear. Patients, many of them aged, sat mute and frightened; children cried. The Outpatient Nursing Officer was escorting a WVS woman with a scalded leg to the casualty department. The first casualty. Along the far wall, a wide expanse of hideous tiles had been sheared off by the shock wave. A row of elderly patients, good-naturedly waiting on a wooden bench beneath, were rubbing their scalps, looking with surprise at the sticky scarlet streaks cloying the grey dust that covered their hands. Harrington turned on his heel, re-entered his consulting-room and lifted the telephone.

What he had played out so often in action-packed daydreams, yet always brought back to reality with a sense of disappointment, his heart racing, had happened. Now excitement left no place for apprehension. This time it was real. Over the phone he calmed an agitated switchboard operator and left her to make her prearranged list of calls. He returned to the waiting-hall and, standing on a chair, gave a few authoritative orders that produced order from chaos. Delaying only to tell Hook to get the Site Officer away as quickly as he could, Harrington then made his way to the operating theatre, striding purposefully through the swing doors to find the theatre staff in groups, gossiping excitedly, along the main corridor. He restrained an impulse to tell them to stop talking, smarten up, look lively. His pace

178

slowed as he approached the group centred around Brookes, Stafford-Wills and David Williams. Anything resembling an order to that lot might well result in an invitation to get stuffed.

'Red alert, Michael. The real thing, this time, it seems. You all know what to do, don't you?'

'Yes, of course, George.'

'What happened, George?' asked David Williams. 'It sounded one hell of a bang.'

'An explosion at Teflo. That's all I know at the moment. They just said very many casualties. Just how many, I have no idea.'

David Williams detached himself from the group and disappeared into the anaesthetic-room. They heard him call to Sister Kay. Harrington turned to his two surgical colleagues.

'Will you stay in "A" theatre, Michael, please, and you in "B", Andrew?' They both nodded. 'I'll keep a general surgeon in one theatre and an orthopod in the other until some sort of pattern emerges. I'd better have young Bond to help me with the triage at first. If we are overrun with general stuff, I'll put him in "B" instead of you, Andrew.'

Robert Bond had been appointed as DGH's third Consultant Surgeon only a month before. Well-trained at thirty-four, he had done the right jobs, written the right papers, made researches into the right animals, kept on the right side of the right professors, ultimately to be rewarded with the prospect of thirty years' hard grind in a small, peripheral hospital. Trained, perhaps; but inexperienced, certainly. What Harrington was saying was that, as yet, no one knew just how much ability lay beneath the arrogance of recently acquired knowledge.

Harrington's gradual assumption of command was tactful. Content that the theatres were ready and well staffed, he turned to go.

'I'll get back to outpatients now, Michael. If you need me, that's where you'll find me. And the best of British to you both. I think you might need it.'

When Harrington reached the waiting-area again, the floor had been cleared. Hook was supervising the stacking of the last chairs in the far corner. When he saw Harrington, he came across.

'All clear in here now, sir.'

'Well done, Mr Hook. Any sign of Mr Bond?'

'Not yet, sir. Having a bit of trouble finding him, I believe.'

'Oh?'

'Yes, sir. Seem to think he may be playing squash somewhere.'

179

'Squash? Did you say squash? At this time on a Thursday morning?'

'You're only young once, sir.'

Harrington grunted.

'And Mr Lithgow?'

'On his way, sir. He came in as soon as he heard the bang. He's gone off in his own car.'

'Wasn't there a police car to take him?'

'Apparently not, sir. All busy. But he took a copper with him.' He hesitated, not looking directly at Harrington as he added, 'Seemed a bit dodgy to me, sir.'

'Who? What?'

'Mr Lithgow, sir.'

'What do you mean?'

'Bit shaky. Know what I mean? Didn't seem to know where to go.'

'He'll be all right.'

'Yes, sir.'

But neither sounded convinced. Harrington looked at his watch. 'I wonder when they will start arriving.'

'Already have, sir. Casualty is heaving. Mainly small stuff brought in by taxis or simply walked in.'

'In that case, I'll . . .'

An ambulance screeched to a halt by the open doors.

'All right, Mr Hook. Get the Nursing Officer to report to me at once. Also get the Records Officer to follow me round with at least two of his girls to document the patients. When you have done that, come back and don't leave at any time without my permission. Right, off you go.'

He did not see Hook leave, his eyes already intent on the first stretcher load of blood-stained humanity to come through the door.

After Harrington left, Brookes sat, tense, in the surgeons' room. He picked up a nursing magazine left behind by the night staff and stared unseeingly at an article that had been some nursing tutor's pride and joy. He got up to pace the corridor restlessly, finally going in to theatre as he heard the sounds of trolley wheels rattling outside. In the theatre, David Williams was drawing up rows of syringes, Sister Kay was scrubbed and gowned, sitting impassively beside the green-draped trays of instruments. The swab nurse shifted from foot to foot, looking uneasily at Brookes. He wondered if she had been too frightened to ask Sister Kay if she could go to the loo.

Brookes went to scrub. There was a rush of footsteps outside, voices raised, trolleys colliding with doorposts. The door from the corridor to the scrub-room burst open and admitted a breathless, dishevelled Gareth Pritchard.

'First one on the way in, sir.' He breathed his excitement as he reached for a scrubbing brush. 'Just a closed abdominal injury as far as I can tell. Not much else wrong with him but he looks pretty clapped out. Mr Harrington has got Shah looking after some of the shambles in casualty so I'm afraid you are stuck with me, sir. Who's the anaesthetist?'

Before Brookes could answer, young Pritchard, looking through the glass panel between scrub-room and theatre, saw David Williams wheeling in a semi-naked torso.

'Dai Jack. Thank God for that.'

Brookes smiled at the mixture of respect and irreverent familiarity. He walked into theatre and waited while the anaesthetist and orderlies settled the patient in position. The anonymous body that lay before Brookes was filthy. The pallor of his face contrasted with the blood caked on his head around a small scalp wound. He still wore his shirt and one wrinkled woollen sock. Someone had put a drip in his arm without removing his shirt and Williams began cutting the sleeve to tear the fabric away. A huge man, his belly was distended, the stretched skin shining. Unshaven, his pubic hair shrouded crumpled genitalia. A narrow, linear third-degree burn ran obliquely across his chest where he must have lain against some hot pipe or metal bar. As Brookes painted the skin, the swab came away fouled with dirt and grease.

The early patients came in straight off the street. The two great emergencies, torrential bleeding and respiratory obstruction, brought their filthy indignity into the theatre, daubing the patients in pallor or cyanosis. The pretty sixth-former stripped near naked by the blast. The virginal spinster, her underclothes in tatters. With no time for the most rudimentary preparation, they were the head-on assault on the theatre team's senses. Their first patient died in a welter of blood almost as Brookes opened the abdomen. But sagging despair gave way to exhilaration as a tube in a flailing chest clawed back a moribund teenager. Slowly, as fatigue had its effect, the amplitude of their emotional swings damped down. Success and failure became as one. Raised voices, rushed movements, uncontrolled feelings of horror: all were subdued as the team strove to conserve its energy. Brookes became numbed to normal emotional stimuli. He was thinking that he would have made a much better job of exteriorising that bit of torn bowel if he hadn't been so rushed, when he felt a tap on his shoulder.

'All right you lot, out. Hop it. You've had your fun. Our turn now, George's orders.'

Brookes looked up to see Stafford-Wills' eyes twinkling at him over his mask. Thankfully, he stripped off his gloves and looked at the clock. Good God; five thirty. He had been operating since nine, had not eaten since an hour before that. He smiled wearily.

'Thanks, Andrew. About time you did a bit.'

'Seems there is a bit of a lull in the general stuff as both Lancaster and Preston are now doing their bit. George reckons we could well have a second wave later on. So I'd make the most of your break if I were you. It looks like being a late night. There's coffee and sandwiches in the rest-room.'

Brookes made his way to the staff-room, squeezing past trolleys, drip stands and portable X-ray machines, to sink thankfully into a chair. Too tired to change his trousers, he hardly noticed the cold wetness of blood-stained fabric against his crotch.

Jonathan. Dear God, Jonathan! He must ring to find out if he was safe. With dismay he realised he had not thought to ring before. And Alison. He knew they were in Shepworth. Surely the explosion could not have done any damage as far away as Shepworth? With sudden panic, he found a telephone only to be told that calls to Shepworth were impossible. Returning to the staff-room, he found Sister Kay in the chair beside him. With red swollen eyes, she looked away from Brookes as he sat down. Neither heard Harrington as he came through the door.

'I'm sorry, Michael. I'm afraid I've got another job for you.'

'What's that, George?' asked Brookes, looking wearily at a shining flushed face. 'Christ,' he thought, 'the man's enjoying this. Look at that smile.'

'They've found someone trapped by the arm out in Teflo. The mobile team is right the other end of town and fully occupied; Bond and Andrew are coping well with what's left here for the moment; so it looks as if you're elected. Do you mind, Michael?'

A wave of adrenalin washed away Brookes' fatigue. He rapidly downed the rest of his coffee and picked up a sandwich as he stood up. 'Not a bit, admiral.' There was enough sarcasm in his voice to wipe the smile from Harrington's face. 'Just tell me where I go and what I do. What about equipment?'

182

'Hook is organising your equipment and getting transport for you. Dai Jack is already there at the main entrance; so as soon as you can, Michael. I'm very grateful. You too, Sister Kay.'

'I don't suppose you know what's happened in Shepworth, George? I tried to phone just now but I was told they can't get through.' Brookes forced a matter-of-fact tone into his voice. 'You haven't had any casualties from Shepworth, have you?'

'None, Michael. I'm told both Westmere and Shepworth have escaped with a few tiles off the roof; nothing worse. Don't worry, Michael. I'm sure everyone there was quite safe.'

He turned to leave.

'And Michael.'

'Yes?'

'I think you've got time to change your trousers. Good luck.'

23

Although it was past six o'clock when they set out for Teflo, the sun was still warm through the windscreen of the police Land-rover. Brookes lowered his window, coughed and closed it again. A grin crazed the patina of dusty sweat on the young driver's face.

'Stinks, doesn't it, sir. You seem to get used to it after a while. I don't notice it any more.' With siren blaring, he cheerfully swerved his way through a traffic jam. Sister Kay, sitting between Brookes and the driver, steadied herself against the dashboard, while David Williams, lapsing into incomprehensible Welsh oaths, fought to protect some of his fragile equipment in the back seat. All four became subdued as they threaded their way with increasing difficulty through the outskirts of Dunbridge towards the coast road and Teflo. The roads, partially blocked by piles of rubble and abandoned cars, became more deserted the nearer they got to Teflo. Soon the twisted, blackened scene took on a nightmarish quality. The only movement was from small groups, usually centred around an ambulance or fire engine, burrowing under a pile of masonry or trying to reach someone stranded on an upper floor. Blanketing all was a silence and a stench.

The driver swore as he swerved to avoid a woman who emerged from the ruins of a house, arms outstretched in an appeal for help. The sight of the woman drew a sob from Sister Kay.

'I only hope this chap in Teflo is worth it.' The policeman's voice was bitter and accusing. 'Perhaps that woman has got a couple of kids under there but my orders are to get you lot to Teflo so I suppose that is what I had better do. All I hope is that she does not recognise me again when all this is over.'

Outwardly Brookes agreed with the young man. 'I know, it isn't easy, is it?' he said. Inwardly he was less sympathetic. 'Orders and anonymity. Lucky man.'

Shortly they broke through to the coast road and Brookes lowered his window to let in the fresh air from the sea. He put his head out to watch a rescue helicopter swish and roar its way inland. A crewman, standing at the helicopter's open door, waved to them. Withdrawing his head, Brookes tried to follow the plane's course by peering through the driver's window, leaning forwards in front of Sister Kay as he did so. He was appalled by what he saw. Monkey Island, less than a quarter of a mile away across the marsh land, was devastated. Even at that distance, it seemed very unlikely that anyone could have survived.

'My God, Sister, look at that.'

Sensing no movement from Sister Kay, he repeated, 'Sister, look at . . .'

Brookes stopped in mid-sentence as he saw Sister Kay's face, tears streaming from eyes that stared stonily ahead. Her crying was soundless, motionless except for the rattling of the Land-rover.

'Are you all right, Sister?' asked Brookes, feeling inept.

There was no reply and Brookes looked back at Williams who shrugged his shoulders. Brookes' left hand, as he offered her his handkerchief, was grasped by Sister Kay with a ferocity which produced no change in her expression, though her head began to tremble, neither did her rigid upright position change as he awkwardly tried to put his right arm around her shoulders.

The jerk as the Land-rover stopped at what remained of Teflo's main gate brought them all back to reality. Brookes heard snatches of conversation, 'Casualty far end . . . near flare stack . . . Impossible through the middle . . . Storage tanks eastern perimeter, leaking, likely to explode.'

The driver turned left towards the wharf and western perimeter, past the pile of rubble that had been the office block. As they circled the complex, it was with difficulty they picked out the roadways between the processing equipment, so hopelessly strewn were they with fallen towers and twisted piping. But the northern half of Teflo, though extensively damaged, at least had been spared the effects of the fireball.

When they reached the far extremity, close to the sandhills beyond, the driver pointed.

'There's the ambulance, sir.'

He pulled the vehicle to the right and drove alongside the flare stack as far as he could. Two ambulancemen approached them as they came to a halt.

'Good evening, Mr Brookes. He's along here.'

No time for pleasantries. Brookes and Williams followed one of the ambulancemen towards the crane while the other helped Sister Kay unload the equipment from the Land-rover. They could see the crane almost completely on its side, still held a few degrees off the ground by the boom enmeshed in the wrecked gantry. The whole crane was covered in debris, mainly from the absorption tower which lay precariously against the uppermost crawler track. It seemed to Brookes that one good push would bring the tower down and crush the crane's cabin like a tin can. Unable to pass to the left of the crane without going up to their thighs in foul-smelling marsh, they made their way to the right, under the sloping tower. When they reached the front of the crane, they saw a wrecked ambulance and a row of six blanket-covered bodies on the roadway leading back into the centre of the plant.

'Looks as if there was an accident here before the explosion. There were six dead around the ambulance and the crane. Seems they must have been trying to get someone out when it happened. That's why we took a second look at the crane and heard this guy groaning. We managed to get close enough to see he was trapped by his arm but that was all. I don't envy you, sir.' The ambulance driver pointed vaguely in the direction of the crane's cab. 'It's all very unstable, sir. I'd say that it is bound to go before very long as the road is still crumbling away in the flood water over on that side. How long do you think it will take you to get him out?'

'I'll give you a better idea when I've seen what is involved,' Brookes replied. Better not tell him that he could not remember when he last amputated an arm, indeed, when he had ever done it, he thought. He climbed on to the track and through gaps in the twisted boom to reach the driver's window, now only jagged fragments around the frame. Williams, fitter and stronger than Brookes, had already reached the cab. He gave Brookes a pull up over the last few feet. As both men held on to each other, the crane gave a lurch with a terrifying sound of twisting metal.

'For Christ's sake, let's get out of here, Michael. Where is the bastard anyway?' He wriggled his way further into the confined space, control levers digging into his back and thighs. 'I've got him; at least I have found his legs. He's outside, Michael. He's trapped somehow on top of the crane. He must have been caught as he was trying to get out. We had better get out again and climb up on top. Oh, bloody hell!'

'David? Are you all right?'

There was no reply from Williams for a moment. As he had struggled for a foothold to get out of the cab again, his shoe had sunk into Albert Crampton's paunch.

'There's another one down here.' Again there was a pause as Williams tugged and gasped. 'He's dead, I'm afraid. Been dead for hours by the look of him. Blast.'

'David?'

'It's all right. I just cut myself. There's glass all over the place down here. I'm coming out.'

As Williams struggled back through the window, Brookes swung himself up on to the steeply sloping side of the overturned crane. For the first time he had a true impression of the size of the tower that was now no more than a few feet above his head. Slipping on the smooth surface and finding footholds only on the surrounding mass of twisted framework, he finally came face to face with the trapped man.

Ashen-faced and only semi-conscious, Larry Barker smiled at Brookes.

It took several seconds for the facts to register in Brookes' stunned mind. Whether Barker was in any fit state to recognise him, Brookes could only but guess. Like a child going to sleep, Barker closed his eyes.

'Oh, my God, no,' was all that Brookes could utter, as he reached for Barker's right arm to find it disappearing, just above the elbow, under the sharp edge of a heavy length of angle iron. One glance showed that there was an almost complete traumatic amputation and that the limb was beyond saving. He looked round to find Williams kneeling by his side, one hand holding the distorted A-frame to keep his balance. He grabbed for the frame with the other hand as the crane gave another lurch. Barker gave a low moan and his eyelids flickered.

'It's Larry Barker.'

186

'Who?'

'Larry Barker. You must have met him; a member at the Royal.'

'Yes, I know him. Had a few beers with him. What will you have to do, Michael?'

'Take his arm off. It's the only way we are going to get him out.'

'Isn't he a neighbour of yours?'

'Next door.'

'Jesus.' Williams shook his head. 'How long will you need?'

'Five minutes. Ten at the most.'

'Fine. We had better get moving.'

'What will you use, David?'

Williams grinned. 'You stick to your job and leave me to mine. In that way we won't come to any harm. Let's get some stuff up here.'

They looked down to find Sister Kay and the ambulance driver no more than a few feet below them, the driver clambering up with Williams' case and Sister Kay laying out a few prepacked instruments in some semblance of order on the mud-encrusted crawler unit. She even produced a bottle of local antiseptic which Brookes massaged into his hands as a token towards sterility.

Williams cut and tore away at the coat and shirt sleeve on Barker's left arm. With a syringe in one hand, the fingers of the other hand swept the skin of the forearm. At a touch it was obvious that there was no hope of an intravenous injection, the veins collapsed and contracted like tight-woven string as a result of shock. He rapidly transferred the needle point to the deltoid muscle, plunging it deep into its substance. Larry Barker's lips moved in two silent words.

'Thank you.'

Brookes wriggled nearer to cut away the tattered clothing from the right upper arm. Handing the scissors back to Sister Kay, he took a scalpel in one hand, a large swab in the other. Sister Kay crawled up as close behind him as was possible. With a patience born of trust, he waited for a sign from Williams. 'Let me know when I can start, Dai. How long does it take?'

'About four or five minutes. After that you will have about fifteen to twenty minutes to play with.' He lifted one of Barker's eyelids, looked at the pupil and gently touched the cornea. 'In fact, I think you can press on.'

With the sounds of the water beneath the road and the creaking of the stricken crane filling his ears, Brookes needed no second invitation. One deep incision over the inner aspect of the arm, as close as he could to the girder, revealed the brachial vessels. Sister Kay exchanged the scalpel for a long curved artery forceps with the points of which Brookes decisively, forcefully tunnelled under the artery until they appeared the other side. He removed the forceps, opened the jaws and thrust one back through the space he had made. With the rasping sound unique to these instruments, the ratchet gripped as he snapped the forceps shut.

Holding the scalpel once more, Brookes passed his hand beneath, then behind and, finally, back above the arm so that the scalpel now pointed directly back towards him. With the *tour de main* of the barber surgeon, he cut boldly away, downwards and, finally, towards himself to sever the crushed limb completely. With the artery forceps still attached, there was little or no bleeding while Sister Kay wrapped the stump in a large swab and rapidly wound on a crêpe pressure bandage.

David Williams muttered, 'Well done, Michael.' The only words spoken.

Sister Kay swept together her instruments and slithered and slipped her way to the ground. Larry Barker was finally lowered, Williams at his head, protecting his airway, Brookes at his shoulders, and his legs held by a sickened but resolute ambulance driver. As Brookes and Williams walked beside the stretcher towards the waiting ambulance, Barker regained a degree of consciousness. With eyes rolling wildly, he became feebly restless.

'Poor bastard is having hallucinations,' said Williams. 'The big drawback with that drug.'

'What was that?' asked Brookes. 'I was most impressed.'

'Ketamine,' replied Williams. 'Bloody marvellous drug. Just the thing for this sort of situation; possibly the only thing. It doesn't matter if you can't get into a vein and you can give a second anaesthetic within a short period without much trouble. The only problem is the hallucinations they often get in the emergence phase. Rather like an alcoholic drying out.'

'That so? In that case he is travelling a road he knows well, poor devil.'

'That's right. I remember you telling me.'

He turned to help lift Barker into the ambulance and climbed in after him.

'I'll go back to the General with him. See you later, Michael.' A broad grin creased his face. 'Why don't you take Sister Kay for a walk on the dunes; do you both good.'

The doors of the ambulance were slammed shut and it disappeared along the perimeter road. Brookes, his hands still tacky with Barker's blood, looked for a pool of water clean enough to wash in. All the water he could reach, whether still or flowing, was covered in a film of oily scum and he cleaned his hands as best he could on a tuft of grass. The young police driver approached him, a new respect evident on his face.

'My instructions are to take you and Sister back to Dunbridge General, sir. I'm ready whenever you are.'

'Can you give us a few moments? Five minutes at the most.'

'Of course, sir.'

The driver climbed back into his seat while Brookes walked over to where Sister Kay stood near the perimeter fence, looking out to sea through its mesh. She did not move her head as he stood beside her, their backs to the plant and Dunbridge.

'It doesn't seem possible, looking out there, does it?' Brookes said quietly. 'Everything is so clean and fresh.'

'That's how it would all look if man hadn't reared his ugly head,' she answered, bitterly. 'There's nothing wrong with the world that man hasn't produced. What a pity we can't find some bacterium that's selective for man. Just wipe us all out. Leave the world to the so-called animals. What a beautiful place it would be.'

She did not move her head when she spoke again, her eyes still focused far out to sea.

'Do you think we could go back through Monkey Island?'

'I don't see why not. At least we can try.' Brookes looked at her enquiringly. He asked, softly, 'Am I allowed to ask why?'

'My husband is in there somewhere.'

'Husband?' Brookes' face showed total disbelief. 'Husband, did you say?'

Sister Kay smiled sadly at him. 'Yes, Mr Brookes, husband. Is that so impossible?'

Through his confusion, Brookes watched her face soften, the usual taut immobility of her features fall away, and, for the first time in all the years he had known her, he saw her as the strikingly handsome woman she was.

'No, of course not. It's just that . . . well, I had no idea.' Brookes blustered. 'What I mean is, how long . . . ? When did . . . ?'

'It's a long story,' Sister Kay broke in. 'Perhaps, one day . . .'

They both returned to staring out over the Irish Sea, their eyes now blind to the sunset. Brookes knew he only had to stay silent. It would come. He turned his head towards her with the stealth of someone anxious not to frighten away some timid creature. When she spoke it was with the slow soft clarity of a childhood catechism, though adult passion took over as she went on.

'My name is Kawalski, Anna Marie Kawalski.' She waited for pretty party dresses and children's laughter to clear from her mind. 'I am Polish. No, that's not true. I was Polish. I was born in Warsaw. My father was Professor of Anatomy in Warsaw before the war.'

This time the mental picture made her catch her breath; that bullet-shattered skull in Katyn forest.

'He must have been a very clever man, my father.' There was a trace of anger in her voice. 'But he made one big mistake. He married a Jewess. She stayed with him and what happened to her . . .' She finished the sentence with a shrug of the shoulders.

'My brothers and I,' Sister Kay went on, 'we were sent east to escape the Germans and ended up in one of Stalin's camps. Down south. We got out; my brothers got me over the border into Persia and then went back to join the partisans. Where they are now . . .' She gave another shrug before turning towards Brookes.

'Am I boring you?'

Brookes shook his head and said nothing. Sister Kay now looked utterly feminine, openly vulnerable. He felt he was managing things badly, that he should be holding her, comforting her. He was still wondering how anyone put their arms around one of the Sister Kays of this world when she moved a few steps forwards to hook her fingers in the mesh of the perimeter fence, her hands above her head. She let her arms hang there, her face close to the wire, her eyes opposite gaps in the mesh so that, to her, there would have seemed to be nothing between her and the fresh seascape beyond. All this she did with the easy movements of someone who had done it countless times before.

'After I got out – into Persia that is – I lived with this British Army sergeant. He looked after me. He was helping deliver supplies to Russia. Lorries and things, up through Persia. In the Queen's. Sergeant in the Queen's Regiment.'

Her eyes softened but there was no suspicion of a tear.

'He was a kind man. Kept telling me how nice it was, living in Ealing. I went to see the house once but I didn't go in.'

She paused as she wondered again whether she could ever have been happy behind that bay window, two-thirds the way down that long identical row.

'Six months later he was posted back to the desert. He took me with him.

190

We were married in Alexandria. He gave me his name and his nationality' – she took a deep, slow breath in – 'and, three months later, a war widow's pension. I don't even know where he was killed.'

'I'm sorry,' Brookes murmured.

Sister Kay unhooked her fingers and turned, smiling. 'Oh, I don't know,' she said. 'I could never really see myself as a Mrs Hockridge, could you?'

'Perhaps not.' Brookes smiled back.

'And then I met him.' Sister Kay's mouth and eyes hardened as she turned her back on the evening sun and nodded her head in the direction of Monkey Island beyond the blackened twisted remains of Teflo. 'I was a final-year student nurse in Dublin and he was a dashing young dental student. The Irish, you know, Mr Brookes – at least, some of them – they make marvellous boyfriends but dreadful husbands.'

'But how –' began Brookes, but Sister Kay didn't appear to be listening.

'We'd been married a year or more before he started . . . I tried. I really did. But when the baby died – cot death, they called it, though I did wonder –' for the first time she looked like cracking, 'then I left him.'

'And came to Dunbridge?' Brookes asked.

'Eventually. I went back to my real name, Kawalski. Can you imagine, Nurse Kawalski, in England? You English, you can never be bothered with foreign names so I became nurse K. And so, it was as Sister Kay I came to Dunbridge. To Dunbridge – where he found me. Drunk, ill and one jump ahead of the bookies' debt collectors, but he found me. I'll spare you the rest, Mr Brookes.'

Michael wondered if that was the end, whether they could now get away, as he sensed the police driver hovering even closer. But he was wrong. As she finally began to cry, he found himself holding her in an awkward, uncomfortable embrace. He saw the embarrassed policeman turn away.

'And I hope he's dead. That's what's so awful. That's how I felt as we drove here, when we saw Monkey Island. I tried to stop myself thinking, "Thank God, he's probably dead", but it kept repeating, over and over, in my mind. I couldn't blot it out. I still can't. And I feel so guilty. Sorrow fades, Mr Brookes; God knows I know that. All I hope is that guilt fades too.'

As she sobbed into Michael's shoulder, he began to walk her towards the police Land-rover.

'Come on. Let me get you back to hospital,' Brookes said, quietly, as if it was the only sort of comfort he could offer.

'But I must find out first.'

'Yes, all right. We'll try.'

The driver stepped forward, about to say something.

'Yes, we're coming,' Michael said, sharply. 'We want to go back via Monkey Island.'

'I'm afraid I can't –' The driver got no further.

'Monkey Island, I said,' Brookes snapped.

The driver took a long look at Sister Kay and back again at Brookes. 'Right, sir. I'll do my best.'

As good as his word, he struggled to get them as close as he could to Piggott Street, finally being brought to a halt at a police road block. A red-eyed and dishevelled police sergeant was terse and uncompromising.

'I'm sorry, sir, but no one is being allowed through now. We are as sure as we can be that there are no survivors in there now and there are gas leaks all over the place. We can't get any heavy lifting gear or oxyacetylene cutters in there until the gas has been cut off to the whole area.' He softened as he saw Sister Kay's face crumble. 'I'm sorry, Sister, if you've got anyone in there but, if you have, I don't think he would have known what hit him.'

The driver drove on, obviously moved as Sister Kay buried her head in Brookes' shoulder. With his arm around her, Michael felt the shuddering sobs.

'May God forgive me.'

24

Michael Brookes helped Sister Kay off the Land-rover and hurried into the outpatient hall. With a brief wave to Harrington, busy at the far end, he took Hook aside.

'I know how busy you are, Mr Hook, but do you think you could get a message through for me?'

'Where to, sir?'

'Shepworth. A Mrs Barker, Old Mill Close, Shepworth. Tell her her husband has been admitted, seriously injured.'

192

Hook pursed his lips, drew air noisily through them. 'Dodgy, sir. We've got a line permanently open for incoming enquiries but they are very few. I imagine the exchange must have copped it. It would probably mean using the police RT. Not popular for that sort of thing at the moment, sir. Difficult to make special cases.'

'It's important, Mr Hook. They are close friends of mine.'

'They would have to find someone the other end to take the message and they are fully stretched as it is.'

'I would consider it a favour, Mr Hook,' Michael persisted.

'Leave it to me, sir. I'll do what I can.'

In the theatre block the atmosphere was still busy but less frenetic than when he had left it. It was just after eight thirty. Brookes glanced through the windows to see Bond and Stafford-Wills operating. No panic. He took a shower, washing away the filth of Teflo, having to work hard to remove the blood dried in the hairs of his forearms and thighs. Only time would rid him of the acrid stench of scorched flesh that would linger for days. Without thinking, he pulled on fresh theatre garb rather than his clothes, sat in a chair and fell deeply asleep in seconds.

Apart from a sagging jaw, he had scarcely moved when David Williams shook him. He gave a snort as he woke, trying to moisten his dry mouth as his eyes opened and rolled blankly.

'Sorry, Michael.' Williams smiled apologetically as he leaned over Brookes.

'T's all right, David.' He yawned noisily. 'What's the time?'

'About half past nine.'

As Brookes grappled with reality, he saw, for the first time, Harrington standing behind Williams.

'Hullo, George. How's it going?'

'Not too bad, Michael. Over the worst, I think, unless we get another batch in. Mostly fracture work now.'

'That's great.'

'Michael,' Williams broke in, now squatting on his haunches in front of Brookes' chair. 'I'm afraid we have got some more work for you.'

Brookes sat forward, looked more alert, shook off vestiges of sleep, forced Williams backwards.

'Not a very pleasant case, I'm afraid.'

'All right, break it to me gently.'

'It's Larry Barker again.'

'Oh, Christ, no. Not him again.'

''Fraid so, Michael.'

Brookes looked up at Harrington. 'Do you know if his wife has come in yet, George? I asked Hook to find her.'

'I know. Not yet. They did get hold of her after a struggle. She must be on the way in but there was no sign of her a few minutes ago. But this can't wait, Michael. We must get on. I'll keep an eye out for her. I promise I'll look after her.'

Beginning to feel trapped, Brookes turned his attention warily to Williams. 'What's the problem?'

'I can't get him fit enough to have his stump tidied up.'

'I'm not surprised. He's an alcoholic. I told you. It's not long since he almost died from liver failure.'

'I know that, Michael, but there is more to it than that.'

'What?'

'We have given him blood but we just can't get his blood pressure up; in fact it seems to be making it worse as his venous pressure has been rising steadily. And then we found this small stab wound on the front of his chest; I must say we all missed it amongst all the other cuts and scratches.'

Brookes, the man, wanted no part in what was going on, did his best to pretend it was not happening. Brookes, the surgeon, reluctantly, inexorably put the evidence together and felt irritation as Williams spelt it all out again as if to a final-year medical student.

'Chest wound, falling arterial pressure, rising venous pressure, very quiet heart.'

'I know,' snapped Brookes, 'cardiac tamponade. But what the hell do you expect me to do about it? Haven't you put a needle in?'

That avenue of escape was also blocked.

'Yes, of course. Got pure blood but virtually no improvement.'

'Oh, shit.'

Brookes could picture what was happening in Larry Barker's chest. He must have a penetrating wound in or near his heart, probably due to a stiletto-sharp piece of glass. The bleeding was being contained partly by the pressure of the overlying breastbone but mainly by the pressure being built up in the pericardium, the glistening, lubricated sac inside which the heart moves as it beats. This sac was now becoming so full of blood that the heart chambers were being compressed by the pressure so that they could not fill when the heart relaxed between beats. Unless this pressure was released and the bleeding stopped, Barker must die. Of that there was no doubt.

'You are the only one here with any real experience of chest surgery,

194

Michael.' Harrington was firm and direct as he closed the ring around Brookes. 'I appreciate what we are asking you to do, particularly as he is a friend of yours. If I thought we could get a chest man here in time, I would gladly do so. If I thought I could do it better than you, I wouldn't hesitate. Unfortunately, there is no other real option, is there? I will explain to his wife what is happening. The least I can do is spare you that.'

'Where is he?' Brookes asked, sullenly.

'On the table.'

No time to go and read the books.

Jerkily, his mind flicked through what he remembered of his two years as a thoracic surgical registrar. Furiously, he tried to re-energise mental circuits that had lain dormant for twenty years. At that time, twenty years ago, cardiac surgery had still been in its infancy. Since then he had been into the chest only in his operations on the oesophagus. A tremor of panic passed through him. He knew what a limited exposure of the heart the usual lateral thoracotomy gave, so that at least he was prepared for the first question fired at him.

'What position do you want him in, Michael?' asked Williams.

'Flat on his back, please, David.' With a feeble attempt at a smile, Brookes added, 'God knows where the bleeding is coming from, so I had better split the sternum; if I can remember how.'

'In that case I'll go and start.'

Gareth Pritchard scrubbed up alongside his chief, high on excitement. No idle chatter now, as he sensed the strain in the older man alongside. Brookes' mind was in turmoil. He knew that time was important but dragged out the scrub a few minutes longer, a few extra minutes to try and compose himself and put the inevitable off a little longer. It was a great relief to see Sister Kay standing at the table.

With the surgical drapes in place, he looked up at David Williams to get an encouraging nod. With the suspicion of a tremor, Brookes took a wide-bore needle and passed it upwards and inwards behind the lower end of Barker's breastbone. Blood dripped immediately and he didn't bother to put a syringe on the end. He pulled it out.

'Not much doubt about that,' Brookes muttered, 'so here goes. Scalpel, please, Sister.'

A moment later the theatre staff looked up in surprise as Brookes said, 'Bloody hell!'

Blood welled from the congested veins on Barker's chest wall. 'We haven't a hope of stopping that.' He spoke urgently. 'Press as hard as you can on each side of the wound with your fingers. We will just have to accept it until the pericardium is opened. Sister, you keep the sucker going just ahead of me.'

He passed his index finger carefully but blindly through a pool of blood to open a tunnel behind the sternum. Inserting a jaw of a bone shears into the tunnel, he grunted and began to sweat with the effort required to split the breastbone from top to bottom. Two or three sharp cracks were heard as ribs cracked and snapped under the power of the screw as the retractor drove the two halves of the sternum apart. The tense, blue pericardium bulged through towards them. Brookes made sure that the essential instruments were to hand and then paused like some high jumper balancing himself both mentally and physically before a leap. He handed the sucker to Pritchard.

'As soon as I open the pericardium, you suck as fast as you can. Sister, you be ready to hand me whichever of those sutures I ask for.' With an obvious intake of breath, he added, 'Right, here we go.'

It took a few seconds only to slit the pericardium from top to bottom and the wound filled with blood. Pritchard plunged the sucker in but it seemed to be having little effect. Brookes waited as long as his straining self-control would allow but finally snatched the sucker from Pritchard's hand.

'For God's sake, give the bloody thing to me.'

With the sucker, he went searching for the source of the bleeding. Released from the constraining pressure, the heart began to beat more forcibly. A jet of brighter, redder blood appeared at the upper end of the wound. Brookes sucked at the area to get a better view. He heard and felt a small clot disappear into the sucker and, too late, jerked his head away as the thrill from a jet of warm blood hit him just below the chin. From instinct as much as from training, he stuck his left index finger over the bleeding point. It took a few more seconds of adjusting both position and pressure before the bleeding came under control. His finger still in place, he handed the sucker back to Pritchard, who cleared the remaining blood from the sac.

'Well done, Michael.' Words of comfort for the second time that day. 'I know it sounds a silly thing to say, but do you think you could keep your finger there, just like that, for a few minutes while I pour some blood into him? He's in desperate need of it and I haven't been able to give him any before because of his venous obstruction.'

Dai Jack busied himself with the intravenous drip, felt Barker's pulse and glanced at the trace on the monitor.

'His circulation is much better already; I reckon another couple of minutes and you will be able to carry on. His pulse pressure is much better. Must have been quite a tough sod in his day.' A grin spread beyond the confines of his mask as he added, 'For an Englishman.'

While Williams continued to force the transfusion, Brookes looked bleakly into the chest. There was the problem; it wasn't going to go away. He was stuck with it. No surgical seventh cavalry was going to ride through the door. He couldn't just take his finger off, say he wasn't going to play any more, and walk away. Remember those surgeons in the air raids when he was still a student? Hadn't he sworn he would be there himself one day? Bugger the surgeons, that's how he felt. His left arm began to ache. Although the pressure required was not great, the slightest movement of his finger in any direction caused a leak.

'For Christ's sake, Dai, buck up.'

The stab wound was not in the heart itself but in the aorta, just where it arose from the left ventricle. The blood which had leaked from it had collected in the pericardium, as this closed sac extended for an inch or more along the major vessels as they left the heart. If the stab wound had been an inch or so further along the aorta, with no pericardium to constrain it, Larry Barker would have bled to death in minutes.

Brookes' mind was so ready to slip off that razor's edge of concentration that would be essential. He wanted to think of anything but the red flood that was going to be released, had to be released, sooner or later, by him. He could put the moment off, ignore the faces that would look at him enquiringly, wondering why he did not just get on with it. He could govern when to take his finger away, stake all, over a time scale of seconds, even minutes. But, there were other faces, ephemeral, smiling, that floated between him and the wound; a beautiful woman, a tall, solemn young man; nebulous shapes that beckoned to him in a drifting world, luring him away from ghastly reality. Think of them tomorrow. Don't think of them now. Get this over, then you can let slip your mind. For the moment, look, see, sharp and clear. Come a week next Sunday, something would have happened; they wouldn't still be here. He would be having his Sunday lunch, time would have passed, all parameters stabilised once more. The man, pulsating under his hand, would be sitting up in bed, sore as hell, or he would be dead. All he had to do was concentrate. Do his best. If only he could concentrate. Voices from the past rang in his head; old chiefs near the end of their days; young contemporaries confiding their fears. 'Damn thing came off in my hand, superior thyroid, right in front of the Moynihan;

talk about bleed!' 'Wandered into this aneurysm; into it before I knew; stuffed a scrubbing-up brush into it in the end; packed it and got out; got a proper vascular wallah to do it a few days later.' 'Honestly, Michael, I was shit scared.' Each voice had a face.

'All right, I think you can go, Michael. I'm not going to get him much fitter than he is now.'

Brookes was tired. He had been working under pressure for over twelve hours, some of it involving physical strains to which he was now quite unaccustomed. He had eaten very poorly and fluid loss during the day had not been adequately replaced; a degree of heat exhaustion augmented his physical tiredness. Added to this, he was no longer a young man and the NHS had already had more than an average surgical mileage out of him. Now he was being asked to tackle a major emergency in a field of surgery he had left over twenty years before.

With a needle holder poised in his right hand, he fought to bring the finger stemming the flow of blood into sharp focus. As he struggled to control his mental turmoil, it began to show outwardly. Brookes' hand started to shake. He saw it shake; imagined everyone watching it. He flushed and a trickle of sweat ran down his back. Tense and jerky, the operation field not crystal clear to him, he inserted the first stitch into the aorta under his finger. With a word of warning to Pritchard he removed his finger. The wound in the vessel disappeared in a swirl of blood and Brookes, in a moment of panic, pulled viciously at the knot. The dark thread cut through the vessel wall like a cheese wire and Brookes looked in dismay at the loop of thread stretching free between his hands. After considerable further blood loss, Brookes regained control with his finger once more.

'Cut out, bugger it.' He straightened an aching back and looked across at David Williams. 'I'm afraid the hole is bigger than before, down at the lower end.'

'He's still not too bad, Michael. His blood pressure has come up remarkably well. Take your time.'

With just the right degree of reassurance, Brookes' professional pride came to his rescue. It drove his mind to think rationally. He must put the stitches in starting from the far end, getting Pritchard to control most of the wound with his finger as Brookes tied the knot. More relaxed, he slowly spelt out to Pritchard each move and soon found himself with two sutures safely inserted.

'I think one more will probably do it. It's going to need a bigger stitch to cover where the first one cut out. Once that is in, our troubles should be over.'

With confidence returning rapidly, Brookes took his finger away for the last time. He inserted the needle deeply and tied the knot swiftly but firmly. After a few moments, while blood spurted between the row of knots, the small gaps clotted and the bleeding stopped.

Brookes, Pritchard and Sister Kay watched intently for a few seconds more and then shuffled their feet and moved stiff joints in relief.

'Problem, Michael.'

The words, curt and incisive, went through Brookes like an ice-cold knife. He had his back to the patient, washing blood off his gloves in a hand bowl, when Williams' voice made him turn. He was suddenly weighed down by a weary premonition of defeat. Patient, colleagues, equipment, all passed before his eyes in a blur as he swung round and it took a few seconds for him to reassemble them into a rational picture again. With an anxious frown creasing his forehead, Williams was looking at the cardiac monitor. Without knowing accurately what he was looking at, Brookes also gazed at the dancing light on the cathode tube.

'He suddenly developed an arrhythmia, just after you finished. I'm afraid they look like ventricular extrasystoles to me,' Williams said.

Brookes looked down at Larry Barker's heart, laid bare before him. Instead of a steady, if rapid, beat, it now jerked erratically, some beats small, some large, all completely uncoordinated. As he watched, the pattern changed before his eyes, the jerks becoming a writhing motion for a matter of seconds and then all motion stopping altogether.

With his eyes still fixed on the monitor, Williams called, 'Cardiac arrest.'

With disbelief, Brookes stared at the lump of muscle lying flaccid in the centre of the wound. He fought against the inertia of fear and self-pity which dragged at him, slowing his reactions.

He heard David Williams repeat, 'Cardiac arrest, Michael.'

'I can see that, David, without all that bloody contraption,' he snarled.

'Make a note of the time, ten forty-five,' he snapped at Pritchard. 'Take it that the heart has now been stopped one minute. Call out the minutes to me. I'm now going to do cardiac massage.'

With his left hand under the heart, his right above it, Brookes began to squeeze rhythmically. If he heard Pritchard call out the two-minute mark, he showed no sign of it. The straight line on Williams' monitor changed to complexes never produced by the normal heart.

'Three minutes.'

There was no sensation of spontaneous movement under his hands, so Brookes continued to massage.

'Just hold on a moment, Michael. Let's see if there is any flicker.'

Brookes took his hands away and joined Sister Kay in willing the heart to move. Williams' eyes did not leave his instruments.

'Four minutes.'

'Nothing,' murmured Williams.

'Oh, Christ, come on.'

As Brookes grabbed the heart again and began massaging in desperate haste, Williams watched anxiously from the head of the table.

'Careful, Michael, or you'll perforate the auricle.'

'Oh, go to hell. Come on, you bastard, come on.'

'Five minutes.'

The House Surgeon was probably a few seconds late in his call as he breathlessly watched a flicker of movement return when Brookes relaxed for a moment.

'Ventricular fibrillation.' Williams turned and snapped at his Registrar. 'Lignocaine, quick as you can.'

'Let's have the defibrillator, Sister.' Brookes put out his right hand without looking up from the chest.

'I'm sorry, sir, but we don't have one; not a sterile one.'

'Six minutes.'

'Oh, shit.'

Over the years, cardiac massage by external compression of the chest had become as much a routine at Dunbridge as anywhere. Gone were the days of the dramatic slash across the chest and the plunge to squeeze the heart with unsterile hands. Gone also were the small electrodes needed for direct application to the heart.

'Hang on, Michael; don't do anything for a moment. I think it may be settling.' A tremor of hope ran through Williams' voice. 'It's still pretty irregular with some ventricular extrasystoles but at least he has got some form of circulation. I can even feel a weak pulse. Let's close him up and get him out of here while we have still got a live patient.'

The heart, now beating quite vigorously, disappeared as Brookes wired the two halves of the breastbone together again. He turned towards the anaesthetist.

'Sorry about the language, David.'

'Language? What language?' Williams grinned. 'Obviously you have never been at the bottom of a Welsh loose maul. Now that, my friend, is language.'

They both laughed but briefly.

'How is he, David?'

The only reply was a shrug of the shoulders.

'What about his pupils?'

'Dilated, I'm afraid.'

Brookes dragged the corners of his mouth down in a grimace of defeat.

'It's early yet, Michael. There's still time for them to improve. At least he is still alive.'

'D'you reckon?' murmured Brookes, as he tied the last skin stitch.

He looked down to see he was standing in a pool of blood. He took one long stride backwards on to a towel laid on the floor by a sweat-bedraggled nurse. He wiped the soles of his boots as if it were a doormat, as he watched Williams help transfer Larry's mass on to the trolley, to be trundled in to the recovery-room and the care of Henry Orme.

'Another customer for you, Henry,' Williams said, stonily. 'He has had cardiac arrest and a long period of massage. He still needs his stump tidied up but that will have to wait. It's the least of his troubles at the moment. His heart is still very irregular but at least he seems to have some sort of a circulation. There are no signs of him breathing spontaneously yet and his pupils are still dilated. So I think you will have to keep him on a respirator for some time.'

'I think we are capable of managing that between us.' Orme smiled with his lips only. 'I realise we are not front-line troops out here but I think we can look after the rest. I am sure you and Michael have done your best.'

Williams made a final check on Barker's airway and the supply of oxygen. 'One of these days,' he thought, 'I am going to hit that slimy little bastard.' Without further word, he left the recovery-room to join Brookes. Close friends; at ease with each other; members of that inner clique of consultants to be found in all hospitals. Restlessness competed with exhaustion. One moment the men sprawled in chairs, their speech clipped and disjointed; the next they paced the corridor, forcing themselves not to enter the recovery-room to feel pulses, lift eyelids, stare neurotically at flickering monitors. Shah helped keep a semblance of normality as Brookes discovered him removing a ruptured appendix from an eight-year-old, flattened by generalised peritonitis.

Brookes looked over his shoulder, smelt the old familiar smell.

'Best operation done here all day, Shah.'

Shah grunted, not impressed.

'You don't think so?'

Another grunt.

'I'm sorry you have been stuck in casualty all day. I expect you feel you have missed all the excitement.'

'Yes, sir.' Shah did not take his eyes from the wound as he sucked out the green, foul smelling pus. 'I would have liked to have been here.'

'I'm sorry the way it has worked out. I can understand how you feel. You could still get your chance. It may not be over yet. We may well get another wave if Preston and Lancaster fill up. But I still mean it about this operation, you know. You will never do a better one. Just think what you are doing. Without this operation she would be dead in two days. And now, what have you given her; sixty, maybe seventy years? Still one of the best operations we do, cardiac transplants and all.'

Michael left his Registrar muttering under his mask, patently unimpressed, to continue his aimless wandering. He saw Williams disappear through the recovery-room door and followed him in. Williams gently but firmly shouldered Orme from the head of the trolley. Orme, still smiling, stood a little to one side and behind.

'Any spontaneous respiration?'

'Virtually none.' Orme's tone hinted of satisfaction.

With an understanding look at Brookes, Williams said, 'Pupils still dilated, I'm afraid. I think we had better arrange for an EEG.'

'Already arranged.' There was no doubt now at the delight in Orme's voice. Michael felt his hackles rise. 'The machine is still here after another case earlier and the psychiatrist is on his way over to do it.'

His stride flagging with the weariness of defeat and failure, shoulders hunched, hands deep in trouser pockets, Michael paced the theatre corridor, jostled by increasingly irritable theatre staff. He stood aside as a trolley went by, heading for the recovery-room. On it a young boy lay, his head swathed in a crêpe bandage, both eyes closed with blue-black bulging eyelids. Blood trickled from one nostril. He was still attached to an anaesthetic machine and Stafford-Wills walked behind.

'What's he got altogether, Andrew?' asked Brookes.

'Nothing much except that head injury. He should do well but he's going to need a respirator for a while and I'm told you have just taken up the last one. Looks as if I may have to fight you for it.'

Stafford-Wills, big and burly even for an orthopaedic surgeon, smiled at Brookes. Brookes tried to smile back but failed. From the corner of his eye, he saw the psychiatrist enter the recovery-room, wearing his theatre garb in that indefinable way that immediately distinguishes visitor from *habitué*. Michael resumed his pacing as the electric clock in the corridor clicked its way into the next day. He did not see the psychiatrist leave. He could put it off no longer.

The scene as he walked through the recovery-room door was one he would be able to recall in minute detail and instantly, for the rest of his days. The neon lighting was ice-blue. The large flat, white clock on the wall showed a quarter past midnight, the slim second-hand sweeping the face silently. In the foreground, the young lad with the head injury was being kept alive by the anaesthetist and his machine. In the next cubicle lay Larry Barker, his shape unbalanced by the hollow under the sheets where his right arm should have been. Pearl-coloured, plastic tubing curved from his face to the squat, box-shaped respirator, the chromium-plated weight moving restlessly up and down, pushing Barker's chest in and out. Around the room stood several nurses, sensing a crisis. At the head of the trolley, Williams and Orme stood, festooned with rolls of broad shiny paper.

Williams looked up as Brookes came in. 'Flat. Not a flicker anywhere, Michael.'

Blurred by hopeless fury, Brookes' eye travelled along the flex to the plug in the wall. He strode across the room and pulled viciously at the plug. The regular beat of the respirator was replaced by the clatter caused by Williams as he rushed to Brookes' side. He replaced the plug and the respirator started to clack away once more. Both were now crouching by the wall.

'Michael, let's think about it for a moment.'

'Think? What is there to think about? The poor beggar is dead. Let him die in peace. Give the respirator to that kid over there.'

Brookes made a grab for the plug once more.

'Michael, just think what you are doing.'

Williams made as if to constrain him again but Brookes brushed his arm away. Unbalanced, Williams fell backwards in an undignified heap. By the time he had regained his balance, the plug had been removed once more and Brookes stood holding it defiantly in his hand.

The whole procedure was etched on Orme's preconditioned mind.

With a shrug of acceptance, Williams disconnected the respirator from Barker's endotracheal tube. He was not surprised to see feeble movements of respiration and the heart continued to beat. There followed over an hour of agonised watching as Barker's breathing became shallower and the neck muscles tugged at the tube in his throat. Finally, all movement stopped and his chest became silent. Tight-lipped and sad, Williams removed his tube, threw it in a wash basin in disgust, and pulled the sheet up over Barker's head.

25

'How much does she know?' Brookes asked.

He sat with Harrington and Williams in the surgeons' room, shortly after Barker's death had become corporal, not just cerebral.

'What have you told her?' he asked Harrington.

'I saw her shortly after she arrived, very soon after you had gone back into theatre, in fact. I told her everything up to that stage; told her about his arm being amputated; told her he had to go back to theatre.'

'Did you say why?'

'Yes.'

'What exactly did you say, George? I had better know. We need to get our stories straight.'

Harrington edged forwards towards Brookes, an opportunity for him to be at his avuncular best.

'My dear chap. There is absolutely no need for you to have to tell her. Let me. I'll do it. You've had enough for one night. Let me handle it.'

'Thank you, George, but no. I'll see her. Does she know I was doing the operation?'

'Yes.'

'And the amputation?'

'Yes.'

'What did you tell her about the second operation?'

'I just said that he was bleeding from somewhere near the heart, that he was a very sick man and that you were doing the only thing possible with a chance of saving him.'

'And how did she take it?'

'Well, you know her a lot better than I do, of course.' There was a smile on Harrington's face, reflected in Williams', which Brookes affected not to notice. 'I've met her once or twice before at parties in your house, in the old days.' He didn't like to say 'in Rosemary's days'. 'But I've never really got to know her. She's a remarkable woman.'

'What do you mean?'

'Well, there was no great show of wifely emotion there. Either that or she has tremendous control. It was almost as if it was no more than she had been expecting. In fact, the first two words I remember her saying were, "Poor Michael".'

There was open curiosity now in Harrington's stare. There must have been enough give-away expression in her face for even Harrington to notice. Williams grinned blatantly from ear to ear.

Brookes had often wondered just how much they knew. Decent, honourable, Senior Service George; even he must have wondered. Dai Jack certainly would have wondered, had joked about it, probing in a kindly way, asking him about his sex life, using his imagination, probably coming to more than the correct conclusions.

'As I say, a remarkable woman. She just asked a few very pertinent questions and then said, quite suddenly, "How can I help?"'

'Help?'

'Yes. So I handed her over to Mrs Richie and when I saw her half an hour later, she had her sleeves rolled up, shoving filthy dressings and clothing into rubbish bags.'

'Where is she now?'

'As far as I know, still in outpatients.' As an afterthought Harrington added, 'And I'm sorry, Michael, I forgot. She asked me to tell you that Jonathan was quite safe. He's staying with her son for the night.'

'Thanks, George.' Brookes stood up. 'Well, I'd better get it over with. What's the time?'

'About two o'clock, I think. Are you sure you don't want me to do it?'

'Sure.'

Harrington didn't look relieved; almost disappointed.

Michael changed his theatre boots for his shoes and threw away his paper theatre cap. He put on a white coat and, for no good reason, turned up the collar. His mask, forgotten and blood spotted, hung on his chest. He stood at the entrance to the waiting-hall and had difficulty in locating Alison across the animated disarray. She saw him immediately but he had to wait while she held a bottle high, a human drip-stand. Relieved of her bottle as the trolley was pushed away, she walked through the litter of catastrophe to reach him.

'How is he, Michael?' She allowed him only a fraction of a second's hesitation before she added, 'Is he dead?'

'Yes, he is, Lissa.'

She stood still, her eyes closed, in utter sadness. No tears, no sobs, no weeping. She stood in the attitude of total pathos that no mime could hope to match. Her face showed that depth of feeling that can only last for moments, seconds, within the limits of sanity. Her neck was blotchy red where the polo neck of a lightweight jumper had been rolled down against the stuffy atmosphere. The fine hairs on her forearms were matted in sweat. Crumpled slacks protruded from under the bottom of a green, disposable, plastic apron.

Michael waited dumbly until she reopened her eyes.

'We can't talk here. Let's try and find somewhere quiet in this madhouse.'

It proved embarrassingly difficult. Room after room was occupied by human flotsam left on the periphery, deposited away from the mainstream to look after themselves for a while. He tried door after door, Alison trailing after him, at times bumping into him as if sleep-walking. They finally found the dental surgeon's room, bare and dark one moment, all formica and glinting stainless steel the next in the glare of neon strip lighting. Brookes perched on the dentist's operating stool; Alison sat on the nurse's chair in the corner. Her knees parted and the apron slipped between them to reveal a thigh stained with someone's vomit. For a while she bent forwards, her elbows on her knees, her head in her hands. Brookes put out his hands to touch her but could not reach. He tried to shuffle the stool forwards but it was fixed to the dental chair.

He sat and watched her slowly come erect, brush the hair from her eyes, blow her nose. She turned towards him as if closing a door behind her.

There was no physical contact between them and she made no effort to establish any. The space that divided them was clinically cold, cruelly lit. Their conversation had nothing to soften it, no kindly ambience. It was just communication between two people physically exhausted, emotionally battered beyond breaking point; two people temporarily stripped of the kindly deviousness that, at other times, would soften words they knew must cut deep.

'And what about you, Michael?'

'Me?'

'Yes.'

'I'm all right.'

'It must have been pretty horrible for you.'

'Part of the job.'

'Part of the job, my foot. What exactly happened?'

'You know we had to take his arm off to get him out from Teflo?'

'Yes. George Harrington told me that.'

'He was trapped under a wrecked crane.'

'Yes, I know. I've already heard rumours about that. I've heard police and ambulance men talking; about an accident with a crane before the explosion. Is that where Larry was?'

'Yes, there was an ambulance amongst the wreckage. It must have been there before the explosion because the driver was dead. It was all tangled up and the crane driver was dead too. It was all quite horrible. Larry was actually up on the crane. We reckoned he must have been trying to help on the crane when the explosion happened.'

'And did Larry . . . ? Was he . . . ?'

'Conscious, do you mean?'

'Yes. Did he know you? Did he realise who it was who . . . ?'

'I don't know. I've wondered about that. He may have but I doubt it.'

'And was it you who . . . ?'

'We got him out between us. Dai Jack gave him an anaesthetic. He did not feel anything.'

'And the second operation? You did that too?'

'Yes. That was downright bad luck. He would probably have been all right except for that. A small sliver of glass had gone into his chest and punctured his aorta. Chance in a million. We had to go in to stop the bleeding.'

'And what happened exactly, Michael? I'm sorry to be asking you all these questions but I want to know. I promise you I'll never bother you again. Just tell me this once. How exactly did he die?'

Alison looked weary and dishevelled but in complete control of her emotions. Michael had not expected hysteria but wondered at the firm voice, the dry eyes.

'Well, we'd managed to stop the bleeding. We were feeling pretty good about it, actually. It hadn't been easy. And then he had a cardiac arrest. Just when everything was over. We managed to get it going again after a fashion. But it took a long time and he never got a really good circulation going again.'

207

'Did he die in the theatre?'

'No. He lived for a couple of hours. In the end we got a brain test done, thing called an EEG. I don't understand too much about them myself but we got a psychiatrist to look at it and he was quite sure that Larry had brain death. He died about an hour later.'

'Isn't life cruel?' Alison said, bitterly. 'I feel so sorry for him. He really was trying so hard to fight back. He was a changed man in many ways, Michael. It was remarkable; the way he had recovered from that other trouble. And then to be killed like that. What a stupid, bloody unnecessary way to die. And how awful for you. Incredible how you two were thrown together yet again.'

'That's one way of putting it, I suppose. I admit it has been strange. God knows, I've wished him dead many times over the last couple of years. But not like this. Why the hell couldn't he have gone off somewhere and done it quietly on his own? Why did he have to involve me? He was a bloody nuisance to me when he was alive and then drags me in at his death. I wouldn't put it past him to come back and haunt me.' He paused, half afraid of what effect his outburst would have on Alison. But he didn't give a damn. Were the dead the only ones who were going to get sympathy that day? 'I'm sorry, Lissa, but it seems a time for honesty, doesn't it? There's been no time for false emotions around this place today. Forgive me if you think I'm being callous.'

'I don't think you are being callous. Look at me. I feel I should be crying or sobbing or something like that. I hardly look the grief-stricken wife, do I? I have cried tonight, but not for Larry. There was plenty I saw out there tonight to make anyone cry. But then I noticed that all those who were doing something useful weren't crying. No. I just feel sad. If he had died up in London a couple of months ago, I wouldn't have been upset, just furious at a man destroying himself. But I am sad for him now; he was trying so hard.'

'What will you do now?'

'What you mean, Michael, is what will we do now, you and I?'

'Lissa, it's hardly the time to talk about that, is it? There will be plenty of time for that.'

'Will there? I'm not so sure. Perhaps this is the time to talk about it; when I'm seeing things pretty clearly. Another week or so and I may not be thinking so straight. As you said, perhaps it is a time for honesty. Death and destruction all around does tend to concentrate the mind, doesn't it?'

'What does that mean?'

208

'What that means, I suppose, is that I am getting out. It's been at the back of my mind for some time. I had a long time to think about it up in London. Yes, I'm getting out.'

'You can't be serious.' Michael looked appalled. 'What about us? What about that – that night? Did that mean nothing? I can't believe you can just turn that on and off.'

'That was two months ago, two months when I've hardly seen you. And I had already decided I couldn't leave Larry. He'd have been drinking again in a week. So I had already got used to the idea. No.' She beat her knee defiantly. 'I'm not going to be trapped again. I want a life of my own.'

'But where would you go?' There was something close to despair in Michael's voice.

'London.'

'London? Why London?'

'Why not? Adrian has been nagging me for ages; says I'm wasting my training. He's offered to help me get a job. He must have got lots of contacts. Why not? Why shouldn't I have a chance? Some feeling of fulfilment. A bit of social standing of my own, not second-hand. Like you've got around here.'

'Then why not get a job around here somewhere?'

'No. I've got to get out. I think it would be good for Robert too. Somehow I have an instinctive feeling that Larry had something to do with the explosion. I may well be wrong but, if that were so, just imagine being his son in the local school; in the same class as some of the orphans; maybe even a few empty desks; I couldn't ask him to face that. If that were true, I would have to get out anyway. But I think Robert deserves a new start too. He was spoilt rotten up until his grandfather died and, since then, he has known nothing but failure. I think it's time he had a taste of success for a change.'

'It doesn't sound as if I fit into your plans much.'

'What you want, Michael, is for us to wait a decent interval, get married and then I come and live with you.'

'And what's so terrible about that?'

'Nothing. That's the problem. The gentle trap; it's there, waiting. What you want is to settle back as you were, happy family, satisfying job, even your sex life sorted out this time. Well, I don't. And that's not true either. I want to be with you, live with you, love you. But' – the next few words were spoken slowly, emphatically – 'I am not going back to that fatuous bloody life I was leading.' She paused. 'I saw a child lose consciousness tonight;

right in front of my eyes. Other women took her away, doing something useful, constructive. And what did I do? Stood there, intelligent, composed and absolutely bloody useless. That's what I have become over the years. And it's not going to happen again. I love you, Michael. I love you very much. You probably won't believe me any more; but I do. But I am not going back to that life for you or for anyone. I am not going to be stifled again, suffocated.'

'For God's sake, stop being so dramatic,' Michael snapped. He wondered how much more he could take. He was so bleary with fatigue he couldn't believe what was being said. 'Suffocated. Stifled. You know it wouldn't be like that.'

'Oh, yes it would. You might turn out to be worse than Larry. You're so conservative.'

'Me? Conservative?' Michael's voice rose in genuine surprise and anger.

'Yes,' Alison replied. 'How can I be sure that you don't just want another Rosemary to look after you.'

'That's ridiculous. I just want to be with you. I wouldn't hold you back.'

'Then come with me.'

'Come with you?'

'Yes. Come with me.'

'Be reasonable, Lissa. You know that's impossible. Middle-aged surgeon trying to get a new consultant post; in the London area at that.'

'Impossible?'

'Well, very, very difficult.'

'Well, have a go. What have you got to lose by trying? You wouldn't have to give up your job here while you were applying. There's no real risk involved. Come and live with me in London. A fresh start for both of us.'

Michael shook his head slowly from side to side. He felt impotent, emasculated. He was a sufficiently reasonable man to see her point of view. He also felt the full force of a powerfully calculating personality he had never suspected before. And he knew that he would never have the courage to do what she had suggested. He realised, as he tried not to listen, that loneliness, once more, was inevitable.

26

The reason for Stephen Gracie's perplexity was plain to see. It stood out against the silver-grey sheen of the stainless steel draining-board where it rested in morbid isolation. The russet-coloured muscle with its striation like coarse grained wood, glistened, moist with the tap water he had used to flush away the post-mortem clots. It lay there, had lain there through several subsequent autopsies, refusing to go away, demanding recognition, challenging Gracie's integrity.

Normally, at eleven thirty on a beautiful Saturday morning in July, he should have been around the tenth green at the Royal Westmere. As it was, two days after the explosion, he had just started his fourth post-mortem with as many still to come as he felt inclined to do or capable of doing. Apart from the sheer numbers involved, there was an added pressure on Gracie to cut away at his grisly workload. The cold-storage facilities at Dunbridge General were quite inadequate to cope with the number of bodies waiting, and high summer was not the time to have corpses, many of them mutilated and burned, lying around for long.

The previous day had been taken up with autopsies on those casualties who had been brought in dead or had died soon after admission. Now many corpses had surgical incisions, some, all hope abandoned, roughly pulled together in the haste of getting to the next case, others quite neatly sutured in the unfulfilled hope of recovery. One such grey, disinterested-looking cadaver that morning had belonged to one Laurence Barker. It was his heart that was causing Gracie's disquiet.

Stephen Gracie was a general pathologist of the old school; one of a dying breed. Although served by an army of technicians, the buck, be it histological, or bacteriological, or haematological, or biochemical, stopped there, at his desk. If he were to die, he could not be replaced except by a histologist and a bacteriologist and a haematologist and a biochemist. They didn't train Stephen Gracies any more. Dunbridge was getting its pathology on the cheap. Yet his accuracy in all his departments was the linchpin of the hospital's entire clinical structure. If he saw black, he must report black. If he saw white, he must report white. If he saw grey, or any shade of it, he must say so; express his doubts, give his reasons for those doubts. But. When he saw nothing but clear-cut black and white and desperately wished it were grey?

Gracie stood aside as his post-mortem room attendant moved forward to reconstruct some degree of humanity out of the empty shell that Gracie had produced. He was drawn back, inexorably, to that lump of flesh, mocking him, inviting him to throw it away, pretend he had not seen it. He leant against the draining-board, propped by outstretched arms; his hands, covered in fouled rubber gloves, rested on the cold metal. His mind travelled back two hours.

The luggage label attached to the string tying both big toes together had identified the naked corpse as being that of Mr Laurence Barker. A hospital number below had been his only epitaph. Gracie had read the clinical notes after checking the number against that on the label. Externally the post-mortem lividity and multiple abrasions had been obvious, as had been the absence of the right arm from above the elbow. He studied the long midline chest incision, neatly closed with a row of black thread sutures, but he wondered if he would have overlooked the tiny separate puncture wound in the chest if he had not read the notes. On opening the body, he had noted the recent loss of body fat but, apart from some evidence of cirrhosis, he had found no evidence of disease. When he had come to the operation site, Gracie had taken extra care, removing the heart and great vessels without disturbing anything likely to be of importance.

He had laid it on a dissecting-board, manoeuvring it with prods and pulls to lie as it would have done inside Larry's chest. He was not surprised to see the small petechial haemorrhages, confluent in places, together with downright bruising. That was only to be expected after internal cardiac massage. He had also noted the neat row of black sutures on the front of the aorta as it arose from the left ventricle.

'Poor bastard,' Gracie had muttered, but whether he had been referring to patient or surgeon, who was to know?

Deft slices with a long-bladed knife had laid the heart open to show normal healthy valves. With movements made automatic by long-standing routine, Gracie had begun to make small transecting cuts along the lengths of the coronary arteries. Two in number and, broadly speaking, supplying the front and the back of the heart, they branched from the aorta

212

immediately it arose from the heart. In fact, Larry Barker, despite the way he had maltreated his body, had had the supple arteries of a man of twenty. Gracie had then turned his attention to the row of stitches Brookes had put in the aorta. Carefully, almost stealthily, he had cut along the length of the aorta down as far as the suture line. The large size of his instruments had made it difficult to cut the tiny sutures but finally they had been removed except for the last one, that nearest the heart. He had cursed softly as, with the aorta laid open, he had searched beneath the aortic valve with a probe to find the mouth of the coronary artery. There had been no doubt that the last remaining stitch had passed round the artery, almost completely occluding it.

Gracie had straightened his back and sighed, his eyes still looking hopefully for some other explanation but finding none. What now? Forget it? Ascribe the cardiac arrest to the initial damage, the period of tamponade? Hell, perfectly healthy adults were known to drop dead from cardiac arrest and have a perfectly normal heart at autopsy. Forget it. Drop it in the bucket. Who's to know? But Gracie had known he couldn't. And the death certificate? Cardiac arrest due to coronary occlusion due to surgical ligature? He had known he couldn't write that either.

With gum boots slapping against his shins, he walked into the tiny office adjoining the post-mortem room, where his secretary typed furiously at her small, inconvenient desk.

'Would you see if Mr Brookes is in hospital. I know it's Saturday but it's not the usual sort of Saturday, is it? If he is in, ask him if he could come down and see me before he goes.'

Gracie was half-way through the next post-mortem when he looked up to see Brookes at the door. Coming in from the summer sun, Michael felt the chill air on the back of his neck. He saw an attendant sewing up one corpse on one table, Gracie delving into someone's cold chest at the other. He walked towards Gracie's table. Although the floor had been swabbed clean, Brookes could not overcome the compulsion to walk on his toes, his hands deep in his white coat pockets as if to avoid contamination with anything he might touch.

'Good morning, Stephen. Keeping you busy, I see.'

'Good morning, Michael.' Gracie smiled. 'How are you? I imagine you have had a pretty hectic time these last two days?'

'You might say that.'

'Been rough, has it?' Gracie sympathised.

'Bloody rough, I don't mind admitting. Still, the worst seems to be over. You don't seem to have been exactly idle yourself.' He peered over the body that Gracie was eviscerating. 'What's the problem?'

'Oh, nothing with this one, Michael.' Gracie scooped up a jumble of viscera on to a wide shallow tray, giving a grunt as he lifted the weight on to the dissecting bench. 'It's this over here.'

He led Brookes down the room to where Barker's heart lay. He saw that the attendant had closed the other body.

'I think it's time you went for lunch, Tommy. Leave that until you come back. I'm sorry to make you work on a Saturday afternoon.'

They waited until the attendant was in the changing-room, out of earshot, before Gracie started again. The slight air of secrecy in Gracie's manner brought anxiety to Brookes' face.

'Something wrong, Steve?'

'Not really. Just something I thought you might want to see.' Gracie's voice was diffident, embarrassed. 'I'm sure it's just one of those things that happen but I thought it would be wiser to let you know about it.'

He picked up Barker's heart and spread the aorta wide with his two thumbs.

'It's that suture there that concerns me a bit, Michael. I haven't removed it so you can see it as I found it.'

Brookes leant closer, his eyes focusing on the small black thread loop as Gracie, once again, tried to pass a probe down the coronary artery.

'Just won't go, I'm afraid. I rather think that stitch has occluded the right coronary, at least virtually occluded it.'

'Enough to kill him?'

'I rather think so, Michael, yes.'

'Nothing else there?'

'Not really.' Gracie turned the heart over, running his thumb along the coronaries, opening up the cuts he had made. 'His coronaries were remarkably normal for a man of his age.'

'There's no sign of an infarct, Steve?'

'Wouldn't really expect to see one, Michael. Not so soon.' Gracie reassembled the heart as far as was possible, smoothing the surface with his fingers. 'How long did he live after the operation, roughly?'

Brookes screwed up his lower lip. 'Few hours.'

'Yes, well you wouldn't expect to see anything. The patient has to survive for at least twenty-four hours for there to be any naked-eye signs of an infarct. It takes twelve to eighteen hours for even histological evidence.

214

No,' Gracie shook his head regretfully, 'I'm afraid that doesn't mean a thing.'

There was silence broken only by the sound of the rattling typewriter.

'So what does all that add up to, Stephen?' asked Brookes, stiffly.

'I have to say, Michael, that the immediate cause of death was a coronary occlusion due to that ligature.'

Once again Gracie had been put in the position of having to give one of his closest friends a cold scientific opinion which he knew would hurt and sadden. And again, just as two years previously, he felt as if he had abjectly failed to soften the impact. He did what he could to help Brookes accept the inevitable.

'I don't see why you should be too upset about it. It's all right for me down here. I operate under the deepest anaesthesia you can get.' He waved at the corpse the attendant had just sewn up. 'Look at the size of the incisions I can make. If I cut an aorta across, what the hell, who cares? What you fellas do through the incisions you use still amazes me. How you manage to stitch up the living aorta at all beats me. I reckon this guy was lucky to get as far as he did.'

A smile of gratitude tweaked at the corner of Brookes' downturned mouth.

'Thanks, Steve.'

There followed a pause that Gracie could find no words to fill. There seemed to be a flat, self-pitying fatalism to the words that ended it.

'So what goes down on the death certificate? What's the official cause of death?'

'Och, no problem there, Michael,' Gracie said, encouragingly. 'Let's see. Cardiac arrest due to operation, due to penetrating wound of the heart. How about that?'

The relief on Brookes' face waned a little as Gracie went on.

'I'll have to record it in the PM findings, of course. I can't just pretend it never happened. But I don't see why the whole wide world should know about it. We normally put a copy of the PM in the clinical notes but, as you know, they often go astray. There'll be no need for this one to go in. I'll ask Pat not to. And my copies are always filed away under lock and key.' Gracie hesitated. 'The Coroner will have a copy, of course,' – Brookes looked at him sharply – 'but I don't see that there need be any trouble. If he picks it up, I'll have a word with him. He's a reasonable enough chap, old Ralston. Bit of a dandy, but he's all right. I'm sure he'd understand, under the circumstances.'

'God, I hope so,' Brookes sighed.

Gracie searched in his mind for some sympathetic way of ending the interview. Visions of the queue of corpses waiting outside flashed before him. But Brookes seemed reluctant to leave.

'Christ! After all that.' Brookes gave a short bitter laugh. 'After all that, I go and put one lousy stitch in the wrong place and kill the poor sod.'

'Rubbish,' Gracie retorted, too tired himself to be in any mood to listen to conscience-stricken surgeons. 'If you want my honest opinion, that man was killed by a bloody great crane falling on him. You did your best and if you have just found out you're not God Almighty, then you are going to have to live with it.'

Moments later, a remorseful Gracie watched Brookes leave the post-mortem room without another word. With a gesture of irritation, Gracie picked up Larry Barker's heart and tossed it into the vacant chest of the corpse he was examining. Who was to know, amongst those standing reverently around the grave, exactly where Larry Barker's heart had finally come to rest?

27

On Thursday, 18 July 1974, Larry Barker was buried. The funeral took place quietly at Shepworth's parish church of St Michael's. There was a creditably professional tone of sincerity in the rector's voice, giving almost an impression of personal involvement, considering that Larry Barker was the fifth resident of Shepworth he had interred that day and that Larry had not seen the inside of St Michael's, even at Christmas, for the last five years of his life. The undertakers were not quite so successful. It was a short-lived boom in a competitive market and shuffling feet and anxious glances showed they were keen to be off.

Alison, dressed in black except for a magenta silk scarf, stood erect at the graveside. Her face showed no emotion as the coffin was lowered into the shallow grave, hastily dug along with many others during the previous three days, around the fringe of the normally neat churchyard. To her left stood Adrian Barker, dressed with the uniformity of the upper echelons of the legal profession. His cold right hand was cupped under Alison's left elbow, the best he could offer in terms of physical comfort. To her right, Alison felt the warmth of her son's body as he pressed against her, his face frowning with the transient intensity of youthful grief. At a respectful distance stood Ivy and Bill Rothwell, Ivy sobbing quietly into a tiny handkerchief, Bill viewing with dismay the fresh-dug clay sticking to his gleaming black shoes.

Jonathan Brookes, his dark suit a size too small for him, stood apart, completing the group. He had not been sure whether it was permissible to smile at Robert, had backed away, embarrassed, from Alison's out-stretched hand. He stood alone, listening to the handfuls of soil rattling on the coffin like flurries of hail on a flat roof. At the first sign from the rector that the proceedings were over, he made his own escape, and it hurt Alison to see his young back disappear amongst the trees.

The rector regretted he could not come back to the house, so busy at the moment; he would call and see Alison soon. Perched on the edge of her chair in the Barkers' lounge, Ivy began to cry again as she watched Robert handing round the sandwiches; he was so like his father. Adrian Barker found no difficulty in showing complete disinterest in anything Bill Rothwell had to say, finally driving him into silence with a frigid intellectual snobbery that left Rothwell mute but impressed. Rothwell would have liked another whisky but he wasn't asked and finally, reluctantly, he and Ivy left. It only remained for Alison to drive a dour brother-in-law to Preston to catch his train.

The case on his knees bulged with briefs he could not wait to get back to, and his left hand hovered over the door handle as Alison brought the car to a halt. He turned his head towards her.

'You'll give me a ring?'

'Yes, I will.'

'Don't leave it too long. Don't go changing your mind.'

'No. I won't do that.'

'Come and stay with me while you are looking for a place to live. There's nothing left here for you now. Just tell me what you want; central London, the City, somewhere outside?'

'Oh, not in the centre,' Alison said, hastily, panic in her voice. 'Some-where near a good school. I was thinking of a day-boy in a good public school. Doesn't have to be a public school. Any good school. Apart from that, I don't care where I go.'

'It'll be assistant solicitor. I can't do better than that. You can't expect anything better with your experience. If you want a partnership, you'll have to work for it.'

'I realise that, Adrian, and thank you.'

He opened the door, put one leg out and, for the first time, smiled the smile that reincarnated his twin.

'Get out now, Alison, while you can. You'll do well, you wait and see. You'll never look back.'

PART THREE

Inquest

28

Henry Orme's obsession was respirators; to be more specific, the humidifying of the gases inhaled by the patients on respirators for any prolonged period. Many methods had been tried and found unsatisfactory, but Orme was convinced that the future lay with introducing water broken up by ultrasonic vibrations. The method was proving so efficient that Orme was concerned that patients were at risk of being drowned.

All the respirators at Dunbridge had been modified to Orme's specifications and the accident at Teflo had given a sudden boost to his statistics. The time had come for him to sit down and analyse what part his respirators had played. It was just before Christmas when everyone else seemed to be enjoying themselves. He tended not to be invited to all those departmental Christmas parties. Resentful and isolated, he tried to convince himself that he'd rather be working on his research.

It was nearly six months after the explosion. Dunbridge General was functioning normally again. Structurally, there were still a few scars, a shored-up ceiling here, a boarded-up window there. But what could not be seen, only felt, was a new sense of pride. Dunbridge General had been tried in the fearsome light of national publicity and not found wanting.

The new camaraderie did not extend, however, to Orme and the clerk in the pathology department office. The girl made no attempt to cross the room when she saw him at the desk.

'Good morning, Janet. Have you been a good girl and found those PM reports I asked you for?'

Sullen-faced, the girl crossed to the desk, reached under it and dropped a pile of papers untidily in front of Orme. She became engrossed in a split finger nail as she leaned against the desk, the sharp edge furrowing across her skirt. The list of names and numbers Orme had given her the previous day lay on top of the pile. He ran his finger down the list, finding it difficult to concentrate.

'One missing here, Janet. Laurence Barker. You haven't ticked him off.'

'I couldn't find no report on him, Dr Orme. Quite sure he's dead, are you?'

The other clerks behind her sniggered.

'Do me a favour, Janet, there's a good girl and look just once more. I've got his PM number if that's any help.'

'No point, Dr Orme. I tell you, there's nothing there under that name.'

The girl was inclined to turn away but Orme's expression changed.

'This man died. There's been an inquest. There must have been a post-mortem. There must be a PM report.'

'Mrs Fielding, Dr Gracie's secretary, will have one but they're away in Preston today. He's giving evidence. But I know she keeps all the reports special for him.'

'Where?'

'In her office.'

'D'you know where she keeps them?'

'Yes.'

'Come on then. Let's go and find it.'

'What me? Go into Mrs Fielding's office? You've got to be joking. I can't go into her office just like that. She'd kill me.'

'I'll put it right with her, if she ever finds out, that is. Don't worry, I'll take the blame.'

'If you say so, Dr Orme.'

Half an hour later, Orme was back in his room, having confirmed during that time all the rumours the clerk had heard about his gropings. He dropped the pile of post-mortem reports, Laurence Barker's now on the top, on his desk. He sat and gazed abstractedly at them. Why didn't he go to the theatre party? He knew it had just started. He knew he didn't have to have a formal invitation. He only had to walk in; take a bottle. That's what everyone else did. Why didn't he go, have a drink, loosen up? Who knows what it might not lead to, all those nurses, staff nurses.

Automatically, his mind full of fantasy, he picked up Barker's report and began to read it.

There was every chance, too, that none of the bastards he really disliked, Williams, Brookes, Harrington, would be there. They would be at the opening of that new extension to the paediatric ward by some fellow from Teflo, another party he had not been invited to. He could see them all, smiling, making speeches. The bastards.

But something else was trying to dislodge the picture from his mind. Orme was so engrossed in his self-pity that he was reluctant to let it go.

Eventually he became aware it was something he was reading in the post-mortem report in his hand that was clamouring for attention. He flicked the page back and looked at the name on the top, Laurence Barker. Just below, the words 'cardiac tamponade' caught his eye. That was enough for someone with Orme's memory. Of course, now he remembered. That was the case where those two Lord Gods Almighty had ended up on the floor, fighting for the plug. Very undignified. But what had he read to make his normally wet-lipped mouth feel dry? Something must have passed subliminally before his eyes to excite him. Without knowing why, he got up and locked his door as stealthily as the noisy catch would allow. Back at his desk he read the report again, word for word. There it was, in the section on the cardio-vascular system. He turned the form over to compare what he had read with the copy of the cause of death as given on the death certificate.

Got them, he thought; got the bastards. His heart thumped noisily and he wiped sweating palms on his thighs. Accidental death, his Aunt Fanny. He imagined Gracie in the witness box. Accidental death, yes; but whose accident? That bastard Gracie, he was just like all the rest. He must have told Brookes, the miserable sod. Well, Brookes had better be nice to him now.

Orme slipped into his favourite world of fantasy where alone he found friendship, peace, success, physical satisfaction. That precious piece of paper would become the means to get even with that bunch of provincial clods who persecuted him. He felt warmed by the sense of power that knowledge gave him. His delusions took him through a score of triumphs against pillars of Dunbridge's establishment. It culminated in an orgasmic vision of himself, alone against the world, denouncing Brookes and Gracie from the witness box. As he fell away from this climax, his insight and intelligence slowly took over from his paranoid wanderings. He knew he wouldn't have the guts, that the facts would remain locked away in his introverted impotence. But it would be fun, he would quite enjoy it, talking to Brookes, to Gracie, knowing their little secret. He locked Barker's report carefully in his desk, went out and headed for the operating theatre.

The room zig-zagged in dancing spectral lights, as Jeremy Whitlam's migraine drilled upwards from the nape of his neck. He had just opened the new mother and baby unit that Teflo had donated to Dunbridge General. Nitromid's senior PR man had politely impressed on Teflo's new Chairman the importance of good community relations if Teflo was ever to be rebuilt.

Where better to start, he had argued, than in the children's ward just before Christmas?

Whitlam had made a speech, competing with the piercing screams of a two-year-old with earache. The local photographer had been there to capture the moment for posterity and there had been a certain amount of jostling by the Mayor of Dunbridge and William Rothwell, the Community Health Council's new Chairman, to get close to the great man in the group photograph. The medical and nursing staff who had felt the full impact of Teflo's disaster, had mixed feelings about the plant being rebuilt and it showed. The Consultant Paediatrician had stood reluctantly on the fringe of the group, refusing to remove his white coat, as if to disassociate himself from such humbug and a staff nurse, widowed by the explosion, had thrust the bawling two-year-old in Whitlam's arms to spray the muco-pus, yo-yoing from his nostrils, over Whitlam's Savile Row lapels.

Whitlam was now increasingly aware that the hospital was going to get the maximum publicity from his visit, and if at first he had nurtured any hopes of escape, he had reckoned without George Harrington.

'Now all the formalities are over, I'd so like you to meet some members of staff, and have arranged a few drinks over in the Boardroom. Particularly like you to meet the surgical side who took the brunt of it.'

How could he refuse? Not to be denied, Harrington propelled Whitlam along the dreary corridors, followed in convoy by the other worthies, to find the Boardroom almost empty. Having forced Whitlam to choose between gin and tonic, cheap cream sherry and orange squash, he turned and whispered fiercely to Gracie.

'Stephen, where the hell is everyone?'

'Still at the theatre party, I imagine.'

'For God's sake go and dig them out, there's a good chap. A bit embarrassing to say the least. Make sure that Michael and Dai Jack come. And make sure you come back too. I need help with Rothwell. He's got Teflo's Chairman, our Chairman and the Mayor all together under one roof. God knows what he might get up to.'

Gracie squeezed his way between the noisy groups that packed the theatre staff rest-room. Trolleys, draped in Government Property sheets, supported stainless-steel dishes which normally held items rather less appetising than peanuts and crisps. In one corner, two staff nurses, their faces flushed beneath the tinsel in their caps, dispensed from a wide choice of bottles. In the other corner Gracie found Brookes and Williams. All he saw of Brookes was his back, Williams and Sister Kay appearing to be pulling at his arms. Brookes was speaking loudly and it was only when he turned as Gracie tapped him on the shoulder that Orme was revealed, wedged in the corner, cowering.

'Come on, you two, you're wanted on deck. Admiral George's orders. He needs your help in the Boardroom.' Gracie had to shout to make himself heard. 'He's got the new Chairman of Teflo there and the Mayor and God knows who. Come on, come and do your stuff.'

'Right,' Brookes snapped. 'Come on, Henry, m'boy. On your feet. Come and meet the top brass. You probably weren't invited but never mind, I'll look after you. New Chairman of Teflo, did you say, Stephen? He's there, is he? I'd like a word with him; tell him what his bloody explosion did to us all. Come on, Henry.'

Roughly, he pulled Orme out of his corner and the babble of conversation hushed as a path was made through the throng to let them cross the room and out. Brookes' voice rang clearly back down the corridor as they disappeared.

'Now then, Henry. This habit of yours of pinching bums. If I'm going to make a proper consultant out of you, it's got to stop, d'you hear? Got to stop. Been spreading your favours around the path lab recently, my spies tell me. That true?'

Gracie and Williams stood for a moment before following them, embarrassed by Brookes' behaviour.

'What the hell's got into him, Dai Jack?' Gracie asked. 'Is he pissed?'

'A bit,' Williams growled, 'but no more than I've seen him before. Never seen him react like this before. Seemed to start with a couple of snide remarks Henry made. Don't quite know what he was on about but it certainly got Michael all steamed up. Whatever he said found a raw spot somewhere. What I do know is that if he had said to me just half of what he said to poor old Henry just now, I'd have thumped him.'

'No, you wouldn't.'

The quiet words came from Sister Kay, standing at their elbows.

'Oh?' Williams smiled at her. 'What do you think's the matter with your favourite surgeon then?'

'The man's lonely, that's all.'

'Oh, come on, Sister; as simple as that?'

'Simple as that, Dr Williams.'

'But, I mean, Rosemary has been dead now, how long is it?' He looked enquiringly across at Gracie. 'Must be all of two years now. He must be over that now. He wasn't like this six months ago.'

'I think the Teflo business took more out of him than we think,' Gracie said. 'He took a real hammering that day.'

'No.' Sister Kay shook her head. 'He's lonely. Christmas isn't the best time of the year for lonely people. A lot of them are glad to see it over and done with. And perhaps he has a particular reason for feeling lonely this Christmas. He'll be all right. Leave him alone. Just be patient with him.'

'What's this, Sister? Feminine intuition?'

'Call it what you want, Dr Williams.'

'Well, well.' Williams grinned across at Gracie, looking for support but finding him serious faced and intent on Sister Kay. 'I never took you for a romantic, Sister. You're going to tell me next he's suffering from a broken heart.'

'I'm surprised you took so long to consider the possibility, Dr Williams. I was given to understand the Welsh were an intuitive race.'

The sight that met Brookes as he entered the Boardroom sobered him, and he discarded Orme. Rothwell was emphasising a point with his index finger on the Mayor's chest, making his chain dance. Stafford-Wills was feigning interest in something the new Area Chairman was saying. In a moment, Brookes' mood swung to one of sullen, watchful mistrust as Harrington beckoned. He was still sufficiently in control of his feelings to realise that he had overreacted to Henry Orme's nasty little digs, made rather a fool of himself. What had he meant anyway, the oily creep? What had he been going on about? 'Nothing is what it seems, is it, Michael? Everyone has his little secrets, hasn't he?' What was going on in that nasty little mind? Something about him and Alison? And now this chap from Teflo, looking so smug and prosperous. How he had the nerve to turn up like that after what Teflo had done to them all. But he must take a grip, behave himself.

'Michael, I'd like you to meet Jeremy Whitlam, Teflo's new Chairman. Jeremy, this is Michael Brookes, one of our senior surgeons.'

'One of, not the, you'll note, Mr Whitlam.' Brookes nodded in Harrington's direction and the three men laughed nervously.

'What you mean is that there's only one boss around here, is that it? Keeps you at it, does he?'

'Regular slave driver.'

There was more nervous laughter and sidelong unwelcoming glances as Rothwell joined them.

'Well, I still think any organisation works better when there's an element of master and man about it, even in the unions.'

226

If Whitlam was hoping for any kind of reaction from Rothwell, he was disappointed.

'Good thing there was only one boss when the casualties started rolling in last July, eh?'

Deprecating noises came from Harrington as Whitlam put his arm on his shoulder.

'When are you hoping to reopen Teflo, Mr Whitlam?' Brookes asked, irritated, jealous.

'We haven't even the roughest date as yet. It's going to take a long time. All we are sure of is that Teflo will reopen. We appreciate how much Dunbridge depends on Teflo for employment, and we're anxious to convince everyone of our intentions to reopen just as soon as it is safe to do so. We will have to wait for the findings of the Court of Inquiry, of course, before approving any new plans. If there are any lessons to be learned from the Court's findings, obviously they must be incorporated into any new plant we build. We must make sure another holocaust like that never happens again.'

Brookes felt he had been on the receiving end of a well-prepared, oft-repeated speech. He felt resentment at the man's confidence.

'I suppose that'll mean another fleeting visit from royalty to this far-flung outpost and an odd knighthood here and there?'

'Could be. Could be.' Whitlam was unperturbed. 'Could be also that there will be a few honours flying round Dunbridge before then. I imagine there'll be quite a local demand for newspapers come 1 January.' Once again Whitlam put his hand on Harrington's shoulder, letting it drop with a dramatic slap. He laughed out loud at Harrington's red-faced blustering.

'You must be joking, Jeremy,' Harrington stuttered unconvincingly. 'Most unlikely. Even if it did happen, it would simply be recognition for a marvellous team effort. I hope everyone will, would, see it in that light.'

'Congratulations, George, you old bastard. What did they do? Look into our mortality rates and you came out top? What does that mean for me? Deportation to a penal colony, perhaps?' A note of the old bitterness returned and Rothwell's eyes darted in Brookes' direction.

'Rubbish, Michael. You took the full brunt of the early severe injuries. By the time I got to theatre, the heat was off. You were front-line defence. You were bound to get the worst of it.'

It was the first time in five months that Harrington had been able to get through Brookes' defence and talk about the accident. Unlike most of his colleagues, Brookes had seemed loath to talk about the catastrophe, had shied away from the subject whenever it was raised, almost as if any mention of the part he had played made him ill at ease. But his reaction to what seemed genuine concern on the part of Rothwell surprised even Harrington.

'Had a bad time, did you, Brookes?' asked Rothwell.

'Bad time, you say? My God, Rothwell, you should have seen us. It was rugged, I tell you. Bodies to the right of us, bodies to the left of us. Up to our ankles in blood. Scalpel in each hand. Saved them all, of course.'

There was more awkward laughter in which neither Brookes nor Rothwell joined. Harrington made an excuse to move Whitlam on, and Brookes curtly turned his back, leaving Rothwell striving not to wince at the spasm of pain that pierced him, high in his belly. Strange, he thought; that pain didn't usually go through to his back like that. He really shouldn't let that man Brookes get under his skin. But to him, Brookes epitomised the old-style consultant, autocratic, superior. Most of the consultants had, at least on the surface, grudgingly accepted more and more lay management of the hospital. But not Brookes. He still remembered his medical superintendent father, whose word had been law. His hostility had been shown by an attitude of cold aloofness which had riled Rothwell from the start. Then there had been Sheila and the baby. Rothwell had never forgiven Brookes about the baby. That still rankled. He should never have got away with that.

'Squeezed you out too, have they?'

Rothwell had barely noticed Orme leaning alongside the drinks trolley. He seemed an odd bod, a non-entity, an outcast from his own tribe. Not someone to bother with if there was someone more important in the room.

'Come and join the club. It doesn't hurt so much once you get used to the idea.'

'No one squeezes me out if I don't want to go, young man. Orme, isn't it? Seen you in medical staff meetings.'

Rothwell took a second look at the lean sardonic figure and instinct told him that a few minutes' chat with this malcontent could be rewarding.

'Your glass is empty, Dr Orme, and you look like a man in need of a drink. Can I get you summat?'

Orme handed his glass over as if he did not care much what Rothwell put in it. Rothwell put his nose to the glass, smelt gin and poured a large measure followed by a little tonic. He made no comment as Orme took a wide-mouthed gulp.

228

'I'd have thought you had all qualifications to join that little lot over yonder, Dr Orme?'

'Qualifications? I've more than that lot put together. But then, I imagine you have this sort of problem in the unions as well. Don't tell me you don't have your élite, your little supreme soviets? I don't imagine your General Secretary stays in a boarding house for the annual conference.'

Rothwell laughed. 'True,' he said, 'but we like to think that only those with ability get to top. Tha can't tell me that doesn't go in medicine too?'

'Balls. Academically speaking, I could make rings around that lot of buggers. No, that's not the answer. There's got to be more to it than that; nothing to do with ability. Either you've got it or you haven't. If you haven't, there's no point in working on it; only seems to make things worse. Best just to go off and do your own thing. Me? I just sit back now and enjoy myself, hating their guts.'

'It certainly seems you have to belong if you want to reap rewards.' Rothwell fuelled Orme's burning resentment. 'There'll be no medals for the likes of you and me.'

'What d'you mean?'

As Rothwell repeated Whitlam's hints about the New Year's Honours List, Orme became increasingly agitated.

'Christ. Just imagine that lot with their OBEs and MBEs. How many do you think they'll hand out?'

'Difficult to say,' Rothwell answered, 'but I suppose there'll be one for heads of all the major departments involved. There'll certainly be something for administrator and I suspect that surgeons will do rather better than anaesthetists, as usual.'

'That's for sure. God, if they only knew.'

The words were ground out from the back of Orme's throat. Rothwell clutched at them but the thread of conversation he wanted to hold snapped.

'What d'you mean exactly?'

'Nothing,' muttered Orme, falling silent.

Rothwell thought for a moment and tried again. 'Tell me, Dr Orme. I've often wondered. What happens in an operation? Who's boss? Happen you have differences of opinion at times, like everyone else. Who has final word?' He got no more than a bitter sound from the back of Orme's throat as a reply. Orme took another mouthful of gin as if to wash it away as Rothwell persisted. 'I always get impression surgeon's boss. He does, after all, take more responsibility like, don't he? Only fair then that he should get reward, don't you think? What's Harrington, surgeon or administrator?'

'Both. Well, let's say an administrator who does a bit of surgery now and again,' Orme sneered.

'So, not surprising if he got major award then. Couldn't really give all surgeons something so they'd probably stop at Harrington. Who's boss of your department?'

'Williams.'

'So he'll get one too, probably, a bit less than Harrington, I fancy. Wouldn't it be interesting,' Rothwell mused, 'if, having done a lot of the work together, Williams got a gong as an anaesthetist and Brookes, the surgeon, got nowt?'

Both Orme and Rothwell fell silent as, following a burst of laughter from near the window, Brookes crossed to the bottles alongside them. Brookes stretched his arm between them to pour himself the remains of a bottle of tonic and returned to his friends. At no time, by word or gesture, did he acknowledge the existence of Orme or Rothwell.

'God forbid that bastard should get anything.' Orme almost spat out the words.

'Why not?'

'It's a good thing you people don't know everything that goes on in theatre.' A picture of Brookes and Williams fighting for the respirator plug filled Orme's mind. 'Very undignified at times.'

'Happen everyone has summat to hide. Difficult to go through life without making mistakes. Doctors can't be any different. And I respect way you doctors stick together. Times when I wish we were as solid in unions. But it must be difficult at times, 'specially if you've any kind of conscience. What does tha say?' The temptation to dive for the secret that Rothwell now knew to be close under the surface was almost unbearable, but he gave his fish a little more line. 'Brookes seems like a man with a conscience. It was interesting. He made some crack about mortality rates earlier on. I wonder what he was thinking about.'

He had to wait a while as a sense of power and alcoholic bravado channelled Orme's thoughts. Orme leaned confidentially towards Rothwell. It was several gins ago that Orme's back had left the wall and he tottered, moving his feet to give himself a wider base.

'This fella, Laurence Barker, wasn't he your boss at Northweir Plant?'

A rising inner excitement made it difficult for Rothwell to make his reply sound matter of fact.

'Yes, he was. I was foreman. What about it?'

'Now, there are some case notes that make interesting reading,' confided Orme. He winked and put his free index finger along his nose, the movements slow and clumsy with gin-induced uncoordination. 'Quite a best-seller if that little story was all told. It would make my day to see Brookes cast as the villain for once, not always the bloody hero.'

'But Brookes did a bloody good job in getting Barker out from that crane, by all accounts. Saved his life at that stage, so they say.'

'Let's just say it's a pity he didn't leave well alone at that stage.'

It would be difficult to say which came first, Rothwell's failure to contain himself any longer or Orme's realisation that he had already said too much. Orme put his glass down as if he had smelt cyanide. The vindictive look on his face was replaced by the old familiar apologetic smile. He looked longingly at the door. Rothwell saw it and moved to block his escape, his head thrust forwards aggressively, his features grim and determined. Gone now was what little subtlety Rothwell possessed, reverting to the attitude of the blunt, forthright Yorkshireman he so favoured.

'Orme, I insist on knowing what went on in theatre that day.'

'Nothing. There was nothing. Forget I ever mentioned it.'

'As Chairman of the Health Council, I have a duty to patients in my area. If case in point was my employer, I have double responsibility. If tha will not tell, then I must find out some other way. It's my duty. I'll not rest until I do, I tell thee.'

Orme was almost cringing. 'Excuse me, I must go.' He made a bolt for the door, brushing Rothwell aside with the outside of his arm. Off balance and surprised by Orme's strength, Rothwell was brought up short as his shoulder hit the wall. He stood for a moment, oblivious to the curious stares of those around him. Ignoring everyone, he followed Orme into the corridor, walking slowly, his eyes narrowed in thought.

29

'Shepworth 720743.'

'Can I speak to Mr Michael Brookes, please?'

'Speaking.'

'Good evening, Mr Brookes. Bill Rothwell here.'

'Good heavens. Good evening. How are you?'

'Mustn't grumble, thank you. And you? Have you had a good Christmas?'

'Not too bad, thank you. Very quiet, of course, with only the two of us. I shall be glad to get back to normal again, though. Christmas goes on too long these days for my liking.' Michael wondered what on earth Rothwell wanted, damn sure the call had nothing to do with the season's goodwill. 'What can I do for you, Mr Rothwell?'

'I'm right sorry to bother you but I wondered if you could help me. I just can't get Teflo accident off my mind, especially over Christmas. I can't help thinking about accident with crane, the one that killed my boss. That were a terrible thing and it still worries me that it might not have happened if I'd been there. And conscience does make cowards of us all, tha knows.'

Brookes simply couldn't believe the penitent tone of Rothwell's voice, it was so out of character.

'I won't argue with you there, Mr Rothwell.'

'Like I said, it's been worrying me for months but seemed worse over Christmas. I'd be grateful if you could put my mind at rest.'

'If I can.'

'Where exactly did you find Mr Barker?'

'He was trapped by his arm on top of the crane, or rather on the side, I suppose, as the crane had toppled over.' Michael was still unsure where this conversation was leading them.

'D'you think he was actually in the cab when it went over? I'd not have allowed him to do that.'

'I have no way of knowing, really, but I wouldn't have thought so from

232

where we found him. I don't think you need worry too much about that.'

'Was it much of a job to get him out?'

'Well, as you know, we had to take his arm off to free him but, after that, there wasn't too much to it.'

'You people are all t'same; you always play things down. Happen you had quite a rough time really.'

Michael began to find Rothwell's manner nauseating.

'That's very good of you to say so, Mr Rothwell, but it really wasn't as difficult as it sounds.'

'And he was alive when you got him back to hospital, I understand?'

'Yes, that's right. He didn't die until several hours later.'

'That was a great shame, weren't it, having got him so far an' all. They tell me you had to operate on him again. Is that right?'

'Yes.'

'So, what did he actually die from, Mr Brookes?'

'Exactly what was written on the death certificate, Mr Rothwell.'

'That's as may be, Brookes, but lesser mortals, like myself, are not allowed access to such documents.' The voice at the other end began to harden, become more the voice Brookes knew of old.

'They've all been produced in the Coroner's Court.'

'I know that but what I'm interested in is what really went on in that second operation. I doubt if everything is written down on death certificate.'

'I'm sure I don't know what you're getting at, Rothwell.'

'Don't you? Then let me spell it out.' Rothwell's voice was back to its normal grinding strength and Michael's breath quickened as his temper flared. 'What I want to know is what exactly it was you found at second operation? I have a feeling everything was not quite straightforward.'

'Everything relevant has been produced in open court, Mr Rothwell. I have no intention of discussing a patient's clinical details with anyone.'

'Barker's dead. He's hardly likely to object.'

'It's possible to invade someone's privacy even after death. Even the dead have rights, you know.' Michael's hand tightened around the phone and his words became pinched as anger tightened his throat and jaw.

'I realise that, but whose privacy are you really worried about, Brookes? Barker's or yours? You'd best take heed. I'm not the sort of person who likes to throw his weight about but you'd better take heed. I'm going to get to bottom of this. I'm not without power now in medical world. We're very

233

concerned in Community Health Council as to what goes on in our hospital.'

By now the mutual bitterness and hostility were quite open. Michael's fury was at a peak but he determined to let Rothwell know that threats would not make him shift his position one iota.

'I don't give a tinker's cuss if you're the bloody Pope, Rothwell. You can do what you damn well like. Good night.'

'Morning, Mr Rothwell. Nice to hear from you.'

'Morning, Whittingham.'

Rothwell found great satisfaction in using his position as Chairman of Dunbridge's Community Health Council to cut through layers of secretarial defences to speak directly to the Area Medical Officer.

'What can we do for you, Mr Rothwell?'

'I'm looking for some information about a patient at Dunbridge General that we're interested in. I wondered if you could help?'

'Of course, if we can. What's his name and address?'

'Laurence Barker, Old Mill Close, Shepworth.'

'Wouldn't have thought there were many social problems in that part of the world.'

'It's no social problem, leastways not in accepted sense of t'word. The man's dead and I want to know why.'

'I see, Mr Rothwell. Is this a personal enquiry or on behalf of the CHC?'

'I'm enquiring in my official capacity as Chairman of Council. We have every right to take an interest in one of our patients, dead or alive. I've tackled surgeon involved already, but as you might expect, I got nowt out of him.'

'So this patient had an operation?'

'He did.'

Whittingham's attitude changed immediately, became more defensive. A weary look came over his face, as if he had been through all this many times before. His voice did not change but his manner became politely obstructive.

'And, no doubt, you've discussed this in Council and you're acting on behalf of the members?'

'As Chairman, no one instructs me, Whittingham. I don't need approval of members for this. I can take action if I think there's any urgency and report back,' Rothwell retorted.

'But why this particular patient? How long ago did he die?'

'He was my boss and he died in explosion. More precisely, he died in your Dunbridge General Hospital and I've reason to think there was something fishy about his death. I warn thee, I'm going to find out truth.'

'But that means he is subject to the adjourned inquest. That alone means we can do nothing to help you until that court has reached its verdict. I'm sorry, Mr Rothwell.'

With stubborn tenacity, Rothwell pursued an able administrator's nimble mind. 'Bloody rubbish,' he growled. 'That's no reason why I shouldn't be allowed to see his notes. After all, they are patient's notes and he's not around to defend himself. Someone has to look into it for him. You have no right to refuse.'

'That's not strictly correct, Mr Rothwell. The notes don't belong to you, the doctor looking after him or even the patient himself. In law, they belong to the Secretary of State and his legal rights are invested in us, here at the Health Authority.' He paused. 'It may save you a great deal of bother, Mr Rothwell, if I were to tell you now that there will be no chance of any clinical details being divulged by this department. Incidentally, what makes you think that there is anything of interest in these notes?'

Though he knew that he had got nowhere, Rothwell was pleased to have the last word.

'That, Whittingham, is confidential.'

'Shepworth 720743.'

'Michael?'

'Yes?'

'Derek Whittingham.'

'Yes, Derek.'

Brookes registered mild surprise. Derek Whittingham frequently rang him at the hospital – they were old friends – but it was unusual to call him at home, late in the evening.

'Michael. What the hell have you been up to?'

'Me? Nothing that I know of. Why?'

The AMO had earned the reputation of being a staunch friend to any member of the medical staff in any kind of trouble. To the outside world he presented an urbane, cultured front. Doctor to doctor he was direct and profane.

'You bloody consultants. Give me half a dozen Pakistani registrars any time. You buggers are more trouble than the rest of the Health Service put together.'

'All right, Derek, what have I done?' Michael smiled to himself.

'What do you know about a patient called Laurence Barker?'

'Oh, God, no. Who's been asking about him, Rothwell?'

'Yes, Rothwell. If you had to do something stupid, why the hell did you let a bastard like Rothwell know about it?'

'I didn't. Come to that, who says I have done anything stupid?'

While Brookes listened with increasing amazement, Whittingham unfolded the whole story starting with the phone call from Rothwell. The AMO had immediately sent for Barker's notes only to find the post-mortem report missing. Gracie had been asked for the report and the empty file had been discovered. An ill-tempered departmental inquisition had resulted in a tearful clerk leading Gracie to Orme's office and the locked drawer.

'Henry?' Michael asked incredulously.

'Yes,' Whittingham answered. 'The story starts with Rothwell and ends with Orme.' He added as an afterthought, 'Or the other way round. How do you get on with our friend Henry?'

'Same as everyone else.'

'As bad as that?'

'Rather worse in fact,' Brookes admitted. 'He's never really forgiven me for being one of the three wise men back when he had that trouble. Remember?'

Whittingham simply grunted. 'Should have sacked the bugger then. Would have saved a lot of trouble.'

'Oh, come on, Derek. That's a bit hard, isn't it?' Brookes remarked.

'Sacked the nurse, didn't we?' Whittingham retorted and Brookes had no reply. They fell silent until Whittingham said quietly, 'Rothwell and Orme. You've picked a right pair. Not the ones to choose if you were looking for compassion and mercy. So tell me, Michael, is there anything in these notes, or anything about the patient at all for that matter, that we need be worried about?'

'Not really.'

'Come on, now, Michael. I've read the notes, including the PM report, and I'm not a complete bloody idiot. Now cut out the bullshit. We've been friends a long time and I'm here to help. What went on?'

'If you must know, I killed the bastard, my close friend and neighbour, by putting a stitch around his coronary artery. And you can't believe what a relief it is to say that to someone after all these months. So now, for Christ's sake, don't say anything nice and kind to me or I'll burst into bloody tears.'

236

'I'm sorry, Michael. I shouldn't have rung you about this. I should have come to see you. But it was the difference between the PM findings and the certified cause of death that stuck out even to a stupid administrator like me. What is certain, is that Orme will have picked it up as well and knows all about it. What isn't so certain is, if Orme and Rothwell have been in cahoots, how much does Rothwell know? Was that the only worry about the case, Michael? There was nothing else, was there?'

'No, unless . . .'

'Yes, Michael? Unless what?'

'There would be nothing in the notes, of course, but there was a slight difference of opinion about switching off the respirator.'

'Between you and Orme?'

'No. Between Dai Jack and myself.'

'But was Orme there?'

'Yes, I rather think he was.'

'Oh, Christ! That's all we need. All right, Michael, leave it with me. I won't do anything unless Rothwell rings again. Perhaps he was trying things on without knowing very much, simply hoping we would let something slip. Knowing that sod, however, I think he'll be back. But don't worry. There'll be no question of us disclosing any information from the notes. But, if Rothwell does ring again, there is one thing you must do.'

'What's that, Derek?'

'Give your Defence Union all the details and send me a copy for our legal department here.'

When Rothwell rang the second time, Whittingham was ready for him.

'Good morning, Mr Rothwell. I've been expecting to hear from you. I have looked into that matter you phoned me about a couple of weeks ago.'

'And what can you tell me about it?'

'Not much more than when you rang last. I've had a look at the notes but, as I said before, there can be no question of discussing any clinical details with you. But I have discussed the case with the consultant concerned . . .'

'Brookes, you mean?'

'Yes, Mr Michael Brookes. And I can find no reason to take any further action. It seems to me that this was just another unfortunate death as a result of the explosion. As such, it is subject to normal legal procedure and I couldn't discuss anything with you that was *sub judice* even if there was anything to discuss.'

It was no more than Rothwell had expected. It was like trying to punch your way out of a sack. It had been the same when he had tried to get to the bottom of things when his Sheila had lost the baby. But he had more power now. He was not going to let it rest. Brookes was not going to get away with it a second time.

'Without going into details, Whittingham, did anything untoward happen to Barker while he was in hospital?'

'I can't discuss a patient with you or anyone else. Be fair, Mr Rothwell. If you had been a patient at Dunbridge General, how would you feel if I were to discuss your case with anyone who happened to ring me up?'

'I appreciate that, but all I want to know is, did anything unusual happen to Barker? I'm not asking you to go into any great detail.'

'Unusual things happen every day in every hospital. A hospital is not a factory, you know, just churning out identical objects.'

'Tha don't have to tell me that. I'm damn sure things happen all the time in hospitals and get hushed up. I'll ask you once more, Whittingham, was there owt irregular in Brookes' management of my boss's case?'

'Unusual, untoward, odd, irregular; it's really coming down to semantics, isn't it, Mr Rothwell?'

'Tha must be daft if tha thinks I'm going to be put off with a few long words, Whittingham. I'm not satisfied and that's a fact. I'm not going to get far with you today, that's for sure. But you can expect a formal application from Health Council for further information on matter.'

'That is your privilege, Mr Rothwell, but I can tell you now that the Authority will be guided by me and by our legal advisers and the answer will be exactly the same.'

Rothwell became flustered as frustration overcame even his dogged determination. He began by talking wildly – 'Then I'll go to law. I'll not rest, I tell thee. Tha's not the only one with law behind him, tha knows . . .' – but his manner became calmer again as if, in his desperation, a new thought had occurred to him.

'Aye, and come to think on it, I know the very chap to ask an' all; the very chap. You'll be hearing from me, Whittingham.'

It took a long time for Rothwell to dial the strange number and he quietly counted out the numbers as he did so. The ringing sound was surprisingly loud and close but was soon replaced by a quiet, cultured voice.

'Wimbledon 9129.'

'May I speak to Mr Adrian Barker, please?'

238

'Speaking.'

'Good evening, Mr Barker. Happen you don't remember me. Name's Rothwell. I was wondering if . . .'

30

Together with Heritage House and the Fire Station, the rectangular, red-brick building formed the first stage of a modest redevelopment scheme for the centre of Dunbridge. It housed the Central Police Station, the Magistrate's Court and the Coroner's Court, its communal entrance-hall staffed by police with friendly smiles and vigilant eyes.

In his court, Hugh Ralston, local solicitor and small-town Coroner, looked down from his dais through circular, gold-rimmed lenses. A small, dapper man in his fifties, his physique was slight to the point of frailty. It was 17 April 1975, exactly a week after the findings of the Ogden Court of Inquiry had been published, and the inquest, adjourned from the prelimi-nary hearing a few days after the explosion, was due to begin. The initial inquest had been a perfunctory affair at which Ralston had officially accepted evidence of identification from the police and evidence as to the cause of death from Gracie, so that he could allow the mortal remains of eighteen victims of the explosion, including Larry Barker's, to be buried or cremated. It had been one of several inquests that Ralston had conducted as a result of the disaster.

It was required by law that inquests be held in public but, whereas Ralston's court was the shop window where the public were permitted to see justice being done, a great deal had already taken place in the room at the back of the store. An hour or so before the initial inquest, nine months previously, Gracie and Ralston had privately gone through the grisly details to be found in the sheaf of post-mortem reports. Gracie had given his cause of death in each case and Ralston had made any queries he had thought necessary. Indeed, the evidence that the pathologist would give in court, and upon which a great deal of the Coroner's verdict would be based, had already been mutually agreed. It was a custom that Ralston had come to accept from long usage. But, as a young law student, he had found it difficult to reconcile with accepted practice in other courts of law. Who could contemplate a High Court judge interviewing an expert witness privately in his chambers and agreeing the evidence in a trial that had not yet begun? It would be unthinkable for a magistrate to discuss a report with a social worker, unseen by the parents, and then walk into court and place their child in care.

It had still pricked at Ralston's conscience when he had been appointed Coroner. It had concerned him that no such access to him was ever achieved by the deceased's family. But the sheer convenience of what was a perfectly acceptable practice had gradually overcome his qualms. Now, in many cases, he did not even see Gracie, the details of what seemed a perfectly straightforward death being settled over the phone. Gracie then gave his evidence in the form of a written report.

Gracie, for his part, had no complaints about the system. To a busy pathologist working single-handed in a large district general hospital, Coroner's post-mortems were a useful source of income, but the court appearances were irritating disruptions to a full timetable. He had no objections to his evidence being passed through the Coroner's filter before being presented to the court. He knew he dared not withhold any of his findings; to be found doing so would be the end of his career. On the other hand, if the Coroner was to place any particular interpretation on the facts presented, that was for him to decide.

But he had often wondered what the families felt about his private conversations with the Coroner. Did they even know about them? He had never had his evidence challenged at an inquest. Didn't they know what an inexact science autopsy was? The average one only took ten minutes or so. Didn't they know that another expert witness might well paint an entirely different picture using the facts presented? And the relatives themselves, might they not have a story to tell? His post-mortem examinations were always preconditioned by a colleague's clinical notes or a policeman's report. When had he thought to interview the relatives before delving into their loved one's body?'

And what if, out there, beyond the law enforcers who huddled round him, beyond the nebulous family that would only acquire substance at the inquest, there stood the shrinking, faceless form of a defendant? With forceful detectives whispering 'murder' in his ear, had Gracie ever insisted on hearing the defendant's side of the story before he started? Only the inquisitors were allowed to stand and watch him dissect, the sweaty young

240

cops as leaden-faced as the corpse. Why shouldn't the defendant be allowed to stand amongst them as Gracie called out his findings? How far had Gracie fallen into the ranks of the Crown's investigators? How far had the calming routine suborned his scientific detachment into becoming 'one of them'? At what point did close co-operation become hand in glove, his hand, the Coroner's glove?

Gracie often saw himself as the lubricant between the local medical and legal professions. Whilst essentially an upright and honest man who gave the facts without fear or favour, he realised that a wrong word here or there from him could suggest negligence on the part of a colleague where none existed. The Coroner was equally anxious to protect a doctor's reputation from vitriolic relatives, unbalanced by grief, as he was to obtain for the widows and orphans the satisfaction of knowing the exact manner of their loved one's death. Gracie still marvelled at the trusting way many families accepted a verdict given by a Coroner, often himself a doctor imbued with professional loyalties, on the probity of another doctor, based on the evidence of yet another doctor. All this with no recourse to legal aid, with their legal representatives, if they could afford them, unable to address either jury or Coroner as to fact, and with the only appeal being a judicial review by the High Court. Even should the legal process get this far, it would be found that no verbatim report would necessarily have been kept to which the Coroner might be held accountable.

Between the two inquests, Basil James Ogden, QC, and his Court of Inquiry, as directed by the Secretary of State for Employment in exercise of his powers under Section 84 of the Factories Act of 1961, had, over ninety days and in five different places, questioned one hundred and ninety witnesses. The time of the explosion had been given accurately by the barometric chart of a glider flying nearby, and confirmed by a lecturer in Manchester University studying the ionosphere. The Atomic Weapons Research Establishment had estimated the explosion to have been the equivalent of seventy tons of TNT. Technical Advisers to the Treasury Solicitor had shown with immaculate clarity that the explosion could be traced back to the fallen crane, how it had blocked the process between the flare stack and the vital safety valves, rendering the latter ineffective. There had been an argument, for the most part academic, as to which pipe between the reactors had finally ruptured, but the skeleton of the disaster had been laid bare for all to see. To get to the bare bones, the court had dissected and displayed layers of human inadequacy.

Although the report was ostensibly a catalogue of cold facts, there had

241

been implicit criticism in every line. The drive to maintain production at all costs, the weakness in management structure, the lack of qualified engineers, the hard-line unions and the nitrogen supply, the bad planning on site, had all been discussed. It was not the function of Ogden and his court to apportion blame, but two witnesses had come in for particular attention. The first was Sir John Anderson, now a pathetic old man, permanently disabled by his stroke. Accordingly, his questions had been put in a quiet, sympathetic tone but their content made no allowance for Anderson's misfortune.

Had he realised the weakness in engineering management? Had he known the Works Engineer had left and not been replaced? On reflection, had the drive to maintain continuous production been taken to the point of recklessness? What were the terms upon which a merger depended? Was Barker desperate to have his contract renewed? Were you equally desperate to complete your merger? Do you think that such hazardous decisions should be made between two desperate men with so much at stake?

Ogden had also questioned Rothwell, whose initial blustering arrogance had spurred him to use his position and greater intellect to crush his witness. Where was he at the time of the explosion? Would it be fair to say that his place should have been at the crane, whether he approved or not? Did he know the level of the nitrogen tanks at the time of the explosion? Was it wise to use Teflo's main safety mechanism as an industrial relations tool? Did he not think that unions should now take as much responsibility as management towards safety, and not use safety measures as a bargaining tool in wage negotiations?

Now, as Ralston reread the white glossy-covered report, he did not detect the fierce emotions aroused during the inquiry. It contained fifty pages of technical jargon, photographs of Teflo taken before and after the explosion, diagrams of towers, valves, reactors and stacks. Ralston found it fascinating; it could almost have been a thriller. All it lacked was a single identifiable villain, and certainly there were no heroes.

Ralston's courtroom was unusually full. Rarely was Dunbridge's Coroner's Court graced by the presence of a jury. He looked at the seven men seated to his left as he turned to the task of swearing them in. The six men in the jury benches had ample space to spread themselves. Solid citizens all, not one looked under sixty-five. The foreman sat apart in a chair. Locked in a rigid curve from knee to neck by arthritis, he could not negotiate the bench. Unfortunately, the only pillar in the room made it impossible for

242

him to sit where he could see both Coroner and witness at the same time and he would have to drag himself painfully from his chair each time Ralston addressed him.

In front of Ralston sat the legal representatives. Although there were empty benches behind them, they squeezed into the front row, hip to hip, elbow to elbow, like swots at the professor's lecture. There were black-jacketed barristers for those who could afford their fees – Teflo and the unions: capital and labour side by side in wary self-interest. No one represented Northweir Plant whose fragile remnant had vanished in the explosion. Grey-suited solicitors kept a respectful distance. To Ralston's right, the only occupant of the Press bench was the young local reporter, learning his trade. Amongst the motley group at the back of his court, Ralston only recognised one, Harrington; one of the surgeons from the hospital who had got the OBE.

Ralston had decided how he wanted the inquest to go. With just enough witnesses to make it look like a mini Court of Inquiry, the evidence would sound like a summary of the Ogden report that he knew would be lying in front of each of the barristers. The session should be finished in the day.

By three in the afternoon things were going well. Experts summarised evidence they had given to Ogden. Union officials and managers were allowed to come and go unchallenged by barristers with a gentleman's agreement.

'I now call Mr William Rothwell.'

Ralston had suspected trouble ever since his officer had handed him that piece of paper from William Rothwell asking, almost demanding, to give evidence. Although Rothwell had not been named in the Ogden report, it was well known that, as plant convenor, he had been held responsible for much of the union trouble at Teflo, especially over the safety measures and the nitrogen supply. Ralston was amazed that he should ask to climb into the witness box again. It would have been more normal had Rothwell tried to fall back into his relative obscurity once again.

All heads turned as Rothwell rose from the back of the court and made his way to the witness box, his head held high in the manner of someone about to do his duty. Militarily correct, he took the oath.

'Your name is William Rothwell?'

'It is, sir.'

'Your occupation, Mr Rothwell?'

'I was foreman of Northweir Plant at the time of the explosion, but I'm retired now.'

'And I understand you have some information that you think would be of interest to this court?'

'I have, sir.'

'I take it that it has something to do with the accident to one of your cranes that triggered the explosion?'

'No, sir.'

Rothwell, with a fine sense of the dramatic, paused until he had the whole of the court's attention.

'No. It's to do with death of Mr Laurence Barker.'

The reporter grasped his notebook a little firmer; counsel stopped packing papers away into bulging briefcases and looked up. George Harrington, sitting in the row behind counsel, found his mouth go dry and wondered why. His view of Ralston and Rothwell became more obscured as counsel sat a little straighter. Ralston's heart sank.

'And what was your relationship with Laurence Barker, Mr Rothwell?'

'He was my boss,' Rothwell answered, and added, 'I worked for him and his father. Both fine men. Highly respected.'

'And what information have you regarding Mr Barker's death that the court does not already have?'

'Tha's just the problem. I just can't get information. Tha's why I'm here. I've grave suspicions of negligence on part of medical staff at General.'

'Mr Rothwell, I advise you to be extremely cautious in what you are saying.' Leaning forwards over his desk, Ralston tried to make each word tell, but Rothwell did not flinch. 'I must remind you also, Mr Rothwell, that you are under oath. Remember you are dealing with the reputations of respected, professional men. While you may or may not know that the proceedings of this court are privileged absolutely against defamation, I am concerned when characters are painted in a certain way and they are not here to defend themselves. I would likewise wish to remind you that the laws of perjury apply in this court as in others. Perhaps you would be wise to take some legal advice before embarking any further in this matter.'

'That I've already done,' Rothwell said, smugly.

'And you still wish to proceed?'

'Aye, I do.'

'So be it.' Ralston took up his pen. 'But, as far as is possible, you will confine yourself to facts. It is for the court to decide whether they amount to reasonable suspicion. Now, what do you know of the death of Laurence Barker?'

244

'Happen there was more to his death than is given in the official cause of death.'

'What do you mean by that exactly?'

'I've been told, on good authority you'll understand, that things went on in operating theatre that shouldn't have.'

'Who told you?'

'Dr Henry Orme, one of consultant anaesthetists.'

Although Rothwell had put on his best suit and white shirt for the occasion, he showed no sign of nervousness. His stance was upright but relaxed, his voice clear and confident. If he had any doubts about the fact that he had no real evidence to give, he did not show them. He felt confident that he only had to get up there and make enough fuss, naming Orme in the process, and they would have to call Orme and then it would all come out – whatever that was.

'What did he tell you?'

'No real facts, you'll understand, sir, but enough to make me very suspicious. He said, in as many words, that there were certain matters in patient's notes that were not generally known, things that certain colleagues of his would not want to become general knowledge. I've tried all ways to get at facts, including in my official capacity as Chairman of Community Council, but I've found out nowt. There's conspiracy of silence, I tell thee. I think it's duty of this court to find out those facts.'

Ralston managed to control his expression with difficulty. 'I have no need to be instructed in the duties of this court, Mr Rothwell. Do you have any solid factual evidence to support your suspicions?'

'None, sir. All I'm certain of is that Orme knows a deal more about Barker's death than he is prepared to admit to. That, sir, you can take for a fact and I felt it my duty to bring it to your attention.'

Ralston leaned once more in Rothwell's direction. 'You must appreciate, Mr Rothwell, that it is not the function of this court to decide liability. That's a civil matter.'

'That's as may be. But that's court job, i'n't it, finding out how they died? You're interested in truth, aren't yer?' Rothwell was beginning to enjoy himself.

'Naturally, Mr Rothwell.'

'Then I say again, this court will not have done its duty if it doesn't look further into death of Laurence Barker.'

Ralston ran his finger down the list and read Barker's cause of death. He picked out Barker's file, feeling everyone's eyes on him, and opened it.

Then he remembered. He remembered talking this one over with Gracie before the initial inquest. He remembered he had agreed not to do that particular piece of dirty washing in public, just so long as Gracie could assure him that the operation would not have taken place had it not been for the explosion. And he had accepted Gracie's cause of death without any reference to that ligature thing. He remembered now. He couldn't even blame Gracie. He hadn't noticed it himself amongst all the other reports. Gracie had pointed it out to him. He could still see Gracie, how relieved he had looked, as if it wasn't on his conscience any more, just glad he had mentioned it and got away without an issue being made out of it. And Ralston now felt certain that this was what this fellow Orme had been shooting his mouth off about. Obviously he hadn't told Rothwell any great detail, just enough to make him suspicious, just enough to cause trouble.

He turned back towards Rothwell. 'And you have nothing more concrete than that to assist the court?'

'No, but I'm sure Orme has. Why don't you ask him?'

Normally Ralston would have known how to deal with Rothwell's truculence but, feeling at a disadvantage, he was glad to get rid of him. 'I'm sure the court is very grateful to you, Mr Rothwell,' he said, drily, 'but, unless you have anything more specific to add, you may stand down.' He paused. 'Is Dr Orme in court?'

As Rothwell, unabashed, made his triumphal way back to his seat, no one stood up. Ralston looked at Harrington who shook his head. The hum of conversation became obtrusive and Ralston felt his control over his court slipping away from him. He made up his mind quickly.

'This court is adjourned until one week from today, at which time I will take further medical evidence to clear up any doubt that may have been raised in evidence today. One week should be sufficient for any witnesses to obtain legal representation should they deem it necessary.'

Rothwell alone did not rise as Ralston left. Grinning broadly, he remained seated, his legs stretched out in front of him. Well pleased with the way things had gone, he couldn't wait to get home and ring young Adrian Barker. Keep him in touch, like. Find out what to do next, you'll understand.

A week later, Brookes found the courtroom oppressive. Morosely, he scuffed his foot along the back of the bench in front, scratching the varnish. The low ceiling, the small, closed windows and crowded benches pressed in on him. He had assumed that he would have to give evidence and he had found a new shirt in the back of a drawer, still in its plastic wrapping, just as Rosemary had bought it. The collar had looked strangely out of fashion in the mirror and he ran his finger around it where the warm air was making it itch. He looked around. Everybody seemed to him to be so bloody friendly; those reporters, joking amongst themselves, looked as if they had seen it all before. This was a bonus for them, Brookes supposed; they must have thought there was nothing left in the Teflo story. He turned in his seat to see who was sitting behind him, only to be faced by Henry Orme and his fixed wet smile.

Brookes did not get a good look at the Coroner until the row of lawyers settled and sat down. Their demarcation disputes had been made worse by the addition of the Area Health Authority solicitor's rump on the front bench.

'Looks like a bloody bank manager,' Brookes whispered to an upright Harrington.

Harrington frowned, anxious not to be associated with such lack of respect, and Brookes slid further down in his seat, chin on chest. Slowly beginning to see himself in the role of martyr, Brookes' mood felt absurdly fatalistic. He could see clearly what was going to happen. Orme was going to be called and he was hardly likely to perjure himself for Brookes.

Ralston, keen to get on with what he knew would be an unpleasant session, cut the preliminaries to a minimum. Within minutes, Orme found himself in the witness box. In the sea of faces staring at him, he saw an island of familiar, hostile features, amongst them those of Harrington, Brookes, Gracie, Williams. He had to clear his throat twice before any recognisable sound emerged to take the oath.

'You are Dr Henry Hilton Orme?'

To Orme it sounded like an accusation. 'Yes, sir.'

'You are a Fellow of the Faculty of Anaesthetists and a Consultant Anaesthetist at Dunbridge General Hospital?'

'Yes, sir.'

'It is the duty of this court, Dr Orme, to investigate the deaths of some of the victims of the Teflo disaster. In particular today, we are looking into the death of a Laurence Barker.'

Ralston's voice was unhurried.

'A previous witness before this court, a Mr Rothwell, has alleged that you told him of some negligence which allegedly took place during the management of Mr Barker's injuries. Is that true?'

'No, sir, I didn't,' Orme replied, quavering.

247

'Did you have a conversation with Mr Rothwell as he claims you did?'

'I may have.'

'Did you or did you not, Dr Orme?'

'Yes.'

Ralston found it distasteful prising admissions out of a squirming doctor. 'Were you present at the operation?'

'No, I wasn't.'

'Were you involved in Mr Barker's treatment in any way?'

'I was partly responsible for looking after him in the recovery-room after the operation.' Orme made every effort to spread the responsibility. 'Dr Williams also took part in this.'

'Dr Williams being your senior colleague?'

'So I'm told,' sneered Orme, resentment overcoming his nervousness for a moment.

'Up to this stage, did you know of any irregularities or mismanagement of any kind?'

Orme was certain that the Coroner was not going to let him out of the witness box until he had said something that would satisfy the suspicion raised by Rothwell, but was equally sure he hadn't the guts to say he knew nothing and stick to it. Wearily he recognised it was going to turn out much as he had expected; no hero, defying the medical establishment and telling all; no hero, defying the outside world, taking his secret to jail if necessary. It had crossed his mind that stubborn perjury in the defence of a colleague might admit him at last to that hospital hierarchy he detested so much. Yet it was almost as if he enjoyed his paranoid isolation, welcoming like an old friend the disfavour of both sides. Resigned to admitting either to the dispute over the respirator or to the post-mortem findings, he weighed up his dislike of Brookes and his fear of Williams. He decided to say nothing about the respirator if he could get away with the post-mortem findings only.

'No, sir, none.'

Ralston tried the only other tack available to him.

'You mentioned Mr Barker's clinical notes in your conversation with Mr Rothwell.'

Orme took that as a statement rather than a question and remained silent.

'Did you have a personal interest in those notes?'

With the first semblance of pride Orme described his research interest. His defensive cringing returned with Ralston's next question.

'What, then, in those notes gave you cause for concern?'

'The post-mortem findings,' Orme blurted out, glad now to say anything to speed the end of his ordeal, whatever or whoever the sacrifice.

'What about the findings?'

'They just seemed unusual. I can't go into details.'

'Can't or won't, Dr Orme? I must warn you of the consequences of withholding evidence wilfully.'

'I'm no expert in this field,' Orme began to whine. 'You can't ask me to give evidence in another field of medicine. You must ask the real experts if you want to know.'

'That I intend doing, Dr Orme. But know what? What are we looking for? Would you agree that there are facts in the post-mortem findings that would be of interest to this court?'

In utter silence, all, save one dozing juryman, waited for Orme's reply.

'Yes, sir.'

Orme had not left the box before he heard Ralston call Gracie again. There was a death-like hush in the court as Orme and Gracie passed like two batsmen. One knew he had let the side down; the other, going in to bat on a very bumpy pitch, was the last man able to defend a team's honour and a captain's reputation.

'Dr Gracie, I'm sure I don't have to remind you that you are still under oath?'

'No, sir.' For all his experience, Gracie looked apprehensive.

'In the light of further evidence you have heard in this court, do you wish to change your opinion as to the cause of death in the case of Mr Laurence Barker?'

'No, sir.'

'You still maintain the cause of his death was his operation?'

'Yes, sir.'

'And, in your opinion, was the operation essential?'

'Yes, sir, absolutely. Without the operation, the patient must surely have died.'

'And the penetrating wound of the heart, that was caused by the accident?'

'Yes.'

'Was it a wound compatible with survival?'

'It was an extremely severe and dangerous injury.'

'But is it uniformly fatal?'

'If not operated on, yes.'

'Yes, yes, Dr Gracie, but is it uniformly fatal if operated on?'

'No, sir.'

'In that case, Dr Gracie, why did this patient die?'

The bastard, thought Gracie. He knows exactly how he died. I told him. And now he's going to grind it out of me as if I've been trying to hide it. Why doesn't he give me a lead?

'As I've mentioned before,' Gracie said out loud, 'cardiac arrest.'

'Was the cardiac arrest due to the injury to the heart?'

'Not directly.'

'What then, in your opinion, was it due to?'

Gracie defended to the end but knew that Ralston was not going to make it any easier for him.

'The heart stopped due to a coronary occlusion.'

'Do you mean he had a coronary thrombosis while under the anaesthetic?'

'No, sir.'

'What then occluded the artery, Dr Gracie?'

Gracie's reluctance to answer was painful to watch.

'One of the stitches used to repair the aorta.'

'Thank you, Dr Gracie.' Ralston showed no emotion as he went on. 'And was there any evidence of disease in the artery?'

'No.'

'Could there have been, in your opinion, any other cause for the occlusion?'

'No.'

'Or the cardiac arrest?'

'Anyone undergoing an operation on his heart runs the risk of an arrest.'

'But this patient, Dr Gracie, did he die as a result of the stitch placed in the heart by the surgeon?'

'Yes,' hissed Gracie.

Ralston faced the court. 'I think that covers all the points I need to bring out at this stage. You are excused, Dr Gracie.'

Ralston turned his head as he heard Gracie speak.

'Sir, perhaps if . . .' started Gracie.

'Yes, Dr Gracie?'

Ralston raised his eyebrows as Gracie's voice trailed away.

'Nothing, sir.'

'Quite so, Dr Gracie. Stand down, please.'

When Michael Brookes had taken the oath, he continued to stand as if he had no intention of being in the box for long.

'Mr Brookes, you are a Fellow of the Royal College of Surgeons and a Consultant Surgeon at Dunbridge General Hospital?'

'I am.'

'You were the surgeon who operated on Mr Laurence Barker?'

'I was.'

'What did you find at operation, Mr Brookes?'

'I found a laceration in the aorta and stitched it up.' There was a tone in the answer that complemented Brookes' suddenly fatalistic attitude.

'What happened after that?'

'The patient had a cardiac arrest which we treated.'

'How long after stitching up the aorta did the arrest occur?'

'A minute or so, no longer.'

'And was the treatment successful?'

'To some degree. He died some time later in the recovery-room.'

'Did he ever recover consciousness?'

'No, he did not.'

'Did you attend Barker's post-mortem?'

'I saw the post-mortem specimens.'

'And are you cognisant of Dr Gracie's findings?'

'Yes.'

Ralston spoke slowly in his effort to make the question as unequivocal as possible. 'Do you accept that this patient died as a result of a stitch placed around the coronary artery?'

'Yes.'

The whole court, Ralston included, waited for some qualifying remark or excuse but there was none. Ralston stared at Brookes as if trying to see the true inner man behind the cool exterior, that look of resignation. Harrington closed his eyes, whispering, 'Oh, Christ.' Orme felt an almighty thrill as he watched someone he hated put on the rack. Williams opened and closed his fist, looking round as if for something to hit.

And Rothwell smiled.

'Do you wish to add anything to what you have said, Mr Brookes?'

'Thank you, sir, no. I think I've said all I need to.'

Ralston paused to marshal his thoughts. 'The court respects the frankness with which you have given your evidence, Mr Brookes. I am sure there are many here today who appreciate the strains that must have been placed upon the medical services that day. But you must also realise that it is the duty of this court to establish the manner of a person's death. Any other consideration is of secondary importance to us. If you have nothing further to add, you may stand down.'

When Brookes had regained his seat next to Harrington, Ralston addressed the front bench.

'Do any learned counsel wish to question any of the medical witnesses?'

Glances were exchanged, heads were shaken but no one moved. No one was there to represent the Barker family, at least not in person. Only indirectly through Rothwell. But Rothwell now knew that there would be another time, another place.

'In that case,' Ralston said, looking at his watch, 'this court will reassemble at 2.15 p.m., when I shall instruct the jury and ask for their verdict.'

Ralston found little enjoyment in the lunch his Officer brought him. It was soured by the thought of how he had drawn the evidence out of Gracie. He knew damn well what Gracie must have been thinking, but there had been no other way of doing it. His decision at the initial inquest not to make a point out of the ligature had been made purely out of consideration for one of Gracie's colleagues. He had genuinely been trying to help. So why should Gracie complain? Nothing would have happened if it had not been for a lot of backbiting amongst the medical staff.

Ralston's main worry now was the verdict. What verdict was he going to allow the jury to feel they had given?

Abstractedly, he found the definitive verdict as elusive as the slithery crème caramel he chased disinterestedly around a cold dish. Several of the verdicts given in the Coroner's Court, such as natural causes or suicide, could be excluded immediately. There were three verdicts only that could be applied, but the final choice tantalised him. Two years previously, four men had died at Teflo when a cradle, hanging from towering scaffolding, had come crashing to earth. Negligence on the part of the inspecting engineers had been admitted and, as a result, he had instructed the jury to return an open verdict. It had worried him ever since. There had been no difficulty in identification and it had been shown when, where and how they had died. Ralston now felt an open verdict had been wrong, and he was not going to make that mistake again.

This left him with accidental death, and death by misadventure, so similar as to be virtually indistinguishable in law. If there was a difference, Ralston saw accidental death as due to an unexpected factor intruding into a regularly performed procedure, while death by misadventure suggested

252

to him some fault in the procedure itself. It sounded easy. Such groomed phraseology. It was harder to explain it convincingly to the jury. What hope did he have of explaining those phrases to the seven worthies out there when he had to learn them verbatim to explain them to himself?

He must differentiate between seventeen deceased where there had been no evidence of medical mismanagement and the one where a mistake had been freely admitted to, amounting to perhaps a considerable degree of negligence. But it had already been counsel's opinion that there had been gross negligence at Teflo. It would seem that no one would have died that day without negligence on someone's part. So, did it matter to the verdict if, in one case, medical negligence had been heaped on engineering? The engineers were going to get away with it, so why not the doctors?

Deaths after operations to which the patient had consented usually attracted a verdict of death by misadventure. To try to indicate some censure on the surgeon, the best he could do was to change that to accidental death. But that was the verdict he already had in mind for the others.

Still undecided, he heard his Officer ask the court to rise. He stumbled as he climbed the dais. He could only hope that the problem would be resolved as he ordered his turbulent thoughts when directing the jury. He stared hard at them, ignoring the rest of the court, before he began to speak.

'Gentlemen, the time has come for you to draw conclusions from this inquest and come to a verdict.' He smiled inwardly as seven wrinkled brows furrowed with painful concentration. 'You have heard all the technical and medical evidence and it is not my intention to go through all that with you again.' He sensed the jury's relief. It was doubtful in Ralston's mind whether they could remember the technical evidence of that morning, let alone that of last week. Not one had taken notes. Was there any need to summarise what they probably hadn't understood before they'd forgotten it? 'It is, of course, entirely up to you what verdict you bring in. You are not bound by any opinions brought in by counsel as regards negligence involved in the causation of the accident at Teflo. Similarly, you are obliged not to express an opinion as to any lack of care you may feel occurred subsequent to the accident. What you are obliged to do is to give your verdict as to the manner in which these eighteen unfortunate people met their deaths.'

Ralston waited for his jury foreman to rearrange his stiff joints.

'What you must remember, is that no one is on trial here today.

Interested parties may have taken note of evidence given here under oath and legal consequences may arise but that is no concern of yours. It is not part of your function to apportion blame or make comment as to civil liability. That may or may not be decided in another court. All that is required of you is that you tell the truth simply as you see it. If there are any legal consequences, so be it. That must in no way influence your decision.'

Honest endeavour was mixed with post-prandial torpidity in the faces of the jurymen as they struggled to absorb and retain every word.

'Now, as to the possible verdicts available to you.'

Seven faces took on the look of grim resolution.

'Under the law as it stands at present, you are entitled to return a verdict of manslaughter if you think that negligence of the grossest nature has taken place.' Ralston was not the only one to detect signs of physical, as well as mental agitation in the jury box. 'But, I must tell you now, that I would be very unhappy with this verdict. It is a verdict resorted to in the rarest of cases and I suggest you may not find it applicable here.'

There was almost audible relief as the jurors looked at each other, nodding their heads. Thank God for that. No need to think about that one again.

'Other verdicts rule themselves out; natural causes, suicide, industrial diseases. That leaves, firstly, an open verdict.' Ralston shifted his position, twitching to a needle prick of conscience. 'There are precedents where this verdict has been brought in where negligence has been the proven cause of an accident but, in many ways, this is an unsatisfactory verdict. Basically it should be reserved for those deaths where some doubt exists as to identity or place, time or manner of death.' He paused 'No such problems exist here. So, what is left?'

One or two of the jurors' faces showed signs of strain, even though they had been invited, instructed, to discard all the options that Ralston had described up to that point.

'That leaves accidental death and death by misadventure, two verdicts which, in law, are almost indistinguishable.'

Ralston heard his inner voice add, behind a mask-like face, 'So how the hell you're expected to tell them apart, I'm damned if I know.'

'I will try to help you in the difficult task of comparing and contrasting the two. An accidental death is one due to some unforeseen event intruding into a regularly performed procedure without the patient's consent,' he paused, 'While death by misadventure is due to some fault in the procedure itself to which the patient has given his consent.'

254

Seven blank features, two with mouths agape, stared back at him. He tried again.

'If a patient, on the advice of the doctor, takes pills and dies from some well-recognised side-effect which is an accepted risk of the treatment, that would be death by misadventure. If he died by reason of being negligently given the wrong drug, or lethal doses of the correct drug, that would be accidental death.'

Sparks of comprehension flickered but were quickly doused. What drugs? There had been no mention of drugs, had there?

'It is, of course, entirely up to you what verdict you think fit to return. However, should you feel, as I do, that in seventeen of the deceased, the deaths were due directly to the accident, then you are free to bring in a verdict of accidental death. In the case of Laurence Barker, however, it would be remiss of the court if no note was taken of his immediate cause of death. It has got to be relevant. But it is a matter for you to decide. The verdict is yours. It is permissible for you to carry out your deliberations without leaving the court but, in this case, I think it would be prudent for you to retire.'

Michael looked bleakly from the Coroner's vacant chair to the empty jury benches, to the crowded court. No one, save the Coroner and the jurors, had left the room. No one expected the jury to be out long. One reporter was reading out his shorthand to a tardy colleague, good for a drink afterwards. One of the barristers glanced up, caught his eye and looked away sharply, as if caught examining someone's birthmark.

As the minutes ticked by, Michael sat, his mind a jumble of faces and backgrounds; Rosemary standing there with blood on the towel; Sister Kay, her fingers hooked in the wire mesh at Teflo; Jonathan and Robert running out of school; Dai Jack's face at the top of the table; and Alison; images thrown up by his feelings of isolation and loneliness. A quarter of an hour later, a decent interval, he watched as the jury foreman stumped stiffly back with his six fellow jurors behind him. Everyone stood and sat to mark Ralston's reappearance. Seventeen verdicts of accidental death were quickly pronounced.

'And in the case of Mr Laurence Barker?' asked Ralston.

'Death by misadventure following an operation resulting from the accident, sir.'

Ralston controlled his desire to roll his eyes to heaven. With the tone of a teacher forced to go over the simplest of points for the dullest pupil in his class, he spoke to the foreman once again. 'If a patient, following an accident, is admitted to hospital and, while in hospital, the roof falls in and kills him, his death cannot be attributed to the accident. If, however, the patient dies as a result of an operation which is itself a direct result of the accident, then that patient's death can be reasonably traced back to the accident. Do you understand that?'

'Yes, sir.'

'In that case, will you please now reconsider your verdict in the case of Mr Laurence Barker.'

Ralston was about to rise and leave once more but hesitated as he saw the foreman turn and whisper to the juryman nearest to him. The remaining five took no part in the short discussion. Within a matter of seconds the foreman jerked his way round to address Ralston again.

'Accidental death, sir.'

Michael had prepared himself to show no emotion at whatever verdict was thundered out to a hushed court. As it was, it was with a sense of having been thwarted that he watched the swing doors thud behind Ralston's back. He had pictured himself as the central figure in a courtroom drama, whereas he felt he had had no more than a few lines in a three-act farce.

31

Wearily, Michael reversed his car into a space near Preston's railway station, switched off the engine and looked at his watch. Eight o'clock. He was early. He tilted his seat back, jammed his head between the headrest and the door pillar, and grasped at sleep that was repeatedly swept away as recollections of Larry's inquest surged through his mind. He was glad Jonathan had missed the last two days. He wondered how he had fared in his interview. His first time in London alone, staying at the Bonnington, where Brookes had stayed when he was taking his Fellowship. How many years ago was it? For a moment, Dunbridge's Coroner's Court gave way in his mind to Southampton Row, that heart-sinking gap into Queen's Square, the tongue-drying steps into the Examination Hall, the seriate ranks shuffling nervously forward to the basement urinals, the dehydration, and Peter's Bar afterwards. And today, some of those 'Fellow' sufferers, lofty teaching hospital staff with greying heads and half-moon glasses, were deciding his son's future.

He flung his door open to pace fretfully up and down the sloping station approach until his son's head and shoulders could be seen bobbing in the midst of the emerging crowd. They walked side by side, with scarcely a word, to the car.

'How did you get on?'

'All right. No problem.'

'Want to drive?'

'Wouldn't mind, Dad.'

Michael threw the car keys across the roof and Jonathan got in, swinging his bag on to the back seat. His seat right back, his long arms and legs at full stretch as if on the starting grid at Monaco, he drove thoughtfully and meticulously out of Preston. The motorway was busy enough to keep a frown of youthful concentration on the face of someone who had only recently passed his driving test. Michael was still staring blankly through the windscreen when they approached Shepworth. His son glanced briefly his way.

'Feel like a pint, Dad?'

Surprise brought life back into Brookes' tired eyes. 'What did you say?'

'A pint, Dad. D'you feel like a pint?'

'What d'you mean?'

'For goodness sake, Dad, come on. You know what I mean.'

'But you're under age.'

'Only a couple of months. Haven't had any trouble so far. How about the Fox and Hounds?'

'But the fellow there is a patient of mine.'

'All the better. Less likely to say anything, isn't he?'

Michael looked at his son anew, saw his maturing physique, warmed to a sensation of strength. 'And how long has this beer drinking been going on then?'

'Hadn't you guessed? I thought you must have. Why d'you think I go to bed so quickly when I come home from away matches? D'you mean to say you've never smelt my breath?'

'Well, I'm damned.' He was genuinely amazed.

'No different from anyone else, Dad. We all do it. You should have seen Robert. He was the worst. The things he got up to after away matches.'

There was a painful silence as memories jarred.

Inside, the bar was crowded. Jonathan turned to his father, raising his voice. 'Go and find a seat. I'll get them. What d'you want? John Smith's do you?'

Brookes nodded vaguely, looking bemused, disorientated, as he slid his son a fiver. He watched from the table as Jonathan confidently pushed his way to the front, shoulder to shoulder, politely assertive. His white shirt was open at the neck. A dark blue crested pullover looked incongruous over the trousers of the formal blue suit he had worn for his interview. The jacket must be crumpled up in the soft bag he had thrown into the car. As Jonathan leaned forward to place the two pint glasses on the table top, pocketing the change, Brookes looked closely at his face.

'You need a shave.'

'I know, Dad,' Jonathan said, rasping his hand over his chin.

'I trust you didn't go into the interview looking like that?'

'No, of course not. That was early this morning. Cheers.'

'Cheers.'

Brookes lifted his glass, sipped his beer, watched his son put his glass down, one-third empty.

'How did things go?'

'Pretty well, I think.'

'Anybody give you a bad time?'

'Not really. One old buffer got a bit tetchy about my rugger. Seemed quite pleased until I told him I was quite happy to stay in the second fifteen. He got a bit upset when I said the lads were always nicer in the second fifteens, but there was another chap there who was very kind. He seemed to know you, asked if I was your son. He wanted to be remembered to you.'

'I wonder who that was. D'you remember his name?'

'No.'

'That's a great help. Are you going to get an offer, d'you think?'

'I think so. But I'm not going.'

Michael was about to drink but put his glass down before it reached his lips. 'You're not?'

'No.'

'Why not?'

'Because I'm going to Liverpool.'

'Why did you bother to go up for the interview then?'

'I thought you'd be a bit upset if I didn't. Plus the fact that I wanted to have a look at the place, and an offer from there would be a good sort of safety net, if you know what I mean.'

258

'But why Liverpool? Your chances of ending up in Harley Street go down by a factor of several thousands, you know, if you don't go to London.'

'Who said I wanted to end up in Harley Street?'

'Just a figure of speech. What I mean is, if you really want to aim for the top . . .'

Jonathan broke in. 'George Harrington, he's a London man, isn't he?'

Brookes nodded.

'And who do you think is the better surgeon, you or him?'

He did not answer but Jonathan was not to be denied.

'Well?'

'That's not the point. If you really want to be a success, you must go to London.'

'Why? What you mean is that if I go to Liverpool, I could well end up in some Dunbridge General like you and, if you don't consider that success, then you must look on it as failure.' Youthful honesty forced Michael out into the open, made him feel ashamed. 'Dad, somewhere like Dunbridge would do me fine. They can keep the rat race; not my scene. In any case, from what you tell me, I'm not going to be short of a bob.'

Glad to deflect the conversation, Brookes said, brightly, 'That's true enough. Another couple of months and you're going to be quite a wealthy young man. There's a lot to be said for being the favourite grandson of a successful builder, eh?'

'Not difficult to be the favourite when you're the only one, Dad.'

'No, I suppose not.' Brookes laughed. 'The only son of his only daughter. Couldn't go wrong, could you really? You don't remember him, do you?'

'Not really. Vague shadowy figure, you know.'

'Pity. He was a great old chap, always very kind to me. Have you thought what you're going to do with all that money?'

'You bet. An old banger, that's top priority. Something to get me to and from Liverpool. I want to get home weekends. I'm going to take my golf seriously. Dai Jack has promised to take me in hand.'

Dai Jack, George Harrington; no more Uncle David, Mr Harrington.

'And, subject to my ex-trustee's approval, of course,' Jonathan smiled, 'a small flat in Liverpool? Just big enough to squeeze your father in if you can ever dig him out from Dunbridge. Go to the theatre or perhaps a meal? What d'you say? And if you really behave yourself, perhaps we'll let you join a student pub crawl. Take you back, eh?'

'But what if you don't get an offer from Liverpool?'

'No problem. I intend getting the sort of grades that I can make them an offer they can't refuse.'

'You cocky young bastard.' Michael looked at his son with open-mouthed astonishment.

Jonathan, enjoying himself, smiled back. 'One out of the three, Dad. Not bad. Young, yes, I'll give you that. Confident, yes, but cocky, no. And a bastard? Well, unless there's something you and Mum should have told me about?'

Michael was still laughing when Jonathan rattled his glass on the table. 'Come on, Dad, you're slow. Drink up.' He held his hand up as he anticipated what his father was about to say. 'I know. Dad, I'm driving. I promise you, never more than two pints, probably shandy, when I'm driving.'

When they had settled again, Jonathan took over the role of inquisitor.

'And how about you, Dad? How did the inquest go?'

'Rough, Jonathan, rough.'

'Want to talk about it?'

And so the whole story flooded out. Michael felt strangely relaxed in the smoke-engrained, rough-stone walls with the artificial brass hanging haphazard and resounding to the clacking fruit machine. The beer absorbed rapidly from his empty stomach and loosened his tongue. He talked of Orme and Rothwell with no hint of bitterness, as if they had been no more than actors in a play he had just seen. He laughed at, made Jonathan laugh at, the jury. He swung naturally to genuine sadness as he described Gracie giving his evidence, regained a factual tone as he related his own. He made the verdict sound trivial, of no consequence, held it back as long as he could, as if he were reluctant to bring the story to an end. He savoured the enjoyment of exploring an intimate communication with this new-found man son.

In return, Jonathan, totally absorbed, made no attempt to interrupt. Not for a moment did his eyes leave his father's face, no flickering away to any noisy distraction around him, his gaze unwavering over the top of his glass as he drank. Only when he had finished did Michael look directly into his son's eyes, in expectation of another verdict.

'I'm sorry, Dad. I really am.'

'That's kind of you. But, what the hell, I'll get over it. It's not the end of the world. Life's got to go on.'

'Oh, I don't mean that.'

260

'Oh?'

'No. That doesn't bother me. You don't imagine I'm going to worry about what other people think, do you? What the hell do they know about it, most of them? I think I know my old man well enough not to worry about any inquest verdict. What I mean is, I haven't been much help, have I? Just didn't understand, I'm afraid. Didn't try to. Not difficult to understand, really. All I had to do was think about it. It would have been bad enough if you hadn't known the chap but, I mean to say, when it was Rob's dad like that. I know how you hate operating on friends; I've seen how you look those mornings. But of all people to have that business of the stitch.'

Michael smiled. 'Known as Sod's Law in the trade,' he said.

'And you've had that hanging over you ever since last July. Did Aunt Lissa . . . ? No, of course not. God, I'm sorry, Dad. I just didn't know. Why didn't you say?'

'Don't be daft; it wasn't your problem. But I must admit this paternal total infallibility bit can be pretty hard going at times, knowing that, sooner or later, your kids are going to find you out. You just hope and pray they'll be old enough to understand when it happens. It comes as quite a relief when your son stops treating you like God incarnate and more like another human being, even if you lose him a bit in the process.'

'I'm sorry about that, too, Dad.'

There was an embarrassed silence as they played with their glasses, smearing beer slops across the table top, fidgeting with beer mats. No names were spoken.

'It was a bit hard to handle at the time, Dad. Well, it was difficult, being so friendly with Robert like that. We couldn't believe it at first, not really. My dad and his mum? We tried to talk about it but it didn't work very well. He was very fond of his dad, you know, whatever he may have done. I hated to see him go, but, in some ways, it was a relief when he did.'

'Have you heard from him?'

'No. What about you? Did you ever hear from Aunt Lissa at all?'

'Couple of letters early on. I didn't reply. Nothing since.'

The conversation hung in the smoky atmosphere.

'D'you love Rob's mum?'

The question was youthfully direct. Michael looked clearly into Jonathan's eyes, and nodded.

'Then why don't you get married? I don't think Mum would have minded, not now, not now that Rob's dad is dead. I don't think she would have wanted you to be lonely. So why don't you? Doesn't she love you?'

'Oh, yes, I think so.'

'Then why don't you?'

'Because she doesn't want to bury herself in Dunbridge again and I can't move. And anyway,' – it was Brookes' turn to peer at his son – 'how would you feel about it?'

'Who, me? Oh, God, Dad, I'd be all for it. Anything to cheer you up. You've been so bloody miserable these last few months.'

Brookes' laugh was free and open as he felt a sudden release from the cramping misery of months. 'That's twice in one day.'

'What d'you mean?'

'That's twice I've been told off about being so miserable,' Brookes replied.

'Oh? Who else . . . ?'

'Dai Jack. He tore great strips off me after the inquest today. Called me spineless, said I was enjoying martyrdom; miserable bastard was about the kindest term he used. Said I should stop thinking about myself so much and think more about you, enjoy you growing up. He was absolutely furious.'

Jonathan did not smile but said, quietly, 'He's still the best friend you've got, you know, Dad.'

'Oh, I know that, Jonathan. And I feel better for it. Have I really been as bad as all that then?'

'Dad, you've been bloody terrible.'

They both laughed again, and Michael raised his right hand as if taking an oath. 'All right, I'm sorry and I hereby swear, as from now, to turn over a new leaf.'

'So what will you do, sell the Old Mill? It's going to be lonely there for you when I go to med school.'

'D'you see me in a bungalow on the seafront in Westmere? Or a semi in Dunbridge?'

Jonathan laughed. 'Frankly, no.'

'Neither do I. No, I'm not going to move.'

'Good.'

As Michael lowered his head to drink, he looked archly at his son from under raised eyebrows. 'And I've no plans for anyone to move in and keep me company either.'

'Fair enough, Dad. And you're going to be happy?'

Brookes hesitated before he answered, as his memory whirled him back to when he had been asked that question before.

'No, Jonathan, I can't promise that. But I will learn to be content, that I promise. That's the best I can do. But no more miseries.'

'What about this other business? You said you thought you would almost certainly be sued. What happens about that?'

'I'm not too sure. I've never been sued before. Something of a novelty, I'm glad to say. I'll ring Derek Whittingham on Monday and find out.'

'But who would be suing you?'

'That again I don't know.'

'I mean, I can't imagine . . .'

'Aunt Lissa or Robert?'

'Well, yes.'

'Neither can I.'

'How soon will you know? How long do these things take?'

'Oh, an action through the courts can take years. It's not unknown for something like this to take up to seven or eight years to come to court. Just think, you could be qualified and have done your house jobs by the time they stick me in jail.'

'Not likely to come to that, is it, Dad?'

'No, of course not. But it's one of those times when the punishment starts long before the verdict. I'm already sentenced to what, five, six, seven, maybe eight years of having a little ghost of Larry Barker sitting on my shoulder wherever I go. I said once, jokingly, that I thought he'd come back to haunt me. I never imagined for a moment it would come true. And now I may have to wait for years to find out whether some judge is going to exorcise my ghost or leave him there as a life sentence.'

PART FOUR

Sub judice

32

15 St Brides Close,
Epsom,
Surrey

8 September 1974

Michael,

As you can see, I have settled at last. The house is not too far from the college for Robert next term, and I am struggling to remember enough law not to get sacked from my new job in Guildford.

I love you. Have I made a ghastly mistake?

Please write to me – though I fear in my heart you will not reply to this.

Forgive me,

Lissa

My dear – Dear Michael – Mr Brookes – Sir,

You will be coming back from London, tired, to find this.

It hasn't worked out, my dear, has it? Not even when Jonathan is away. You are a good kind man and you would never admit it but you will be glad. I know you will and you must not think badly of yourself for doing so.

I love you but you only need me.

And so, dear, dear man, from tomorrow we shall be Mr Brookes and Sister Kay once more. And you must not be upset or embarrassed. All I ask is, in the hospital, please no sign in any way. Look after Jonathan and please, please don't do anything that would mean I couldn't go on working with you.

If you need me that much, I will not be difficult to find.

Anna

The Clinic,
Opposite the Roxy Cinema,
Poona,
Maharashtra,
India

3 September

Dear Dad,

I'm sorry I haven't written more often but I have been very busy. I am fit and well – I have not fallen foul of any of the local bugs as yet, nor any of the local dusky maidens either, in case you're worrying.

I have no regrets about choosing to spend my elective out here. I'll tell you all about it when I get home. It's not at all what I expected. I really am most impressed with what Mr Shah manages to do in his clinic with such limited back up. He must have learned a thing or two when he was with you, Dad. He has asked me to send his most respectful kind regards to my esteemed father. He keeps telling me you were like a father to him too. He has tried hard to get some sort of post in the medical school here but has failed, though he has taken me to a few of their lectures.

But it's what they have to leave alone that is upsetting, especially the children. And the streets in Bombay – I had no idea. If nothing else, it has taught me just how much we take for granted at home.

Hope to see you in three weeks' time. Mr Shah says, why don't you come out to visit him? I didn't tell him I can't get you as far as Liverpool. Just looking forward to two things – a pint in the Fox and Hounds and the chance to be on my own, just for an hour.

Cheers, Dad. See you in three weeks.

Jonathan

The Old Mill,
Shepworth,
Nr. Dunbridge
9.11.79

Dear Alex,

Forgive me for writing to you personally like this, but I feel sure that we have been friends long enough for you not to be offended.

Jonathan, all being well, should qualify next June and is hoping to do his preregistration posts in Liverpool. He has told me how he would welcome the chance to work for you, but he tells me also that there is considerable competition for your jobs. It seems you have developed quite a reputation as a teacher in your old age!

Jonathan has had a pretty good student career, as you may have heard, and, although perhaps I shouldn't say it, he's not a bad lad.

I am sure he will quite understand if you have already promised your jobs to others, and I appreciate that, these days, such things should go through some computer or other, but I hope you have not minded my taking advantage of our friendship (once more) like this.

My kindest regards to Mary. I hope you are both well.

Yours sincerely,

Michael

PART FIVE

Judgment

33

Brookes' ward sister took an instant dislike to the short, fat man walking so confidently down her corridor. She was used to the tentative steps of relatives, as they glanced anxiously from side to side, hoping their best behaviour would ensure good news. This man, dressed in a thick dark jacket and black striped trousers, in spite of the heat of mid-June, limped as if he had a pebble in his right shoe. Oblivious to the nurses he forced to one side, deviating not one inch for the wheelchair that had to be backed into a doorway to let him pass, he descended on a bristling, hostile Sister.

'Yes?'

'Good morning, Sister. Warm, isn't it? Do you mind if I sit down?'

Without hesitating, he walked past and into her office. The chair alongside her desk disappeared beneath his bulk. As she followed him in, his large, thick-lipped mouth drew back in a broad grin to show massive white teeth. She had been wrong. He was not fat but thick-set and powerful. He took a handkerchief from his breast pocket to wipe his forehead, and she saw the coarse black hairs on the backs of stubby fingers. Thick tight curls of youth festooned his head, with no suggestion of a parting, yet the short crescents of grey were more consistent with a man of near sixty.

'Where's the big white chief then, Sister?'

'If you are referring to Mr Brookes, he's not on the ward at the moment.'

There was about him an aura of physical power that overawed her, prevented her from barking at him, but she resisted the temptation to call him 'sir'. His dark clothes were obviously expensive but crumpled, his trousers baggy.

'D'you have an appointment?' she asked.

'We arranged to meet, if that's what you mean, Sister.' He looked at a heavy gold watch, the bracelet cutting into a thick-skinned hirsute wrist. 'A quarter of an hour ago.'

'Mr Brookes is in theatre. He was called down to do an intussusception.'

Somehow she expected him to know what that meant. 'And who exactly are you?' she asked.

'Name's Stern. Ben Stern. I'm the guy who's got the unenviable task of keeping your beloved boss's name on the Medical Register so that he can go on being late for appointments like this. I'm here to protect him from the wrath of someone he appears to have orphaned.' He smiled, as if relishing his irreverence. He picked up the phone from her desk and held it towards her. 'Ask him to put a move on' – he grinned again – 'just so long as he doesn't go cutting anything he shouldn't again.'

The grin only widened as he watched her dial a number, her face and neck blotchy with suppressed fury. A few words and she dropped the phone back on its stand.

'Mr Brookes will be up in about ten minutes.'

'So, what about a cup of coffee then, Sister? I'm parched. No sugar.'

When she returned with the coffee, the Sister found Stern reading a patient's clinical notes. He did not look up but neither did he resist as she took them from him.

'I think, Mr Stern, you'd better wait in the patients' sitting-room.'

'That's all right, Sister. This will do me fine; nearer the heart of things, if that's not too insensitive a way of putting it on this ward.' He laughed, though the Sister did not. 'Tell me,' he said, taking his first cautious sip from the thick mug, 'were you on duty here at the time of the accident?'

'Your appointment, Mr Stern, is with Mr Brookes, not me. If you'll excuse me, I've got work to do.'

The ward sister thought she had made rather a good exit until she heard Stern chuckle throatily as she closed the door. As he sat drinking the murky, tasteless NHS coffee, made without caring, Stern tried to visualise the man he must defend. What should he expect? What would anyone expect in one of the NHS's more distant outposts? Some surgical rough diamond? Coarse surgery to Wimpole Street as reservoir fishing to the Spey? Solid but hard-working, unimaginative surgical hack? Or perhaps some surgical inadequate, his ineptitude protected for years by his obscurity? All right for the run of the mill cases – not up to the big stuff – found wanting on the day – laid bare by the big event – panics under pressure – fails in the eye of a surgical typhoon – a veritable Captain Queeg?

Brookes' appearance as he entered the room was much as Stern had expected. He was dressed in sports coat and brown trousers, his woollen shirt clean but worn, the collar lax from want of a button. At least he was not a Gladstone bag and morning-coat man; they always got up judges' noses. But, God, to turn up in court looking like that would be a disaster. Hardly a judge's impression of a successful, competent surgeon. Local vet, maybe. Perhaps he had a couple of Labradors in the car, wellington boots and trout rods in the boot.

On seeing Stern, Brookes' face took on that narrow-eyed defensive mask that always appeared when anyone now talked about the Teflo disaster. Over the years since the explosion, any mention of those eventful days saw Brookes reacting with mute withdrawal. If the discussion was prolonged, he would make some excuse and leave. His other aching unhappiness he had succeeded in encasing within a shell of apparent contentment. He had become once more the friendly but authoritative pillar of the hospital establishment. Some of the older nursing sisters still shook their heads – he'd never been the same since his wife died. And Sister Kay smiled. Only two others knew the truth. Only once had his unhappiness poured out, when alcohol had freed his tongue and a devoted son and a compassionate Celt had put him to bed after Jonathan's twenty-first birthday party.

Brookes and Stern glowered at each other in silence as if to speak first would have been a sign of weakness. Neither proffered a hand to the other. Stern broke first as he watched Brookes sit behind the Sister's desk.

'I hope you won't be this late at your trial tomorrow,' Stern growled.

'Somewhat tardy yourself, I understand. I trust your excuse was as good as mine?'

Stern would have preferred it if the words had been spoken with venom, not in that apathetic monotone. It was going to be easier to get Brookes to change his clothes than that martyr's smile.

'How can I help you?' Brookes asked, apparently more interested in a pile of pathology reports on the desk.

Stern scowled. 'Let's establish one fact before we go any further, shall we?' he said. 'You need the help, not I. You're on trial tomorrow, not I. All I'm doing is visiting the scene of the crime.'

'And the criminal?'

'That helps at times. I don't suppose it crossed your mind to come and see me?'

'Why should it? I hadn't even heard of you until a couple of weeks ago. One or two letters to my Defence Union just after the accident and what happens? Seven years later you turn up. What the hell took you so long? Seven years. If I keep a rupture waiting seven months, people play hell. And now you dig me out, seven years later, to have your bit of fun with me tomorrow. If I'm such a bloody awful surgeon, haven't you been worried what I've been up to during the last seven years?'

'Due process of law,' Stern said. 'Due process of law. Perhaps you surgeons feel you should be above the law?'

'Of course not.'

'But you do tend to think you're a little bit special, don't you – singled out from the common herd?'

Brookes looked unmoved as he swung his chair back, using both hands to play with his tie, but his voice rose as he answered. Here was a chance to burnish his resentment, keep it alive. He took his time, choosing his words. 'Yes. I reckon a surgeon is a bit special. Just imagine me operating on someone as fat as you with something bleeding like hell down in the depths of his belly. If it was your ulcer that was bleeding, you'd hope the surgeon was someone rather special, wouldn't you? Just as they put you to sleep, how much would you pay to make sure the surgeon was a bit special? Do you belong to BUPA? You look the sort. And how special do you think parents hope the surgeon is when they see their only child being wheeled into theatre after a road accident? Yes, I think I'm a little bit special at times.'

'Been trained to do it, haven't you? God knows you get paid well enough for it.'

'That's no answer and you know it.' Anger began to replace whining cynicism in Brookes' voice. 'Try taking anyone at random off the street and training him to do it. Not everyone could do it. Could you do it?'

'Perhaps I will when I get fed up with the law.'

'Balls.'

'Perhaps you consider yourself a bit special amongst surgeons?' Stern asked.

'Better than some, worse than others.'

'And do you reckon you're the only surgeon that has ever killed his patient?'

'No.'

'Then why the Greek tragedy?' Stern raised his voice. 'Perhaps you think you're so goddam good that it couldn't happen to you? Perhaps you think you're so goddam good that, if it does happen to you, everyone should forgive you and pretend it didn't happen? Why the resentment? What are you really afraid of? Something you've never had the guts to face, that you just weren't up to the job? Are you scared that your brood of idolising nurses and devoted patients, all cooped up in this cosy little world of yours' – Stern waved an arm around vaguely, warming to his theatrical oration – 'are going to see you for what you are? Are you worried we're going to crack open the big, tough surgeon tomorrow and they're going to see your soft centre? Not just feet of clay but clay right through? True or untrue?'

Brookes stood up, his fists clenched. 'No. Not true.'

Stern stood up and the two squared up across the table. The veins in Stern's short neck filled as he pressed home his point. 'The trouble with you surgeons is that you strut around this little world of yours with the power of life and death, until you think you're God. You get to feel you can do what you bloody well like; make a balls of an operation and kill your best friend in the process and then expect no one to take any notice.'

Brookes had never been closer to striking anyone in his life. But, in Stern's face, close to his as they stretched towards each other across the table, Brookes saw no more than his own conscience, shut away, suppressed, for years behind a veneer of apparent indifference. Driven into a corner from which he could find no logical escape, he spat out the only reply he could muster. 'What makes you think you know anything about it? Why don't you fuck off.'

To Brookes' surprise, a grin spread slowly over Stern's face, replacing the angry congestion of his features. 'Good. That's better. At least now I know I'm going to have a man in the box tomorrow, not some martyred, fucking teddy bear. Now take me down and show me the theatres.'

The exchange of obscenities became a bond. Michael warmed to Stern as he realised he had been summed up and manipulated by an expert. Within a matter of minutes, he had instilled in Michael absolute confidence, and their rapport grew from there. Stern's catechism showed no sign of relenting as they made their way to the theatre block, but Brookes' answers lost their overtones of resentment.

'What about this anaesthetist fellow, Orme, the one that seems to have stolen all the limelight at the inquest?'

'That bastard? He hates my guts.'

'Why?'

Brookes found it difficult to answer the simplest of questions.

'Why?' repeated Stern. 'One of your congenital misfits, is he? Not one of your healthy outdoor types, I'm told. Not a queer by any chance, or have you never dared to get close enough to find out? I don't imagine he has much chance of being elected captain of your local golf club?'

Michael was ashamed by his inability to answer. He finally muttered a few words. 'No good reason. He's just a sweaty little creep, that's all.'

'And I imagine you miss no opportunity to make him aware of the fact,' Stern added drily. 'What about the others? Williams, Dai Jack you call him? How would he stand up in court?'

Brookes looked at Stern with a new respect. How much did he know about them, if he even knew their nicknames? How the hell could he have learned that?

'Salt of the earth,' he replied. 'No worries there. I would trust him completely.'

'And Harrington?'

'Solid as the Bank of England.'

'Got himself a gong out of the mess?'

'Yes. And deserved it.'

'Loves to walk the corridors of power, I believe, narrow and dim as they might be up here? Got the committeeman's corns on his arse, no doubt?'

'Someone's got to do it. Nothing much would get done if it was left to the likes of me.' Michael was genuinely irritated that he should have to listen to Stern criticising George Harrington.

Taking care over each word, Stern said, 'And if it came to a direct conflict of loyalties between you and the hospital, which way do you think your friend Harrington would jump?'

The answering silence was sufficient for Stern.

'No other friends?'

'I like to think I'm on pretty good terms with the rest of the staff.'

'What about this chap, Gracie, the pathologist fellow?'

'Oh, of course, Steve. I'd forgotten him.'

'Oh, I'd forgotten him,' Stern mimicked. 'One of the guys whose evidence could be crucial to you and you forget him altogether. I'm surprised. I thought, of all people, the surgeon would want to make a friend out of the pathologist. I imagine you've had more than a passing interest in many a post-mortem over the last twenty years. Wouldn't do to have the pathologist bearing you a grudge, now would it?'

'Don't believe in pulling your punches, do you?' Michael said. There was no bitterness now in his voice, just admiration. He found relief in Stern's scourging tongue.

'Look, if you want some ponced-up counsel who will just make the noises you want to hear, tell me and I can find you half a dozen. I have more briefs than I can handle without coming to this God-forsaken part of the world to wet-nurse a surgeon who is too bloody pathetic to stand up straight. If I don't suit, just say the word.'

'No thanks. You'll do.' Michael smiled. 'You'll do me fine.'

Stern walked into the theatre block of Dunbridge General as if he had been working there for years. He headed for an empty theatre to find his way barred by Sister Kay. Greek met Greek.

'You don't go into there dressed like that. Go and change.'

'Sister Kay, this is Mr Stern, my defence counsel for tomorrow. He's very anxious to visit the scene of my crime.'

'I don't care if he's the Pope, Mr Brookes. No one goes into my theatre dressed like that.'

They walked to the surgeons' changing-room to emerge with Stern's dusty clothes inadequately concealed behind a straining gown, and his shoes thrust into pale blue plastic overshoes.

'Change, I said, Mr Stern.' Sister Kay once more barred his way.

Chuckling, Stern returned to the changing-room. He re-emerged to hobble into theatre, one footless leg sliding his theatre boot across the floor. They were joined by David Williams. Celt and Jew, not unlike in build and temperament, eyed each other warily and declared a truce with silent nods. Stern insisted on standing at the operating table where Brookes had stood. The questions he asked were aimed at building up a sense of atmosphere in his mind. The answers he used to fuel a vivid imagination trying to break out of the ambient, sterile calm. He drove himself to feel the heat, hear the noises of clacking anaesthetic machines, urgent suckers and short, clipped conversation, see the litter of surgical battle, the green drapes stained black by the wound's red overflow, taste the dry mouth of controlled fear. Brookes answered his questions with amused tolerance, Sister Kay with ill-concealed hostility.

'You don't like me, Sister.'

'Nothing personal, Mr Stern. I don't like lawyers.'

'Not even when they're trying to help?'

'Help?' said Sister Kay. 'Why don't you let the poor man alone? Why do you have to treat him like a criminal?' Her voice became guttural as she ground out the last word.

'You were taking table at the time, I believe?'

'Yes, I was.'

'Do you think what Mr Brookes did was negligent?'

'No.'

'Do you know the legal definition of negligence, Sister?'

'All I know is that Mr Brookes is incapable of doing anything negligent, whatever fancy words you use to wrap it up in.' Sister Kay stared with uncompromising defiance at Stern. She had seen more frightening sights than him.

Stern nodded approval but made a mental note not to call her as a witness. The woman was so emotionally involved that no one in court would believe a word she said.

In the recovery-room they found George Harrington waiting for them, full of nautical *bonhomie*, his file on the accident under his arm. Facts and figures flowed; how many had been operated on by Brookes before the Barker case, the number of casualties waiting for surgery at the time, how many had died, how many had been treated in the recovery-room.

'I must congratulate you on your records, Harrington. You seem to have coped pretty well.'

'Thank you, Mr Stern. I don't think the hospital has any reason to feel ashamed of the way it behaved that day.'

'Really?' Stern suddenly sounded desperately tired. 'Perhaps you should write a book about it.'

Harrington lacked the sensitivity to detect the hint of asperity in Stern's voice. 'Actually, I have written it up in a couple of the journals. I thought perhaps our experiences might help others in similar circumstances, you know.'

'With Mr Harrington as sole author, no doubt?'

Harrington's wrinkled face slowly sagged behind the thick lenses as his smile gave way to a look of bemused wonder. He stepped back, almost at attention, and swung his file under his arm like a swagger stick, trying to fathom the meaning behind this untidy little man's innuendo, his sense of self-importance disturbed by the challenge.

Stern bent to wipe his forehead on the front of his theatre gown, looking up again to smile haggardly at Sister Kay. 'Sister, d'you think you could find me one of those hot sweet drinks that your profession is so famous for? I rather think I forgot to have breakfast this morning.'

'Yes, of course, Mr Stern.' With a nod of her head in the direction of the corridor, she spoke to Michael. 'You'd better take him into my room while I get the drink. I'll bring you both some sandwiches, but I'll get that drink first.'

Brookes sat silently, watching Stern improve, and by the second sandwich the lawyer's colour had returned and he had stopped sweating.

'How long have you been a diabetic?' Brookes asked.

280

'Five years.'

'On insulin?'

'Yes.'

'And you forgot, as you call it, to have your breakfast?'

'Oh, for God's sake, don't you start nagging as well.'

'How often do you test your urine?'

'Now and again, mostly again.'

'Then, sooner or later, you're going to be in trouble.'

'I know, but I can't be bothered. I've got some trouble already, actually. That's how it came to light. I get ulcers on my stump; a Symes, I think you people call it.'

'Yes, I noticed. It's not an operation you see very often these days. How did you come to lose your foot?'

Subliminally, there flashed across Stern's mind the picture of a rebellious student, dressed in the uniform of the 5th East Yorks, staring in disbelief at what a German land mine had just done to his foot, on a short, crowded midsummer visit to la Rivière.

'Let's just say I put my foot in it once too often,' Stern replied, briskly. He belched and changed the subject.

'Did you say you hadn't seen a solicitor?'

'That's right,' replied Brookes. 'As I said, a few letters after the inquest and nothing more.'

Stern made a short sucking noise between tongue and palate, as if irritated that a colleague had let him down.

'But shouldn't he be here with you?' Brookes asked. 'Bit unethical for you to see your client like this without the solicitor being present, isn't it?'

'Ignorant medic,' Stern scowled, good-humoured again. 'Barristers don't have clients. Stick to something you're meant to know something about. Tell me how it feels to operate on your best friend. You'd better give me something to work on if I'm going to come up with some sort of sob story for the judge tomorrow. What is it like?'

'Depends on what you're doing.' The answer was not designed to be evasive. Their initial episode of flagellating intercourse had left Brookes strangely at peace with himself.

'Does it have any effect on you at all?'

'What a bloody stupid question.'

'Is it? Everyone's guts are the same, aren't they?'

'Yes, of course, but there is a difference.'

'What difference?'

'Who would you rather defend on a murder charge, your best friend or a complete stranger?'

'That's no answer. I'm not on trial, you are. I've got to know whether you were affected by the knowledge of whom you were operating on, and how, and why.'

Brookes sat forward to answer, began to use his hands to make his point. 'Young man of twenty comes off his motorbike while going for a burn up the M6. You're called in. He's bleeding like hell. You do your best and you get lucky. He survives. No great song and dance if he does. You might not be so lucky. He dies. Everyone is upset for a while. Awful waste of a young life and all that. Five lines in the local rag. Motorcycles ought to be banned, et cetera. If you're really lucky, you get away without even having to interview heartbroken parents. You may never even get to know his name.' He paused and then went on. 'Telephone goes. Big flap. Prince of Wales in road accident while travelling north. Internal injuries. Critical. No time to get the big boys from London. All yours. You're the end of the line. Line of accession running through your fingers. Everyone is looking at you. D'you mean to say that would be the same? Barker was hardly the heir to the throne but he was important to me.'

'All right. Fair enough. All that I can understand,' Stern said, 'but what I'm interested in is what you are thinking about at a moment of utter crisis in an operation. Are you still conscious of whom you are operating on? Does it still affect you then?'

At least Stern looked as if he cared, but there was no way Michael could tell whether his concern was genuine or not. Stern was, after all, a competent professional. This was probably the way he looked with all his clients, that mask of ersatz concern Brookes showed at the end of a long outpatient clinic. He continued, and Stern made no attempt to cut him short, did not seem anxious to get away.

'I think,' Brookes said, thoughtfully, 'that most VIPs run the risk of surgeons being, perhaps, a bit too cautious, too concerned that nothing should go wrong. It can get to the point of timidity, the muscles all tensed up, your movements jerky. Occasionally it can give rise to one of these utter crises, as you call them, in an operation the surgeon might normally do quite happily once or twice a week. There have been famous examples. Naturally, they occur much more frequently when you're a junior. As time goes on you learn how to avoid them and, when they do occur, you become more experienced in dealing with them. Many of the mishaps that I would have thought the end of the world as a junior, I would handle without much sweat now. But they still happen, even now, try as you will to avoid them, perhaps once or twice a year. I've often said that I earn my salary about twice a year and then I earn every penny in about three minutes flat.'

'Yes, but in that couple of minutes,' Stern persisted, 'what are you thinking about? Are you conscious of whom you are operating on then?'

Michael hesitated. 'No, probably not,' he conceded.

'What are you thinking of then?'

'Nothing. Just a blank.' He gave a short laugh of embarrassment. 'What I mean by "nothing", is that you seem to step beyond the edge of reality. You seem to be standing to one side, watching, a high-pitched screaming noise in your mind's background against which you can hear yourself saying, "Oh, God, get me out of this", or, sometimes, just a stream of foul language.'

'Panic, you mean.'

'No.' Brookes barked out the word, angrily, lowering his voice again and looking about him as if afraid he had been overheard. 'No,' he repeated. 'Not panic. Because, all the time this is going on, you can hear yourself quietly asking for instruments, telling the houseman what to do, making them all take their time, not get flustered. It's quite different from panicking. You can always tell when a surgeon is panicking, and don't imagine it never happens. Either he freezes and lets the poor bastard bleed to death or he becomes hyperactive, inefficient, usually getting himself deeper and deeper into trouble. It's striking the happy medium when the shit hits the fan, that's the problem.'

'And in your operation on Barker, d'you reckon you did that; struck a happy medium?'

Michael looked straight at Stern. 'I think so.'

Stern held his stare for a moment and grunted. He looked down at his empty cup as if he would have liked another one but did not want to break the thread of conversation. 'And you reckon the fact that the patient's name was Barker had no influence on you?'

Michael sighed in exasperation, as if he had already made his point. 'Look,' he said. 'You still don't seem to have grasped what I'm trying to say. There was a phantom Laurence Barker, fit and well, peering over my shoulder, whispering in my ear, very interested in what I was doing to him. It's the same whoever you're operating on. There's always someone looking over your shoulder, watching. If you don't know the patient, then at least these ghosts don't have faces, personalities. But, at times, they're the only company you've got, even though the room is full of people only too eager to help. Perhaps they are there for a purpose. Perhaps the surgeon who has managed to get rid of them has finally convinced himself he's God and immediately, of course, becomes a bloody menace.' Suddenly aware of the fervour in his voice, he apologised. 'Sorry. Don't take too much notice of the paranoid ramblings of a self-pitying surgeon.'

'And if Barker was looking over one shoulder, who was looking over the other?'

'What do you mean?'

'I mean his wife. Barker's wife. A very attractive lady, by all accounts. Was she keeping an eye on you too?'

Brookes began to look flushed. 'Why on earth should you think that?'

'Oh, come on,' Stern said. 'Stands out a mile. Small, enclosed society; big, healthy widower living next door to an intelligent, good-looking woman, whose husband is on the skids. Shouts at you. Doesn't have to be *Peyton Place*. Only have to put two and two together. Was there anything between you? I need to know.'

'We were friendly, naturally. But why d'you need to know? What the hell is it to do with all this?'

'Friendly,' Stern mocked. 'Did you have an affair with her?'

'I suppose you could say we did, yes,' Brookes growled. 'But that's all over now. It didn't exactly last very long,' he added, bitterly. 'I don't see that it's relevant.'

'You don't?' Stern replied. 'Well, perhaps you will when I tell you who the plaintiff's counsel is.'

'Who is it?'

'Adrian Barker.'

There was a long pause. 'Oh, my God.'

The whispered words came from deep inside Brookes' chest.

'Exactly. And he's good, very good indeed. Also quite capable of counting up to four. Is there anything to suggest he knows?'

Michael still seemed utterly shocked by Stern's revelation. He answered slowly.

'Not that I know of. I've always kidded myself that no one knew about it.'

'What, in a place like this?'

'Yes, except, that is . . .'

'Except?'

'My son. My son and hers.'

'They knew?'

284

'Yes.'

Stern's look of disapproval suggested a puritan core to this worldly man.

'I've never met Adrian Barker,' Brookes said, almost in a whisper. 'He's not likely to bring anything like that up in court, is he? Surely not.'

'I wouldn't have thought so, but it's not exactly designed to make him love you any the more, is it? But just imagine how it would sound coming from someone as good as Adrian Barker. You've admitted to an act which has killed someone you must have wished dead many times.' He paused as he seemed to become intensely preoccupied with something in the bottom of his cup. 'Don't suppose it crossed your mind, by any chance?' Stern raised his eyes to concentrate on Brookes' face: his question had not been an entirely frivolous one.

'Don't be so bloody stupid.'

The reply seemed to satisfy Stern. 'I understand she ran out on you in the end?'

He expected a brisk retort but Michael did not respond for a moment. 'No,' he said, pensively. 'I thought so at the time. But, looking back, if anyone ran away, I did. You couldn't really expect her to go on living here after the results of the inquiry came out. Imagine her son having to go to school and sit next to some of the orphans. He would have had a hell of a time. No, she wanted me to go with her and I chickened out. Too stuck in my ways. Too afraid of what might happen.'

'She's a solicitor?'

'Yes.'

'Where?'

'South London somewhere.'

'And you don't know where in London?'

'No. The last I heard, some years ago, she'd been made a partner in a firm in Guildford.'

'And you haven't seen her since?'

'No.'

'Not since the disaster?'

'No.'

Stern smiled, shaking his head from side to side as if he never ceased to be amazed by his fellow man.

'They must have been thinking of people like you,' he said, 'when they coined that phrase up here – how does it go? – something like "There's nowt as strange as folk."'

34

The Hon. Sir Iestyn ap Owen Lloyd, DSO, DFC, was a vain man. Aged sixty-five, he was proud of the mass of silver hair that had made him so easily recognisable during his years at the Bar and he regretted now its relative obscurity beneath the judge's wig. The son of a wealthy Caernarvonshire landowner, he once was proud of the Welsh lilt to his voice, but consciously suppressed it, first at Shrewsbury and later at Cambridge, only to cultivate it again, within limits, for the benefit of judges and juries. After a distinguished career in Pathfinders, flying Lancasters and Mosquitoes, his promotion through the legal ranks had been rapid, firstly as Recorder of Caernarvon and of Chester, and later, in 1971, to the Queen's Bench Division. But Sir Iestyn still nurtured ambitions.

As he sat, isolated, in the back of the official Daimler, which was purring its way sedately towards the centre of Preston, he peered through round, gold-rimmed glasses at the *Weekly Law Reports* of 6 March 1981. Abstractedly, he drew a circle around 'House of Lords' with a red felt-tipped pen. The headings of 'Whitehouse, Appellant', and 'Jordan and Another, Respondents', he passed over rapidly but resisted the temptation to draw a ring around the names below. Lord Fraser of Tullybelton, Lord Russell of Killowen, Lord Bridge of Harwich; names to be conjured with. Sir Iestyn relished their sound as they rolled off his tongue.

Negligence was always difficult to try, medical negligence particularly so. There was no black and white statute law to rely on. No Queen's Regs. He could not try this man Brookes by the book because there was no book to try him by. From the pleadings, the fellow looked as guilty as hell. The evidence was factual, clear cut, admitted, not contested. But it was not going to be that easy. No case with that man Stern ever was. Stern had appeared before him many times. A persuasive bastard. Needed to be kept in line. Intelligent lot. Frightening. He remembered that fat little Bavarian Jew boy during his last year in school, the one who had run away to England, the one who had escaped from the Gestapo into the arms of the fourth-form *fascisti*, the one he used to turn away from, pretending not to see the upper-class brutality.

Sir Iestyn had had his fair quota of verdicts overturned over the last two years and any other additions would inevitably incur unfavourable attention from their Lordships. And so the decision of the Law Lords in the matter of *Whitehouse* v. *Jordan*, three months earlier, had been a godsend in that it represented the most up-to-date definition of medical negligence. It was going to be a comfort to quote their Lordships in his judgment. Thereby he could comply with precedent, dispense justice without incurring their Lordships' displeasure and defend his judgment if contested. Even so, it was all very difficult. He slid the papers into a briefcase as the car drew silently to a halt.

While the judge was waiting for his chauffeur to open the door, Michael Brookes was negotiating the tight curves of the concrete ramp up to Preston's central car park.

He felt tense, and for a brief moment he was reminded of the fear and excitement which examinations always engendered in him years ago. The only difference was that, this time he would be the only candidate, with nothing but a viva to see him through. He had fantasised briefly that people would behave with great respect towards someone going for trial, standing back, making way for him with pitying looks on their faces, but no one in the shopping arcade seemed to notice him. Two small children even jostled him out of their way in their race to get to the escalator. Too early, he joined the window-shoppers and watched an elderly man buy the local newspaper with the time-passing deliberation of someone surplus to society's requirements. Brookes wondered whether to introduce himself, tell the stranger to look out for him in tomorrow's edition.

He crossed the Lancaster Road, took a last deep breath of fresh air and tentatively pushed open the swing doors into the green-tiled entrance-hall to the Law Courts. It could have been the entrance-hall at the DGH. As he stood, undecided, feeling the strangeness of the place, the doors slapped and thudded behind him as dark-suited men walked purposefully past him, nodding to the pipe-smoking police sergeant behind the desk. It was just as Brookes had nodded to Hook a thousand times, but now they were the consultants and he the patient.

'Number two court, please?'

'Along the corridor. Can't miss it.' The policeman took the pipe from his mouth but did not say 'sir'.

Brookes felt dwarfed by Preston's number two court. Heavy oak panelling rose above the green tiles to a high ceiling surrounded by an ornate cornice. What little light filtered through a stained-glass window at the ceiling's centre was the sole testimony to the existence of a world outside. Steps led downwards, out of view, from a forbidding, brass-railed dock. Subliminally, Brookes saw the prisoner between the uniforms, saw the black cap, heard the voice of doom. Seriate ranks of seats, split in three by two aisles, rose behind him like a small, intimate theatre, the acoustics being so good as to make audible the tick of a large clock on the back wall. It was 10.20 a.m.

The court usher gossiped with the shorthand writer and showed no interest in a defendant who looked around vaguely, not knowing where to sit. Brookes finally chose a seat in the row in front of Williams and Gracie, who stopped their hushed whisper to give Brookes a nod and a few words of encouragement. In the second row of the central block, Brookes saw Stern in earnest conversation with a young barrister behind him. Brookes smiled. Stern looked back as if Brookes were a total stranger. Beyond Stern a bewigged head was bent over some papers. No doubt that would be Adrian Barker. Brookes' eyes scanned the remainder of the court, hopefully. But he saw no one else he recognised. She was not there.

A thin young man in a Marks and Spencer suit rose from the row behind Stern and crossed over to Brookes.

'Good morning, Mr Brookes. Higgins, legal department at Area.'

They shook hands.

'Sorry about this, Mr Brookes. Very unpleasant for you, I'm sure, but you're in good hands. I'll see you later.'

Brookes wondered how often he had heard an anaesthetist say that and realised, for the first time, that it did nothing to allay fear or lessen the feeling of utter loneliness.

Behind the judge's high chair stood a heavy-panelled door with a magnificently carved architrave surmounted by an ornate coat of arms. But it was from a small side door that a tall man, indistinguishable from any five-star head waiter, entered and, with short, important movements, tidied some papers and dog-eared books. He nodded loftily to the usher and disappeared once more from the stage.

'Will the court please rise.'

There was a hissing flurry of silk as the judge made his appearance at a velocity that indicated a studied entrance begun deep inside the room behind, the action of someone anxious to make an immediate impact on the court below. Deep bows were followed by more rustling sounds as judge and counsel sat. Sir Iestyn gave his standard smile to the bewigged head just below him which had turned and said 'Good morning, my Lord', before announcing to the court that 'The Queen's Bench Division . . .' What had taken seven years to come to court started two minutes late. Adrian Barker stood up.

'My Lord, I appear for the plaintiff in this case and my learned friend . . .'

'Yes, Mr Barker. Now tell me all about this.'

With an imperceptible sigh, Barker began again.

'It is the plaintiff's case, my Lord, that, on the night of 11–12 July 1974, Mr Laurence Barker, in the town of Dunbridge, died as a result of a negligent act carried out by the defendant, Michael Brookes, in the performance of a surgical operation which, though severe, was compatible with survival. If I could first take your Lordship back to the events of Thursday, 11 July 1974, to the occasion of one of the worst, if not the worst disaster in . . .'

Barker's words drifted away into the background as Brookes saw, for the first time, the speaker. The likeness to Larry Barker was staggering. The strangeness of the wig and the gown detracted nothing from the uncanny feeling that Larry Barker was back from the dead. All Brookes could see for the moment was the profile, severe and aloof, but the physical similarity was remarkable. It was only with a conscious effort that he could concentrate on what Barker was saying.

'. . . and so, with respect, my Lord, I suggest you may find that most of the evidence pertaining to the facts will not be the subject of dispute and –'

'Yes, Mr Barker, a great deal of this appears to be common ground.'

Once more, Barker held his breath in silent irritation before going on.

'. . . and it will be the interpretation of the facts that will be at issue. No doubt you will hear from the defence, my Lord, all the extenuating circumstances, but it will be the plaintiff's case that, accepting the extra-ordinary conditions that applied that night, the defendant did not bring to the operation that standard of care that could be reasonably expected of him. At this point, therefore, I call my first witness, Dr Stephen Gracie.'

In law, Adrian Barker had a straightforward case and he couldn't see how he could influence the case one way or the other. Present the facts, clear cut and uncontested, and miss no chance to pre-empt the inevitable pleas of extenuating circumstances. He couldn't see what Stern could do about it. There were no hazy edges to the clinical facts with which to blur the images in lay minds. It would simply be a matter for the judge to decide whether putting a stitch around a man's coronary artery constituted a negligent act. He had considered carefully whether it was right for him to appear for the plaintiff, and he had decided that since he bore Brookes no malice, there was nothing wrong in trying to obtain justice for his brother's family. Such was his dispassionate love of the law that one surge of emotion within him would have caused him to stand down. Yet now, as Gracie took the oath, he looked across at Brookes and he was quite sure he saw the man who had killed his brother by his negligence.

'Dr Gracie, why did Laurence Barker die?'

'He died following a major operation.'

'Quite so, Dr Gracie, but then many patients have major operations and do not die. Is that not so?'

'Of course.'

'So, I repeat my question. Why did Laurence Barker die?'

'He had a cardiac arrest from which he did not recover.' Stephen Gracie was no stranger to the witness box and he knew, better than most, that the manner in which a witness gave his testimony was almost as important as the quality of the evidence. He consciously made the effort to speak clearly and firmly without giving the impression of being on the defensive, as if he had something to hide.

'And this was the cause of death you gave at the initial inquest, I believe. Let me see.' Barker lifted a sheet from the lectern in front of him. 'Yes, here it is. Cardiac arrest from an operation due to penetrating wound of the heart. Is that correct, Dr Gracie?'

'Yes.'

'And you still stand by this cause of death?'

'Of course.'

'Even though you were obliged to elaborate in rather greater detail at the adjourned inquest, I understand?'

'Yes, but I have no reason to regret the cause of death I gave. It would be the same today.'

'But would you agree, Dr Gracie, that the certified cause of death can be, at times, no more than a three-line précis of a whole chapter of accidents?'

Gracie looked at the judge, at a loss as to how to answer. 'I agree it is often difficult to condense all the post-mortem findings into a single cause of death.'

'But you know, and I know, that the central issue in this case is the fact that the defendant tied off one of his patient's coronary arteries, a fact totally ignored in your cause of death.'

Gracie began to feel cornered. Why was he standing there, taking all the flak? What had he done? All he'd done was find the damned ligature. He'd put it in the post-mortem report, hadn't hidden it from the Coroner. He wondered where the Coroner was. Why didn't they call Ralston, put him in the box? There was anger in his voice as he replied.

'The fact was recorded in my post-mortem findings and made available to the Coroner. The Coroner was aware of the facts and was quite happy to accept my cause of death.'

'I don't dispute that, Dr Gracie, but would it not be true to say that the fact would not have come to light except for information, if one can use contemporary political jargon, leaked to certain interested parties?'

Gracie said nothing and Barker was quite happy with the response. After a carefully timed pause, he continued.

'So let's get the real cause of death quite clear in everyone's mind, shall we? It was?'

'Cardiac arrest,' Gracie answered doggedly.

'Due to?'

'Cardiac infarction.'

'Due to?'

'Coronary occlusion.'

'Due to?'

With the faultless timing of long practice, the judge raised his forearm, his elbow still resting on the bench, his palm turned towards Barker.

'Mr Barker, a little laboured, if I might say so.' He turned towards Gracie. 'Dr Gracie, did Laurence Barker die as a result of a stitch or ligature placed around one of his coronary arteries by the defendant?'

'Yes, my Lord.'

The judge grunted and returned to his writing.

'I am obliged to you, my Lord,' Barker said, though he didn't look it. 'And his remaining injuries, Dr Gracie, would he have died from any of these?'

'Well, of course, he had already undergone major surgery once before that day. He had lain in the open, shocked, with his arm trapped, and had undergone the amputation of a limb to free him.'

'And this is inevitably fatal?'

'No,' Gracie conceded grudgingly. 'And he was found also to have evidence of liver disease.'

'But I am prepared to call expert evidence to state that this is compatible with survival for many years. Is that not so?'

'Yes.'

'So, I put it to you, Dr Gracie – if I may be permitted my own précis of the cause of Laurence Barker's death – that he died as a result of the ligature placed round the coronary artery, no other diseases or injuries being found that were not compatible with survival for many years?'

'Yes,' muttered Gracie.

'Speak up, Dr Gracie,' the judge said, sharply. 'What did you say?'

'That's correct, my Lord.' Gracie looked back towards Barker, submissive now to any question he might put, but Barker had sat down.

'Mr Stern?'

'No questions, my Lord.'

Adrian Barker stood again, briskly, crisply relaxed, exuding confidence in the justice of his case.

'I now call Mr Hugo Latimer.'

Barker's two expert witnesses were London heavyweights whose task it was to sit on the lid of the coffin that he felt Gracie had already screwed down. The first was a brash Australian who had come to the old country to learn his surgery and had decided that his considerable talents would be most profitably applied amongst the Poms he never failed to deride. Garrulous and opinionated, he was, however, an accepted authority on cardiovascular surgery. Barker drew from him what an accepted risk of surgery on the aorta the occlusion of one of the coronary arteries was. Latimer drove home the point with quotations from his own textbook on the subject, a work, he explained, which now had become standard reading for all surgeons, even general surgeons, who professed to keep abreast of recent advances. Stern let him come and go unchallenged.

The second was Mr Geoffrey Henniker-Boyce, a handsome, imposing figure, immaculately dressed and mannered; a man whose traverse of a teaching hospital ward had resembled that of a brilliant comet, and who was more at home in the pillared halls of Royal Colleges or Societies, or the carpeted hush of private clinics just south of Regent's Park, than grinding out the third gall bladder of the day in a London suburb or West Country market town. Now retired, he found the limelight of the professional witness a great boon in warding off boredom, grooming his evidence with great care to suit prosecution or defence.

He modestly agreed the string of appointments Barker read out and went on to explain what a splendid job most surgeons at the periphery were doing under, at times, quite primitive conditions and that, of course, such a mistake would have been unthinkable at his old hospital, as there would have been suitably qualified experts immediately to hand to look after that sort of thing.

This time Stern stood up.

'Mr Henniker-Boyce, have you ever done the operation in question?'

'No, actually I haven't.'

'Mr Henniker-Boyce, are you a thoracic surgeon?'

'No.'

'Mr Henniker-Boyce, do I take it from what you have just said, that if such a patient was admitted to your hospital, you would get someone else to do it?'

'Yes, that is true.'

'Someone who would do it better than you would?'

'I don't know that I would put it quite like that,' Henniker-Boyce replied. He looked towards the judge but there was no sign of help from that quarter.

'Mr Henniker-Boyce,' – Stern drew the name out longer and longer – 'do you mean that you would do the operation just as well, if not better than your thoracic surgical colleagues?'

'Well, no.'

'So what I said previously was true?'

'Yes,' he agreed, uncomfortably.

'So, Mr Henniker-Boyce, you are giving evidence today as an expert on an operation you have never done and one you would get someone else to do for you if confronted with it?'

Stern gave him no chance to answer and left Barker to repair his witness's dignity with a few adulatory questions the judge showed no sign of heeding. As Henniker-Boyce stood down, mentally resolving that no fee would ever lure him so far north again, Barker closed his case.

The judge made little attempt to hide his feelings as Stern rose to present his case. Stern's shirt stuck out above his trousers and his gown had slipped so far down his back that, had he dropped his arms, it would have slid in a heap at his feet.

'Yes, Mr Stern?'

'My Lord, I appreciate that it is a little unusual but I would, with your permission, like to call one of my expert witnesses first. They are both busy men but one has come a considerable distance and I am sure he would welcome the opportunity to get home tonight.'

'Very well, Mr Stern.'

'I am obliged, my Lord. Call Sir John Biggar.'

When Michael had come into the courtroom, he thought he had recognised the man who was now moving up to the witness box, but he could not bring himself to believe that a recent ex-President of the Royal College of Surgeons could possibly be there, let alone give evidence in his, Brookes', defence. He couldn't conceive that his case was that important. By nature iconoclastic, he respected Biggar completely. He was a surgeon's surgeon whose integrity Brookes had never heard challenged. He wondered how Stern had managed it. And yet it was only in keeping with the man in the box, someone whose appointment book read like a page out of *Debrett* but was known to operate with equal care on the aristocracy and the unemployed alike. His evidence was in character.

He began by saying that it was almost impossible for even an experienced surgeon to visualise the difficulties in a one-off situation like this. No one could claim to be an expert on an operation so rarely performed; it was quite possible to go through a surgical lifetime without being put in that position. Of course it was a tragic mistake but quite understandable in the circumstances, one he might well have made himself. Was it even correct to call it a mistake? Was it not more of an error of judgment? Wasn't there a difference? It was remarkable that more such errors had not been made that day and a tribute to the standard of surgery to be found in the periphery nowadays; the reason for the dearth of clinical material at London's teaching hospitals now.

When Stern sat down, Barker was not so foolish as to prolong Sir John's influence from the box. As Biggar passed on his way out he gave Michael a broad smile of encouragement. The smile he gave in return seemed to Brookes to be limp and inadequate, a poor return for what Biggar had done for him. He wanted to get up and shake his hand, to thank him, but that was patently impossible under the circumstances. Perhaps he could write to him after it was all over. He became conscious of the judge and Stern talking.

'. . . and I imagine your examination might last some time, Mr Stern?'

'Yes, my Lord.'

'In that case, I think this a suitable time to adjourn until two this afternoon.'

Outside the courtroom Brookes found his colleagues grouped in the corridor between himself and the hall beyond. Gracie and Williams stepped forward, extending friendship, but Brookes smilingly disengaged himself, sliding between the group and the shiny green tiles to make for the comforting anonymity of the street. For half an hour he window-

294

shopped, dyspeptic from a greasy Welsh rarebit and a cup of tea, wondering whether he should have had a word with Stern, asked him how things were going.

Immediately the court had reassembled, Stern called Brookes to the witness box. Michael felt the shield of indifference, which he had built so assiduously around himself in the preceding weeks, shattering in seconds. He had fondly imagined he would be allowed to give his evidence in a manner as scientific, as unemotional, as he was capable of, leaving the court to make a judgment that he would accept, whatever the verdict. He had convinced himself that he had produced in himself a trance-like immunity that would protect him from what he saw as a loathsome assault on his personal and professional integrity and dignity. For those uniformed legal technicians to rip out his feelings, examine them publicly, measure his competence, perhaps even question whether he should continue to practise his profession, was as obscene to Brookes as discussing with colleagues in front of an unanaesthetised, conscious patient, what to do with a cancerous colon he had just withdrawn from the abdomen and draped in front of the patient's eyes. These learned professionals, utterly at home in surroundings as frightening as any operating theatre, dressed up in their operating clothes, gowns and caps, were dissecting away at parts of Brookes that were every bit as vital and as private to him as any patient's glistening viscus. But he had been determined they were not going to hurt him, had long since come to terms with the judgment he had passed on himself a hundred times. In short, he had resolved to tell the truth and ignore the verdict.

But when he walked up to the box and saw the two faces his resolve melted away. There was to be no clinical detachment for him after all. In seconds he was taken back seven years, years that might not have existed. It was as if the trial was now taking place shortly after the explosion, the inquest, her departure. In a wave of emotion he had been determined to dam back, Brookes heard again Larry Barker's drunken, bubbling snigger and felt again that deep longing for Alison. He felt betrayed. This was not how he had planned it. He had been prepared to hand over his beloved surgical reputation to an impersonal legal system, to do with it what they would. What he had not expected was to be confronted by the dead man and his wife.

Sitting where he had been previously, low down in the corner of the large courtroom, he had seen Barker only in profile and from some distance away. In the witness box, Brookes had now turned through a right-angle and stood only a matter of feet from Barker, who faced him squarely. Over Barker's right shoulder the upper far corner of the courtroom now came into view also. In the poorly lit benches near a rear entrance sat Alison Barker. There could be no doubt about it. Brookes' focus, zooming back and forth between the two faces, had the effect of projecting Alison forwards, making it seem in his imagination as if she were sitting alongside Adrian Barker. Once again Michael was unnerved by the likeness between Adrian and his identical twin. It was Larry in fancy dress. Michael almost expected him to grin, wink and raise a glass to his lips. He heard himself speaking uncomfortable, staccato sentences in a voice he scarcely recognised. For a few moments he felt the ragged cover of a book in his hand. His feet scuffed the wooden panels of the witness box as he struggled to maintain some sort of peripheral communication in the blur that was everywhere except around those two faces. Finally, the scowling face of his defence counsel broke through to his left, and the judge's laconic but incisive tones to his right.

'Mr Brookes, are you feeling unwell?'

'No, my Lord,' Michael answered, surprised by the question.

'Would you care to sit?'

'Thank you, my Lord, but I would rather stand.'

'As you wish, Mr Brookes. I would point out, however, the gravity of the question your counsel has just put to you and advise you, in your own interest, to consider the answer carefully.'

A vertical furrow of dumb concentration appeared between Brookes' eyebrows.

'Mr Stern, I think you had better repeat that question.'

'I agree, my Lord, it would seem to be necessary.' Stern turned his face towards Brookes, his features tense with irritation. 'I ask you again, Mr Brookes, have you at any time contested the fact that Laurence Barker died as a result of a technical mishap on your part?'

'No.'

'Thank you.' Exasperated at the effect on the judge Brookes' wool-gathering must be having, Stern sounded as if he had just ground out a confession from a hostile witness. His tone softened, became more persuasive.

'Now, Mr Brookes, it is the plaintiff's contention that this mishap was the result of a negligent act on your part. It could well be argued that this alleged act of negligence was the temporary lack of competence on your part, brought about by a few moments of panic. Obviously, therefore, it would be of considerable assistance to the court if you could describe what goes on in your mind at such a time.'

'That's something I find very difficult.'

'Let me try to help you.' Stern picked up his notes. 'Essentially, the problem you were confronted with was a lacerated aorta from which there was torrential bleeding. Would that be a reasonable description?'

'Yes, it would.'

'So, tell me, under those conditions, would you see everything as clearly as, say, a thoracic surgeon who might be operating on the aorta every day?'

'No.'

'What is your speciality, Mr Brookes?'

'General surgery.'

'But your own pet operation? You must have a favourite?'

'Gall bladder surgery, I suppose.' Brookes' modesty provoked a glare from Stern.

'When you operate on the common bile duct, do you see that clearly?'

'Mr Stern, what is a common bile duct?'

Stern was not surprised to see the raised arm as he looked up to answer. 'My Lord, it is a tube alongside the gall bladder, not unlike an artery though, of course, containing bile not blood.'

'Very well, Mr Stern, but I would be obliged to you if you would avoid technical jargon as far as is consistent with the proper presentation of your case.'

The arm fell back as if allowing the traffic to flow again.

'As your Lordship pleases.' Stern turned to Brookes once more. 'Do you see the bile duct clearly, Mr Brookes?'

'Most times, yes, but there are occasions when it can be so obscured by disease as to be very difficult to operate on with safety.'

'When accidents can occur?'

'Yes, certainly.'

'Fatal accidents, Mr Brookes?'

'Yes. Very rarely immediately fatal, but mistakes can be made that can result in prolonged ill-health and death months, maybe years, later.'

'And under these difficult conditions, who would you think would be more likely to make such a mistake, a general surgeon such as yourself, or a plastic surgeon, or a neurosurgeon, or, let us say, a thoracic surgeon?'

'I think an abdominal surgeon would be least likely to make a mistake.'

'Even though the thoracic surgeon would almost certainly have done, let us say, two or three years' abdominal surgery as a junior?'

'Yes.'

'Now, let us take another operation you probably perform regularly but not as commonly as a gall bladder. Take, for instance, a vagotomy.' Stern had anticipated the judge and he spoke before the forearm had reached forty-five degrees. 'A vagotomy, my Lord, is the division of the vagus nerve where it lies alongside the oesophagus, or gullet, in the treatment of stomach ulcers.' Stern waited for the arm to fall before he went on. 'Would you say that you see the vagus nerve as clearly as you do the common bile duct? Would you say you see it as clearly as a surgeon working in a centre that specialises in the treatment of stomach ulcers, operating on them every day?'

'No.'

'Even though you are performing the operation yourself fairly regularly?'

Michael was opening up, relaxing. Stern gave him confidence. He laughed. 'At times, in a big fat man with a deep chest, I'm glad to find the oesophagus let alone the vagus.'

'During which time the adrenalin begins to flow?'

'Yes.'

'More than when you are taking a gall bladder out?'

'Yes.'

'Why do you think that happens?'

'I don't know. Some surgeons are better at some operations than others, surgeons of equal overall ability. I imagine it happens in other professions. I imagine most counsel would prefer to argue some points of law than others, get a reputation for it, get chosen for a narrower and narrower field.'

'Would I be right in assuming therefore, Mr Brookes, that the adrenalin flows more readily in some operations than in others, even though you may be doing them regularly?'

'Yes,' Brookes agreed. 'I suppose, up to a point, it brings out the best in a surgeon, rather like an athlete.'

'But an athlete is pushing himself to his limit. Are you suggesting that this is the best way to do your operating?'

'No.'

'Surely you operate best when you are relaxed, finding it easy?'

298

'Not necessarily. You can get too relaxed, too complacent. You get careless.'

'What are you implying, Mr Brookes, that there is an optimum level of tension in any operation?'

'Exactly.'

'That this tends to be increased above the optimum in operations you don't like doing or don't do very often?'

'Yes. I would have thought it easy to understand that a surgeon's performance must be affected when that tension within him rises abnormally high.'

'Mr Brookes, does it lower the threshold at which these effects come into play if the patient you are operating on is one of your close friends?'

'It doesn't help.'

Sir Iestyn neither looked up nor stopped writing as he said, 'Mr Brookes, that is a question which can be answered with a simple yes or no.'

'I'm sorry, my Lord. Yes.'

'As when you operated on Laurence Barker?' Stern asked.

'Yes, I suppose so. But that doesn't mean that surgeons who are operating on their best friends, or find themselves in all sorts of trouble operating on someone they have never met before, ever throw their hands in the air and run out of the theatre, shouting they can't cope. All surgeons who make it to consultant rank these days would come up with some sort of a result. But the tendency is either to rush it or slow down with rather turgid, frozen movements, depending perhaps on your basic personality.'

'Into which category would you place yourself?'

'I rather tend to slow down.'

'Do you agree then that, from your description, your movements during the operation in question would have been slower than normal? I put it to you, Mr Brookes, were you putting the stitches in with more than the usual degree of care?'

The judge's head came up as he looked quizzically at Adrian Barker but there was no response. Michael looked up to see Alison nodding.

'I put them in with far greater deliberation than if I had been sewing up a common bile duct, if that's what you mean.'

Stern dropped his notes on the desk in front of him as if he were almost finished.

'We were discussing earlier the comparison with an athlete; the tension, the adrenalin, the effect on efficiency. But it was couched mainly in physical terms. I would ask you now to consider the effect on your mental capacity. Do you think it could affect you mentally?'

'Yes.' Brookes answered cautiously now, unsure suddenly where Stern's line of questioning was leading him. If it had not been for the confidence he had gained in Stern during their dry-run the previous day, he would probably have answered 'no'.

'Tell me,' asked Stern, 'I'm sure you have seen the pictures of Sir Roger Bannister completing the first four-minute mile?'

'Yes, of course.' Brookes appeared as surprised as the rest by the question.

'What do you think he had in his mind as he broke the tape?'

'Not a lot,' smiled Brookes.

'As you are well aware, Mr Brookes, Sir Roger is now a physician of international renown. But, if someone had presented him then with some complicated neurological problem to solve, do you think his ability to do so would have been impaired?'

'Yes, I do.'

'And what about putting in a stitch? At the risk of sounding Irish, over a matter of seconds, perhaps even minutes, would his mental state have impaired his physical ability to put a simple stitch in the back of a man's hand?'

'Absolutely.'

'And so, I put it to you, Mr Brookes, would it have been possible for you, having been physically stressed for nearly twelve hours, to have been driven to the point of physical exhaustion where, even though taking every care, and I stress again' – Stern thumped the desk – 'taking every care, to have been blind to the fact of how deeply you were putting in that stitch?'

'Yes.'

'And could you – having had seven years to think it over, as well as the trauma of these proceedings to impress it in your memory – could you guarantee absolutely, under identical conditions, never to make the same mistake again?'

'No.'

Michael's eyes followed Stern as he sat, sweating profusely, his hand searching for his trouser pocket through the confusion of his gown. He looked up and beyond Stern. Even from that distance he could see her mouth distorted as she bit her lower lip.

'Mr Stern.'

Stern got to his feet unsteadily, looking ill.

'Mr Stern, I think you owe it to your learned friend that he has not objected to the degree of leading that you have indulged in when examining the defendant. For my part, I have let it pass out of appreciation of the difficult point you were endeavouring to make. I felt, however, that it should not pass unnoted.'

'I am obliged, my Lord.'

As Stern slumped back in his seat, Barker rose.

'Mr Brookes, you have heard Dr Gracie's evidence. Do you accept his findings?'

'I do.'

'In their entirety?'

'Yes.'

'And you agree with his opinion that Laurence Barker died as a result of the stitch you placed around his coronary artery?' The judge's arm rose again like an old-time railway signal. Michael now gave the impression of someone interested only in getting the matter settled as quickly as possible. 'Mr Brookes, I hope you appreciate the seriousness of the charges brought against you? I would only say again that, while the question is a right and proper one,' he glanced for a moment towards Barker, 'if somewhat repetitive, you should, in your own interest, think before you answer.'

'I understand, my Lord.'

Sir Iestyn nodded and he searched Brookes' face intently as Adrian put the question again.

'Yes.' There was sufficient defiance in Michael's answer to make it clearly heard around the court. Barker stood, silently running his finger down his notes until he felt he had milked every drop of dramatic effect out of the pause that followed that single word. Sir Iestyn had done it often enough himself as an advocate not to let Barker overplay the part.

'Yes, Mr Barker.'

'Mr Brookes,' Barker resumed, 'did you panic at the point of putting those stitches in the aorta?'

'No.'

'Would you agree that a surgeon is more likely to panic when he is tired?'

'I imagine so.'

'Were you tired, Mr Brookes?'

'It had been quite a long day,' Brookes answered, drily.

'I imagine other surgeons in Dunbridge worked equally long hours that day?'

'Yes. I'm sure they did.'

'And yet you seem to have been the only one to have given way to panic.'

'Mr Barker' – the judge peered down – 'I cannot allow this repeated use of the word panic. As yet, there has not been a shred of evidence that the defendant panicked.'

'As your Lordship pleases. I will rephrase the question. Is it true to say that, out of all the medical and nursing care given that day, by very tired doctors and nurses, no other action for negligence has been taken as far as is known?'

'Yes.'

'So there must have been perhaps a dozen or more surgeons involved over the north-west of England during those few days without finding themselves being sued for negligence?'

'Yes.'

Barker looked at his notes, giving Michael a chance to glance once again at Alison. She was leaning forward, intent, chin in hand. She saw him look at her. He saw her smile. Throughout Stern's questioning, Brookes had been aware of her reactions. There had been almost imperceptible nods and smiles, a feeling that she was pressing forwards towards him, encouraging him. This was no predatory angel come to hover over the remains of a past lover. He had also been wrong about Adrian Barker. Brookes looked back at him. This was no Larry Barker reincarnate either.

Even if Larry had been right in saying the brothers had gone their several ways from the moment the single ovum, fertilised by a sperm so zestfully provided by Tom Barker, had split in two to form their own complete individuals, he had been wrong when he had claimed that Adrian had taken all the talents with him. Perhaps Larry had taken more than his fair share of warmth and generosity and that innate friendliness that his cold, withdrawn twin must, at times, have envied. The more Brookes looked at Adrian Barker the less he feared him. He saw nothing more than a legal robot, programmed to dispense the law without feeling except, perhaps, for the law itself. He just happened to look like Larry. But Larry would have been more restive, his face more alive, his eyes mocking as he asked the questions, hoping the answers would not be too serious.

'Have you ever operated for that length of time before, Mr Brookes?'

'Yes, on occasions.'

'What sort of occasions?'

'Well, if emergencies start coming in at the end of a long operating day, it

302

can happen that you have to go on into the next night. With breaks, of course.'

'When, naturally, you would be tired?'

'Naturally.'

'Mr Brookes, have you ever been sued for negligence before?'

The judge reacted sharply but Brookes forestalled him.

'I don't mind answering that, my Lord. No, never.'

'So it is possible for you to work long hours, be very tired and not make mistakes?'

'Yes, except the nature of the cases that day were rather unusual, to say the least.'

Barker waited for the judge to catch up with his notes before putting the next question. 'You had some considerable training in thoracic surgery as a junior, I understand, Mr Brookes?'

'A long time ago.'

'For how long did you work in a thoracic surgical unit?'

'Two and a half years.'

'Would you say there are many general surgeons with that length of specialised training in thoracic surgery?'

'Probably not. But, as I say, it was a long time ago, when most of the surgery was pulmonary.'

'Surgery of the lungs rather than the heart?'

'Yes.'

'But you were involved in some heart operations?' Barker persisted.

'Yes.'

'And did you perform any of these yourself, by any chance?'

'One or two patent ductuses and the odd mitral valvotomy, yes.'

Barker repeated the answer word for word, mouthing 'ductuses' as if he found it singularly offensive. 'And perhaps these operations involved putting stitches in or near the heart?'

'Yes.'

'Which ones?'

'The valvotomies.'

'What do you mean by that exactly?'

'In those days, we used to make a hole in the wall of the heart to put our finger through and then stitch it up again.'

'Quite so.' Again Barker paused as if he had made an important point. The next question, when it came, was abrupt. 'Did you know where the coronary artery lay?'

'I think so.' Brookes laughed. 'I certainly do now.'

'The Medical Directory informs us, Mr Brookes, that you were an outstanding student of human anatomy? Is that correct?'

'That was even longer ago.'

'It mentions a distinction and a medal.'

'Someone's got to win the medal every year.'

'But it signifies an above average knowledge of anatomy?'

'I suppose so.'

'And this would, of course, include the area of the heart and great vessels?'

'Of course.'

'So you would have been conscious of the proximity of the coronary artery to the site of the operation?'

'I can't say it figured very large in my thoughts at the time.'

Michael felt instantly that he had not answered that very well and was about to do what he could to retrieve it when Barker cut him short. 'What you are saying, Mr Brookes, is that you were aware of the fact that the coronary artery lay close by but did not take it into account at the time. Is that correct?'

'No.' Brookes began to stutter. 'What I mean was that when you have someone bleeding to death in front of your eyes, that is not the time to be bothered with anatomical minutiae.'

'You would consider the exact position of one of the coronary arteries an anatomical minutia, Mr Brookes?'

Brookes floundered for an answer only to find that Barker had not waited for one but had sat down in one precise movement. Barker knew he would not have another opportunity to leave Brookes at such a disadvantage and sacrificed one or two other minor questions he had intended asking.

Sir Iestyn peered down at Stern. 'D'you wish to re-examine, Mr Stern?'

'No, my Lord. I would like to call my second expert witness, Mr William Francome.'

Almost as an aside and without a flicker of emotion, Sir Iestyn dismissed Brookes. As Francome passed Michael on his way to the box, he hesitated as he heard the judge address Stern. Michael's relief at having given his evidence was such that he scarcely registered any surprise he may have felt at seeing Francome. He knew Francome in the same way all surgeons within a radius of thirty miles know each other, no more, no less. He knew him to be a good, sound surgeon, but why Stern had called him as an expert witness Michael could not imagine and he suddenly felt too weary to summon the energy to try.

'Are you contemplating a lengthy examination of this witness, Mr Stern?' asked Sir Iestyn. 'Time is getting on.'

Stern had to look back over his shoulder to see the clock. 'No, my Lord. Mr Francome is also a very busy man and I'm sure he would appreciate not having to return to court tomorrow.'

'Very well.'

Bill Francome stepped into the witness box and took the oath.

'You are William John Francome?' asked Stern.

'I am.'

'You are a Fellow of the Royal College of Surgeons?'

'I am.'

'And you are Consultant Surgeon at Lancaster Royal Infirmary?'

'Yes.'

Bill Francome, dressed in the suit he kept for dining out with people he did not know very well, was not sure what to do with his hands. Finally he settled for holding the front of the witness box as if he were afraid of fainting.

'Mr Francome, why do you think you have been called as an expert witness?' Stern said.

'Frankly, I haven't a clue.' Francome looked sideways at the judge as if expecting a rebuke.

'Are you a thoracic surgeon?'

'No.'

'Have you ever performed the operation in question?'

Francome's answer was forestalled by the judge.

'Do you really want me to take notes of this line of questioning, Mr Stern? It can scarcely be seen to favour the defendant's cause, you know.'

Stern acted out his irritation by twitching at his gown, pulling one side temporarily over one shoulder. 'With respect, my Lord, I am well aware of the implications of my line of questioning.'

The judge allowed himself a smile, happy that he had broken up Stern's theatrical posturing. It was bad enough at times keeping ahead of some of these successful advocates in matters of law without feeling threatened by personalities as well.

'Mr Francome, do you have any personal experience of this operation?'

'None.'

'And what would your feelings be if you were faced with having to perform such an operation this afternoon?'

This time Francome looked at the judge before answering and decided not to use the words that had come immediately to mind. 'I wouldn't relish the prospect one bit.' Stern did not follow up and Francome glanced round apologetically. 'It's one of those operations that lurks at the back of a surgeon's mind. Every surgeon wonders how he would cope; a bit like finding a child choking to death in front of you on a bead or a marble; would you have the bottle to do a tracheostomy with kitchen scissors?'

'Bottle?' asked the judge.

'Sorry, my Lord. Courage, guts,' Francome replied.

'Courage will do nicely, Mr Francome. Yes, Mr Stern.'

'I'm obliged, my Lord. Mr Francome, are you a personal friend of the defendant?'

Stern scowled at the judge's raised arm indicating they were going too fast. Francome watched it drop.

'No.'

'But you have met him before?'

'Briefly, now and again. Usually in local clinical meetings and lectures.'

'Just as in other professions, Mr Francome, I imagine a surgeon has two reputations, one amongst his patients and another amongst his colleagues?'

Francome nodded, not quite sure he understood exactly what Stern was getting at.

'And what is Mr Brookes' reputation like amongst his colleagues locally?'

'First class,' Francome replied, sounding genuine.

'In what way?' Stern asked.

'Well, it's one of the perks of the profession. You get to know, over a radius of about thirty miles or so, who's good, who isn't quite so good; who's good for this operation, who's good for that. Patients by and large have to take pot luck. At least we can choose. I know for a fact that Mr Brookes operates on many of his colleagues and their families. For certain conditions I would be more than happy to have him look after me.'

'And the hospital you work in in Lancaster, Mr Francome, is that very similar to Dunbridge General?'

'Well, yes and no. Naturally, as you can imagine, there is a certain amount of local rivalry – everyone likes to think his hospital is the best – but essentially the work done in the two hospitals is very similar. Dunbridge is

306

slightly different, slightly bigger, I suppose, as my appointment is split between Lancaster and Morecambe.'

'But, apart from being split in two, the surgical services are roughly comparable?'

'Oh, yes.'

'Then I ask you, Mr Francome' – Stern pushed his wig forward on to his forehead to audibly scratch his thick hair as he put his last question together with great care – 'if the same thing had happened to you but the fact had never come to light, as, I imagine, many such facts do not,' – Francome nodded – 'how would you have felt?'

'Sorry, upset, sad. Difficult to describe just how one feels. I would have taken it as being downright bad luck and pressed on. You've got to, otherwise you go crazy.' He looked round modestly and saw Stern nodding encouragement. 'It's the sort of thing where your colleagues smile, say "bad luck" and change the subject. Unless, that is, they think you want to talk about it, get it off your chest, so to speak. You soon know if they think you've been negligent, they don't mention the subject. If they're reluctant to talk about it, sort of turn away, then you know. They'll never tell you you've been negligent, they'll never do that, never put it into words. Too frightened they'll go out and do the same thing the next day, I suppose, like tempting fate. No, there's never any doubt when your colleagues think you've done wrong. But you've got to keep going. All surgeons make mistakes. The best you can do is do your damnedest not to make the same mistake twice.'

Francome's sudden eloquence pleased Stern as much as it amazed Francome himself, prompting Stern to ask one more question.

'Knowing as you do the circumstances of this case, if you had been aware of the post-mortem findings a few days after the operation, what would your reaction to the defendant have been? Would you have said "bad luck" or turned away?"

'Said "bad luck",' Francome answered, without hesitation.

'Thank you, Mr Francome.'

Stern sat down, visibly delighted, and Barker rose, slowly, allowing Francome time to fidget his feet but not relinquish his grasp on the box in front of him.

'You mentioned bad luck, Mr Francome. Would you agree that the bad luck was not all the surgeon's, that the patient was deserving of some commiseration also?

'Yes, of course,' Francome licked dry lips.

'But, unfortunately for him, he was not around to be patted on the back?'

Francome stayed silent.

'No?' Barker persisted but drew a reply only from the judge.

'A somewhat rhetorical question, don't you think, Mr Barker?'

'As your Lordship pleases.' Barker bowed. 'Mr Francome, have you had any training in thoracic surgery?'

'No.'

'Not at any time?'

'No.'

'So any venture into the chest would be much more of a stressful procedure than if you had benefited from some considerable period of training?'

'Yes, of course.'

'And the mistakes you mentioned, the ones all surgeons make. Would you agree that there are mistakes and mistakes?'

'Yes.'

'And one can hardly imagine one more major than tying off someone's coronary artery?'

'I agree that it would have very dramatically fatal results, but it's possible for a patient to die just as surely, if less dramatically and over a longer period, from what seems at the time an almost insignificant technical error.'

Francome was beginning to enjoy himself, fending off everything Barker put to him, and it was with something close to disappointment that he saw Barker sit down. Exhilarated, he walked out of the court, deaf to everything but his own words ringing in his ears.

'Will you be calling any further witnesses, Mr Stern?'

'No, my Lord.'

'In that case, I will hear both counsels' summing-up tomorrow morning. The court is adjourned until 10.15 tomorrow.'

With abrupt finality, it was over. Brookes stood, bowed and watched the judge's back disappear. The door had not closed behind the judge before Brookes had turned, raising himself on his toes, to look obliquely over the heads of counsel towards the far corner of the room.

She had gone.

35

At the door of the court, an usher handed Brookes a note, the expression on his face implying that he did not do that sort of thing very often. It was equally obvious that he had read it. It would not have taken him long. All it said was, 'Staying at Esplanade. Please come and see me. Alison.'

Brookes drove home, rang his son, cooked and ate a frozen cottage pie without registering its predictable taste. He washed and dried his face, changed his mind and showered and put on a clean shirt. The courtroom had been hot and his beard had grown. He considered shaving again, twice in a day, something he had not done for years, and decided against it.

It was nearly nine o'clock, the air still hot, the sea as flat as a child's painting, as he walked from the car park to the Esplanade's front entrance. Since Brookes' last visit to the hotel, many years previously, alcoves had been built along one wall of the lounge, each alcove looking out over the promenade and beach. In each alcove the soft plush of the semicircular seats contrasted with the circular tables' unforgiving hardness of cast iron and stone. In the alcove farthest from the door he found Alison, a cold, empty coffee cup before her.

He stood over her, awkward and embarrassed. She clasped her hands firmly in her lap as if afraid they might make some involuntary sign.

'Hullo. How are you?'

'I'm fine. And you?'

'Fine, thanks.'

Seven years and that was the best they could do.

'Can I get you a drink?' Michael pointed with a nervous twitch towards the bar.

'No, thank you, Michael. But I'd love another cup of coffee, if that's possible.'

She watched his back as he stood at the bar, saw the same familiar movements as he reached for his money. His pint glass was brim-full and he drank a little as he walked back.

'Your coffee's coming.'

'Thanks.'

He sat facing her but within range of the perfume he had always found stimulating.

'Well, what brings you so far north? You've come a long way just to see the fun.'

'I'm sorry. I wondered how you'd feel about it. I just wanted to be there. Did you mind very much?'

'Not really. I did wonder whether you'd come. I was glad to see you.'

'You were? Truly?'

'Yes. Why didn't you stay after it finished?'

'I wasn't too sure what sort of reception I'd get.'

'You needn't have worried. The natives are quite friendly up here. We haven't eaten any southerners for years now.'

Alison was glad to look away and smile at the waiter bringing her coffee whilst Michael felt no better for playing the role of rejected lover and martyred surgeon.

'And how's the big city? Lived up to your expectations, has it?'

'Yes, mostly it has. It's been nice to know I can stand on my own feet. I'm not sorry I did it.'

'Good,' Brookes said, his voice as unyielding as the sound of his beer glass on the cold table top. 'It's been a success then?'

'Yes,' Alison answered, no vestige of compromise in her tone. 'I've been an equity partner now for some years. In a very big firm. If you consider that success, well then, yes, it has been a success.'

'In Guildford?'

'In Guildford.'

'Bully for you.'

Ill at ease, they looked out of the window. They watched two T-shirted skinheads, bored with another day's sun and sea air, overturn an already overflowing rubbish basket, darting away into the dusk amongst the evening strollers.

'Place hasn't changed much.' Brookes laughed.

'No,' Alison agreed. 'I'm glad.'

'Oh?'

'Yes. Somehow it's a comfort. I've had a picture of this place in my mind for years. Nice to know it's been fairly true to life.'

'Haven't forgotten us altogether then?'

'No. I think of the old days very often, wonder what's happened to

310

everyone. They all seemed so important in those days. I couldn't imagine life without them. Never thought I'd miss them. Sir John Anderson. How is he?'

'Dead. Only lasted a year or so.'

'Poor man. When I think how frightened we were of him. Poor Larry . . . And Maggie?'

Brookes laughed. 'Still going strong. Took her breast off a year or so ago but she's all right. Still smoking like hell.'

'And that other chap? The Canadian. I think Larry was even more frightened of him. What was his name?'

'I know. I remember Larry talking about him. I never met him.'

'Looking back, he was the villain of the plot, wasn't he? And he was the only one to survive completely unscathed. Just vanished from the scene.'

Alison gazed out to sea as if wondering where he had gone. 'And who else was there?' She paused thoughtfully, turning to sip her coffee. 'Oh, your theatre sister. What about her? What was her name? Sister Kay? Yes, that's right, Sister Kay. How's she?'

Her tone was too studiedly nonchalant to ring true.

'She is now Theatre Superintendent. Except they don't call them that any more. She's a number six or seven or eight, or something daft like that. Anyway, she's the boss now.'

'But still adores you?'

Brookes pulled a face but didn't answer.

'Oh, come off it.' There was bitterness in her voice. 'You know she does and you love it.'

Brookes felt uncomfortable and thrust the conversation away. 'Robert. How is he?'

'He's very well.' There was a coldness in the reply that surprised Brookes. 'He got an engineering degree in Southampton and he's stayed on to do a course in nautical studies. I believe he's talking about accountancy after that. A very, very, determined boy is Robert. Sailing crazy. Very much in demand as crew in these cross-Channel races. I imagine he'll end up some sort of marine engineer, build oil rigs or an Admiral's Cup winner, perhaps.' Alison laughed. 'One thing's for sure, he doesn't need me any more.' Now there was no doubting the icy tone. 'And Jonathan? Where is he now?'

'In Liverpool. He's coming up tomorrow. He couldn't get away today but he said he'd be in court tomorrow. Wants to be around on the day of judgment, as he calls it.'

311

'And what did he do afterwards? Did he do medicine?'

'Yes. He's done very well, seems to take everything in his stride. He'll be twenty-four next month. He's Alex Tibbs' House Physician at the moment. Do you remember Alex?'

'Yes, of course. I'm not likely to forget him, he was so kind. And is Jonathan still the quiet thoughtful one?'

'No, not altogether.'

'Oh?' Alison sounded surprised.

'No. I must admit he rather surprised me. He's still pretty quiet but he changed, sort of grew up, about the time it all happened.'

'Yes,' Alison said, making sure now that they faced each other as she answered. 'I don't think any of us realised what a strain we put on those boys. People can be very selfish at times, can't they?'

Brookes' mouth hardened as the old bitterness crept back. 'I like to think I haven't done too badly by Jonathan.'

'And Dai Jack? And George?' she asked, as if Jonathan had only been one of a list.

How kind of you to take an interest, Michael thought sarcastically, after all these years. 'Much the same as ever,' he said. 'Both within a couple of years of retiring now. Both very fit though George lost his wife a year or so back.'

'I'm sorry,' Alison murmured, sounding sincere.

'I take it you came up with your brother-in-law.' Michael made it sound like a sneer.

'Adrian?'

'How many brothers-in-law have you got?'

'My God,' Alison said, her face flushing. 'You really are bitter, aren't you?'

'How the hell d'you expect me to feel?' Brookes replied, roughened with anger. He waved his empty glass at her. 'I'm going to have another pint. Would you like a drink now?'

Tight-lipped, Alison shook her head. Both felt their anger rising as Brookes returned, glass in hand. Alison began to throw words at him before he sat down again.

'Why shouldn't I come up with Adrian, if I wanted to? What's it to you?'

'Nothing really. I thought the Barker family might come up in force, looking for its pound of flesh, that's all. I was surprised Robert wasn't there today.'

'Adrian, if it's any comfort to you, must have come up by train. He's

312

probably in a hotel in Preston. As a matter of fact he doesn't own a car.'

'Poor chap,' Brookes snapped.

'Don't be so damned patronising,' Alison snapped back, her voice rising. 'He's very much his own man. If he's chosen to be an intellectual monk, so what? It's his choice and he doesn't give a damn what anyone else thinks about it. That's what was wrong with you. You're, you're . . . a damned sight too concerned with what people think of you. Your b-blasted image.' She began to splutter furiously. 'And who for? These people?'

She swung her arm around in the direction of the bar. As they both looked up, they saw that their raised voices had attracted attention.

'I still have a son.'

'Oh, for God's sake. We're not back to him again, are we?' Alison jerked her head vertically to add venom. 'He always was your excuse for everything. He's old enough to look after himself.'

'He wasn't alw–'

'Oh, God.' Alison tried to cut him short but he fought back. Though he found every word hateful, though he could hardly bear to look at a face he loved hardened with anger, this was one fight he was not going to run away from. There was another thought that drove him on, the thought that, unless these things were said, unless the slate could be wiped clean of all the recrimination that had smouldered away for the past seven years, there was no hope of anything beyond it, no going back to the tenderness they had both felt for each other.

'At least he doesn't go round suing people. At least I think I've still got that much influence with him. And, if he did, I think he'd at least have the decency to turn up in court. Where the hell was Robert today? Or perhaps he sent you up just to keep an eye on things for him.' That hurt and Brookes saw her lower lip begin to tremble and a sadistic pleasure drove him on. 'And what about this image you're on about? What about your image?' he snarled, inwardly incredulous at the intensity of his feelings, physically shaking with a rage he had never felt before. He felt himself skating uncontrollably on a verbal plateau over whose edge physical violence lurked. In a moment of terror he realised that, if he went on as he was, he might conceivably strike Alison. The thought appalled him, forced his fury to abate, and his last few sentences stuttered like a burned-out motor jerking to a halt. 'Didn't fancy your image much as a Shepworth housewife, did you? Don't tell me . . . But the successful career woman, that's different, isn't it? More your style. Circle of friends . . . Law Society dinners . . .'

And the sad jealousies of years flooded in to damp down his fury. Brookes saw them all, all male, all handsome, solicitors, barristers, doctors, accountants. Perhaps one of the Guildford surgeons. The hesitation at the doorway. 'Won't you come in for a nightcap? No, there's no one here. My son's away at the moment.' Perhaps she had arranged for Robert to be away, as she had done once before.

He sat glowering down at his beer, preparing himself to ward off the next tirade, feeling he could no longer sustain his level of anger, that he would either have to get up and leave or become ill in some way. The silence was broken by a sudden movement and Brookes looked up to see Alison snatch at a handkerchief in her bag alongside her. He saw her tears, and it crossed his mind that she was resorting to the ultimate feminine weapon. But no; this was genuine enough.

'Lissa. I'm sorry. I had . . . I'm sorry.'

He watched her sniff, swallow and dab, all with the staccato movements of irritation. It made him smile, brought back that ache.

'I'm sorry too,' Alison said. 'It's so stupid.'

'What?'

'Us. Bawling at each other like that.'

'Wasn't very pleasant, was it?'

'No.' Alison hesitated as a secondary surge of defiance swept over her. 'But I meant what I said. These things are probably best said and over and done with, don't you think? Out in the open?'

'Maybe,' Michael answered as if he was not quite sure – yet. 'Now, can I get you that drink?'

Now, tenderness was transmitted via the most banal of requests.

'Mmm. Please.'

'It used to be vodka and lemonade.'

'Still is. Plenty of lemonade.'

'And ice?'

'Please. By the time you get back, perhaps I will have dried myself out.'

Brookes did something he rarely did, ordered himself a whisky over a bar, and carried the drinks back. Alison, smiling, had moved the seat around and Michael moved an equal distance to sit closer though still without touching.

'Not exactly in keeping with my image that, was it?' she laughed.

314

'Oh, please.' Brookes spread his hands and closed his eyes. 'I'm sorry. I shouldn't have . . . Anyway – cheers.'

'Cheers.'

They both sipped their drinks and waited. They both knew there were explanations, excuses, confessions, confidences to come. But they didn't fear them any more. They knew they would be made in the intimate tones of loving friends if not lovers. Michael was still gazing at Alison, just realising how much he still loved her, when she began.

'I don't know what your mental picture of things in Guildford is but it probably isn't anything like the truth.'

'Oh? You seem to have been pretty successful.'

'Oh, yes. I've done pretty well but –' She stopped, reluctant to go on. 'Well, it's been – oh, what the heck, there's nothing to be ashamed of about it – I've been lonely.' She avoided looking at Brookes. 'Desperately lonely.'

'But Robert, Adrian? You must have made friends? In seven years?'

'It hasn't been that easy. Adrian I never see. He lives in Wimbledon and has his chambers in the Temple. I live in Epsom, near the college, and work in Guildford. He tried to help at first, with Robert, but he didn't get far.'

'And Robert?' Brookes asked, quietly.

'Yes, Robert.' Alison looked briefly but sadly out of the window, as if unsure where to start. 'I was never party to the action against you. You know that, don't you, Michael?'

'Yes. I know that.'

'I refused.' There was another pause. 'And, of course, Robert was under age at the time and Barclays Bank, as executors, had no choice when Adrian informed them about the inquest.'

'But how did Adrian come to know about it?'

'Oh, I think he would have found out anyway. An inquest on his identical twin? But it was Bill Rothwell who kept him in the picture.' She smiled, glad of a diversion. 'Bill Rothwell,' she said. 'There's another name from the past. Is he still alive?'

'As far as I know,' Brookes replied, 'though I haven't heard of him for years, not since he was Mayor.'

'Bill Rothwell, Mayor of Dunbridge,' Alison mused. 'Well, well.'

'You were saying about Robert.' Brookes brought her back.

'Yes,' Alison's voice dulled with sadness again. 'Robert. It was when he came of age – I think that was the first inkling I had.'

Brookes looked puzzled but kept silent.

'I asked him to withdraw the writ. But he refused, refused point blank. In fairness, Adrian did advise him that withdrawal at that stage would probably involve him in considerable costs – Adrian really did try, you know, to help Robert after Larry died – but I don't think it was that. In fact, I'm sure it wasn't.'

'Then why?' asked Brookes.

'Money. Simple as that. I'm afraid I've bred a son who worships money. What Larry would have thought, I can't imagine. Imagine Larry having a Beaupré for a son. Beaupré, that was the name. Beaupré.' She looked up at Brookes. 'It seemed as if, from the day Larry died, his son became utterly and totally ruthless. I rarely see him now. I wouldn't say we've quarrelled but he hardly ever comes home. He has his own flat.'

'I'm sorry.' Brookes could think of nothing else to say.

'Make no mistake about it, Robert is going to end up a millionaire. This court action, I'm sure he sees it as a means to getting a considerable amount of cash out of some faceless Defence Society, cash he will put to very good use, believe me.'

'I almost feel like wishing him luck,' Brookes said with a paper-thin smile, 'if it's going to be the first step to him making a fortune. At least some good would have come out of it all. But I'm sorry. I had no idea it had worked out like that. When did you see him last?'

Alison shrugged her shoulders. 'Six, seven months ago.'

'But why? Does he . . . What I mean is, have I something . . .'

'D'you mean, does he still hold it against us, having an affair while his father was so ill?'

'Yes.'

'I wouldn't rule it out. I certainly don't think he has ever forgiven me.' Looking vulnerable, she went on, sadly rather than with self-pity. 'And so it's been difficult. No husband and no son, it hasn't been easy to make friends. Widow on her own. I had plenty of offers but friendship didn't figure very high on the list. If you go out on your own, people think you're only after one thing, and I fought shy of those bunches of spinsters and widows that go round together.'

Brookes smiled.

'There was the occasional man, of course,' she said, abstractedly, as if Brookes wouldn't be interested, 'over seven years. But, I don't know . . . It wasn't the same.'

316

Brookes kept his smile intact in spite of the pain he suddenly felt in his gut.

Abruptly, Alison sat more upright, looked brighter, as if she was determined to put all that behind her. 'Come on, let's talk about something a bit more cheerful. I hope Robert doesn't get a penny. Do him good. Not that he will if that defence counsel of yours has anything to do with it. Where did you find him?'

'Stern? I didn't. The Medical Defence people just came up with him. Not a very prepossessing sight, is he? I can't say I was very impressed at first. The inevitable prejudice, I suppose. We had one hell of a barney within a few minutes of meeting each other but, after a while, he had me eating out of his hand.'

'Well, I thought he was fantastic today.'

'He was rather good, wasn't he?'

'Rather good? Is that all you can find to say about him?' She looked at him, slowly shaking her head from side to side. 'But then, I don't suppose you would have noticed.'

'Noticed? Noticed what?'

'The game of chess that was going on. Between Stern, Adrian and the judge. You were just the pawn. And he didn't miss a trick. Sorry,' she laughed, 'move, I suppose I should say. Your Mr Stern, I mean. And there was nothing the judge could do about it. It really was masterly.' Alison laughed as Brookes frowned. 'The way he brought on the ex-President of the College of Surgeons just after those two city slickers of Adrian's. Snuffed them out. "Anxious to get back to London." "Very busy man." My foot. Stern wouldn't think twice about keeping him hanging around for days if it suited him. No, he wanted him in immediately after the plaintiff's experts and just before lunch. That's important. Let his words stay with the judge over his lunch.'

Alison shifted her position and Michael followed her movements, his eyes admiring her. She still held an attraction for him that no other woman ever had and his face now showed it. Lissa recognised the look and there was a flush in her cheeks and a trace of excitement in her voice that had nothing to do with the law.

'The same with your other expert witness. Good yeoman surgeon, honest and true. He was brilliant. Said all the right things. And that's how Stern has managed to leave things overnight. Managed to get him in as the last witness of the day. As I say, Stern hasn't missed an opportunity so far. The way he chewed up that old buffer with the buttonhole.'

317

'Henniker-Boyce?' Brookes laughed. 'That pompous old bastard? I rather think he's been asking for that for years. Couldn't have happened to a nicer guy. I wouldn't lose too much sleep over him.'

'And your lovely man from Lancaster; that was brilliant.'

'Was it?' There was an element of banter in Michael's remark as if he was anxious for her not to be so intense, for her to change the subject, move on to something less professional, more intimate.

'Oh, come on, Michael. You're not as naïve as that. You don't think that was an accident? Or that Stern couldn't think of anyone else? If anyone's evidence is going to get you off, it's his.'

Brookes frowned. 'How d'you mean?'

One moment Alison was an intensely interested, animated professional, the next a soft, caring woman. 'How on earth have you managed to survive, you and that dreamer son of yours, for how many years now? How long is it since Rosemary died?'

'Nine years.'

'Nine years,' Alison repeated, slowly. There was a pause as if someone had asked for a few seconds' silence in memory of a loved one. 'If you get off, the first thing you must do is go to Lancaster and buy him a drink.'

'Who, Francome?'

'Yes.'

'If I get off? You don't sound so sure. Is that how you feel? Don't you reckon I'm going to get off?'

'Darling,' – she blushed and looked away as the word slipped out – 'it has nothing to do with the way I feel, or you, or Stern, or Adrian. It all depends on how the judge feels tomorrow. He alone will decide and I think sometimes it's safer to put your money on the dogs than on the judges. Who knows which way he'll jump tomorrow.'

'He'll give his judgment tomorrow, d'you think?'

'I should imagine so. It depends a bit on how long Stern takes to sum up but he can hardly go on later than lunch-time, and Adrian has virtually nothing to sum up. So it all depends on how long Stern takes.'

'And what d'you think he'll say?'

'Who, Stern?'

'No, the judge.'

'Anyone's guess.'

'Oh, come on, you must have some sort of idea.'

'No.'

'But faced with those PM findings?'

318

'Still anyone's guess. Look, you've got the typical layman's idea of a judge, all-wise, incapable of a mistake, dehumanised. You take it from me, there's just another man beneath those robes.'

'Listen.' She turned in her seat, tucking her leg under her again. The long curve of her thigh, stretching taut the thin velvet skirt, led down to a silk-smooth knee, now only inches from Brookes' reach. She put her left elbow on the window ledge and her head in her hand, her fingers disappearing into her hair. 'Say today, he, the judge that is, has heard that he has just inherited a thousand-acre estate with the best claret cellar outside France, at a time when he is still in those rosy early stages of a new love affair.'

'D'you mean to say judges do that sort of thing?' Brookes interrupted, smiling in mock disbelief.

'Consultant surgeons do, don't they, so why not judges?' Alison smiled back as she went on. 'Under those circumstances, do you expect him to come into court in the same frame of mind as if he had heard that his house had just burned down together with the Château-Latour, and his girlfriend had just told him to get lost after five years of a discreet and highly satisfying arrangement? No, you take it from me, they suffer from piles and ulcers and nagging wives just like everyone else.'

Brookes sat and gazed at her in wonder. The same face, older but just as beautiful, exquisitely feminine, but the manner changed, the restless drive behind the calm exterior now muted with subtle variations in expression and tone. Less urgency. More alluring. She had always been physically attractive to him, but now there was something more. She seemed more vulnerable now, needing him other than physically too. It made him feel protective. As if she wanted to come in out of the cold. He edged his hand along the bench seat but the gap was still too great.

'There've been times when I've sat behind counsel who are quietly fuming at a judge who has obviously already made up his mind long before all the evidence has been presented. I've heard judgments that make you wonder whether you've been sitting in the same court. And, of course, there can be quite definite personality clashes. At least he seemed to dislike both counsel equally today.'

'He did?' asked Brookes.

'Didn't you watch him? I suspect he feels threatened by Adrian, wouldn't relish a slugging match on points of law with him. And Stern isn't exactly your Winchester and Cambridge man, is he? But you've got one thing going for you. I'm told this judge is very much an establishment man and ambitious into the bargain.'

'How do you know all this?' Brookes looked at her quizzically. It produced the fluster of someone who realises that she has said more than she intended.

'I've been . . . I was talking . . . It's just gossip around the courts.'

'What, in Guildford?'

'No. But it is important.' Alison was clearly anxious to change the subject. 'You must have heard of the recent House of Lords ruling in the *Whitehouse* v. *Jordan* case?'

'What surgeon hasn't?'

'Well, I'm sure the judge will have read that report very carefully and he's not likely to fly in the face of their Lordships, not unless, of course, he's decided the time has come for him to make a name for himself.'

Flushed, excited, Alison stopped to find Brookes laughing gently at her.

'It must be fun to have a lawyer in the family. Would you like a walk before bed?' Both laughed as Brookes closed his eyes and raised his hands as if in surrender. 'Sorry. I think they call that a Freudian slip. Let me rephrase that.'

'I'd love a walk. Let me get a jacket.'

As Michael paced the hall, waiting, the night porter glanced up from the reception desk where he was reading the evening paper. He wondered briefly whether the porter recognised him and how big a write-up they had given him, then realised he did not give a damn. There was excitement in his belly once more, as Alison came down the stairs.

Outside, the promenade's flagstones were still giving out the heat they had stored from the day's sun. There had been no rain for several days and their feet felt the gentle crunching of a covering of fine dusty sand transported by a thousand children's feet. Walking slowly, Alison with her hands thrust deep in the pockets of a dark velvet jacket, they found it difficult not to touch without maintaining a wide gap between them. They had gone several hundred yards before Alison broke the silence.

'Is it really as bad as you said it was?'

'What?'

'What Stern and you were going on about this afternoon. Is that really how you feel?'

'No.'

'I just don't believe you. It sounded too genuine. In any case, you couldn't tell a lie on oath in front of a judge if your life depended on it.'

'Oh, for goodness sake, what does it matter? It's over now. Let's forget

320

it.' Michael wanted to savour his every moment with Alison, not over-shadow it with the trial.

'And that's just what you'd like, isn't it? Go back to that great big house of yours and feel sorry for yourself. Sit there, enjoying yourself, mulling it all over, all on your own.'

'Oh, what the hell,' Michael growled, his mind in conflict. That was the last thing he wanted to do, go back to that dreary existence. What he wanted more than anything was for her to go back there with him, then and there, that moment. But there was still that shell of pride that frustrated him, made it impossible for him to say it. He made a conscious effort to do so and no words came out. He was still struggling, furious with himself when they stopped to face each other, hard-mouthed again, but searching for a hint of love, then moved on erratically, walking crab-wise as they clawed at each other's feelings.

'There are times when I could hit you,' Alison said, almost laughing in her exasperation. 'There is always that last little bit that you won't give, isn't there?' Michael felt her hand in his. 'Let me in, Michael. Try to understand. I was desperate to get away all that time ago. This place was stifling me. I had to try. At least I have the satisfaction of knowing I could do it. But I'm lonely, Michael. And I miss you very much.'

'But seven years, Lissa. Has it taken you seven years to find that out?' Michael wondered again at his total inability to tell Alison what he was really thinking, that he missed her too, that he had missed her more over the last seven years than she would ever know, certainly more than he would ever be able to tell her.

'I know. It's been crazy, hasn't it? Such a waste. Pride, I suppose. God knows, I've been so miserable.'

They strolled on, now as close as they had been on that beach years before. Several slow, luxurious strides later . . .

'*Was* it true?'

'What?' Brookes asked.

'What Stern dragged out of you in court today?'

'You never really give up, do you?' Brookes laughed affectionately.

'Darling, I'm a woman. And I love you, Michael. And I want to know how you feel; share it with you. Please.'

'Yes, it's true. But for God's sake don't imagine it happens every day. It's only once in a blue moon. But, as I say, now and again, you earn your salary in about ten seconds. But most of the time, it's pretty routine.'

321

'And this must have happened quite a few times since Larry's operation?'

'Oh, yes.'

'And what do you do then?'

'Probably have a good old curse and swear with Dai Jack, maybe talk it over with George, people who would understand, say the right things.'

'And then you go back to that big empty old house?'

'Yes.'

By now, they were beyond the far end of the sagging loops of coloured fairy lights, out on the darkened stretch of road that led to the Royal Westmere, where the flagstones and tarmac gave way to a grassy headland, cool under their feet. Her head was on Brookes' shoulder and his arm around her waist when he asked her when she was going back to Guildford. He made it sound as if Guildford was a place from which there was no return.

'Would you mind if I stayed up for your day of judgment? I'd like to see Jonathan again; make my peace with him.'

'Don't be ridiculous.'

'I'm not. There must have been a time when he hated me, just after Rosemary died. He must have thought I was going to take his beloved dad away from him.'

'Well, I'm sure he doesn't feel like that now.'

'In that case, I'll stay until the day after tomorrow, if that's all right with you?'

'Of course, but can you take time off just like that?'

'I've taken ten days of my holiday, so there's no problem.'

'So that means you don't have to go back for a week or so?'

'Well, yes, I do. I've only a couple of days left.'

There was childlike disappointment in Brookes' reaction as he asked, 'When did you come up then?'

Alison answered in flat, frightened words, as if bracing herself for Brookes' response. 'About a week ago.'

'A week ago?' Brookes' voice rose in surprise as he pushed her away to seek out her eyes in the darkness. 'Do you mean to say that you've been walking round here for a week without telling me?'

'Yes.'

'Why?'

Alison did not answer until she had got her head safely back against his shoulder, her eyes hidden. 'Michael, I didn't come up just for the trial.'

322

'So?'

'You know Reggie Craxford?'

'Yes.'

'Well, I'm not sure you remember, but I did my articles with his father, old Tom Craxford.'

'Yes, I knew that.'

'Old man Tom is still alive. He's a poppet. I think he was quite fond of me. I think, at one time, he had plans for Reggie and me.'

'Yes, but what has this got to do with you?'

'Well, I've been keeping in touch with them from time to time.' She stopped, edging her way into Brookes' mind like someone hesitating on a narrow path alongside a precipice.

'They've offered you a partnership?' Brookes asked.

'No.' She felt his sagging disappointment as she turned to stop him walking any further. 'But the job of Magistrate's Clerk in Dunbridge becomes vacant next month. There have been vacancies once or twice over the last few years that the Craxfords have written to me about. But I wasn't sure.'

'But this time you've decided to apply?' Brookes held her elbows excitedly.

'I have.'

'And when's the interview?'

'I've had it, earlier this week.'

'And?'

'They offered me the job.'

Brookes tightened his grip and began gently to rock her back and forth. 'And you've accepted?'

'No.'

'No?' Brookes shouted.

'No. I wasn't quite sure. I had to be sure. I didn't know how you'd feel about it. I've got until the end of the week to let them know. Shall I take it?'

Her only answer was the sight, as she began to cry, of Brookes racing off into the night, where she heard, coming from the summer darkness, noises she would have expected more from a young drunken medical student. As she called to him to be careful, he emerged, breathless, to lift her off her feet and whirl her round. With a yelp, he put her back on the ground and clasped one hand to his back. As they leaned on each other, their gasping sounds of laughing and crying merged.

36

The next morning there was a spring in Michael's step as, without a glance at the police sergeant, he walked through the entrance-hall and entered number two court. As he descended the aisle he nodded cheerfully to Stern. He took his seat and turned to chatter to George Harrington. His spirits were high. There was nothing they could do now to touch him, not since last night. The one thing that he had dreamed about for years had happened. Alison had come back. Nothing else mattered. Feeling a tap on his shoulder, he turned back to find a furious defence counsel's face no more than inches away from his own.

'What the hell is the matter with you? Take that great grin off your face. What d'you think the judge is going to believe if he sees you looking like that? For God's sake, try to behave as if you were on trial.'

Reacting like a scolded child, Brookes scarcely had time to apologise before Stern had recrossed the aisle, his limp accentuated as he negotiated the row of seats. Brookes was still consciously searching for the appropriate facial expression, when a smile broke through again at the sight of Alison and Jonathan coming through the door together. This time they traversed the sloping court to take their seats, side by side, a few rows behind him. Dai Jack looked up from talking to Francome, caught his eye and winked.

Stern had every cause to be bad tempered. A phantom foot hurt like hell. There had been talk recently about something called neuroma and mention had been made of injections, maybe explorations. And so, he had not slept very well, in spite of the brandy. And his mind had been churning over, late into the night, the legal precedent on which he must base his defence. High on his reference list was the report of the House of Lords' opinion in *Whitehouse* v. *Jordan*. Other precedent dated back to 1839. Selected phrases lay before him, printed in clear red letters on a small clipboard.

Lord Wright in 1934 in *Lochgelly Iron and Coal Company* v. *McMullen* had stated that no negligence could be found where a mistake had given rise to no damage. Stern wondered why he had included that one – you can't damage a man much more than kill him. Stern rather fancied Lord Justice Scott in 1939 in *Manon* v. *Osborne* but had already decided that the bedrock of his defence was to be the words of Lord Denning in *Hatcher* v. *Black and Others*. In 1954 Lord Denning had said, 'The jury must therefore not find him negligent simply because one of the risks inherent in the operation actually took place. They should only find him guilty when he has fallen short of the standard of reasonable medical care, when he is deserving of censure.' Stern had underlined 'deserving of censure'.

Also, set carefully aside beneath the clipboard, was a small grey-green book, a bewigged head with an impish face challenging from the cover.

Stern knew that the plaintiff did not have to prove Brookes' negligence beyond reasonable doubt but simply as a matter of probability. Neither did they have to worry about proving any degree of negligence. Being a civil case, once negligence had been proved, the degree was immaterial. There was no question of Barker having to prove gross or criminal negligence. To prove that, Barker would have had to show that Brookes had been operating when he was drunk or under the influence of drugs. It would have been different if, just before the operation, he had been found slumped in the corner or staggering about the theatre, his face black and his voice modulated by anaesthetic gases. There had never been any suggestion of that.

Michael, bewildered with new-found happiness, made a brave effort to concentrate his mind on his own trial. 'Come on,' he muttered to himself. 'For God's sake take a grip. This is your trial. It's you they're talking about. Listen. They are going to tell you shortly whether you are guilty or not. And it matters now. You're not on your own any more. It's going to matter to her so it has got to matter to you. And Jonathan too.'

What Stern was saying began to register.

'My Lord, it is not my intention to burden you with any tedious repetition of the facts, facts which, from the earliest stages of these proceedings, have not been contested by the defendant. But your Lordship may consider that his open admission to the facts is only in keeping with the defendant's character. I submit, my Lord, that the attitude of the defendant throughout his trial has been that of an honest man, a thoughtful man, someone unlikely to shirk the responsibilities of an onerous profession. As an indication of this sense of duty, I would invite your Lordship to place to the defendant's credit the fact that, earlier on the day in question, he had already saved the man's life at the site of the explosion, not without some considerable risk to himself.'

Sir Iestyn looked unimpressed. Stern knew that Brookes' saving a man's life once had no bearing on whether his negligence had killed the same man later in the day. The judge looked even less impressed as Stern extolled Brookes' local reputation and his thirty years of practice without previous litigation. As if to show Stern how little he thought of his argument so far, he opened a book on his desk, looking down as he flicked through the pages, nodding his head as if to say, 'Carry on. I'm listening.'

'If I might deal first, my Lord, with what may be parcelled together as extenuating circumstances; the operating field to which the defendant is not now accustomed, the tiredness both mental and physical, and the emotional element in the type of operating that day, the youthfulness of many of the casualties, the high mortality rate.'

Sir Iestyn closed the book and looked up as if this might be a bit more interesting.

'The operation was a highly complex one, carried out through the thoracic cavity by someone who is now predominantly an abdominal surgeon, though my learned friend has argued that the defendant should still be considered an expert in this field. In answer, I would ask you what value you would place upon counsel's opinion, forced from him against his wish, derived within minutes, without time to refer to the printed word, without appeal, upon which a client's life or liberty might depend and in a branch of the law he had not practised for over ten years. I submit, my Lord, that not only do memories go but that special skills need to be kept sharp by constant practice.

'Turning next to the matter of fatigue, my Lord, the question is, does tiredness and emotional stress constitute mitigation when considering a possibly negligent act? Respectfully, my Lord, I put it to you that if a surgeon is urged by his colleagues not to embark, due to his obvious fatigue, on a difficult operation for a condition that would not deteriorate while the surgeon rested, and if the surgeon insisted on proceeding with the operation during which some mishap occurred, would this not be accepted by all as lacking in care? Surely to operate wilfully on a patient when the surgeon's faculties are dulled by fatigue might be considered as culpable as operating under the influence of alcohol? If such liability was agreed, how then may a court disregard fatigue that has been honourably sustained by someone who, according to the urgent promptings of his colleagues, is the only surgeon available to perform an operation that cannot be delayed by so much as a few minutes? Would the law have him say, "Let him die. I am too tired"?'

Stern let the words float in the atmosphere.

'I am much encouraged in this view, my Lord, by a ruling of Mr Justice Paull who took favourably into account a young doctor's tiredness at the time of failing to get a patient X-rayed. It has to be accepted that at times tired doctors have to take on responsibilities they cannot avoid.'

As Michael watched, now totally engrossed, Stern took a sip from a glass of water.

'An understanding of the effect of such fatigue is, I respectfully suggest, my Lord, germane to the decision you will be called on to make. As far as is possible, the defendant has taken us into his mind at a time of surgical crisis. He has striven in evidence to describe to those who have never had that experience, the moments of crisis perhaps better understood by others in those walks of life that take them periodically through the eye of an emotional storm. The state of mind he depicts must not be confused with panic. Everyone has experienced blind panic and the defendant's description of his feelings has nothing in common with that.'

The judge extended his arms rigidly down the sides of his chair, the muscles of his neck and jaw tensing in the suppression of a yawn.

'I have taken pains,' Stern went on, hurrying a little in reaction to the judge's sign of boredom, 'to stress these points, my Lord, in answer to those who might argue, "Is it possible to make such a fatal mistake without it being a negligent act?" In other words, is negligence inherent in the act? I submit it is not. In evidence, my Lord, you have heard an ex-President of the Royal College of Surgeons state that, in his opinion, it was no more than an error of judgment. If this were true, is negligence inherent in all errors of judgment? I submit it is not. It is perhaps as fortunate for the legal profession as for the medical if it is not, my Lord, for, if applied to the law, would not logically the Court of Appeal become a punitive body with erring judges as defendants?'

Sir Iestyn sat forward, suddenly full of interest, but Stern sped on.

'With your permission, my Lord, it is my intention now to examine the evidence of the expert witnesses. Lord Denning in *Hatcher* v. *Black and Others*, has stated that we should only find the defendant guilty "when he has fallen short of the standard of reasonable medical care, when he is deserving of censure". Deserving of censure, my Lord. But whose censure? Regrettably, in 1954, Lord Denning didn't specify whose censure. So we turn to the medical profession for help in this matter. Did the expert witnesses think the defendant "has fallen short of the standard of reasonable medical care"? Did they think him "deserving of censure"? At first glance, two said "yes" and two said "no". If I might be forgiven for reducing such an important matter to Saturday afternoon parlance, a drawn game, two all. But is it not always thus? Neither plaintiff nor defence is likely to call expert medical evidence not favourably disposed to his case. Is it not so that, provided we are prepared to pay the fees, we can always find supportive medical evidence? How many unfavourable medical reports are left in chambers for each one produced in court? With such manicured expert evidence, given by opposing witnesses of equal eminence, being so finely balanced as to be mutually exclusive, what can be the consequences?'

Stern slid from a transparent plastic folder, a sheaf of papers already folded over at the appropriate page. He held them as if about to sing.

'I propose, my Lord, to quote a short paragraph from the transcript of the trial of *Whitehouse* v. *Jordan*.' He took a deep breath and spoke with the voice of authority. 'I quote, "I am satisfied on the balance of probabilities that this is a case of intrapartum asphyxia or anoxia. There are two ways in which asphyxia and cerebral malfunction can be related. Firstly the asphyxia may damage the brain cells by depriving them of the oxygen they need. As respiratory function is controlled by the brain, respiration is normally further impaired when the brain is damaged; the worse the asphyxia the more the brain is damaged, the more the brain is damaged the worse the asphyxia. On the other hand, the brain may have developed abnormally so that it is incapable of regulating the respiration at birth. Asphyxia then occurs and this asphyxia further damages the brain."'

Stern slowly and deliberately replaced the transcript in its folder.

'I accept, my Lord, the dangers of quoting out of context but it is my contention that this extract could readily be mistaken for the words of a medical witness, whereas it was an opinion being expressed by a learned judge. Does it not demonstrate that the introduction of diametrically opposing views of equally distinguished doctors can force the judge into the role of some kind of super specialist? Can it not be argued from the extract that I have just quoted that the learned judge was being obliged to make a choice of an essentially clinical nature? And on what criteria, based on what training, did he make his decision? Did he have sufficient medical expertise to remain unaffected by the eminence, qualifications, bearing, personality, persuasiveness of one or other of the witnesses? My Lord, is it not true that, usually, the bigger the gun, the heavier the shell?

328

'And so, it is with this danger in mind that I commend to you, with respect, the evidence of one of the expert witnesses for the defence, Mr William Francome. While he is a man much respected locally by patients and colleagues alike, Mr Francome would be the first to agree that he has none of the national and international repute of the other experts. But it is my argument, my Lord, that he alone was the most knowledgeable as to the conditions that pertain to an operating theatre in a district general hospital under great duress. I commend to you his evidence as being that of the only true expert in this matter. I submit that his evidence is based on long personal experience in the milieu of a district hospital that surrounds and permeates every aspect of this case.'

The courtroom fell silent and Brookes saw the tell-tale sweat and the tremor as Stern lifted the grey book, inserting a finger at a page marked with a white card and stretching it flat.

'In conclusion, my Lord, I beg leave to read one further quotation.' He held the book aloft for the judge to see. 'My Lord, it is from Lord Denning's *Discipline of Law* and I quote from that chapter in his writing on medical negligence and malpractice. In it he now states who, in his opinion, should bear the burden of censure that I have discussed previously. He says, "A medical man, for instance, should not be found guilty of negligence unless he has done something of which his colleagues would say, 'He really did make a mistake there. He ought not to have done it.'"'

Closing the book with the utmost reverence, Stern put it on the desk and tidied all the notes and folders he could, giving time for Lord Denning's words to sink in.

'My Lord, since the dawn of our legal system, the common man has clung to his inalienable right to be tried by his peers. When he enters a court, he has always been entitled to look around and find, among his judges, those with whom he can identify himself. In the presence of a jury, he need look no further. He is happy to let them act as his collective conscience, to accept their censure if required. But, in the absence of a jury, with whom does the defendant identify himself? Let us try to see this place of trial through the eyes of the defendant. We are as accustomed to courts of this kind, my Lord, as a surgeon is to an operating theatre. One might almost say that this is our operating theatre. Look, my Lord,' – Stern flicked his fingers towards his head before sweeping his hand downwards to display his garments – 'do we not also wear our caps and gowns? And, surely, masks too. Do not we all assume a mask the moment one of your Lordships enters a court? And masks of what, my Lord? Infallibility, perhaps? Are we not all trying to give the defendant the same feeling of confidence in the rectitude of a procedure that a surgeon strives to instil in his patient? I suggest, my Lord, that we would feel very different if we were suddenly transported to the surgical theatre. We would look round for objects and persons to whom we could relate, from whom we could draw comfort. And the defendant in this case, during these two days, when he has searched about him for the men of his world who are going to try him, whom has he seen? A representative of the judiciary; counsel, half of whom are openly hostile to him; and so-called experts, some of whom, to a surgeon working in a far-flung district general hospital, might as well have come from a different planet

'I humbly submit, my Lord, that Mr Brookes, looking round this court, has seen only one of his genre, only one man whose verdict he would unquestioningly accept. Safe in the knowledge that you will construe nothing but respect in my closing remark, my Lord, let Mr Francome, the defendant's peer, be his judge.'

Stern slumped, almost fell back, into his seat. His chin on his chest, he felt the trickle of sweat under his collar. The seat pressed a cold wet shirt to his back. Sir Iestyn craned his neck forwards to lean on his elbows and peer down at Stern. It was a minute or more before he made any decisive movement. He, the Hon. Sir Iestyn ap Owen Lloyd, DSO, DFC, had not once been mentioned in person during the defence but, obvious to everyone sitting in his court and couched in indirect implications, Stern had attacked his competence to judge. There was little doubt in the judge's mind that those faces down there, looking up at him expectantly, wondering why he was taking so long, saw this now not so much as *Barker* v. *Brookes* as *Stern* v. *Lloyd*. This was no longer a judge choosing between the case for and the case against the defendant. Stern had deflected the question of the defendant's guilt by raising doubts about the competence of the court in general and the judge in particular.

Adrian Barker's summing-up, predictable and precise, did not take its place in series with the recognised court procedure so much as in parallel with the duel of personalities that was still oscillating between the judge and defence counsel. The judge maintained his minatory hunch without allowing his eyes to waver from the dishevelled heap below him, as if any movement might diminish his influence. If he was listening to Barker, speaking as if intoning some *missa privata*, he gave no indication of doing so. Barker's words lay against the senses like cold, polished marble whereas Stern's phrases had had the rubefacient chafe of weathered stone on a climber's hands. The judge could feel the glow that Stern had stimulated throughout the court. It was not his court any longer. It was Stern's. It was Stern, Stern, Stern.

Sir Iestyn had no intention of passing judgment in that atmosphere. It would take time in that windowless court for the air to change.

Without acknowledging that Barker had sat down, without a word of explanation, the judge, his eyes still fixed on Stern, spoke as if there was a hidden threat in every word.

'I will require time to consider the arguments put forward today. This court will reassemble at ten thirty tomorrow morning when I will give my judgment.'

He rose, bowed and was gone.

37

Brookes wandered in a fantasy world of disbelief, afraid to accept his happiness, like a child who refuses a toy he fears will only be taken from him later. He was still stunned by the suddenness of it all. He couldn't believe that, only twenty-four hours before, he had still been the withdrawn, superficially emotionless man that seven years' loneliness had produced. And now, in a matter of hours it had all changed. He couldn't believe it.

On their way back from Preston they had lunched, together, the three of them, with wine and talk of the future. Then there had been the telephone call as Alison had accepted her new job, followed by the mutual composition of her letter of confirmation. The old house had creaked its welcome back to booming hi-fi, slamming doors and shouted messages. Jonathan had accepted Alison's return with the adaptability of youth. His attitude had been, 'Well, thank God for that. Why the hell you didn't get on and do it years ago beats me.' Alison had cooked the men her first evening meal, sending them out into the garden while she cleared up, enabling her to explore her new kitchen, peering and prodding into cupboards and drawers, musty from disuse. Memories of Rosemary, evoked at every touch, were not discordant and a spirit who had watched over two lonely men for so long, seemed to step back, content.

Out in the courtyard, she rounded the corner of the house to see Michael and Jonathan, father and son, pacing slowly on the long lawn, intent on their own company. Forcing down a swell of jealousy, she drew back unseen.

Jonathan looked sideways at his father, a cheerful, encouraging smile on his face. 'I hope all goes well tomorrow, Dad. I'm sure it will. I'm sorry I shan't be around to hold your hand. Find your way around Preston now, can you?'

'Cheeky young beggar. I don't know what's come over you in the last few years. You were much nicer when you were a kid.' He grinned affectionately. 'Started going to the dogs as soon as you got into the sixth form. And to think they give you real live patients to play with now. How do you get on with Alex?'

'Alex? He's all right. Gets a bit stuffy now and again but he's pretty good on the whole. I keep an eye on him – you know – keep him up to date.'

Michael was still laughing as Jonathan went on. 'That's why I have to get back tonight. God knows what sort of a mess he's made of things while I've been away. It's quite true what they say, you know. It is the junior staff that do all the work while these consultants are all sitting on their fat wallets.'

'Yeah, yeah,' Michael drawled. 'Wait until you're a consultant.'

Totally relaxed and at ease with each other, they felt no awkwardness in the ensuing silence.

'Joking apart, Dad, I hope all goes well tomorrow. You're not too worried about it, are you?'

'No, not really.'

It took time for Jonathan to frame his next remark; Brookes sensed it and waited.

'Don't get me wrong, Dad, but one thing I've . . . Well, how can I put it? You don't seem all that concerned about the verdict tomorrow. Never have. It's been strange. You've never mentioned it – ever. Never talked about it. Never heard you talk to anyone else about it.'

'I know,' Brookes said. 'I didn't really want to bother you with it.'

'Oh, come on, Dad. It can't just be that. Hang it all, I'm over twenty-one – or perhaps you hadn't noticed? I'm all grown up now. I know about girls – all that sort of thing.' There was gentle reproof in every word.

Michael was torn. His immediate instinct was to close down, mutter and mumble until this unwelcome intrusion into his mind went away. But he also yearned for that fellowship his son was offering, open handed. How to break out of the black, introspective bedlam of thoughts that had been his constant emotional milieu for years? He would actually have to put into words his opinions, feelings, judgments that he had found so convenient to leave whirling round in comfortable disarray in his brain. He knew that if he could not do it now, with the help of a son's young, open mind, he would never do it.

'It's not easy,' he said.

'I know. But how do you feel about tomorrow? Are you really as unconcerned as you seem?'

'Well, yes and no.'

Brookes reacted sharply to his son's grunt of frustration. Now he really wanted to explain and he suddenly feared his son's rejection.

'No, Jonathan, please. Be patient. It's very difficult to explain. Yes, I am concerned about the verdict, in a way, in so far as it would reflect on my reputation, I suppose, but also for your sake and now, of course,' he smiled and nodded towards the house, 'for Alison's sake.'

'You needn't worry about me, Dad. I'm not going to worry about it.'

'I know that, Jonathan, but there'll be a few nods and winks around the common-room, you know, if they hear your old man's been found guilty of negligence.'

'Oh, to hell with them, and I wouldn't have thought . . .' – he paused, smiling – 'What do I call her now? Can't really call her Aunt Lissa any more, can I? It will have to be Lissa if that's all right with you? I wouldn't have thought Lissa would lose much sleep over it. She knows you better than that.'

'Oh, I know that.' Michael stopped suddenly. Jonathan walked on a pace or two before he too stopped, turned and listened with youthful concentration. 'D'you know, Jonathan, but I think this is the first time I've really passed judgment on myself. I've told myself many times that I know how I feel and that that is the only thing that matters and that I couldn't give a damn what the outside world thinks. But I've never really done it – not really.' He smiled affectionately at Jonathan. 'Who was it – was it Aneurin Bevan who said, "If you can't say it, you don't know it"? If he didn't say it, he should have. It's very true, you know.' He paused and when he spoke again his words were slow, distinct and discrete, as if he was paying out a heavy chain, link by link. 'Yes, I was negligent. I could have done better. I know, inside me, that I am a better surgeon than that. Oh, I know –' He raised his arm as he saw Jonathan begin to sympathise. 'I know. Things

333

were tough. OK, so some surgeons might not even have got so far. But I got frightened – no, that's not it – I let fear get the better of me. There's a difference. That first stitch I put in, the one that cut out, the one that made me put that extra deep one in, that was because I snatched at it. I panicked just for that split second and I shouldn't have. I know I'm better than that. I know that if only I could have another run at it now, I would make a better job of it. Yes,' – he nodded his head slowly – 'I reckon I'm guilty.'

It was a while before Jonathan answered, as if he sensed what it must have taken out of his father to speak like that. 'I suppose it all depends on what you mean by guilty,' he said, softly, 'what you feel inside or what the judge might say tomorrow.'

'That's a remarkably profound statement for a house physician, young man.'

'Yeah, maybe,' Jonathan said, without smiling. 'But what you're really saying is that everyone, judges and all, will make their own minds up about it but that only you really know.'

'Yes, I think so. Or possibly someone who has been in exactly the same position. And even the surgeon himself might get away without ever really judging himself unless he's got a son who's interested enough to prise it out of him. Not everyone is quite as fortunate.' He paused. 'I've got an interesting project for you.' Michael looked at his son's frown of concentration. 'Very shortly now, when you are a registrar, you will be in on all sorts of controlled experiments and double blind trials. Why don't you take six actions for negligence, put them before six judges, chosen at random, hear the evidence *in camera* and then compare the verdicts. Might be interesting.'

'I'll think about it, Dad.' Jonathan laughed, his features finally relaxing. But now it was Brookes' turn to look serious, serious and sad.

'The strange thing is that I've been more negligent than that in my career and no one has said a word. In some ways that's more difficult to handle, if you've got any conscience at all, that is. And it'll happen to you.' And there's nothing I can do now to prevent it and I probably won't be around to comfort you, Brookes thought, lapsing into a reverie of bruised knees, grazed hands and a young boy's tears. He was taken completely by surprise by his son's next question, the only possible indication of his sudden change of topic being his shifting of his weight from one leg to the other.

'Dad, what am I going to do about Robert?'

334

'Robert?'

'Yes.'

'How d'you mean?'

'Well, with Lissa and everything. I'll never forgive him – for what he's done to you, I mean.'

'Oh, don't be silly.'

'I'm not being silly. I don't understand you, Dad. You always were a soft touch but this is ridiculous. He's been a right bastard, bringing this action. We're bound to meet each other again now and, honestly, Dad, I don't know how I'm going to handle it, I really don't.'

'Well, try and think about it from my point of view,' Brookes said. 'Very shortly now, God willing, Lissa will be my wife. Robert is her son. What does that make him to me?' He watched Jonathan's lips thin out. 'Perhaps more important, what does that make him to you? It's possible you may have to come to terms with a step-brother who has made a considerable amount of money out of your father. But it may not be as difficult as you think.'

Brookes explained how Alison now rarely saw her son but Jonathan remained unmoved.

'Dad,' he said, measuring his words, 'I promise you I'll do nothing that will upset you and Lissa. I'd never forgive myself. I couldn't be happier for you. But what Robert and I are going to say to each other in private, I don't know. I just don't know.'

'Fair enough,' Brookes said, 'but we'd better leave it there for now. We'll talk about it again.'

They both turned their heads as they saw Alison approach them, her step tentative, her face appealing. Michael held his hand out to her, put his arm around her, kissed her, all to Jonathan's obvious delight. As they crossed the courtyard, Jonathan smiled at them both.

'As I said, good luck tomorrow, Dad. I'll ring you tomorrow night. See you in a week or so.'

He hesitated for a moment and then hurried around the car to give Alison a kiss that made her cry out loud. Jerky with embarrassment, he punched his father gently on the shoulder. 'See you, Dad.'

They watched him drive away, as studiously careful as ever. As the sound of the car's engine died away, they heard the telephone ring.

'Shall I answer it?' asked Alison, afraid to intrude too quickly, anxious to put down early, tender roots.

'Yes, of course.'

A few minutes later, she came out once more, smiling and blushing.

'It's Dai Jack. He wants a word with you. He doesn't change much, does he?'

'No, not much,' Brookes laughed. 'Why? What did he say?'

'I'm not telling you,' Alison answered, her blush deepening.

'What does he want?'

'He didn't say.'

Brookes walked into the house.

'Hullo, Dai. What d'you want?'

'Evening, Michael. Sorry to butt in but I'm afraid your services are required.'

'Oh, no, Dai, not tonight. In any case, I'm not on call. What is it?'

'A haematemesis. A nasty one.'

'But where's Bob Bond? He's on call.'

'Er – on holiday, I believe.'

'That's news to me.'

'Decided to go suddenly today.'

'Bastard. What about George? I'm sure he wouldn't mind, just this once?'

'George? He's, let me see, oh yes, he's away at a symposium in Manchester or somewhere like that.'

'Can't be, Dai. He was in court this morning.'

'That's true. In that case, he broke his leg this afternoon.'

'Dai, what the hell's going on?'

'Michael, just get in your car and come in. Don't ask questions. This one's for you. I'll explain when you get here or perhaps I won't need to.'

'But it's very difficult, Dai.'

'You mean Alison?'

'Yes.'

'Bring her along. Tell her to bring a book. We'll put her in the surgeons' room with a cup of coffee. She'll be all right. Shouldn't take you more than half an hour. If you don't take too long, I'll buy you both a drink somewhere afterwards.'

'Yes, well . . .'

'Michael, I'm taking it you're on your way in. And you'd better get a move on; he's over seventy and bleeding like a tap.'

Brookes was still holding the phone to his ear when it clicked and went dead. He called to Alison, locked the house and jumped into his car. On

336

the way, he explained as far as he could why he was driving so fast. In the theatre corridor, they were met by David Williams, a broad smile on his face as he kissed Alison.

'Your Houseman and Registrar are both scrubbed up, Michael, so go and get changed while I look after Alison.'

'Is the patient in?'

'No, not yet.'

'Well get going, it won't take me long to change.'

'I think you ought to see this one before I anaesthetise him. Just get a move on, that's all I ask.'

'Oh? Any particular problem? Do we know where he's bleeding from?'

'Yes. No problem. He's been in under the physicians for a few days. He's got a bloody great DU shown on barium meal. Had it for years, apparently. Now, hurry up.'

Brookes was still tying a length of bandage around his waist as he entered the anaesthetic-room. Williams stood at the foot of the trolley, syringe in hand. Two blood drips, one in each arm, bracketed the patient, and the air was heavy with the smell of vomited, partly digested blood and black, tarry diarrhoea. Brookes had experienced the sights and smells countless times but it was only when he went over to speak the platitudes demanded of the occasion that the patient took on an identity. He recognised first the heavy dark moustache. The usual red plethora was replaced by the sweaty grey of haemorrhagic shock but there was no mistaking William Rothwell. Brookes looked sideways to see Williams delighting in his reaction. He turned back as he heard Rothwell speak, the words pleading, the tone submissive.

'I'm right glad to see it's you, Brookes. What are t'chances, d'you think?'

'Have you had trouble for long, Mr Rothwell?'

'Bit of pain, now and again you'll understand, but never anything like this.'

'No problem, Mr Rothwell. You'll be up and about in a few days, you mark my words. Nothing to it.'

As Brookes walked into theatre, he was surprised to see Sister Kay, scrubbed, gloved hands resting patiently on the instrument trolley.

'Sister Kay, what are you doing here? Shouldn't you be off duty?'

'I wasn't going to miss this one, Mr Brookes,' she said, making no attempt to hide her satisfaction.

Brookes scrubbed, and watched Williams wheel Rothwell in. Within minutes, he was standing, knife in hand, his Registrar opposite him, his

House Surgeon alongside. As he was about to make his incision, Williams laughed.

'Take care now. Don't forget he's a VIP.'

Brookes chuckled as he worked his way through the abdominal wall, at the same time cursing at the uncoagulating blood of some Liverpool docker or Preston housewife that now coursed through Rothwell's veins. Once in the abdomen, he palpated the distended stomach, felt the characteristic sensation as the huge blood clot within it broke up between his squeezing fingers. With the tip of his index finger, he invaginated the front wall of the duodenum and felt the wide irregular crater of a posterior duodenal ulcer, penetrating deep into the pancreas. He didn't have to ask for the catgut sutures, the needles were already in Sister Kay's hand.

With a stay stitch inserted above and below to hold the cut edges upwards, Brookes opened the front of the duodenum along its length and extended the incision into the stomach. Dishes were filled with the clot that Brookes squeezed, scooped and sucked from the stomach. The grey-brown ulcer was now plain to see, the lining of the duodenum ragged around its edges. There was no fresh bleeding and the artery in the base of the ulcer could be seen, the hole eroded in its side blocked for the moment by a small, dark, hard clot.

As Brookes manoeuvred the duodenum to demonstrate the problem to his House Surgeon, the plug of clot blew off and a jet of red blood spurted. Half expecting it, Brookes pulled his head away as his left index finger instinctively searched for the spot. In doing so, inadvertently he deflected the stream on to his Registrar's face and neck. The blood loss controlled, Brookes looked across at his Registrar and smiled.

'Sorry about that. Nothing personal.' Keeping his left hand still, he used his right to clear the field of the fresh blood that had collected. Satisfied that he could get conditions no better, he held his hand out towards Sister Kay without raising his eyes from the wound.

'Thank you, Sister. A fully curved atraumatic thread, please.'

Brookes felt the pressure of the needle holder in his palm. He knew it would be the right way up. Pronating his wrist, he chose his spot and applied the tip of the needle to the base of the ulcer, just above his left index finger. The point disappeared a millimetre or so. Brookes stopped, looked up and saw Williams, blue cap on the back of his head, his mask fallen away, his teeth bared in a face-splitting grin. 'Takes you back, doesn't it?' Brookes slowly shook his head from side to side.

338

'I must admit,' said Williams, 'that human anatomy was not my strongest subject and you must correct me if I'm wrong, but isn't there something called a common bile duct just under where your needle is now?'

'Yes,' Brookes replied, his eyes above his mask seeming to egg Williams on to say what he wanted to hear.

'And, if you stick that needle in too far, you'll pick it up and damage it?'

'Yes.'

'And what happens then?'

'A biliary fistula and dead in a couple of weeks or perhaps a biliary stricture, jaundice, biliary cirrhosis and dead in six, maybe twelve months.'

'And, if you don't put it in deep enough, he's going to start bleeding again in the middle of the night and that will be curtains for our friend, Rothwell?'

'That's about it, yes.'

They stared at each other, relishing the moment.

'Tell you what I'll do,' Williams said. 'You stay there, just like that, and I'll go and give the judge a ring; ask him to come over and tell you just how deep to put that stitch in.'

Brookes found it necessary to remove the needle holder from the abdomen as his shoulders shook with laughter and it took a few more minutes for the atmosphere to tighten up again. Williams knew it was a time to be serious again and acknowledged it by rechecking his dials and gauges. But he was watching closely as Brookes, with absolute concentration, once again sank the needle point into the ulcer bed. A slow supinating roll of his wrist and the needle point showed as a glinting millimetre of stainless steel on the other side of his finger. Releasing the needle holder, he used it to grasp the point and gently ease it out, millimetre by millimetre, pulling it through tissues that had the consistency of thick, sodden cardboard. The needle safely through, he carefully drew a length of thread after it, long enough to tie a knot. With the instrument set aside, one-handed he arranged the two ends of the thread, the needle still dancing on one end, so that he could pick them up rapidly. Quickly but unhurriedly, Brookes took up the two ends of the thread. As he took his left index finger away to do so, the ulcer disappeared into the fizzing pool of blood. Brookes tied a knot and pulled it down into the depths of the pool, alongside the spluttering sucker wielded by his Registrar. With the theatre in total silence except for the metronome-like anaesthetic machine, he pulled the knot tight, the left index finger judging the tension against the right thumb. If he didn't pull it tight enough, it would not stop the bleeding.

Jerk it viciously and it would cheese-wire through, increasing the bleeding ten-fold.

Eyes half-closed, Brookes measured the tension in the knot against graduations etched into his brain by experience. Satisfied, he locked the knot. Rapid movements of his left hand and two further locking turns were run down. Taking the sucker from his Registrar, he cleared the base of the ulcer, was relieved to see no further bleeding and knew in his heart that the stitch was firmly around the artery. He took a scissors, cut away the excess thread, leaving a dark tufted knot where the clot had been. He leaned, straight-armed, on Rothwell's body as he stared into his belly.

The roar Brookes gave as he threw his head back, startled Alison where she sat in the surgeons' room, across the corridor. It drew out of Williams a smaller, secondary shout, like two old lions roaring defiance over a bloody kill. Intermixed with the snarl of defiance and victory was the cry of fear, exhilaration, tiredness, loneliness, bloody-mindedness. There were two loud snapping punctuating sounds as Brookes stripped off his gloves and walked away.